Praise for James Kelman's *Busted Scotch*

"These are bleak and beautiful stories . . . so various and brilliant in such crazy ways that it is impossible to encapsulate this book's many splendors."   —James DeRossit, *Review of Contemporary Fiction*

"Common to these portraits of the downtrodden and the self-defeated are a dark hilarity and a lyricism . . . slashing through with razor-sharp emphasis."   —*Kirkus Reviews*

"James Kelman [should be] a household name in America. . . . *Busted Scotch* is filled with compelling, arresting portraits."
—David W. Madden,
San Francisco Examiner and Chronicle Book Review

"[Kelman's] stories are a prose poetry of unparalleled vividness and pungency."   —Ray Olson, *Booklist*

"Kelman is a brilliant aural portraitist . . . and a writer utterly unfazed by risk."   —*Publishers Weekly* (starred review)

"[A] treat for American readers. . . . No one writes stories like these."   —Corey Mesler, *Memphis Commercial Appeal*

"Kelman is a hero to the newer generation of Scottish writers . . . and it's easy to see why. . . . In a word, he's brilliant."
—Jeff Baker, *Portland Oregonian*

An old pub near the Angel, and Other Stories
Three Glasgow Writers (with Tom Leonard and Alex Hamilton)
Short Tales from the Nightshift
Not not while the giro, and Other Stories
The Busconductor Hines
Lean Tales (with Agnes Owens and Alasdair Gray)
A Chancer
Greyhound for Breakfast
A Disaffection
Hardie and Baird and Other Plays
The Burn
Some Recent Attacks: Essays Cultural and Political
How late it was, how late

Busted Scotch

Selected Stories

By JAMES KELMAN

W · W · NORTON & COMPANY

NEW YORK · LONDON

First published as a Norton paperback 1998

The text of this book is composed in Adobe New Caledonia, with the display set in Adobe Present Roman. Composition and manufacturing by The Haddon Craftsmen, Inc. Book design by Marjorie J. Flock.

Library of Congress Cataloging-in-Publication Data

Kelman, James, 1946–
        Busted scotch: selected stories / by James Kelman.
        p.   cm.
        ISBN 0-393-04072-0

        I. Title.
        PR6061.E518B88   1997
        823'.914—dc20   96-35251
                                                         CIP

ISBN 0-393-31777-3 pbk.

W. W. Norton & Company, Inc., 500 Fifth Avenue, New York, N.Y. 10110
        http://www.wwnorton.com

W. W. Norton & Company Ltd., 10 Coptic Street, London WC1A 1PU

1 2 3 4 5 6 7 8 9 0

To Tillie Olsen, June Jordan and Mary Gray Hughes

Contents

———————

Letter to My Editor

Dear Gerry,

You asked me to write an introduction . . . *nothing extravagant, just a tight statement on my own ideas about the aesthetics of the short story and my working methods, and my political point of view about language, plus a bit of an autobiography, how I came to be a writer, the literary milieu I inhabit, how these stories came to be published and where . . .*
It took me three weeks' work to discover that that is the story of my life. I have now given up the project and content myself with the following comments:

> It was from an admixture of two literary traditions, the European Existential and the American Realist, allied to British rock music (influenced directly from Blues music, with an input from Country and Western), that I reached the age of twenty-two in the knowledge that certain rights were mine. It was up to me what I did. I had the right to create. I didn't have to write as if I was somebody not myself (e.g. an imagined member of the British upper middle classes). Nor did I have to write about characters striving to become other persons (e.g. imagined members of the British upper middle classes). I could sit down with my pen and paper and start making stories of my own, from myself, the everyday trials and tribulations; my family, my boss, the boy and girl next door; the old guy telling yarns at the factory; whatever. It was all there. I was privy to the lot. There was no obligation to describe, explain or define myself in terms of class, race or community. In spite of dehumanising authority people around me existed as entire human beings; they carried on with their lives as though "the forces of evil" did not exist. My family and culture were not up for evaluation. Neither was my work, not unless I so chose. Self-respect and the determination of self, for better or for worse. Some of this was intuitive, but not all.

All the best

He knew him well

The old man lowered the glass from his lips and began rolling another cigarette. His eyes never strayed until finally he lit up, inhaling deeply. He stared at me for perhaps thirty seconds then cleared his throat and began speaking. "Funny places—pubs. Drank in here for near enough twenty years." He paused, shaking his head slowly. "Never did get to know him. No. Never really spoke to him apart from Evening Dennis, Night Dennis. Been in the navy. Yeh, been in the navy alright. Torpedoed I hear. 1944." He paused again to relight the dead cigarette. "One of the only survivors too. Never said much about it. Don't blame him though." He looked up quickly then peered round the pub. "No, don't blame him. Talk too much in this place already they do. Never bloody stop, it's no good." He finished the remainder of his drink and looked over to the bar, catching the barman's eye who nodded, opened a Guinness and sent it across.

"Slate," said the old guy, "pay him pension day." He smiled. "Not supposed to drink this, says it's bad for me gut—the doctor."

"Yeh?"

"Oh yeh." He nodded. "Yeh, said it would kill me if I weren't careful." He was looking at me over the tops of his spectacles. "Seventy two I am, know that? Kill me! Ha! Bloody idiot."

"Did you like old Dennis though?" I asked.

"Well never really knew him did I? I would've though. Yeh, I would've liked old Dennis if we'd spoke. But we never talked much, him and me. Not really." He paused for a sip of the beer, continued, "Knew his brother of course—a couple of years older than Dennis I think. And a real villain he was. Had a nice wife. I used to work the racetracks then and sometimes met him down there." The old man stopped again, carefully extracting the long dead roll-up from between his lips and putting it into his waistcoat pocket. He took out his tobacco pouch and rolled another. "Yeh, Dennis' brother." He lit the cigarette. "He was a villain.

He used to tell me a few things. Yeh, he made a living alright. Never came in here except to see old Dennis."

"How did they get on together, okay?"

"What was that? Well . . ." He scratched his head. "Don't really know. Didn't speak much to each other—some brothers don't you know." He was looking over the glasses at me. "No, they'd usually just sit drinking, sometimes laughing. Not speaking though. Not much anyhow, probably said everything I suppose. Course, maybe old Dennis would ask after his wife and kids or something like that."

"Was he never married himself then?"

"Maybe. I don't rightly know. Guvnor'd tell you."

"Who, him?" I pointed at the barman.

"What. Him! Ha." The old guy snorted into his drink. "Guvnor! He would like that. Bloody guvnor. No, his brother-in-law, Jackie Moore, he's the guvnor. But he's been laid up now for nearly a year. Broke his leg and it's never healed proper, not proper. Him!" He gestured at the barman. "Slag thinks he'll get this place if Jackie has to pack it in. . . ." The old guy's voice was beginning to rise in his excitement. "No chance, no bleeding chance. Even his sister hates his guts."

He was speaking too loudly now and I glanced across to see if the barman was loitering, but he seemed engrossed in wiping the counter. The old guy noticed my concern and he leaned over the table. "Don't pay no attention." He spoke quietly. "He hears me alright. Won't let on though. Bloody ponce. What was I saying though—old Dennis, yeh, he could drink. Scotch he liked, drank it all the time. Don't care much for it myself. A drop of rum now and then, yeh, that does me." He paused to puff on the cigarette, but had to relight it eventually. "Used to play football you know, old Dennis. Palace I think or maybe the Orient. Course he was getting on a bit when the war went on. Just about ready to pack it in. And he never went back after."

"Cause of his arm?"

"Yeh, the torpedo." The old man was silent for several moments, puffing on the roll-up between sips at the black rum I'd got him. "Funny he should've waited so long to do it. Nearly as bleeding old as me he was! Course, maybe the arm had something to do with it. Maybe not." He scratched his head. "Talk in this place they do. Wouldn't if Jackie was here. No, not bloody likely they wouldn't." He sucked on his teeth. "No, not if Jackie was here behind the bar." He inhaled very deeply before looking at me over the glasses. "Where d'you find him then . . . I mean what like was he when." He stopped and swallowed the last of the rum.

"Well, just like it said in the paper. I was a bit worried cause I hadn't seen him for a couple of days so I went up the stair and banged his door. No answer, so off I went to the library to see if I could see him there."

"The library?"

"Yeh, he used to go up before opening time, nearly every day."

"Yeh, expect he would," said the old man, "now I think on it."

"Anyway," I continued, "I got home about half five and saw the landlord's daughter. She was worried so I said did she want me to force open the door or what, before her dad came back—should I wait maybe. She said to do what I thought so I went ahead and broke it in, and he was lying there, on the bed. The wrist sliced open."

"Yeh . . ." The old guy nodded after a moment, then added, "And the eating, it said in the paper . . ."

"That's right. The doctor, he said old Dennis couldn't have been eating for nearly a week beforehand."

"Bloody fool," he sighed. "He should've ate. That's one thing you should do is eat. I take something every day, yeh, make sure of that. You got to. A drop of soup's good you know."

I ordered two more drinks just on the first bell, we stayed silent, smoking then drinking, until I finished and rose and said, "Well, I'm off. See you again."

"Yeh," he muttered, staring into his glass. He shook his head. "Old Dennis should've ate eh!"

An old pub near the Angel

Charles wakened at 9.30 A.M. and wasted no time in dressing. Good God it's about time for spring surely. Colder than it was yesterday though and I'll have to wash and shave today. Must. The face has yellow lines. I can't wear socks either. Impossibility. People notice smells though they say nothing.

Think I will do a moonlight tonight, I mean five weeks' rent—he has cause for complaint. Humanity. A touch of humanity is required. He has fourteen tenants paying around £3.00 each for those poxy wee rooms, surely he can afford to let me off paying once in a while. Man I've even been known to clean my room on occasion with no thought of rent reduction.

Still he did take me for a meal last night. Collapsed if he hadn't. Imagine that bloody hotel porter knocking me back from their staff canteen. Where's your uniform? Are you a washer-up? These people depress me. What's the difference, one meal more or less. You'd think they were paying for the actual grub themselves. Old Ahmed though—what can I say—after the bollicking he gives me for not even trying to get a job and some bread together, who expects him to come back half an hour later saying, "Okay you Scotch dosser, come and eat." No, nothing to be said apart from "Fancy a pint first Ahmed?" Yes, he has too many good points. Suppose I could give him a week's money. Depends on what they give me though. Anyway.

Charles left the house and made his way towards the Labour Exchange up near Pentonville Road. It was a twenty-five minute walk but one he didn't mind at all as he normally received six and a half quid for his trouble, later on, from the N.A.B.

Yes, spring is definitely around the corner man. Look at that briefcase with the sports jacket and cavalry twills. Already. Very daring. Must be a traveler. Best part of the day this—seeing all the workers, office and site and the new middle-class tradesmen, yes, all going about their business. It pleases me.

Can't say I'm in the mood for long waits though. Jesus Christ I forgot a book. Man man what do I do now? Borrow newspapers? Stare at people's necks and make goo goos at their children. Good God! the money's going to be well earned today.

Charles stopped outside the Easy Eats Cafe and breathed in deeply. This fellow must be the best cook in London, without any doubt at all. My my my. Every time I pass this place it's the same, smells like bacon and eggs and succulent sausages with toast and tea. Never mind never mind soon be there.

Charles arrived at the Labour Exchange and entered door C to take up position in the queue under D.

Well, I can imagine it this morning, "Yes Mr. Donald there is some back money owing to you. Would you sign here for £43.68?" I'd smile politely, "Oh yes thank you, I had been beginning to wonder if it'd ever come through. Yes. Thank you. Good day." Then I'd creep out the door and run like the clappers before they discovered the error. God love us! What's this? Can't be somebody farting in a Labour Exchange surely! Bloody Irish, don't understand them at all. Think they delight in embarrassing the English just. Everybody kids on they didn't hear. But surely they can smell it?

Charles stepped out the queue and tapped the culprit on the shoulder. "Hey Mick that's a hell of a smell to make in a public place you know."

"Ah bejasus," he sighed, "it's that bloody Guinness Jock. Sure I can't help it at all."

"Terrible stuff for the guts right enough."

"Ah but it's better than that English water they sell here. Bitter!" He shook his head. "It's a penance to drink it altogether."

"Aye. You been waiting long?"

"Not at all." He shook his head again and spat on the floor, wiping it dry beneath his boot. "Want a smoke?"

"You kidding?"

"What you going on about. Here." He took out a packet of Woodies and passed it to Charles. "Take a couple Jock—I've plenty there and I'll be getting a few bob this morning."

Charles accepted, sticking one behind his ear. He said, "You been over long?"

"Ah too long Jock, too long." He gave a short laugh. "Still skint." He struck a match off the floor and they lighted the cigarettes. "Aye, if I'd been buying that Guinness in shares instead of pints I'd be worth a fortune and that's a fact—the hell with it."

"Heh, you're next Mick."

The Irishman went to the counter and received the signing-on card from the young girl clerk. He signed and was handed his pay slip then he walked over to the cashier where he was soon receiving the money, and he vanished. Charles followed the man who was next in line and was astonished to receive a pay slip. Normally he got a B1 form for the N.A.B. He asked the girl whether he would still be getting it. She smiled. "Not this week anyway Mr. Donald."

Charles strode to the money counter and stole a quick look at the pay slip. Good God! He looked again. He studied it. "God love us," he said loudly.

£23.82. Jesus. Oh you good thing. Nearly twenty-four quid. Man man that must be near eighteen back pay! What can one say God? Mere words are useless.

He passed the slip under the grill to the older woman with the fancy spectacles. Once he had signed at the right place she counted and passed him the bundle of notes and coins.

"My sincere thanks madam," he said.

The cashier smiled. "That makes a change."

"You have a wonderful smile," continued Charles, folding the wad. "I shall certainly call back here again. Good morning."

"Good morning." The cashier watched him back off towards the exit.

He closed the door. Yes, maybe chances there if I followed it through. A bit old right enough. Maybe she just pities me. With that smile she gave me! Impossible.

He walked up Pentonville Road and decided to go for a pint rather than a breakfast. Half past eleven. Not too early.

"Pint of bitter and eh—give me . . ." Charles stared at the miserable gantry, "just give me one of your good whiskies eh!"

The ancient bartender peered at him for a moment then bent down behind the bar to produce a dusty bottle of Dimple Haig. "How's this eh?"

"Aye," replied Charles, "that's fine. How much is it?"

"Seven bob," muttered the bartender rubbing his ear thoughtfully.

"Well give me twenty Players as well and that's that."

The bartender passed over the cigarettes and grabbed the pound

note, mumbling to himself. Very friendly old bastard. Must hate Scots-
men or something. He brought back the change and moved around the
counter tidying up. "Hoy!" called Charles after a time. "Any grub?"

"What's that?" cried the bartender, left hand at his ear.

"Food, have you any food?"

"What d'you want, eh?"

"Depends. What've you got?"

"Don't know." He thought for a moment. "Potato crisps?"

"No chance," said Charles. "Is that it?"

"Shepherd's pie? The missus makes it," he added with a strange
smile.

Wonder why he's smiling like that. Poisoned or something?

"Homemade eh . . ." Charles nodded. "Aye, I'll have some of that."

"Now?"

"Yes, now for heaven sake." He shook his head.

"Okay okay, just take a seat a minute, I'll go and tell her eh?" He
shuffled away. As he passed through the door in the partition he glanced
back at Charles who gave him a wave.

Kind of quiet place this. Wonder when it gets busy. Strange I'm the
only customer at nearly twelve o'clock on a Thursday morning. The ancient bartender returned and cried, " 'Bout ten fifteen minutes eh?"
Charles nodded. The other resumed wiping some glasses.

Man man who would've thought of me getting paid back money like
that. Brilliant. Let me see. 11.50 A.M. By rights I should still be sitting
in the second interview queue at the N.A.B. The fat woman's kids'll be
rolling on the floor and she'll be reading the *Evening Standard* dog-
section. Yes, I'll be missed. They'll think I've gone to Scotland. Or maybe
been lifted by the busies. No, won't have to go back there for a while.
Thank Christ for that.

A huge woman appeared from behind the partition holding a great
plateful of steaming shepherd's pie. "One shepherd's pie!" she shouted.
Her chins trembled and her breasts rested on her knees as she bent to
plonk it down in the center of Charles' table.

"This looks wonderful," he said, sniffing at it. He smiled up at her.
"Madam, you've excelled yourself. How much do you ask for this deli-
cious fare?"

"Fourteen pee." She pointed to her husband. "He'll give you the
condiments. Just shout, he's deaf occasionally."

"Many thanks," replied Charles, placing thirty pence on her tray. "Please have a drink on me."

"Ta son," she said and toddled back through to the kitchen.

Charles ate rapidly. He thoroughly enjoyed the meal. "Hoy!" he called. "Hoy!"

The bartender was standing, elbows propped on the counter, staring up at the blank television screen. "Hoy!" shouted Charles, getting out of his seat. He walked to the bar.

"Yeh yeh, yeh! What's up eh?"

"Another pint of bitter. And have one yourself."

"What's that?"

"Jesus what's up here at all. Listen man get me a pint of bitter please and have one with me, eh! How's that. Eh?"

"Fine son, I'll have a half. Nice weather eh . . ." The ancient fellow was showing distinct signs of energy while pulling the beer taps. "Pity about the Fulham though eh! Yeh, they'll be back, they'll be back." He took a lengthy swig at his half pint, eyes closed, a slow stream trickling down his partly shaven chin and winding its way round the Adam's apple on down beneath his frayed shirt collar. "Yeh," he said, "Poor old Chelsea." And he finished the rest of the drink.

"What about the old Jags though eh? I mean that's even worse than the Fulham surely!"

"What's that Jock?"

"The Thistle man, the old Patrick Thistle, they were relegated last season."

"Ah, Scotch team eh! Don't pay much heed."

"Yeh, you're right and all. Not much good up there."

"Bloody Celtic and Rangers, "he shook his head in disgust. "Get them in here sometimes. And the bloody Irish. Mostly go down Kings Cross they do. Bloody trouble they cause eh?"

"Give us another of these Dimples."

"Yeh." He smiled awkwardly. "Like them do you?" He pursed his lips.

Charles got it and returned to his table near the wall, and sat quietly for about five minutes. "Hoy!" he shouted.

The bartender had regained his former position beneath the television set. He gave no indication of having heard.

"HOY!"

The old fellow jumped and turned angrily. "What's up then? What's this bleeding hoy all the time eh?"

"Well you're a bit deaf for Christ sake."

"No need to bloody scream like that though."

"Alright alright, sorry. Look, I'm just going to go out for a paper a minute. Keep your eye on my drink eh?"

The bartender began muttering then started to polish glasses.

Charles had to visit three newsagents before obtaining a copy of the *Sporting Life*. Nothing else could possibly do with all that back money lying about. When he returned to the pub he noticed another customer sitting at a table facing him, just at the corner of the room. She was around ninety years of age.

"Morning," called Charles. "Good morning missus."

The old lady was sucking her gums and smiled across at him, then she looked up at the bartender. "Goshtorafokelch," she said.

The bartender looked from her to Charles and back again before replying, "Yeh, I'll say eh?"

Bejasus thank God I've got a paper to read. This must be an old folk's home in disguise. He quickly swallowed the remains of the whisky and then the remains of the beer. "Hoy!" he shouted. "What time is it? I mean is that the right time there or what?"

The bartender frowned. "Must be after twelve I reckon eh?"

Charles got up and carried the empties across. "Think I'll be going," he said.

"You please yourself," he muttered. "Going to another shop are you eh?"

"No, it's not that man, I've just got to go home, get a bath and that."

"Will you be back then eh?"

"Well, not today. Maybe tonight though, but if not I'll definitely be back sometime."

"Ah—who cares eh?" The bartender poured himself a gin then said, "Want a short do you eh?"

"WHAT?"

"Another short, one of them." He pointed at the dusty Dimple Haig. "Bleeding thing's been there for years," he said and poured a fair-sized measure out. "Yeh, glad to get rid of it eh?"

Charles took the tumbler and looked at it. The bartender watched him drink some and asked, "You really like it then eh Jock?"

"Aye, it's a good whisky."

The barman opened a bottle of sweet stout and pushed it across to him. "You pass that down to her," he said.

"Right you are." Charles walked over to the corner and put it down next to the old woman's glass. "Here you are missus, the landlord sent it."

She looked up and glanced at him with a smile and a nod of the head. "Patsorpooter," was what she said.

"Aye," Charles grinned. "Fine." He went back to the bar to finish the whisky. "Okay then," he said, "that's me, I'll be off. And I'll be back in again, don't worry about that."

"Hm." The bartender polished the counter. He moved on to another part of it.

"Listen," called Charles, "I'll be back."

The ancient fellow was now polishing a large glass and seemed unable to hear for the noise of the cloth on it.

"I'll see yous later!" shouted Charles hopelessly.

He collected the newspaper and cigarettes from the table and made for the door. Christ this is really terrible. Can't understand what it's all about. Maybe . . . No, I haven't a clue. Sooner I'm out the better.

He stopped at where the old lady was sitting. "Cheerio missus, I'll be in next week sometime. Okay?"

She wiped a speck of foam from the tip of her nose. "Deef!" she cried, "deef." And she burst into laughter. Charles had a quick look round for the bartender but he must have gone through the partition door, so he left immediately.

Nice to be Nice

Strange thing wis it stertit oan a Wedinsday, A mean nothin ever sterts oan a Wedinsday kis it's the day afore pey day an A'm ey skint. Mibby git a buckshee pint roon the *Anchor* bit that's aboot it. Anywey it wis eftir 9 an A wis thinkin aboot gin hame kis a hidny a light whin Boab McCann threw us a dollar an A boat masel an auld Erchie a pint. The auld yin hid 2 boab ay his ain so A took it an won a couple a gemms a dominoes. Didny win much bit enough tae git us a hauf boattle a Lanny. Tae tell ye the truth A'm no fussy fir the wine bit auld Erchie'll guzzle till it comes oot his ears, A'm tellin ye. A'll drink it mine ye bit if A've goat a few boab A'd rethir git a hauf boattle a whisky thin 2 ir 3 boattles a magic. No auld Erchie. Anywey—nice tae be nice—every man tae his ain, comes 10 and we wint roon the coarner tae git inty the wine. Auld Erchie waantit me tae go up tae his place bit Jesus Christ it's like annickers midden up therr. So anywey A think A git aboot 2 moothfus oot it afore it wis done kis is A say, whin auld Erchie gits stertit oan that plonk ye canny haud him. The auld cunt's a disgrace.

A left him ootside his close an wint hame. It wis gittin cauld an A'm beginnin tae feel it merr these days. That young couple wir hinging aboot in the close in at it as usual. Every night in the week an A'm no kiddin ye! Thir parents waant tae gie thim a room tae thirsel, A mean everybody's young wance—know whit A mean. They waant tae git merrit anywey. Jesus Christ they young yins nooadays iv goat thir heid screwed oan merr thin we ever hid, an the sooner they git merrit the better. Anyhow, as usual they didny even notice me goin up the sterr. Bit it's Betty Sutherland's lassie an young Peter Craig—A knew his faither an they tell me he's almost as hard as his auld man wis. Still, the perr iv thim ir winchin near enough 6 month noo so mibby she's knoaked some sense inty his heid. Good luck tae thim, A hope she his, a nice wee lassie— aye, an so wis her maw.

A hid tae stoap 2 flerrs up tae git ma breath back. A'm no as bad as

A wis bit A'm still no right; that bronchitis—Jesus Christ, A hid it bad. Hid tae stoap work cause iv it. Good joab A hid tae, the lorry drivin. Hid tae chuck it bit. Landid up in the Western Infirmary. Nae breath at aw. Couldny fuckin breathe. Murder it wis. Still, A made it tae the toap okay. A stey in a room an kitchen an inside toilet an it's no bad kis A only pey 6 an a hauf a month fir rent an rates. A hear they're tae come doon right enough bit A hope it's no fir a while yit kis A'll git buggir aw bein a single man. If she wis here A'd git a coarpiration hoose bit she's gone fir good an anywey they coarpiration hooses urny worth a fuck. End up peying a haunful a week an dumped oot in the wilds! Naw, no me. No even a pub ir buggir aw! Naw, they kin stick them.

Wance in the hoose A pit oan the kettle fir a pot iv tea an picked up a book. A'm no much ay a sleeper at times an A sometimes end up readin aw night. Hauf an oor later the door goes. Funny—A mean A dont git that minny visitors.

Anywey it wis jist young Tony who'd firgoat his key, he wis wi that wee mate ay his an a perr a burds. Christ, whit dae ye dae? Invite him in? Well A did—nice tae be nice—an anywey thir aw right they two; sipposed tae be a perr a terraways bit A ey fun Tony aw right, an his mate's his mate. The young yins ir aw right if ye lea thim alane. A've eywis maintained that. Gie thim a chance fir fuck sake. So A made thim at hame although it meant me hivin tae sit oan a widdin cherr kis A selt the couch a couple a months ago kis ay that auld cunt Erchie an his troubles. They four hid perred aff an were sittin oan the ermcherrs. They hid brung a cerry-oot wi thim so A goat the glesses an it turned oot no a bad wee night, jist chattin away aboot poalitics an the hoarses an aw that. A quite enjoyed it although mine you A wis listenin merr thin A wis talkin, bit that's no unusual. An wan iv the burds didny say much either an A didny blame her kis she knew me. She didny let oan bit. See A used to work beside her man—aye she's nae chicken, bit nice tae be nice, she isny a bad lookin lassie. An A didny let oan either.

Anywey, must a been near 1 a cloak whin Tony gits me oan ma ain an asks me if they kin aw stey the night. Well some might ay thoat they wir takin liberties bit at the time it soundit reasonable. A said they kid sleep ben the room an A'd sleep here in the kitchen. Tae tell the truth A end up spennin the night here in the cherr hell iv a loat these days. Wan minute A'm sittin readin an the nix it's 6 a cloak in the moarnin an ma neck's as stiff as a poker ir somethin. A've bin thinkin ay movin the bed frae the room inty the kitchen recess anywey—might as well—A mean it looks hell iv a daft hivin wan double bed an nothin else. Aye, an A mean nothin else, sep the lino. Flogged every arra fuckin thin thit wis in the room an A sippose if A wis stuck A kid flog the bed. Comes tae that A kid even sell the fuckin room ir at least rent it oot. They Pakies wid jump at it—A hear they're sleepin twinty handit tae a room an mine's is a big room. Still, good luck tae thim, they work hard fir their money, an if they dont good luck tae thim if they kin git away wi it.

A goat a couple a blankets an that bit tae tell the truth A wisny even tired. Sometimes whin A git a taste ay that bevy that's me—awake tae aw oors. An A've goat tae read then kis thir's nae point sterring at the waw—nothin wrang wi the waw right enough, me an Tony done it up last spring, aye, an done no a bad joab tae. Jist the kitchen bit kis A didny see the point ay doin up the room wi it only hivin wan double bed fir furniture. He pit up a photy iv Jimi Hendrix oan the waw, a poster. A right big yin.

Whit's the story wi the darkie oan the waw? says auld Erchie the first time he comes up eftir it wis aw done. Wis the greatest guitarist in the World ya auld cunt ye! says Tony an he grabs the auld yin's bunnet an flings it oot the windy. First time A've seen yir heid, he says. Nae wunnir ye keep it covered.

The Erchie filla wisny too pleased. Mine you A hidny seen him much wioot that bunnet masell. He's goat 2 ir 3 strans a herr stretchin frae the back iv his heid tae the front. An the bunnet wis still lyin therr oan the pavement whin he wint doon fir it. Even the dugs widny go near it. It's a right dirty lookin oabject bit then so's the auld yin's heid.

Anywey, A drapped aff to sleep eventually—wioot chinegin, well it wid be broo day the morra an A wis waantin tae git up early wi them bein therr an aw that.

Mibby it wis the bevy A dont know bit the nix thin Tony's pullin ma erm, staunin oor me wi a letter frae the tax an A kid see it wisny a form tae fill up. A'd nae idear whit it wis so A opind it right away and oot faws a cheque fir 42 quid. Jesus Christ A near collapsed. A mean A've been oan the broo fir well oor a year, an naebody gits money eftir a year. Therr ye ur bit—42 quid tae prove me wrang. No bad eh!

Wiv knoaked it aff Stan, shouts Tony, grabbin it oot ma haun.

Well A mean A've seen a good few quid in ma days whit wi the hoarses an aw that bit it the time it wis like winnin the pools so it wis.

A'm no kiddin ye. Some claes an mibby a deposit tae try fir that new HGV yiv goat tae git afore ye kin drive the lorries nooadays.

Tony gits his mate an the burds up an tells thim it's time tae be gaun an me an him wint doon the road fir a breakfist. We winty a cafe an hid the works an Tony boat a *Sporting Chronicle* an we dug oot a couple. Well he did kis A've merr ir less chucked it these days. Aye, long ago. Disny bother me much noo bit it wan time A couldny walk by a bettin shoap. Anywey, nae merr ay that. An Tony gammils enough fir the baith ay us. Course he wid bet oan 2 flies climbin a waw whirras A wis eywis a hoarsy man. Wance ir twice A mibby took an intrist in a dug bit really it wis eywis the hoarses wi me. A sippose the gammlin wis the real reason how the wife fukt aff an left me. Definitely canny blame her bit. I mean she near enough stuck it 30 year by Christ. Nae merr ay that.

A hid it aw figird oot how tae spen the cash. Tony wint fir his broo money an I decidet jist tae go hame fir merr iv a think.

Whin A goat therr Big Moira wis in daein the cleanin up fir me bit she wisny long in puttin oan a cup a tea. Jist aboot every time ye see her she's either drinkin tea ir jist aboot tae pit it oan. So wir sittin an she's bletherin away good style aboot her weans an the rest ay it whin aw iv a sudden she tells me she's gittin threw oot her hoose—ay an the 4 weans wi her. Said she goat a letter tellin her. Canny dae it A says.

Aye kin they no, says Moira. The coarpiration kin dae whit they like Stan.

Well A didny need Moira tae tell me that bit A also knew thit they widny throw a single wummin an 4 weans oot inty the street. A didny tell her bit—in case she thoat A wis oan therr side ir somethin. Big Moira's like that. A nice lassie, bit she's ey gittin thins inty her heid aboot people, so A said nothin. She telt me she wint straight up tae see the manager bit he wisny therr so she seen this young filla an he telt her she'd hivty git oot an it wisny cause ay her debts (she owes a few quid arrears). Naw, it seems 2 ir 3 ay her neighbours wir up complainin aboot her weans makin a mess in the close an shoutin an bawlin ir somethin. An thir's nothin ye kin dae aboot it, he says tae her.

Well that wis a diffrint story an A wis beginnin tae believe her. She wis aw fir sortin it oot wi the neighbours bit A telt her no tae bother till she fun oot fir certain whit the score wis. Anywey, eftir gittin the weans aff her maw she wint away hame. So Moira hid tae git oot ay her hoose afore the end ay the month. Course whether they'd cerry oot the threat ir no wis a diffrint story—surely the publicity alane wid pit thim aff. A must admit the merr A wis thinkin aboot it the angrier A wis gettin. Naw—nice tae be nice—ye canny go aboot pittin the fear a death inty folk, speshly a wummin like Moira. She's a big stroang lassie bit she's nae man tae back her up. An whin it comes tae talkin they bastirts up it Clive House wid run rings roon ye. Naw, A know whit like it is. Treat ye like A dont know whit so they dae. A wis gittin too worked up so I jist opind a book an tried tae firget aboot it. Anywey, A fell asleep in the cherr—oot like a light an didny wake up till well eftir 5 a cloak. Ma neck wis hell iv a stiff bit A jist shoved oan the jaiket an wint doon the road.

The *Anchor* wis busy an A saw auld Erchie staunin near the dominoe table wherr he usually hings aboot if he's skint in case emdy waants a drink. Kis he sometimes gits a drink himsel fir gaun. A wint straight tae the bar an asked John fir 2 gless a whisky an a couple a hauf pints an whin A went tae pey the man A hid fuck aw bar some smash an a note sayin, Give you it back tomorrow, Tony.

40 quid! A'll gie ye it the morra! Jesus Christ Almighty. An he wis probly hauf wey oor tae Ashfield right noo. An therrs me staunin therr like a fuckin numbskull! 40 notes! Well well well, an it wisny the first time. A mean he disny let me doon, he's eywis goat it merr ir less whin he says he will bit nice tae be nice, know whit A mean! See A gave him a sperr key whin we wir daein up the kitchen an A let him hing oan tae it eftirwirds kis sometimes he's naewherr tae kip. Moira's maw's git the other yin in case ay emergencies an aw that. Bit Tony drapped me right in it. John's staunin therr behind the bar sayin nothin while A'm readin the note a hauf dozen times. The bill comes tae aboot 70 pence—aboot 6 boab in chinge. A leans oor the counter an whispers sorry an tells him A've come oot wioot ma money.

Right Stan it's aw right, he says, A'll see ye the morra—dont worry aboot it.

Whit a showin up. A gave the auld yin his drink oor an wint oor tae sit oan ma tod. Tae be honest, A wisny in the mood fir either Erchie's patter or the dominoes. 40 sovvies! Naw, the merr A thoat aboot it the merr A knew it wis oot ay order. Okay, he didny know A firgoat aboot ma broo money kis ay me hivin that kip—bit it's nae excuse, nae excuse. Aw he hid tae dae wis wake me up an A'd iv gied him the fuckin money if he wis needin it that bad. The trouble wis A knew the daft bastirt'd dae somethin stupit tae git it back if he wound up losin it aw at the dugs.

Jesus Christ, aw the worries iv the day whit wi big Moira an the weans an noo him. An whit wid happen if they did git chucked oot! Naw, A couldny see it. Ye never know bit. I decidet tae take a walk up tae the coarpiration masell. A kin talk whin A waant tae, bit right enough whin they bastirts up therr git stertit they end up blindin ye wi science. Anywey, I git inty John fir a hanfill oan the strength ay ma broo money an wint hame early wi a haufboattle an a big screwtap wioot sayin a word tae auld Erchie.

Tony still hidny showed up by the Monday, that wis 4 days so A knew A'd nae chance ay seein him till he hid the cash in his haun ready fir me. An it wis obvious he might hiv tae go tae the thievin gemms inty the bargin an thir wis nothin A could dae aboot it, A'd be too late. Big Moira's maw came up the sterr tae see me the nix moarnin. Word hid come aboot her hivin tae be oot the hoose by the 30th ir else they'd take immediate action. The lassie's maw wis in a hell iv a state kis she couldny take thim in wi her only hivin a single end. A offirt tae help oot bit it didny make matters much better. An so I went roon as minny factors as A could. Nae luck bit. Nothin, nothin at aw. Ach A didny expect much anyhow tae be honest aboot it. Hopeless. I jist telt her maw A'd take a walk up Clive House an see if they'd mibby offer some alternit accommodation—an no tae worry kis they'd never throw thim inty the street. Single wummin wi 4 weans! Naw, the coarpiration widny chance that yin. Imagine expectin her to pey that kinna rent tae! Beyond a joke so it is. An she says the rooms ir damp an aw that, and whin she cawed in the sanitry they telt her tae open the windaes an let the err in. The middle ay the fuckin winter! Let the err in! Ay, an as soon's her back's turnt aw the villains ir in screwin the meters an whit no. A wis ragin. An whin A left the hoose oan the Wedinsday moarnin A wis still hell iv a angry. Moira wis waantin tae come up wi me bit A telt her naw it might be better if A wint oan ma tod.

So up A goes an A queued up tae see the manager bit he wisny available so A saw the same wan Moira saw, a young filla cawed Mr Frederick. A telt him whit wis whit bit he wisny bothrin much an afore A'd finished he jumps in sayin that in the furst place he'd explained everythin tae Mrs Donnelly (Moira) an the department hid sent her oot letters which she'd no taken the trouble tae answer—an in the second place it wis nane iv ma business. Then he shouts: Nix please.

A loast ma rag at that an the nix thin A know A'm lyin here an that wis yesterday, Thursday—A'd been oot the gemm since A grabbed the wee cunt by the throat. Lucky A didny strangle him tae afore A collapsed.

Dont even know if A'm gittin charged an tae be honest A couldny gie 2 monkeys whether A am ir no. Bit that's nothin. Moira's maw comes up tae visit me this moarnin an gies me the news. Young Tony gits back Wedinsday dinner time bit no findin me goes doon tae Moira's maw an gits telt the story. He says nothin tae her bit jist goes right up tae the coarpiration wherr he hings aboot till he finds oot whit's whit wi the clerks, then whin Mr Frederick goes hame a gang iv young thugs ir supposed ta iv set aboot him an done him up pretty bad bit the polis only manages tae catch wan ay thim an it turns oot tae be Tony who disny even run aboot wi embdy sem sometimes that wee mate iv his. So therr it is an A'll no really know the score till the nix time A see him. An big Moira an the weans, as far as A hear they've still naewherr tae go either, A mean nice tae be nice, know whit A mean.

Remember Young Cecil

Young Cecil is medium-sized and retired. For years he has been undisputed champion of our hall. Nowadays that is not saying much. This pitch has fallen from grace lately. John Moir who runs the place has started letting some of the punters rent a table Friday and Saturday nights to play Pontoons, and as an old head pointed out the other day: that is it for any place, never mind Porter's.

In Young Cecil's day it had one of the best reputations in Glasgow. Not for its decoration or the rest of it. But for all-round ability Porter's regulars took some beating. Back in these days we won the "City" eight years running with Young Cecil Number 1 and Wee Danny backing up at Number 2. You could have picked any four from ten to make up the rest of the team. Between the two of them they took the lot three years running; snooker singles and doubles, and billiards the same. You never saw that done very often.

To let you know just how good we were, John Moir's big brother Tam could not even get into the team except if we were short though John Moir would look at you as if you were daft if you said it out loud. He used to make out Tam, Young Cecil and Wee Danny were the big three. Nonsense. One or two of us had to put a stop to that. We would have done it a hell of a lot sooner if Wee Danny was still living because Young Cecil has a habit of not talking. All he does is smile. And that not very often either. I have seen Frankie Sweeny's boy come all the way down here just to say hello; and what does Young Cecil do but give him a nod and at the most a how's it going without even a name nor nothing. But that was always his way and Frankie Sweeney's boy still drops in once or twice yet. The big noises remember Cecil. And some of the young ones. Tam!—never mind John Moir—Young Cecil could have gave Tam forty and potting only yellows still won looking round. How far.

Nowadays he can hardly be annoyed even saying hello. But he was never ignorant. Always the same.

I mind the first time we clapped eyes on him. Years ago it was. In those days he used to play up the YM, but we knew about him. A hall's regulars kind of keep themselves to themselves and yet we had still heard of this young fellow that could handle a stick. And with a first name like Cecil nobody needed to know what his last one was. Wee Danny was the Number 1 at the time. It is not so good as all that being Number 1 cause you have got to hand out big starts otherwise you are lucky to get playing, never mind for a few bob—though there are always the one or two who do not bother about losing a couple of bob just so long as they get a game with you.

Wee Danny was about twenty-seven or thirty in those days but no more than that. Well, this afternoon we were hanging around. None of us had a coin—at least not for playing with. During the week it was. One or two of us were knocking them about on Table 3, which has always been the table in Porter's. Even John Moir would not dream of letting anyone mess about on that one. There were maybe three other tables in use at the time but it was only mugs playing. Most of us were just chatting or studying form and sometimes one would carry a line up to Micky at the top of the street. And then the door opened and in comes this young fellow. He walks up and stands beside us for a wee while. Then: Anybody fancy a game? he says.

We all looks at one another but at Wee Danny in particular and then we bursts out laughing. None of you want a game then? he says.

Old Porter himself was running the place in those days. He was just leaning his elbows on the counter in his wee cubbyhole and sucking on that falling-to-bits pipe of his. But he was all eyes in case of bother.

For a couple of bob? says the young fellow.

Well we all stopped laughing right away. I do not think Wee Danny had been laughing at all; he was just sitting up on the ledge dangling his feet. It went quiet for a minute then Hector Parker steps forward and says that he would give the young fellow a game. Hector was playing 4 stick at that time and hitting not a bad ball. But the young fellow just looks him up and down. Hector was a big fat kind of fellow. No, says the young yin. And he looks round at the rest of us. But before he can open his mouth Wee Danny is off the ledge and smartly across.

You Young Cecil from the YM?

Aye, says the young fellow.

Well I'm Danny Thompson. How much you wanting to play for?

Fiver.

Very good. Wee Danny turns and shouts: William . . .

Old Porter ducks beneath the counter right away and comes up with Danny's jar. He used to keep his money in a jam-jar in those days. And he had a good few quid in there at times. Right enough sometimes he had nothing.

Young Cecil took out two singles, a half quid, and made the rest up with a pile of smash. He stuck it on the shade above Table 3 and Wee Danny done the same with his fiver. Old Porter went over to where the mugs were playing and told them to get a move on. One or two of us were a bit put out with Wee Danny because usually when there was a game on we could get into it ourselves for a couple of bob. Sometimes with the other fellow's cronies but if there was none of them Wee Danny maybe just covered the bet and let us make up the rest. Once or twice I have seen him skint and having to play a money game for us. And when he won we would chip in to give him a wage. Sometimes he liked the yellow stuff too much. When he got a right turn off he might go and you would be lucky to see him before he had bevied it all in; his money right enough. But he had to look to us a few times, a good few times—so you might have thought: Okay I'll take three quid and let the lads get a bet with the deuce that's left. . . .

But no. You were never too sure where you stood with the wee man. I have seen him giving some poor bastard a right sherricking for nothing any of us knew about. Aye, more than once. Not everybody liked him.

Meanwhile we were all settled along the ledge. Old Porter and Hector were applying the brush and the stone; Wee Danny was fiddling about with his cue. But Young Cecil just hung around looking at the photos and the shield and that, that Old Porter had on full view on the wall behind his counter. When the table was finally finished Old Porter began grumbling under his breath and goes over to the mugs who had still not ended their game. He tells them to fuck off and take up bools or something and locks the door after them. Back into his cubbyhole he went for his chair so he could have a sit-down to watch the game.

Hector was marking the board. He chips the coin. Young Cecil calls it and breaks without a word. Well, maybe he was a bit nervous, I do not know; but he made a right mess of it. His cue ball hit the blue after disturbing a good few reds out the pack on its way back up the table. Nobody could give the wee man a chance like that and expect him to

stand back admiring the scenery. In he steps and bump bump bump—
a break of fifty-six. One of the best he had ever had.

It was out of three they were playing. Some of us were looking dag-
gers at Danny, not every day you could get into a fiver bet. He broke
for the next and left a good safety. But the young fellow had got over
whatever it was, and his safety was always good. It was close but he took
it. A rare game. Then he broke for the decider and this time it was no
contest. I have seen him play as well but I do not remember him playing better all things considered. And he was barely turned twenty at the
time. He went right to town and Wee Danny wound up chucking it on
the colors, and you never saw that very often.

Out came the jam-jar and he says: Same again son?

Double or clear if you like, says Young Cecil.

Well Wee Danny never had the full tenner in his jar so he gives us
the nod and in we dived to Old Porter for a couple of bob till broo day
because to tell the truth we thought it was a bit of a flash in the pan.
And even yet when I think about it, you cannot blame us. These young
fellows come and go. Even now. They do not change. Still think they
are wide. Soon as they can pot a ball they are ready to hand out J.D.
himself three blacks of a start. Throw their money at you. Usually we
were there to take it, and we never had to call on Wee Danny much either. So how were we supposed to know it was going to be any different this time?

Hector racked them. Young Cecil won the toss again. He broke and
this time left the cue ball nudging the green's arse. Perfect. Then on it
was a procession. And he was not just a potter like most of these young
ones. Course at the time it was his main thing just like the rest but the
real difference was that Young Cecil never missed the easy pot. Never.
He could take a chance like anybody else. But you never saw him miss
the easy pot.

One or two of us had thought it might not be a flash in the pan but
had still fancied Wee Danny to do the business because whatever else
he was he was a money-player. Some fellows are world beaters till there
is a bet bigger than the price of renting the table then that is them—all
fingers and thumbs and miscueing all over the shop. I have seen it many
a time. And after Young Cecil had messed his break in that first frame
we had seen Wee Danny do the fifty-six so we knew he was on form.
Also, the old heads reckoned on the young fellow cracking up with the

tenner bet plus the fact that the rest of us were into it as well. Because Wee Danny could pot a ball with a headcase at his back all ready to set about his skull with a hatchet if he missed. Nothing could put the wee man off his game.

But he met his match that day.

And he did not ask for another double or clear either. In fact a while after the event I heard he never even fancied himself for the second game—just felt he had to play it for some reason.

After that Young Cecil moved into Porter's, and ever since it has been home. Him and Wee Danny got on well enough but they were never close friends or anything like that. Outside they ran around in different crowds. There was an age gap between them right enough. That might have had something to do with it. And Cecil never went in for the bevy the way the wee man did. In some ways he was more into the game as well. He could work up an interest even when there was no money attached whereas Wee Danny was the other way.

Of course after Young Cecil met his he could hardly be bothered playing the game at all.

But that happened a while later—when we were having the long run in the "City." Cleaning up everywhere we were. And one or two of us were making a nice few bob on the side. Once Cecil arrived Wee Danny had moved down to Number 2 stick, and within a year or so people started hearing about Young Cecil. But even then Wee Danny was making a good few bob more than him because when he was skint the wee man used to run about different pitches and sometimes one or two of us went along with him and picked up a couple of bob here and there. Aye, and a few times he landed us in bother because in some of these places it made no difference Wee Danny was Wee Danny. In fact it usually made things worse once they found out. He was hell of a lucky not to get a right good hiding a couple of times. Him and Young Cecil never played each other again for serious money. Although sometimes they had an exhibition for maybe a nicker or so, to make it look good for the mugs. But they both knew who the 1 stick was and it never changed. That might have been another reason for them not being close friends or anything like that.

Around then Young Cecil started playing in a private club up the town where Wee Danny had played once or twice but not very often. This was McGinley's place. The big money used to change hands there.

Frankie Sweeney was on his way up then and hung about the place with the Frenchman and one or two others. Young Cecil made his mark right away and a wee bit of a change came over him. But this was for the best as far as we were concerned because up till then he was just too quiet. Would not push himself or that. Then all of a sudden we did not have to tell him he was Young Cecil. He knew it himself. Not that he went about shouting it out because he never did that at any time. Not like some of them you see nicking about all gallus and sticking the chest out at you. Young Cecil was never like that and come to think about it neither was Wee Danny—though he always knew he was Wee Danny right enough. But now when Young Cecil talked to the one or two he did speak to it was him did the talking and we did not have to tell him.

Then I mind fine we were all sitting around having a couple of pints in the Crown and there at the other end of the bar was our 1 and 2 sticks. Now they had often had a drink together in the past but normally it was always in among other company. Never like this—by themselves right through till closing time. Something happened. Whenever Young Cecil went up McGinley's after that Wee Danny would be with him, as if he was partners or something. And they started winning a few quid. So did Sweeney and the Frenchman; they won a hell of a lot more. They were onto Young Cecil from the start.

Once or twice a couple of us got let into the club as well. McGinley's place was not like a hall. It was the basement of an office building up near George Square and it was a fair-sized pitch though there was only the one table. It was set aside in a room by itself with plenty of seats round about it, some of them built up so that everybody could see. The other room was a big one and had a wee bar and a place for snacks and that, with some card tables dotted about; and there was a big table for Chemmy. None of your Pontoons up there. I heard talk about a speaker wired up for commentaries and betting shows and that from the tracks, but I never saw it myself. Right enough I was never there during the day. The snooker room was kept shut all the time except if they were playing or somebody was in cleaning the place. They kept it well.

McGinley and them used to bring players through from Edinburgh and one or two up from England to play exhibitions and sometimes they would set up a big match and the money changing hands was something to see. Young Cecil told us there was a couple of Glasgow fellows down there hardly anybody had heard about who could really handle a stick.

It was a right eye-opener for him because up till then he had only heard about people like Joe Hutchinson and Simpson and one or two others who went in for the "Scottish" regular, yet down in McGinley's there was two fellows playing who could hand out a start to the likes of Simpson. Any day of the week. It was just that about money-players and the rest.

So Young Cecil became a McGinley man and it was not long before he joined Jimmy Brown and Sandy from Dumfries in taking on the big sticks through from Edinburgh and England and that. Then Sweeney and the Frenchman set up a big match with Cecil and Jimmy Brown. And Cecil beat him. Beat him well. A couple of us got let in that night and we picked up a nice wage because Jimmy Brown had been around for a good while and had a fair support. In a way it was the same story as Cecil and Wee Danny, only this time Wee Danny and the rest of Porter's squad had our money down the right way and we were carrying a fair wad for some of us who were not let in. There was a good crowd watching because word travels, but it was not too bad; McGinley was hell of a strict about letting people in—in case too many would put the players off in any way. With just onlookers sitting on the seats and him and one or two others standing keeping an eye on things it usually went well and you did not see much funny business though you heard stories about a couple of people who had tried it on at one time or another. But if you ask me, any man who tried to pull a stroke down McGinley's place was needing his head examined.

Well, Young Cecil wound up the man in Glasgow they all had to beat, and it was a major upset when anybody did. Sometimes when the likes of Hutchinson came through we saw a fair battle but when the big money was being laid it was never on him if he was meeting Young Cecil. Trouble was you could hardly get a bet on Cecil less he was handing out starts. And then it was never easy to find a punter, and even when you did find one there was liable to be upsets because of the handicapping.

But it was good at that time. Porter's was always buzzing cause Young Cecil still played 1 stick for us with Wee Danny backing him up at Number 2. It was rare walking into an away game knowing everybody was waiting for Young Cecil and Porter's to arrive and the bevy used to flow. They were good days and one or two of us could have afforded to let our broo money lie over a week if we had wanted though none of us ever did. Obviously. Down in McGinley's we were seeing some rare tussles; Young Cecil was not always involved but since he was Number 1 more often than not he was in there somewhere at the windup.

It went well for a hell of a long while.

Then word went the rounds that McGinley and Sweeney were bringing up Cuddihy. He was known as the County Durham at that time. Well, nobody could wait for the day. It was not often you got the chance to see Cuddihy in action and when you did it was worth going a long way to see. He liked a punt and you want to see some of the bets he used to make at times—on individual shots and the rest of it. He might be about to attempt a long hard pot and then just before he lets fly he stands back from the table and cries: Okay. Who'll lay me six to four to a couple of quid?

And sometimes a mug would maybe lay him thirty quid to twenty. That is right, that was his style. A bit gallus but he was pure class. And he could take a drink. To be honest, even us in Porter's did not fancy Young Cecil for this one—and that includes Wee Danny. They said the County Durham was second only to the J.D. fellow though I never heard of them meeting seriously together. But I do not go along with them that said the J.D. fellow would have turned out second best if they had. But we will never know.

They were saying it would be the best game ever seen in Glasgow and that is something. All the daft rumors about it being staged at a football ground were going the rounds. That was nonsense. McGinley was a shrewdie and if he wanted he could have put it on at the Kelvin Hall or something, but the game took place in his club and as far as everybody was concerned that was the way it should be even though most of us from Porter's could not get in to see it at the death.

When the night finally arrived it was like an Old Firm game on New Year's Day. More people were in the cardroom than actually let in to see the game and in a way it was not right for some of the ones left out were McGinley regulars and they had been turned away to let in people we had never clapped eyes on before. And some of us were not even let into the place at all. Right enough a few of us had never been inside McGinley's before, just went to Porter's and thought that would do. So they could not grumble. But the one or two of us who would have been down McGinley's every night of the week if they had let us were classed as I do not know what and not let over the doorstep. That was definitely not fair. Even Wee Danny was lucky to get watching as he told us afterwards. He was carrying our money. And there was some size of a wad there.

Everybody who ever set foot in Porter's was onto Young Cecil that night. And some from down our way who had never set foot in a snooker hall in their lives were onto him as well, and you cannot blame them. The pawnshops ran riot. Everything hockable was hocked. We all went daft. But there was no panic about not finding a punter because everybody knew that Cuddihy would back himself right down to his last penny. A hell of a man. Aye, and he was worth a good few quid too. Wee Danny told us that just before the marker tossed the coin Cuddihy stepped back and shouts: Anybody still wanting a bet now's the time!

And there were still takers at that minute.

All right. We all knew how good the County Durham was; but it made no difference because everybody thought he had made a right bloomer. Like Young Cecil said to us when the news broke a week before the contest: Nobody, he says, can give me that sort of start. I mean it. Not even J.D. himself.

And we believed him. We agreed with him. It was impossible. No man alive could give Young Cecil thirty of a start in each of a five-frame match. It was nonsense. Wee Danny was the same.

Off of thirty I'd play him for everything I've got. I'd lay my weans on it. No danger, he says: Cuddihy's coming the cunt with us. Young Cecil'll sort him out proper. No danger!

And this was the way of it as far as the rest of us were concerned. Right enough on the day you got a few who bet the County Durham. Maybe they had seen him play and that, or heard about him and the rest of it. But reputations are made to be broke and apart from that few, Cuddihy and his mates, everybody else was onto Young Cecil. And they thought they were stonewall certainties.

How wrong we all were.

But what can you say? Young Cecil played well. After the event he said he could not have played better. Just that the County Durham was in a different class. His exact words. What a turn-up for the books. Cuddihy won the first two frames then Young Cecil got his chance in the next but Cuddihy came again and took the fourth for the best of five.

Easy. Easy easy.

What can you do? Wee Danny told us the Frenchman had called Cecil a good handicapper and nothing else.

Well, that was that and a hell of a lot of long faces were going about our side of the river—Porter's was like a cemetery for ages after it. Some of the old heads say it's been going downhill ever since. I do not know. Young Cecil was the best we ever had. Old Porter said there was none better in his day either. So, what do you do? Sweeney told Young Cecil it was no good comparing himself with the likes of Cuddihy but you could see it did not matter.

Young Cecil changed overnight. He got married just before the game anyway and so what with that and the rest of it he dropped out of things. He went on playing 1 stick for us for a while and still had the odd game down McGinley's once or twice. But slowly and surely he just stopped and then somebody spoke for him in Fairfield's and he wound up getting a start in there as a docker or something. But after he retired he started coming in again. Usually he plays billiards nowadays with the one or two of us that are still going about.

Mind you he is still awful good.

No longer the warehouseman

What matters is that I can no longer take gainful employment. That she understands does not mean I am acting correctly. After all, one's family must eat and wear clothes, be kept warm in the winter, and they must also view television if they wish—like any other family. To enable all of this to come to pass I must earn money. Thirteen months have elapsed. This morning I had to begin a job of work in a warehouse as a warehouseman. My year on the labour exchange is up—was up. I am unsure at the moment. No more money was forthcoming unless I had applied for national assistance which I can do but dislike doing for various reasons.

I am worried. A worried father. I have two children, a wife, a stiff rent, the normal debts. To live I should be working but I cannot. This morning I began a new job. As a warehouseman. My wife will be sorry to hear I am no longer gainfully employed in the warehouse. My children are of tender years and will therefore be glad to see me once more about the house although I have only been gone since breakfast time and it is barely five o'clock in the afternoon so they will scarcely have missed me. But my wife: this is a grave problem. One's wife is most understanding. This throws the responsibility on one's own shoulders however. When I mention the fact of my no longer being the warehouseman she will be sympathetic. There is nothing to justify to her. She will also take for granted that the little ones shall be provided for. Yet how do I accomplish this without the gainful employment. I do not know. I dislike applying to the social security office. On occasion one has in the past lost one's temper and deposited one's children on the counter and been obliged to shamefacedly return five minutes later in order to uplift them or accompany the officer to the station. I do not like the social security. Also, one has difficulty in living on the money they provide.

And I must I must. Or else find a new job of work. But after this morning one feels one . . . well, one feels there is something wrong with one.

I wore a clean shirt this morning lest it was expected. Normally I dislike wearing shirts unless I am going to a dinner dance etcetera with the wife. No one was wearing a shirt but myself and the foreman. I did not mind. But I took off my tie immediately and unbuttoned the top two buttons. They gave me a fawn dusk or dust perhaps coat, to put on— without pockets. I said to the foreman it seemed ridiculous to wear an overcoat without pockets. And also I smoke so require a place to keep cigarettes and the box of matches. My trouser pockets are useless. My waist is now larger than when these particular trousers were acquired. Anything bulky in their pockets will cause a certain discomfort.

One feels as though one is going daft. I should have gone straight to the social security in order to get money. Firstly I must sign on at the labour exchange and get a new card and then go to the social security office. I shall take my B1 and my rent book and stuff, and stay calm at all times. They shall make an appointment for me and I shall be there on time otherwise they will not see me. My nerves get frayed. My wife knows little about this. I tell her next to nothing but at other times tell her everything.

I do not feel like telling my wife I am no longer the warehouseman and that next Friday I shall not receive the sum of twenty-five pounds we had been expecting. A small wage. I told the foreman the wage was particularly small. Possibly his eyes clouded. I was of course cool, polite. This is barely a living wage I told him. Wage. An odd word. But I admit to having been aware of all this when I left the labour exchange in order that I might commence employment there. Nobody diddled me. My mind was simply blank. My year was up. One year and six weeks. I could have stayed unemployed and been relatively content. But for the social security. I did not wish to risk losing my temper. Now I shall just have to control myself. Maybe send the wife instead. This might be the practical solution. And the clerks shall look more favorably upon one's wife. Perhaps increase one's rate of payment.

I found the job on my own. Through the evening times sits vac col. It was a queer experience using the timecard once more. Ding ding as it stamps the time. I was given a knife along with the overcoat. For snipping string.

I am at a loss. At my age and considering my parental responsibilities, for example the wife and two weans, I should be paid more than twenty-five pounds. I told the foreman this. It is a start he replied. Start fuck all I answered. It is the future which worries me. How on earth do I pay the monthly rent of £34.30. My wife will be thinking to herself I should have kept the job till securing another. It would have been sensible. Yes. It would have been sensible. Right enough. I cannot recall the how of my acceptance of the job in the first instance. I actually wrote a letter in order to secure an interview. At the interview I was of course cool, polite. Explained that my wife had been ill this past thirteen months. I was most interested in the additional news, that of occasional promotional opportunities. Plus yearly increments and cost of living naturally. Word for word. One is out of touch on the labour exchange. I knew nothing of cost of living allowance. Without which I would have been earning twenty-two sixty or thereabouts.

It is my fault. My wife is to be forgiven if she . . . what. She will not do anything.

There were five other warehousemen plus three warehouselads, a forklift driver, the foreman and myself. At teabreak we sat between racks. An older chap sat on the floor to stretch his legs. Surely there are chairs I said to the foreman. He looked at me in answer. Once a man had downed his tea I was handed the empty cup which had astonishing chips out of its rim. It was kind of him but I did not enjoy the refreshment. And I do not take sugar. But the tea cost nothing. When I receive my first wage I am to begin paying twenty-five pence weekly. I should not have to pay for sugar. It does not matter now.

Time passes. My children age. My wife is in many ways younger than me. She will not say a word about all this. One is in deep trouble. One's bank account lacks money enough. I received a sum for this morning's work but it will shortly be spent. Tomorrow it is necessary I return to the labour exchange. No one will realize I have been gone. Next week should be better. If this day could be wiped from my life or at least go unrecorded I would be happy.

The warehousemen were discussing last night's television. I said good god. A funny smell. A bit musty. Soggy cardboard perhaps.

The boss, the boss—not the foreman—is called Mr Jackson. The foreman is called George. The boss, he . . . The trouble is I can no longer. Even while climbing the subway stairs; as I left the house; was eating my breakfast; rising from my bed; watching the television late last night: I expected it would prove difficult.

Mr Jackson, he is the boss. He also wears a shirt and tie. Eventually the express carriers had arrived and all of we warehousemen and warehouselads were to heave to and load up. It is imperative we do so before lunch said Mr Jackson. I have to leave I said to him. Well hurry back replied George. No, I mean I can no longer stay I explained. I am going home. And could I have my insurance cards and money for this morning's work. What cried Mr Jackson. George was blushing in front of Mr Jackson. Could I have my cards and money. It is imperative I go for a pint and home to see the wife.

I was soon paid off although unable to uplift my insurance cards there and then.

The problem is of course the future—financing the rearing of one's offspring etcetera.

Busted Scotch

J had been looking forward to this Friday night for a while. The first wage from the first job in England. The workmates had assured me they played Brag in this club's casino. It would start when the cabaret ended. Packed full of bodies inside the main hall; rows and rows of men-only drinking pints of bitter and yelling at the strippers. One of the filler acts turned out to be a scotchman doing this harrylauder thing complete with kilt and trimmings. A terrible disgrace. Keep Right On To The End Of The Road he sang with four hundred and fifty males screaming Get Them Off Jock. Fine if I had been drunk and able to join in on the chants but as it was I was staying sober for the Brag ahead. Give the scotchman his due but—he stuck it out till the last and turning his back on them all he gave a big boo boopsidoo with the kilt pulled right up and flashing the Y-fronts. Big applause he got as well. The next act on was an Indian Squaw. Later I saw the side door into the casino section opening. I went through. Blackjack was the game until the cabaret finished. I sat down facing a girl of around my own age, she was wearing a black dress cut off the shoulders. Apart from me there were no other punters in the room.

Want to start, she asked.

Aye. Might as well. I took out my wages.

O, you're scotch. One of your countrymen was on stage tonight.

That a fact.

She nodded as she prepared to deal. She said, How much are you wanting to bet.

I shrugged. I pointed to the wages lying there on the edge of the baize.

All of it . . .

Aye. The lot.

She covered the bet after counting what I had. She dealt the cards.

Twist.

Bust . . .

Acid

In this factory in the north of England acid was essential. It was contained in large vats. Gangways were laid above them. Before these gangways were made completely safe a young man fell into a vat feet first. His screams of agony were heard all over the department. Except for one old fellow the large body of men was so horrified that for a time not one of them could move. In an instant this old fellow who was also the young man's father had clambered up and along the gangway carrying a big pole. Sorry Hughie, he said. And then ducked the young man below the surface. Obviously the old fellow had had to do this because only the head and shoulders—in fact, that which had been seen above the acid was all that remained of the young man.

learning the Story

J once met an old lady sitting under a bridge over the River Kelvin. She smoked Capstan full-strength cigarettes and played the mouthorgan.

The moon was well up as I had passed along the footpath listening to the water fall at the small dam beyond the old mill. Aye, cried the voice, you are there are you! If I had spotted her before she had me I would have crept back the way I had come. Aye, she cried again. And rising to her feet she brought out the mouthorgan from somewhere inside the layers of her clothing, and struck up the tune: Maxwelton Braes Are Bonny was the name of it. Halfway through she suddenly stopped and she stared at me and grunted something. She sat down again on the damp grass with her back against the wall at the tunnel entrance; she stared at her boots. Very good that, I said to her. From her shopping bag she pulled out the packet of Capstan full-strength cigarettes. She sniffed. And I felt as if I had let her down. I always liked that tune, I told her. She struck a match and lighted a cigarette. She flicked the match a distance and it landed with smoke still rising from it. Drawing the shopping bag in between her raised knees she inhaled deeply, exhaled staring at her boots. Cheerio then, I said. I paced on beneath the bridge aware of my footsteps echoing.

The old lady wore specs and had a scarf wrapped round her neck. Her nose was bony. Her skirt may have showed under the hem of her coat. When she was playing the mouthorgan she had moved slightly from foot to foot. Her coat was furry.

Away in Airdrie

During the early hours of the morning the boy was awakened by wheezing, spluttering noises and the smell of a cigarette burning. The blankets hoisted up and the body rolled under, knocking him over onto his brother. And the feet were freezing, an icy draft seemed to come from them. Each time he woke from then on he could either smell the cigarette or see the sulfur head of the match flaring in the dark. When he opened his eyes for the final time the man was sitting up in bed and coughing out: Morning Danny boy, how's it going?

I knew it was you.

Aye, my feet I suppose. Run through and get me a drink of water son will you.

Uncle Archie could make people laugh at breakfast, even Danny's father—but still he had to go to work. He said, If you'd told me you were coming I could've made arrangements.

Ach, I was wanting to surprise yous all. Uncle Archie grinned: You'll be coming to the match afterwards though eh?

The father looked at him.

The boys're through at Airdrie the day.

Aw aye, aye. The father nodded, then he shrugged. If you'd told me earlier Archie—by the time I'm finished work and that . . .

Uncle Archie was smiling: Come on, long time since we went to a match the gether. And you're rare and handy for a train here as well.

Aye I know that but eh; the father hesitated. He glanced at the other faces round the table. He said, Naw Archie. I'll have to be going to my work and that, the gaffer asked me in specially. And I dont like knocking him back, you know how it is.

Ach, come on—

Honest, and by the time I finish it'll be too late. Take the boys but. Danny—Danny'll go anywhere for a game.

Uncle Archie nodded for a moment. How about it lads?

Not me, replied Danny's brother. I've got to go up the town.

Well then . . . Uncle Archie paused and smiled: Me and you Danny boy, eh!

Aye Uncle Archie. Smashing.

Here!—I thought you played the game yourself on Saturdays?

No, the father said, I mean aye—but it's just the mornings he plays, eh Danny?

Aye. Aw that'll be great Uncle Archie. I've never been to Broomfield.

It's no a bad wee park.

Danny noticed his mother was looking across the table at his father while she rose to tidy away the breakfast stuff. He got up and went to collect his football gear from the room. The father also got up, he pulled on his working coat and picked his parcel of sandwiches from the top of the sideboard. When the mother returned from the kitchen he kissed her on the cheek and said he would be home about half past two, and added: See you when you get back Archie. Hope the game goes the right way.

No fear of that! We'll probably take five off them. Uncle Archie grinned, You'll be kicking yourself for no coming—best team we've had in years.

Ach well, Danny'll tell me all about it. Okay then . . . He turned to leave. Cheerio everybody.

The outside door closed. Uncle Archie remained by himself at the table. After a moment the mother brought him an ashtray and lifted the saucer he had been using in its stead. He said, Sorry Betty.

You're smoking too heavy.

I know. I'm trying to . . . He stopped; Danny had come in carrying a tin of black polish and a brush, his football-boots beneath his arm. As he laid the things in front of the fireplace he asked: You seen my jersey mum?

It's where it should be.

The bottom drawer?

She looked at him. He had sat down on the carpet and was taking the lid off the tin of black polish. She waited until he placed an old newspaper under the things, before leaving the room.

Hey Danny, called the Uncle. You needing any supporters this morning?

Supporters?

Aye, I'm a hell of a good shouter you know. Eh, wanting me along? Well . . .

What's up? Uncle Archie grinned.

Glancing up from the book he was reading Danny's brother snorted: He doesnt play any good when people's watching.

Rubbish, cried Danny, it's not that at all. It's just that—the car Uncle Archie, see we go in the teacher's car and there's hardly any space.

With eleven players and the driver! Uncle Archie laughed: I'm no surprised.

But I'll be back in plenty of time for the match, he said as he began brushing the first boot.

Aye well you better because I'll be off my mark at half twelve pronto. Mind now.

Aye.

It's yes, said the mother while coming into the room, she was carrying two cups of fresh tea for herself and Uncle Archie.

Danny was a bit embarrassed, walking with his uncle along the road, and over the big hill leading out from the housing scheme, down towards the railway station in Old Drumchapel. But he met nobody. And there was nothing wrong with the scarf his uncle was wearing, it just looked strange at first, the blue and white, really different from the Rangers' blue. But supporters of a team were entitled to wear its colors. It was better once the train had stopped at Queen Street Station. Danny was surprised to see so many of them all getting on, and hearing their accents. In Airdrie Uncle Archie became surrounded by a big group of them, all laughing and joking. They were passing round a bottle and opening cans of beer.

Hey Danny boy come here a minute! Uncle Archie reached out to grip him by the shoulder, taking him into the middle of the group. See this yin, he was saying: He'll be playing for Rangers in next to no time. The men stared down at him. Aye, went on his uncle, scored two for the school this morning. Man of the Match.

That a fact son? called a man.

Danny reddened.

You're joking! cried Uncle Archie. Bloody ref chalked another three off him for offside! Eh Danny?

Danny was trying to free himself from the grip, to get out of the group.

Another man was chuckling: Ah well son you can forget all about the Rangers this afternoon.

Aye you'll be seeing a *team* the day, grunted an old man who was wearing a bunnet with blue and white checks.

Being in Broomfield Park reminded him of the few occasions he had been inside Hampden watching the Scottish Schoolboys. Hollow kind of air. People standing miles away could be heard talking to each other, the same with the actual players, you could hear them grunting and calling out names. There was a wee box of a Stand that looked like it was balancing on stilts.

The halftime score was one goal apiece. Uncle Archie brought him a bovril and a hot pie soaked in the watery brown sauce. A rare game son eh? he said.

Aye, and the best view I've ever had too.

Eat your pie.

The match had ended in a two-all draw. As they left the terracing he tagged along behind the group Uncle Archie was walking in. He hung about gazing into shop windows when the game was being discussed, not too far from the station. His uncle was very much involved in the chat and after a time he came to where Danny stood. Listen, he said, pointing across and along the road. See that cafe son? Eh, that cafe down there? Here, half a quid for you—away and buy yourself a drink of ginger and a bar of chocolate or something.

Danny nodded.

And I'll come and get you in a minute.

He took the money.

I'm just nipping in for a pint with the lads . . .

Have I to spend it all?

The lot. Uncle Archie grinned.

I'll get chips then, said Danny, but I'll go straight into the cafe and get a cup of tea after, okay?

Fair enough Danny boy fair enough. And I'll come and get you in fifteen minutes pronto. Mind and wait till I come now.

Danny nodded.

He was sitting with an empty cup for ages and the waitress was looking at him. She hovered about at his table till finally she snatched the cup out of his hands. So far he had spent twenty-five pence and he was spending no more. The remaining money was for school through the week. Out from the cafe he crossed the road, along to the pub. Whenever the door opened he peered inside. Soon he could spot his uncle, sitting at a long table, surrounded by a lot of men from the match. But it was impossible to catch his attention, and each time he tried to keep the door open a man seated just inside was kicking it shut.

He wandered along to the station, and back again, continuing on in the opposite direction; he was careful to look round every so often. Then in the doorway of the close next to the pub he lowered himself to sit on his heels. But when the next man was entering the pub Danny was onto his feet and in behind him, keeping to the rear of the man's flapping coattails.

You ready yet Uncle Archie?

Christ Almighty look who's here.

The woman's closing the cafe.

Uncle Archie had turned to the man sitting beside him: It's the brother's boy.

Aw, the man nodded.

What's up son?

It's shut, the cafe.

Just a tick, replied Uncle Archie. He lifted the small tumbler to his lips, indicated the pint glass of beer in front of him on the table. Soon as I finish that we'll be away son. Okay? I'll be out in a minute.

The foot had stretched out and booted the door shut behind him. He lowered himself onto his heels again. He was gazing at an empty cigarette packet, it was being turned in abrupt movements by the draft coming in the close. He wished he could get a pair of wide trousers. The mother and father were against them. He was lucky to get wearing long trousers at all. The father was having to wear short trousers and he was in his last year at school, just about ready to start serving his time at the trade. Boys nowadays were going to regret it for the rest of their days because they were being forced into long trousers before they needed to. Wide trousers. He wasnt bothered if he couldnt get the ones with the pockets down the sideseams, the ordinary ones would do.

The door of the pub swung open as a man came out and passed by the close. Danny was at the door. A hot draft of blue air and the smells of the drink, the whirr of the voices, reds and whites and blues and whites all laughing and swearing and chapping at dominoes.

He walked to the chip shop.

Ten number tens and a book of matches Mrs, for my da.

The woman gave him the cigarettes. When she gave his change he counted it slowly, he said: Much are your chips?

Same as the last time.

Will you give us a milky-way, he asked. He ate half of the chocolate and covered the rest with the wrapping, stuck it into his pocket. He smoked a cigarette; he got to his feet when he had tossed it away down the close.

Edging the door ajar he could see Uncle Archie still at the table. The beer was the same size as the last time. The small tumbler was going back to his lips. Danny sidled his way into the pub, but once inside he went quickly to the long table. He was holding the torn-in-half tickets for the return journey home, clenched in his right hand. He barged a way in between two men and put one of the tickets down on the table quite near to the beer glass.

I'm away now Uncle Archie.

What's up Danny boy?

Nothing. I'm just away home . . . He turned to go then said loudly: But I'll no tell my mother.

He pushed out through the men. He had to get out. Uncle Archie called after him but on he strode sidestepping his way beyond the crowded bar area.

Twenty minutes before the train would leave. In the waiting room he sat by the door and watched for any sign of his uncle. It was quite quiet in the station, considering there had been a game during the afternoon. He found an empty section in a compartment of the train, closed the door and all of the windows, and opened the cigarette packet. The automatic doors shut. He stared back the way until the train had entered a bend in the track then stretched out, reaching his feet over onto the seat opposite. He closed his eyes. But had to open them immediately. He sat up straight, he dropped the cigarette on the floor and then lifted it up and opened the window to throw it out; he shut the window and sat down, resting his head on the back of the seat, he gazed at the floor. The train crashed on beneath the first bridge.

The hitchhiker

I t was a terrible night. From where we were passing the loch lay hidden in the mist and drenching rain. We followed the bend leading round and down towards the village. Each of us held an empty cardboard box above his head. The barman had given them to us, but though they were saturated they were definitely better than nothing. We had been trudging in silence. When we arrived at the bridge over the burn Chas said, There's your hitchhiker.

I glanced up, saw her standing by the gate into one of the small cottages. She appeared to be hesitating. But she went on in, and chapped at the door. A light came on and a youngish woman answered, she shook her head, pointed along the road. The three of us had passed beyond the gate. About 30 yards on I turned to look back, in time to see her entering the path up to the door of another cottage. A man answered and shut the door immediately. The girl was standing there staring up at the window above the door; the porchlight was switched off. Two huge rucksacks strapped onto her back and about her shoulders and when she was walking from the cottage she seemed bent under their weight. Young lassie like that, muttered Sammy. She shouldnt be walking the streets on a night like this.

Aye, said Chas, but she doesnt look as if she's got anywhere to go. It's a while since we saw her.

I nodded. I thought she'd have had a lift by this time. Soaked as well, I said. Look at her.

She's no the only one that's soaked, replied Sammy. Come on, let's move.

Wait a minute, Christ sake.

The girl had noticed us watching her, she quickened her pace in the opposite direction. Sammy said: She's feart.

What?

He grinned at me, indicating the cardboard boxes. The three of us standing gaping at her! what d'you expect son? Sammy paused: If she was my lassie . . . Naw, she shouldnt be out on a night like this.

Not her fault she cant get a lift.

Single lassies shouldnt go hitching on their tod.

Sammy's right, grinned Chas. No with bastards like us going about.

Come on yous pair . . . Sammy was already walking away: Catch pneumonia hanging about in weather like this.

Just a minute, wait till we see what happens.

He paused, glowering at me and grunting unintelligibly. Meanwhile the girl was in chapping on the door of the next cottage. The person who answered gestured along the road in our direction; but once the door had closed she gazed at us in a defiant way and carried on in the opposite direction.

Dirty bastards, I shook my head, not letting her in.

Chas laughed: I'd let her in in a minute.

Away you ya manky swine ye, cried Sammy. His eyebrows rose when he added, Still—she's got a nice wee arse on her.

These specs of yours must have X-ray lenses to see through that anorak she's wearing.

Sammy grinned: Once you reach my age son . . .

Bet you she's a foreigner, said Chas.

A certainty, I nodded.

The girl had just about disappeared into the mist. She crossed over the bridge and I could no longer distinguish her. And a moment later the older man was saying: Right then I'm off.

Chas agreed, Might as well.

The pair of them continued on. I strode after them. Heh Sammy, can the lassie stay the night with us?

Dont be daft son.

How no?

No room.

There is, just about.

Nonsense.

Christ sake Sammy how would you like to be kipping in a ditch on a night like this, eh? fuck sake, no joke man I'm telling you.

God love us son; sharing a caravan with the three of us! you kidding? Anyhow, the lassie herself'd never wear it.

I'll go and tell her it'll be okay but. I mean she can have my bunk, I'll kip on the floor.

Chas was grinning. Sammy shook his head, he muttered: Goodsa-fuckingmaritans, I dont know what it is with yous at all.

Ach come on.

Sammy grunted: What d'you say Chas?

Nothing to do with me, he grinned.

Good on you Chas, I said.

Ah! Sammy shook his head: The lassie'll never wear it.

We'll see.

I passed him the carry-out of beer I had been holding and ran back and across the bridge but when I saw her I slowed down. She had stopped to shrug the rucksacks up more firmly on her shoulders. A few paces on and she stopped again. I caught up to her and said, Hello, but she ignored me. She continued walking.

Hello.

She halted. To see me she twisted her body to the side, she was raging. Glaring at me.

Have you no place to stay? I said.

She hoisted the rucksacks up and turned away, going as fast as she could. I went after her. She was really angry. Before I got my mouth open she stopped and yelled: What.

Have you not got a place for the night?

Pardon . . . She glanced along the road as she said this but there was nobody else in sight. Never anybody in sight in this place, right out in the middle of the wilds it was.

Dont worry. It's okay. You need a place for the night. A house, a place out the rain—eh?

What?

A place to stay the night?

You know?

Hotel, there's a hotel.

Yes yes yes hotel, hotel. She shrugged: It is too much. She looked at me directly and said, Please—I go.

Listen a minute; you can come back to our place. I have place.

I . . . do not understand.

You can come to our place, it's okay, a caravan. Better than hanging about here getting soaked.

She pointed at my chest: You stay?

Aye, yes, I stay. Caravan.

No! And off she trudged.

I went after her. Listen it's okay, no bother—it's not just me. Two friends, the three of us, it's not . . . I mean it's okay, it'll be alright, honest.

She turned on me, raging. What a face. She cried: 1 2 3 . . . And tapped the numbers out on her fingers. 1 2 3, she cried. All man and me.

She tapped 1 finger to her temple and went on her way without hesitation. At the lane which led up to the more modern cottages used by the forestry workers she paused for an instant, then continued along it and out of sight.

Inside the caravan Chas had opened a can of lager for me while I was finishing drying my hair. Both he and Sammy were already under the blankets but they were sitting up, sipping lager and smoking. The rain battered the sides and the roof and the windows of the caravan.

Chas was saying: Did you manage to get through to her but?

Get through to her! Course I didnt get fucking through to her—thought I was going to rape her or something.

Hell of a blow to your ego son, eh! Sammy grinned.

Fuck my ego. Tell you one thing, I'll never sleep the night.

Aye you will, said Chas. You get used to it.

You never get used to it. Never mind but, Sammy chuckled, you can have a chug when we're asleep . . . He laid the can of beer on the floor next to his bunk and wiped his lips with his wrist; he took another cigarette from his packet and lighted it from the dowp-end of the one he had been smoking. He was still chuckling as he said: Mind fine when I was down in Doncaster . . .

Fuck Doncaster.

Chas laughed. Never mind him Sammy—let's hear it.

Naw, better no. Sammy smiled, Wouldnt be fair to the boy.

When I had dried my feet I walked into the kitchenette to hang up the towel. The top section of the window was open. I closed it. If anything the rain seemed to be getting heavier. And back in the main area Chas said: She'll be swimming out there.

Thanks, I said.

Thanks! Sammy snorted, You'd think it was him swimming!

I drank a mouthful of lager, sat down at the foot of my bunk, and lifted the cigarette one of them had left for me. Chas tossed me the matches. A few moments passed before Sammy muttered: Aye, just a pity you never thought to tell her about next door.

I looked at him.

The sparks, he said, they're not here tonight. Had to go back down to Glasgow for some reason.

What?

I'm no sure, I think they needed a bit of cable or something.

Jesus Christ! How in the name of fuck could you no've told me already ya stupid auld . . . I was grabbing my socks and my boots.

Sammy had begun laughing. I forgot son honest, I forgot, I forgot, honest.

Chas was also laughing. The two of them, sitting spluttering over their lager. Fine pair of mates yous are, I told them. Eh! Fuck sake, never've signed on by Christ if I'd known about yous two bastarn comedians. Aye, no wonder they keep dumping yous out in the wilds to work.

Will you listen to this boy? Sammy was chortling.

And Chas yelling: Aye, and me about to lend him my duffel coat as well.

Keeping to the grass verge at the side of the track I walked quickly along from the small group of caravans. The center of the track was bogging. It was always bogging. Even during the short heatwave of the previous week it was bogging. Plastered in animal shit. Cows and sheep and hens, even a couple of skinny goats, they all trooped down here from the flearidden farm a couple of fields away. By the time I got to the road my boots and the bottoms of my jeans were in a hell of a mess. I headed along to the village. Village by Christ—half a dozen cottages and a general store cum post office and the bastards called it a village. Not even a boozer. You had to trek another couple of miles further on to a hotel if you wanted a pint.

Over the bridge I went up the lane to the modern cottages. Although the mist had lifted a bit it was black night but it wasnt too bad, the occasional porchlight having been left on. Where the lane ended I turned back. If she was here she was either sheltering, or hiding.

Round the bend I continued in the direction of the hotel. The rain had definitely lessened, moonlight was glinting on the waters of the loch. I saw her standing at a wee wall next to the carpark entrance, she was with a very old man who was dressed in yellow oilskins, a small yap of a terrier darted about in the weeds at the side of the road. My approach had been noted. The girl finished muttering something to him, and he nodded. She made a movement of some kind, her face had tightened; she stared in the direction of the loch.

Well, I said. Has she not got a place yet?

What was that? The old man leaning to hear me.

I said has she not got a place yet, the lassie, she was looking for a place.

O aye aye, a place.

Aye, a place, has she got one yet?

He waited a moment before shaking his head, and while he half gazed away from me he was saying: I've been telling her try up at Mrs Taylor's house.

Were you?

Aye, aye I was telling her to try there. You know Mrs Taylor's I would think.

Naw, I dont, I dont at all.

Is that right . . . He had glanced at me. You dont know her house then, aye, aye. No, I dont think she'd have any rooms at this time of night. Mrs Taylor, he shook his head. A queer woman that.

The girl turned her head, she was gazing in through the carpark entrance. But her gaze had included me in its maneuver. Look, I told the old man. I'm living on that wee caravan site along past the village. There's a spare one next to where I am. Tell her she'd be alright in there for the night.

He looked at me.

Look it's empty, an empty caravan, she'll be on her tod, nothing to worry about for Christ sake.

The old man paused then stepped the paces to begin chattering to her in her own language. Eventually she nodded, without speaking. She'll go, he said to me.

I told him to tell her I would carry her rucksacks if she wanted. But she shook her head. He shrugged, and the two of us watched her hitch them up onto her shoulders; then she spoke very seriously with him, he smiled and patted her arm. And she was off.

I nodded to him and followed.

She stared directly in front of her thick hiking boots. We passed over the bridge and on to the turnoff for the site. A rumble from the mountains across the loch was followed by a strike of lightning that brightened the length of the bogging track. A crack of thunder. Look, I said, I might as well get a hold of your rucksacks along here, it's hell of a muddy . . . I pointed to the rucksacks indicating I should carry them. I helped them from her. She swung them down and I put one over each of my shoulders. Setting off on the grass verge I then heard her coming splashing along in the middle of the bog, not bothering at all.

The light was out in our caravan. I showed her to the one next, and opened the door for her, standing back to let her enter but she waved me inside first. Dumping the rucksacks on the floor of the kitchenette we went into the main area, it was the same size as the one shared by the three of us. These caravans were only really meant for two people. A stale smell of socks and sweat about the place, but it was fine apart from this, fairly tidy; the sparks must have given it a going-over before returning to Glasgow, and they had taken all their gear with them.

The girl had her arms folded and her shoulders hunched, as if she had recently shivered. She stood with her back to the built-in wardrobe. I nodded and said: I'll be back in a minute.

Chas was snoring. I could see the red glow from Sammy's cigarette. He always had trouble getting to sleep unless drunk; this evening we'd only had 4 or 5 pints each over a period of maybe 3 hours. He said: I heard yous.

Any tea bags?

My jacket pocket.

I also collected two cups and the tin of condensed milk from the cupboard in the kitchenette. It's still teeming down out there, I whispered.

Aye.

She's soaked through. I hesitated. Okay then Sammy—goodnight.

Goodnight son.

I chapped on the door before entering. She was now sitting on a bunk but still wore both her anorak and her hiking boots, her hands thrust deep inside the anorak pockets. When I had made the tea she held the cupful in both hands. No food, I said.

Pardon?

Food, I've no food.

Ah. Yes . . . She placed the tea on the floor, drew a rucksack to her, unzipped it and brought out a plastic container from which she handed me a sandwich. Then she closed the container without taking one for herself.

After a few sips of tea she said, Tea very good.

Aye, you cant beat it.

She looked at me.

The tea, I said, you cant beat it—very very good.

Yes.

She refused a cigarette and when I had my own smoking she asked: You work.

Aye, yes.

Not stay? She gestured at the window. The rain pounding at it.

Naw, not stay. I grinned: I stay in Glasgow.

Ah, she nodded, my friend is Glasgow.

Great place Glasgow. You like it?

Glasgow very good.

Great stuff, have another cup of tea immediately.

She looked at me.

Tea—more tea?

She shook her head. You ah . . . You . . . She continued in french and finished with a shrug: I cannot say this with english.

I shrugged as well and as soon as I had swallowed the last of the tea I rose to put the cups on the draining board at the sink. The girl said, You go now.

I smiled. I go now.

Yes.

In the morning, tomorrow morning I'll be here.

Yes.

I paused at the door.

She half smiled. Tired, tired tired tired.

I nodded and said, Goodnight.

Both of them were washed and ready to leave when I woke up next morning. When Sammy was out of earshot I asked Chas if he thought he would mind if I was a bit late in. Ask him and see, was the reply. Sammy scratched his head when I did. He said: Okay but dont be all morning. I pulled the blankets up to my chin but as soon as I heard the car engine revving I got out of the bunk and dressed. Brushed my teeth, shaved.

Outside it was dry, fresh, a clear morning in June. Across the loch puffy clouds round the Ben. In the hotel bar the previous night Sammy had forecast a return of the warm weather, and it looked like he was going to be right. There was no reply when I chapped the door. I chapped again and went inside. Clothes strewn about the place, as if she had unpacked every last item. And her smell was here now.

She was sleeping on her side, facing into the wall. I stepped back out and chapped the door loudly. Rustling sounds. I clicked the door open.

No!

It's me.

No!

I remained with my hand on the doorknob.

Come!

Her hair rumpled, a pair of jeans and a T-shirt she was wearing, eyes almost closed; she moved about picking things up off the floor and folding them away into the rucksacks; so much stuff lying it seemed odds against the rucksacks being able to take it all. I filled the kettle and shoved it on to boil the water. She looked up: Tea?

Aye, yes, tea.

Your friends?

Work.

Ah.

She stopped clearing up, she yawned while sitting down on the bunk with her back to the wall and her legs drawn up, resting her elbows on her knees. She gazed over her shoulder, out of the window, murmuring to herself in french.

You sleep okay?

Yes, she replied.

She had the plastic container out, the sandwiches ready, when I came back with the tea.

I said, It's a great morning outside, really great. The morning, outside, the weather, really beautiful.

Ah, yes . . . She looked out of the window again and spoke in french, she shrugged.

Tea good?

Very very good, she smiled. She passed me the plastic container.
Fine sandwiches, I told her. What kind of stuff is this?

Pardon?

I parted the 2 slices of bread.

O. Sausage. You like?

It's good.

Yes. Suddenly she laughed, she laughed and held up the sandwich
she was eating: In Glasgow piece—a piece. Yes?

Christ.

She laughed again, flicking the hair from her face: My friend in Glasgow she say peez, geez peez pleez.

That's right geeza piece, I grinned. Heh, more tea? Fancy some more
tea?

She nodded.

At the turnoff for the Mallaig Road we shook hands in a solemn sort
of way, and she headed along in that direction, her gaze to where the
boots were taking her. I watched until she reached the first bend on the
road. She hadnt looked back at all.

When I banged out the signal the hammering halted and I crawled
through the short narrow tunnel into the big chlorine tank we were re-
lining. I climbed the scaffolding. The two of them were now sitting on
the edge of the platform, their legs dangling over, having a smoke. Without speaking I got the working gear on; pulled the safety helmet, the
goggles and the breathing mask into their right positions about my head.
While tugging the sweatband down to my brow a loud snort came from
Sammy, and he said: Looks like he's decided not to speak.

Aye, said Chas.

Waiting for us to ask I suppose.

Must be.

God love us.

A moment later Chas glanced at me: Well?

Well what?

Well?

Well well well.

Hh, Christ.

Ach never bother with him, grunted Sammy.

But Chas said: Did you or didnt you?
What? What d'you mean?
Did you or fucking didnt you?
Did I or didnt I what?
Sammy sighed: Aye or naw, that's all he's asking.
Is it? I laughed.
Orange bastard, muttered Sammy.
So you did then, Chas asked.
Did what?
Ah fuck off.
What's up.
What's up! Chas said, Are you going to tell us? aye or naw!

I had a look at the hammer to make sure it was properly adjusted onto the pressurized air-hose, then got myself a chisel. By the way, I said, thanks for bringing my gear up from below, makes a difference having good mates on a job like this.

Sammy gazed at me. He said to Chas: You wouldnt credit it—look at him, he's not going to tell us anything right enough. Tell you something for nothing Chas it's the last time the cunt'll even smell one of these tea bags of mine.

That goes for my duffel coat, grunted Chas.

I fixed the chisel into the nozzle of the hammer, and began whistling.

Fuck off, cried Chas.

Ach. Never bother, muttered Sammy, never bother. Who's interested anyhow!

I slung the hammer across my shoulder, tugging the air-hose across to the place I had stopped at the day before. Both of them were watching me. I winked before pulling the goggles down over my eyes, triggered off the hammer.

Wee horrors

The backcourt was thick with rubbish as usual. What a mess. I never like thinking about the state it used to get into. As soon as a family flitted out to the new home all the weans were in and dragging off the abandoned furnishings & fittings, most of which they dumped. Plus with the demolition work going on you were getting piles of mortar and old brickwork everywhere. A lot of folk thought the worst kind of rubbish was the soft goods, the mattresses and dirty clothing left behind by the ragmen. Fleas were the problem. It seemed like every night of the week we were having to root them out once the weans came in. Both breeds we were catching, the big yins and the wee yins, the dark and the rusty brown. The pest-control went round from door to door. Useless. The only answer was keeping the weans inside but ours were too old for that. Having visitors in the house was an ordeal, trying to listen to what they were saying while watching for the first signs of scratching. Then last thing at night, before getting into bed, me and the wife had to make a point of checking through our own stuff. Apart from that there was little to be done about it. We did warn the weans but it was useless. Turn your back and they were off downstairs to play at wee houses, dressing up in the clothes and bouncing on the mattresses till all you were left hoping was they would knock the stuffing out the fleas. Some chance. You have to drown the cunts or burn them. A few people get the knack of crushing them between thumbnail and forefinger but I could never master that. Anyway, fleas have got nothing to do with this. I was down in the backcourt to shout my pair up for their tea. The woman up the next close had told me they were all involved in some new den they had built and if I saw hers while I was at it I was to send them up right away. The weans were always making dens. It could be funny to see. You looked out the window and saw what you thought was a pile of rubble and maybe a sheet of tarpaulin stuck on the top. Take another look and you might see a wee head poking out, then another, and another, till finally maybe ten of them were standing there, thinking the coast was clear. But on this occasion I couldnt see a thing. I checked out most of the possibilities. Nothing. No signs of them anywhere. And it was quiet as well. Normally you would've at least heard a couple of squeaks. I tramped about for a time, retracing my steps and so on. I was not too worried. It would have been different if only my pair was missing but there was no sight nor sound of any description. And I was having to start considering the dunnies. This is where I got annoyed. I've always hated dunnies—pitchblack and that smell of charred rubbish, the broken glass, these things your shoes nudge against. Terrible. Then if you're in one and pause a moment there's this silence forcing you to listen. Really bad. I had to go down but. In the second one I tried I found some of the older mob, sitting in a kind of circle round two candles. They heard me come and I knew they had shifted something out of sight, but they recognized me okay and one of the lassies told me she had seen a couple of weans sneaking across to Greegor's. I was really angry at this. I had told them umpteen times never to go there. By rights the place should've got knocked down months ago but progress was being blocked for some reason I dont know, and now the squatters and a couple of the girls were in through the bar-ricading. If you looked over late at night you could see the candle glow at the windows and during the day you were getting the cars crawling along near the pavement. It was hopeless. I went across. Once upon a time a grocer had a shop in the close and this had something to do with how it got called Greegor's. Judging from the smell of food he was still in business. At first I thought it was coming from up the close but the nearer I got I could tell it was coming from the dunny. Down I went. Being a corner block there were a good few twists and turns from the entrance lobby and I was having to go carefully. It felt like planks of wood I was walking on. Then the sounds. A kind of sizzling—making you think of a piece of fucking silverside in the oven, these crackling noises when the juice spurts out. Jesus christ. I shouted the names of my pair. The sound of feet scuffling. I turned a corner and got a hell of a shock—a woman standing in a doorway. Her face wasnt easy to see because of the light from behind her. Then a man appeared. He began nodding away with a daft smile on his face. I recognized them. Wineys. They had been dossing about the area for the past while. Even the face she had told a story, white with red blotches, eyes always seeming to water. She walked in this queer kind of stiff shuffle, her shoes flapping. When she stepped back from the doorway she drew the cuff of her coat sleeve across her mouth. The man was still giving his daft smiles. I followed. Inside the room all the weans were gathered round the middle of the floor. Sheets of newspaper had been spread about. I spotted my pair immediately— scared out their wits at seeing me. I just looked at them. Over at the fireplace a big fire was going, not actually in the fireplace, set to about a yard in front. The spit was fashioned above it and a wee boy stood there, he must've been rotating the fucking thing. Three lumps of meat sizzled away and just to the side were a few cooked bits lined in a row. I hadnt noticed the woman walk across but then she was there and making a show of turning the contraption just so I would know she wasnt giving a fuck about me being there. And him—still smiling, then beginning to make movements as if he wanted to demonstrate how it all worked. He was pointing out a row of raw lumps on the mantelpiece and then reaching for a knife with a thin blade. I shook my head, jesus christ right enough. I grabbed for my pair, yelling at the rest of the weans to get up that effing stair at once.

Roofsliding*

The tenement building upon which the practice occurs is of the three-storey variety. A section of roof bounded on both sides by a row of chimney stacks is favored. No reason is known as to why this particular section should be preferred to another. Certain members of the group participating are thought to reside outwith this actual building though none is a stranger to the district. *Roofsliding*, as it is termed, can take place more than once per week and will always do so during a weekday midmorning. As to the season of the year, this is unimportant; dry days, however, being much sought after.

The men arise in single file from out of the rectangular skylight. They walk along the peak of the roof ensuring that one foot is settling on either side of the jointure which is beveled in design, the angle at the peak representing some 80 degrees. During the walk slates have been known to break loose from their fixtures and if bypassing the gutter will topple over the edge of the building to land on the pavement far below. To offset any danger to the public a boy can always be seen on the opposite pavement, from where he will give warning to the pedestrians.

When the men, sometime designated *roofsliders,* have assembled along the peak they will lower themselves to a sitting posture on the jointure, the legs being outstretched flatly upon the sloped roof. They face to the front of the building. *Roofsliding* will now commence. The feet push forward until the posterior moves off from the jointure onto the roof itself,

---

*This account has been taken more or less verbatim from a pamphlet entitled *Within Our City Slums;* it belongs to the chapter headed "Curious Practices of the Glaswegian." The pamphlet was published in 1932 but is still available in a few 2nd hand bookshops in the south of England.

the process continuing until the body as a whole lies prone on the gradient at which point momentum is effected.

Whether a man "slides" with arms firmly aligned to the trunk, or akimbo, or indeed lying loosely to the sides, would appear to be a function of the number of individuals engaged in the activity at any given period (as many as 32 are said to have participated on occasion). Legs are, however, kept tightly shut. When the feet come to rest on the gutter *roofsliding* halts at once and the order in which members finish plays no part in the practice.

A due pause will now occur. Afterwards the men maneuver themselves inch by inch along the edge of the roof while yet seeming to maintain the prone position. Their goal, the line of chimney stacks that stand up right to the northside of the section. From here the men make their way up to the jointure on hands and knees. It is worth noting that they do so by way of the *outside,* unwilling, it would appear, to hazard even the slightest damage to the "sliding" section that is bounded between here and the line of chimney stacks to the southside. When all have gathered on the jointure once again they will be seated to face the rear of the building. Now and now only shall conversation be entered upon. For up until this period not a man amongst them shall have spoken (since arrival by way of the skylight).

At present a ruddy-complexioned chap in his 44th year is the "elder statesman" of the *roofsliders.* Although the ages do vary within the group no youth shall be admitted who has yet to attain his 14th birthday. On the question of alcohol members are rightly severe, for not only would the "wrong doer" be at mortal risk, so too would the lives of each individual.

As a phenomenon there can be no doubt as to the curious nature of the practice of *roofsliding.* Further observation might well yield fruits.

Not not while the giro

say not talkin about
not analysin nuthin
is if not not

Tom Leonard, *Breathe deep and regular with it*

Of tea so I can really enjoy this 2nd last smoke which will be very very strong which is of course why I drink tea with it in a sense to counteract the harm it must do my inners. Not that tea cures cancer poisoning or even guards against nicotine—helps unclog my mouth a little. Maybe it doesnt. My mouth tastes bad. Hot and kind of squelchy. I am smoking too much old tobacco. 2nd hand tobacco is stiff, is burnt ocher in color and you really shudder before spluttering on the 1st drag. But this is supposed to relieve the craving for longer periods. Maybe it does. It makes no difference anyway, you still smoke them 1 after the other because what happens if you suddenly come into a few quid or fresh tobacco—you cant smoke 2nd hand stuff with the cashinhand and there isnt much chance of donating it to fucking charity. So you smoke rapidly. I do—even with fresh tobacco.

But though the tea is gone I can still enjoy the long smoke. A simple enjoyment, and without guilt. I am wasting time. I am to perambulate to a distant broo. I shall go. I always go. No excuse now it has gone. And it may be my day for the spotcheck at the counter. Rain pours heavily. My coat is in the fashion of yesteryear but I am wearing it. How comes this coat to be with me yet. Not a question although it bears reflecting upon at some later date. Women may have something to do with it. Probably not, that cannot be correct. Anyway, it has nothing to do with anything.

I set myself small tasks, ordeals; for instance: Come on ya bastard ye and smoke your last, then see how your so-called will fucking power stands up. Eh! Naw, you wont do that. Of course I wont, but such thoughts often occur. I may or may not smoke it. And if it does come down to will power how the hell can I honestly say I have any—when circumstances are as they are. Could begin smacking of self pity shortly if this last continues. No, yesteryear's coat is not my style. Imitation Crombies are unbecoming these days, particularly the kind with narrow lapels. This shrewd man I occasionally have dealings with refused said coat on the grounds of said lapels rendering the coat an undesired object by those who frequent said man's premises. Yet I would have reckoned most purchasers of 2nd hand clothing to be wholly unaware of fashions current or olden. But I have faith in him. He does fine. Pawnshops could be nationalized. What a shock for the smalltrader. What next that's what we'd like to know, the corner bloody shop I suppose. Here that's not my line of thought at all. Honest to god, right hand up that the relative strength of the freethinkers is neither here nor there. All we ask is to play up and play the game. Come on you lot, shake hands etcetera. Jesus what is this at all. Fuck all to do with perambulations to the broo.

Last smoke between my lips, right then. Fire flicked off, the last color gone from the bar. Bastarn rain. The Imitation Crombie. And when I look at myself in the mirror I can at least blow smoke in my face. Also desperately needing a pish. Been holding it in for ages by the feel of things. Urinary infections too, they are caused by failing to empty the bladder completely ie. cutting a long pish short and not what's the word—flicking the chopper up and down to get rid of the drips. Particularly if one chances to be uncircumcised. Not at all.

In fact I live in a single bedsitter with sole use of confined kitchenette whose shelves are presently idle. My complexion could be termed gray. As though he hadnt washed for a month your worship. Teeth not so good. Beard a 6 dayer and of all unwashed colors. Shoes suede and stained by dripping. Dripping! The jeans could be fashionable without the Imitation Crombie. Last smoke finished already by christ. Smile. Yes. Hullo. Walk to door. Back to collect the sign-on card from its safe place. I shall be striding through a downpour.

Back from the broo and debating whether I am a headcase after all and this has nothing to do with my ambling in the rain. A neighbor has left a child by my side and gone off to the launderette. An 18 month old child and frankly an imposition. I am not overly fond of children. And this one is totally indifferent to me. The yes I delivered to the neighbor was typically false. She knew fine well but paid no attention. Perhaps she dislikes me intensely. Her husband and I detest each other. In my opinion his thoughts are irrelevant yet he persists in attempting to gain my heed. He fails. My eyes glaze but he seems unaware. Yet his wife appreciates my position and this is important since I can perhaps sleep with her if she sides with me or has any thoughts on the subject of him in relation to me or vice versa. Hell of a boring. I am not particularly attracted to her. A massive woman. I dont care. My vanities lie in other fields. Though at 30 years of age one's hand is insufficient and to be honest again my hand is more or less unused in regard to sexual relief. I rely on the odd wet dream, the odd chance acquaintance, male or female it makes no difference yet either has advantages.

Today the streets were crowded as was the broo. Many elderly women were out shopping and why they viewed me with suspicion is beyond me. I am the kind of fellow who gets belted by umbrellas for the barging of so-called "infirm" pensioners while boarding omnibuses. Nonsense. I am polite. It is possible the Imitation Crombie brushes their shoulders or something in passing but the coat is far too wide for me and if it bumps against anything is liable to cave in rather than knock a body flying. Then again, I rarely wear the garment on buses. Perhaps they think I'm trying to lift their purses or provisions. You never know. If an orange for example dropped from a bag and rolled in my direction I would be reluctant to hand it back to its rightful owner. I steal. In supermarkets I lift flat items such as cheese and other articles. Last week, having allowed the father of the screaming infant to buy me beer in return for my ear, I got a large ashtray and two pint glasses and would have got more but that I lacked the Imitation Crombie. I do not get captured. I got shoved into jail a long time ago but not for stealing cheese. Much worse. Although I am an obviously suspicious character I never get searched. No more.

My shoes lie by the fire, my socks lie on its top. Steam rises. Stomach rumbles. I shall dine with the parents. No scruples on this kind of poncing. This angers the father as does my inability to acquire paid employment. He believes I am not trying, maintains there must be something. And while the mother accepts the prevailing situation she is apt to point out my previous job experience. I have worked at many things. I seldom stay for any length of time in a job because I cannot. Possibly I am a hopeless case.

I talk not at all, am confined to quarters, have no friends. I often refer to persons as friends in order to beg more easily from said persons in order that I may be the less guilty. Not that guilt affects me. It affects my landlord. He climbs the stairs whenever he is unwelcome elsewhere. He is a nyaff, yet often threatens to remove me from the premises under the misapprehension I would not resort to violence. He mentions the mother of this infant in lewd terms but I shall have none of it. Maybe he is a secret child molester. I might spread rumors to pass the time. But no, the infant is too wee. Perhaps I am a latent molester for even considering that. Below me dwells the Mrs Soinson, she has no children and appears unaware of my existence. I have thought of bumping into her and saying, Can I watch your television.

Aye, of course I'll keep the kid for another bastarn half hour. Good christ this is pathetic. The damn parent has to go further messages. Too wet to trail one's offspring. I could hardly reply for rage and noises from the belly and sweet odors from the room of a certain new tenant whom I have yet to clap eyes upon though I hear she is a young lady, a student no doubt, with middle-class admirers or fervent working-class ones or even upper-class yacht drivers. I cannot be expected to compete with that sort of opposition. I shall probably flash her a weary kind of ironic grin that will strike her to the very marrow and gain all her pity/sympathy/respect for a brave but misguided soul. What sort of pish is this at all. Fuck sake I refuse to contemplate further on it although I only got lost in some train of thought and never for one moment contemplated a bastarn thing. I daydream frequently.

This infant sleeps on the floor in an awkward position and could conceivably suffocate but I wont rouse her. The worst could not happen with me here. Scream the fucking place down if I woke her up.

I am fed up with this business. Always my own fault with the terrible false yesses I toss around at random. Why can I not give an honest no

like other people. The same last time. I watched the infant all Friday
night while the parents were off for a few jars to some pub uptown where
this country & western songster performs to astonishing acclaim. Now
why songster and not singer. Anyway, they returned home with a 1/2 bottle of whisky and a couple of cans of lager so it wasnt too bad. This country & western stuff isnt as awful as people say yet there are too many
tales of lost loves and horses for my liking although I admit to enjoying
a good weepy now and then unless recovering from a hangover in which
case—in which case . . . Christ, I may imagine things more than most
but surely the mother—whom for the sake of identity I'll hereon refer
to as Greta. And I might as well call him Percy since it is the worst I can
think of at present—displayed her thigh on purpose. This is a genuine
question. If I decide on some sort of action I must be absolutely sure of
my ground, not be misled into thinking one thing to be true when in
fact the other thing is the case. What. O jesus I have too many problems to concentrate on last week and the rest of it. Who the hell cares.
I do. I do, I wish to screw her, be with her in bed for a lengthy period.

Oxtail soup and insufficient bread which lay on a cracked plate. Brought
on a tray. Maybe she cant trust herself alone with me. Hard to believe
she returned to lunch off similar fare below. I cant help feeling nobody
would offer someone soup under the title of "lunch" without prior explanation. Tea did of course follow but no further bread. I did not borrow from her. I wanted to. I should have. It was necessary. I somehow
expected her to perceive my plight and suggest I accept a minor sum to
tide me over, but no. I once tried old Percy for a fiver on his wages day.
He looked at me as if I was daft. Five quid. A miserable five. Lend
money and lose friends was his comment. Friends by christ.

Sucked my thumb to taste the nicotine. A salty sandish flavor. Perhaps
not. In the good old days I could have raked the coal embers for cigarette ends. Wet pavements. I am in a bad way—even saying I am in a
bad way. 3:30 in the afternoon this approximate Thursday. I have until
Saturday morning to starve to death though I wont. I shall make it no
bother. The postman comes at 8:20—7:50 on Saturdays but the bastarn
postoffice opens not until 9:00 and often 9:05 though they deny it.

I refuse to remain here this evening. I will go beg in some pub where
folk know me. In the past I have starved till the day before payday then

tapped a handful on the strength of it and . . . christ in the early days I
got a tenner once or twice and blew the lot and by the time I had repaid this and reached the Saturday late night I was left with thirty bob
to get me through the rest of the week ie. the following 7 days. Bad bad.
Waking in the morning and trying to slip back into slumber blotting out
the harsh truth but it never works and there you are wide awake and
aware and jesus it is bad. Suicide can be contemplated. Alright. I might
have contemplated it. Or maybe I only imagined it, I mean seriously considered it. Or even simply and without the seriously. In other words I
didnt contemplate suicide at all. I probably regarded the circumstances
as being ideal. Yet in my opinion

No more of this shite. But borrowing large sums knowing they have to
be repaid and the effects etc must have something to do with the deathwish. I refuse to discuss it. A naive position. And how could I starve to
death in two days, particularly having recently lunched upon oxtail soup.
People last for weeks so long as water is available.

Why am I against action. I was late to sign-on this morning though prepared for hours beforehand. Waken early these days or sometimes late.
If I had ten pence I would enter supermarkets and steal flat items. And
talking about water I can make tea, one cup of which gives the idea if
not the sustenance of soup because of the tea bag's encrustation viz
crumbs of old food, oose, hair, dandruff and dust. Maybe the new girl
shall come borrow sugar from me. And then what will transpire. If

Had to go for a slash there and action: the thing being held between middle finger and thumb with the index slightly bent at the first joint so that
the outside, including the nail, lay along it; a pleasant, natural grip. If I
had held the index a fraction more bent I would have soaked the
linoleum to the side of the pot. And the crux is of course that the act is
natural. I have never set out to pish in that manner. It simply happens.
Everyman the same I suppose with minute adjustments here and there
according to differing chopper measurements. Yet surely the length of
finger will vary in relation. Logical thought at last. Coherence is attain-
able as far as the learned Hamish Smith of Esher Suffolk would have
us believe. I am no Englishman. I am for nationalization on a national
scale and if you are a smalltrader well

No point journeying forth before opening time.

It is possible I might eat with the neighbors as a last resort and perhaps watch television although in view of the oxtail soup a deal to hope for. But I would far rather be abroad in a tavern in earnest conversation with keen people over the state of nations, and I vow to listen. No day-dreaming or vacant gazing right hand up and honest to god. Nor shall I inadvertently yawn hugely. But my condition is such company is imperative. I can no longer remain with myself. And that includes Percy, Greta and the infant, let us say Gloria—all three of whom I shall term the Nulties. The Nulties are a brave little unit gallantly making their way through a harsh uncaring world. They married in late life and having endeavored for a little one were overwhelmed by their success. The infant Gloria is considered not a bad-looking child though personally her looks dont appeal. She has a very tiny nose, pointed ears, receding hair. Also she shits over everything. Mainly diarrhea that has an amazingly syrupy smell. Like many mothers Greta doesnt always realize the smell exists while on the other hand is absolutely aware so that she begins apologizing left right and center. Yet if everybody resembles me no wonder she forgets the bastarn smell because I for the sake of decency am liable to reply: What smell?

Greta is a busy mum with scarce the time for outside interests. There is nothing or perhaps a lot to say about Percy but it is hell of a boring. The point is that one of these days he shall awaken to an empty house. The woman will have upped and gone and with any sense will have neglected to uplift the infant. Trouble with many mothers is their falling for the propaganda dished out concerning them ie. and their offspring— Woman's Own magazines and that kind of shite. Most men fall for it too. But I am being sidetracked by gibberish. No, I fail to fit into their cozy scene for various reasons the most obvious of which is 3's a crowd and that's that for the time being.

But dear god I cannot eat with them tonight. They skimp on grub. One Saturday (and the straits must have been beyond desperation if Saturday it truly was) they sat me down and we set to on a plate of toast and tinned spaghetti. For the evening repast! My christ. But what I said was, Toast and spaghetti, great stuff. Now how can I tell such untruths and is it any wonder that I'm fucking languishing. No, definitely not. I deserve all of it. Imitation tomato sauce on my chin. And after the meal we turn to the telly over a digestive smoke and pitcher of coffee essence & recently boiled water; and gape our way to the Late Weather. I could make the poor old Nulties even worse by saying they stand for God Save The Queen Of The Great English Speakers but they dont to my knowledge—it is possible they wait till I have departed upstairs.

I have no wish to continue a life of the Nulties.

Something must be done. A decisive course of action. Tramping around pubs in the offchance of bumping into wealthy acquaintances is a depressing affair. And as far as I remember none of mine are wealthy and even then it is never a doddle to beg from acquaintances—hard enough with friends. Of which I no longer have. No fucking wonder. But old friends I no longer see can no longer be termed friends and since they are obliged to be something I describe them as acquaintances. In fact every last individual I recollect at a given moment is logically entitled to be termed acquaintance. And yet

Why the lies, concerning the tapping of a few bob; I find it easy. Never in the least embarrassed though occasionally I have recourse to the expression of such in order to be adduced ethical or something. I am a natural born beggar. Yes. Honest. A natural born beggar. I should take permanently to the road.

The pubs I tramp are those used by former colleagues, fellow employees of the many firms which have in the past employed me for mutual profit. My christ. Only when skint and totally out of the game do I consider the tramp. Yet apparently my company is not anathema. Eccentric but not unlikable. A healthy respect is perhaps accorded one. Untrue. I am treated in the manner of a sick younger brother. It is my absolute lack of interest in any subject that may arise in their conversation that appeals to them. I dislike debates, confessions and New Year resolutions. I answer only in monosyllables, even when women are present: Still Waters Run Deep is the adage I expect them to use of me. But there are no grounds for complaint. Neither from them nor from me. All I ask is the free bevy, the smoke, the heat. It could embarrass somebody less sensitive than myself. What was that. No, there are weightier problems. The bathwater has been running. Is the new girl about to dip a daintily naked toe. Maybe it is Mrs Soinson. Or Greta. And the infant Gloria. And Percy by christ. But no, Percy showers in the work to save the ten pence meter money. Petty petty petty. I dont bathe at all. I have what might be described as an alloverbodywash here in the kitchenette sink. I do every part of my surface bar certain sections of my lower to middle back which are impossible to reach without one of those long-stemmed brushes I often saw years ago in amazing American Movies.

Incredible. Someone decides to bathe in a bath and so the rest of us are forced to run the risk of bladder infection. Nobody chapped my door. How do they know I didnt need to go. So inconsiderate for fuck sake that's really bad. Too much tea right enough, that's the problem.

No, Greta probably entertains no thoughts at all of being in bed with me. I once contemplated the possibility of Percy entertaining such notions. But I must immediately confess to this strong dislike as mutual. And he is most unattractive. And whereas almost any woman is attractive and desirable only a slender few men are. I dont of course mean slenderly proportioned men, in fact—what is this at all. I dont want to sleep with men right hand up and honest to god I dont. Why such strenuous denials my good fellow. No reason. Oho. Honest. Okay then. It's a meal I need, a few pints, a smoke, open air and outlook, the secure abode. Concerted energy, decisive course of action. Satisfyingly gainful employment. Money. A decidable and complete system of life. Ungibberishness. So many needs and the nonexistent funds. I must leave these square quarters of mine this very night. I must worm my way into company, any company, and the more ingratiatingly the better.

Having dug out a pair of uncracked socks I have often made the normal ablutions and left these quarters with or without the Imitation Crombie. Beginning in a pub near the city center I find nobody. Now to start a quest such as this in a fashion such as this is fucking awful. Not uncommon nevertheless yet this same pub is always the first pub and must always be the first pub in this the quest.

Utter rubbish. How in the name of christ can one possibly consider suicide when one's giro arrives in two days' time. Two days. But it is still

Thursday. Thursday. Surely midnight has passed and so technically it is tomorrow morning, the next day—Friday. Friday morning. O jesus and tomorrow the world. Amen. Giro tomorrow. In a bad way, no. Certainly not. Who are you kidding. I have to sleep. Tomorrow ie. tonight is Friday's sleep. But two sleeps equal two days. What am I facing here. And so what. I wish

To hell with that for a game.

But I did move recently. I sought out my fellows. Did I really though. As a crux this could be imperative, analogous to the deathwish. Even considering the possibility sheds doubt. Not necessarily. In fact I dont believe it for a single solitary minute. I did want to get in with a crowd though, surely to christ. Maybe I wasnt trying hard enough. But I honestly required company. Perhaps they had altered their drinking habits. Because of me. In the name of fuck all they had to do was humiliate me—not that I would have been bothered by it but at least it could have allayed their feelings—as if some sort of showdown had taken place. But to actually change their pub. Well well well. Perhaps they sense I was setting out on a tramp and remained indoors with shutters drawn, lights extinguished. My christ I'm predictable. Three pubs I went to and I gave up. Always been the same: I lack follow-through. Ach.

Can I really say I enjoy life with money. When I have it I throw it away. Only relax when skint. When skint I am a hulk—husk. No sidesteps from the issue. I do not want money ergo I do not want to be happy. The current me is my heart's desire. Surely not. Yet it appears the case. I am always needing money and I am always getting rid of it. This must be hammered home to me. Not even a question of wrecking my life, just that I am content to wallow. Nay, enjoy. I should commit suicide. Unconsecrated ground shall be my eternal resting spot. But why commit suicide if enjoying oneself. Come out of hiding Hamish Smith. Esher Suffolk cannot hold you.

Next time the landlord shows up I shall drygulch him; stab him to death and steal his lot. Stab him to death. Sick to the teeth of daydreams. As if I could stab the nyaff. Maybe I could pick a fight with him and smash in his skull with a broken wine bottle and crash, blood and brains and wine over my wrist and clenched fist. The deathwish after all. Albeit murder. Sounds more rational that: ie. why destroy one's own life if enjoyable. No reason at all. Is there a question. None whatsoever, in fact I might be onto something deep here but too late to pursue it, too late. Yet it could be a revelation of an extraordinary nature. But previously of course been exhausted by the learned Smith of Esher decades since and nowadays taken for granted—not even a topic on an inferior year's O-level examination paper.

He isnt even a landlord. I refer to him as such but in reality he is only the bastarn agent. I dont know who the actual landlord really is. It might be Winsom Properties. Winsom Properties is a trust. That means you never know who you are dealing with. I dont like this kind of carry-on. I prefer to know names.

Hell with them and their fucking shutters and lights out.

It isnt as bad as all that; here I am and it is now the short a.m.'s. The short a.m.'s. I await the water boiling for a final cup of tea. Probably only drink the stuff in order to pish. Does offer a sort of relief. And simply strolling to the kitchenette and preparing this tea: the gushing tap, the kettle, gathering the tea bag from the crumb strewn shelf—all of this is motion.

My head gets thick.

One of the chief characteristics of my early, mid and late adolescence was the catastrophic form of the erotic content. Catastrophic in the sense that that which I did have was totally, well, not quite, fantasy. And is the lack by implication of an unnatural variety. Whether it is something to do with me or not—I mean whether or not it is catastrophic is nothing to do with me I mean, not at all. No.

Mr Smith, where are you. No, I cannot be bothered considering the early years. Who cares. Me of course it was fucking lousy. I masturbated frequently. My imagination was/is such I always had fresh stores of fantasies. And I dont wish to give the impression I still masturbate; nowadays, for example, I encounter difficulties in sustaining an erection unless another person happens to be in the immediate vicinity. Even first thing in the morning. This is all bastarn lies. Why in the name of fuck do I continue. What is it with me at all. Something must have upset me recently. Erotic content by christ. Why am I wiped out. Utterly skint. Eh. Why is this always as usual. Why do I even

Certain clerks behind the counter.

I mend fuses for people, oddjobs and that kind of bla for associates of the nyaff, tenants in other words. I am expected to do it. I allow my— I fall behind with the fucking rent. Terrible situation. I have to keep on his right side. Anyway, I dont mind the oddjobs. It gets you out and about.

I used to give him openings for a life of Mrs Soinson but all he could ever manage was, Fussy Old Biddy. And neither he nor she is married. I cant figure the woman out myself. Apart from her I might be the longest tenant on the premises. And when the nyaff knows so little about her you can be sure nobody else knows a thing. She must mend her own fuses. I havent even seen inside her room or rooms. It is highly possible that she actually fails to see me when we pass on the staircase. The nyaff regards her in awe. Is she a blacksheep outcast of an influential family closely connected to Winsom Properties. When he first became agent around here I think he looked upon her as easy meat whatever the hell that might mean as far as a nyaff is concerned. And she cant be more than fifty years of age, carries herself well and would seem an obvious widow. But I dispute that. A man probably wronged her many years ago. Jilted. With her beautiful 16 year old younger sister by her as bridesmaid, an engagement ring on her finger just decorously biding her time till this marriage of her big sister is out the way so she can step in and get married to her own youthful admirer, and on the other side of poor old Mrs Soinson stood her widowed father or should I say sat since he would have been an invalid and in his carriage, only waiting his eldest daughter's marriage so he can join his dearly departed who died in childbirth (that of the beautiful 16 year old) up there in heaven. And ever since that day Mrs Soinson has remained a spinster, virginal, the dutiful but pathetic aunt—a role she hates but accepts for her parents' memory. Or she could have looked after the aged father till it was too late and for some reason, on the day he died, vowed to stay a single lassie since nobody could take the place of the departed dad and took on the title of Mistress to ward off would-be suitors although of course you do find men more willing to entertain a single Mrs as opposed to a single Miss which is why I agree with Womens Lib. Ms should be the title of both married and single women.

In the name of god.

Taking everything into consideration the time may be approaching when I shall begin regularly paid, full-time employment. My lot is severely trying. For an approximate age I have been receiving money from the state. I am obliged to cease this malingering and earn an honest penny. Having lived in this fashion for so long I am well nigh unemployable and if I were an Industrial Magnate or Captain of Industry I would certainly entertain doubts as to my capacity for toil. I am an idle goodfornothing. A neerdowell. The workhouse is too good for the likes of me. I own up. I am incompatible with this Great British Society. My production rate is less than atrocious. An honest laboring job is outwith my grasp. Wielding a shabby brush is not to be my lot. Never more shall I be setting forth on bitter mornings just at the break of dawn through slimy backstreet alleys, the treacherous urban undergrowth, trudging the meanest cobbled streets and hideously misshappen pathways of this gray with a heart of gold city. Where is that godforsaken factory. Let me at it. A trier. I would say so Your Magnateship. And was Never Say Die the type of adage one could apply to the wretch. I believe so Your Industrialness.

Fuck off.

Often I sit by the window in order to sort myself out—a group therapy within, and I am content with a behaviorist approach, none of that pie-in-the-sky metaphysics here if you dont mind. I quick-fire trip questions at myself which demand immediate answers and sometimes elongated thought-out ones. So far I have been unsuccessful, and the most honest comment on this is that it is done unintentionally on purpose, a very deeply structured item. Choosing this window for instance only reinforces the point. I am way way on top, high above the street. And though the outlook is unopen considerable activity takes place directly below.

In future I may dabble in psychiatry—get a book out the library on the subject and stick in, go to nightschool and obtain the necessary qualifications for minor university acceptance whose exams I shall scrape through, industrious but lacking the spark of genius, and eventually make it into a general sanatorium leading a life of devotion to the mental health of mankind. I would really enjoy the work. I would like to organize beneficial group therapies and the rest of it. Daily discussions. Saving young men and women from all kinds of breakdowns. And you would definitely have to be alert working beside the average headbanger or disturbed soul who are in reality the sane and we the insane according to the learned H. S. of Esher S. But though I appear to jest I give plenty thought to the subject. At least once during their days everybody has considered themselves mad or at least well on the road but fortunately from listening to the BBC they realize that if they really were mad they would never for one moment consider it as a possible description of their condition although sometimes they almost have to when reading a book by an enlightened foreigner or watching a heavy play or documentary or something—I mean later, when lying in bed with the lights out for example with the wife fast asleep and 8 1/2 months pregnant maybe then suddenly he advances and not too accidentally bumps her on the shoulder all ready with some shite about, O sorry if I disturbed you, tossing and turning etc but I was just wondering eh . . . And then it dawns on him, this, the awful truth, he is off his head or at best has an astonishingly bad memory—and this memory under the circumstances may actually be at worst. And that enlightened foreigner is no comfort once she will have returned to slumber and you are on your own, alone, in the middle of the night, the dark recesses and so on dan d ran dan. But it must happen sometimes. What must fucking happen.

The postoffice may be seeking reliable men. Perhaps I shall fail their medical. And that goes for the fireservice. But the armed forces. Security. And each branch is willing and eager to take on such as myself. I shall apply. The Military Life would suit me. Uplift the responsibility, the decision making, temptations, choices. And a sound bank account at the windup—not a vast sum of course but enough to set me up as a tobacconist cum newsagent in a small way, nothing fancy, just to eke out the pension.

But there should be direction at 30 years of age. A knowing where I am going. Alright Sir Hamish we cant all be Charles Clore and Florence Nightingale but at least we damn well have a go and dont give in. Okay we may realize what it is all about and to hell with their christianity, ethics, the whole shebang and advertising but do we give in, do we Give Up The Ghost. No sirree by god we dont. Do you for one moment think we believe someone should starve to death while another feeds his dog on the finest fillet of steak and chips. Of course not. We none of us have outmoded beliefs but do we

I cannot place a finger somewhere. The bastarn rain is the cause. It pours, steadily for a time then heavier. Of course the fucking gutter has rotted and the constant torrent drops just above the fucking window. That bastard of a landlord gets nothing done, too busy peeping through keyholes at poor old Mrs Soinson. I am fed up with it. Weather been terrible for years. No wonder people look the way they do. Who can blame them. Christ it is bad, the weather, so fucking consistent. Depresses everything. Recently I went for a short jaunt in the disagreeable countryside. Fortunately I got soaked through. The cattle ignored the rain. The few motor cars around splished past squirting oily mud onto the Imitation Crombie. I kept slipping into marshy bogs from whence I shrieked at various objects while seated. It wasnt boring. Of yore, on country rambles, I would doze in some deserted field with the sun beating etc the hum of grasshoppers chirp. I never sleep in a field where cattle graze lest I get nibbled. The countryside and I are incompatible. Everybody maintains they like the countryside but I refuse to accept such nonsense. It is absurd. Just scared, to admit the truth—that they hate even the idea of journeying through pastureland or craggyland. Jesus christ. I dont mind small streams burning through arableland. Hardy fishermen with waders knee-deep in lonely inshore waters earn my total indifference. Not exactly. Not sympathy either, nor pity, nor respect, envy, hate. Contempt. No, not at all. But I heroworship lighthousekeepers. No. Envy is closer. Or maybe jealousy. And anyway, nowadays all men are created equal. But whenever I have had money in the past I always enjoyed the downpour. If on the road to somewhere the rain is fine. A set purpose. Even the cinema. Coat collar upturned, street lights reflecting on puddles, arriving with wind-flushed complexion and rubbing your damp hands, parking your arse on a convenient convector heater. But without the money. Still not too bad perhaps.

According to the mirror I have been going about with a thoughtful expression on one's countenance. I appear to have become aware of myself in relation to the field by which I mean the external world. In relation to the field I am in full knowledge of my position. And this has nothing to do with steak & chips

Comfortable degrees of security are not to be scoffed at. I doff the cap to those who attain it the bastards. Seriously, I am fed up with being fed up. What I do wish

I shall not entertain daydreams
I shall not fantasize
I shall endeavor to make things work

I shall tramp the mean streets in search of menial posts or skilled ones. Everywhere I shall go, from Shetland Oilrigs to Bearsden Gardening Jobs. To Gloucestershire even. I would go to Gloucestershire. Would I fuck. To hell with them and their cricket & cheese. I refuse to go there. I may emigrate to The Great Englishes—o jesus christ Australia & New Zealand. Or America and Canada.

All I'm fucking asking is regular giros and punctual counter clerks.

Ach well son cheer up. So quiet in this dump. Some kind of tune was droning around a while back. I was sitting clapping hands to the rhythm and considering moving about on the floor. I used to dream of playing the banjo. Or even the guitar, just being able to strum but with a passable voice I could be dropping into parties and playing a song, couple of women at the feet keeping time and slowly sipping from a tall glass, 4 in the a.m.'s with whisky on the shelf and plenty of smokes. This is it now. Definitely.

black and white consumer and producer parasite thief come on shake hands you lot

Well throw yourself out the fucking window then. Throw myself out fuck all window—do what you like but here I am, no suicide and no malnutrition, no fucking nothing in fact because I am leaving, I am getting to fuck out of it. A temporary highly paid job, save a right few quid and then off on one's travels. Things will be done. Action immediate. Of the Pioneering Stock would you say. Of that ilk most certainly Your Worship. And were the audience Clambering to their Feet. I should think so Your Grace.

The fact is I am a late starter. I am

I shouldnt be bothering about money anyway. The creditors have probably forgotten all about my existence. No point worrying about other than current arrears. The old me wouldnt require funds. A red & white polkadot handkerchief, a stout sapling rod, the hearty whistle and hi yo silver for the short ride to the outskirts of town, Carlisle and points south.

It is all a load of shite. I often plan things out then before the last minute do something ridiculous to ensure the plan's failure. If I did decide to clear the arrears and get a few quid together, follow up with a symbolic burning of the Imitation Crombie and in short make preparations to mend my ways I could conceivably enlist in the Majestic Navy to spite myself—or even fork out a couple of months' rent in advance for this dump simply to sit back and enjoy my next step from a safe distance and all the time guffawing in the background good christ I am schizophrenic, I never thought I acted in that manner yet I must admit it sounds like me, worse than I imagined, bad, bad. Maybe I could use the cash to pay for an extended stay in a private nursing home geared to the needs of the Unabletocope. But can it be schizophrenia if I can identify it myself. Doubtful. However, I regard

I was of the opinion certain items in regard to my future had been resolved. Cynical of self, this is the problem. Each time I make a firm resolution I end up scoffing. Yes. I sneer. Well well well, what a shite. That really does take the biscuit. And look at the time look at the time.

Captains of Industry should create situations for my ilk. The Works Philosopher I could be. With my own wee room to the left of the Personnel Section. During teabreaks Dissidents would be sent to me. Militancy could be cut by half, maybe as much as 90%. Yet Works Philosophers could not be classed as staff, instead they would be stamping in & out like the rest of the troops just in case they get aspirations, and seek reclassification within Personnel maybe. Gibberish. And yet fine, that would be fine, so what if they got onto the staff because that would leave space for others and the Dissident next in line could become the new Works Philosopher and so on and so forth. And they would stick it, the job, they would not be obliged to seek out square squarters whose shelves are crumb-strewn.

I shall have it to grips soon. Tomorrow or who knows. After all, I am but 30, hardly matured. But fuck me I'm getting hell of a hairy these days. Maybe visit the barber in the near future, Saturday morning for instance, who knows what is in store. Only waiting for my passion to find an object and let itself go. Yes, who can tell what's in store, that's the great thing about life, always one more fish in the sea, iron in the fire; this is the great thing about life, the uncertainty and the bla

Jesus what will I do, save up for a new life, the mending of the ways, pay off arrears, knock the door of accredited creditors, yes, I can still decide what to do about things concerning myself and even others if only in regard to me at least it is still indirectly to do with them and yet it isnt indirect at all because it is logically bound to be direct if it is anything and obviously it is something and must therefore be directly since I am involved and if they are well

well well, who can tell what the fuck this is about. I am chucking it in. My brain cannot cope on its own. Gets carried away for the sake of thought no matter whether it be sense or not, no, that is the last fucking thing considered. Which presents problems. I really do have a hard time knowing where I am going. For if going, where. Nowhere or somewhere. Children and hot meals. Homes and security and the neighbours in for a quiet drink at the weekend. Tumbling on carpets with the weans and television sets and golf and even heated discussions in jocular mood while the wives gossip ben in the kitchen and

Now then: here I am in curiously meager surroundings, living the life of a hapless pauper, my pieces of miserable silver supplied gratis by the Browbeaten Taxpayer. The past ramblings concerning outer change were pure invention. And comments made about one's total inadequacy were done so in earnest albeit with a touch of pride. Even the brave Nulties are abused by me, at least in respect to grub & smokes. And all for what. Ah, an ugly sight. But this must be admitted: with a rumbling stomach I have often refused food, preferring a lonely smoke and the possible mystery of, Has he eaten elsewhere . . . and if so with whom. Yet for all people know I have several trunks packed full of articles, clothes and whatnot. Apart from a couple of clerks nobody knows a thing about me. I could be a Man about Town. They probably nudge each other and refer to me as a bit of a lad. I might start humping large suitcases plastered with illegible labels. Save up and buy a suit in modern mode. Get my coat dyed, even stick with its symbolic burning. Or else I could sell it. A shrewd man I occasionally have dealings with rejected this coat. But I did ask a Big price. Shoes too I need. Presently I have what are described as Bumpers. Whereas with real leather efforts and a new rig out I could travel anywhere and get a new start in life. I could be a Computer Programmer. But they're supposed to reach their peak at 21 years of age. Still and all the sex potency fucking peak is 16. 16 years of age by christ you could not credit that. Ach. I dare say sex plays more of a role in my life than grub. If both were in abundance my problems could only increase. Yet one's mental capacities would be bound to make more use of their potential without problems at the fundamental level.

But

the plan. From now on I do not cash giros. I sleep in on Saturday mornings and so too late for the postoffice until Monday mornings by which time everything will be alright, it will be fine, I shall have it worked out and fine and if I can stretch it out and grab at next Saturday then the pathway shall have been erected, I shall have won through.

Recently I lived in seclusion. For a considerable period I existed on a tiny islet not far from Toay. Sheep and swooping gulls for companions. The land and the sea. After dark the inner recesses. Self-knowledge and acceptance of the awareness. No trees of course. None. Sheer drops from mountainous regions, bird shit and that of sheep and goats as well perhaps, in that kind of terrain. No sign of man or woman. The sun always far in the sky but no clouds. Not tanned either. Weatherbeaten. Hair matted by the salt spray. Food requires no mention. Swirling eddies within the standing rocks and nicotine wool stuck to the jaggy edges, the droppings of the gulls.

Since I shall have nothing to look forwards to on Saturday mornings I must reach a state of neither up nor down. Always the same. That will be miserable I presume but considering my heart's desire is to be miserable then with uncashed giros reaching for the ceiling I can be indefinitely miserable. Total misery. However, to retain misery I may be obliged to get out and about in order not to be always miserable since— or should I say pleasure is imperative if perfect misery is the goal; and, therefore, a basic condition of my perpetual misery is the occasional jaunt abroad in quest of joy. Now we're getting somewhere Sir Smith, arise and get your purple sash. And since ambling round pubs only depresses me I must seek out other means of entertainment or henceforth desist this description of myself as wretch. And setbacks and kicksintheteeth are out of the question. Masochism then. Is this what

Obviously I am just in the middle of a nervous breakdown, even saying it I mean that alone

But for christ sake saving a year's uncashed giros is impossible because the bastards render them uncashable after a 6 month interval.

Walking from Land's End to John O'Groat's would be ideal in fact because for one thing it would tax my resistance to the utmost. Slogging on day in day out. Have to be during the summer. I dislike the cold water and I would be stopping off for a swim. Yet this not knowing how long it takes the average walker . . . well, why worry, time is of no concern. Or perhaps it should be. I could try for the record. After the second attempt possibly. Once I had my bearings. Not at all. I would amble. And with pendants and flags attached to the suitcase I could beg my grub & tobacco. The minimum money required. Neither broo nor social security. The self-sufficiency of the sweetly self-employed. I could be for the

rest of my life. The Land's End to John O'Groat's man. That would be
my title. My name a byword, although anonymity would be the thing to
aim for. Jesus it could be good. And far from impossible. I have often
hitched about the place. Many times. But hitching must be banned otherwise I shall be saving time which is of course an absurdity—pointless
to hitch. And yet what difference will it make if I do save time because
it can make no difference anyway. None whatsoever. Not at all. And if
it takes 6 weeks a trip and the same back up I could average 4 return
trips a year. If I am halfway through life just now ie. a hundred and
twenty return trips then in another hundred and twenty trips I would
be dead. I can mark off each trip on milestones north & south. And when
the media get a grip of me I can simply say I'll be calling a halt in 80
trips time. And I speak of returns. That would be twenty years hence
by which time I would have become accustomed to fame. Although I
could have fallen down dead by then through fatigue or something. Hail
rain shine. The dead of winter would be a challenge and could force me
into shelter unless I acquire a passport and head out to sunnier climes,
Australia for example to stave off the language barriers yet speech need
be no problem since communication will be the major lack as intention
perhaps. No, impossible. I cannot leave The Great British Shores.
Comes to that I cannot leave the Scottish ones either. Yes, aye, Scotland
is ideal. Straight round the Scottish Coast from the foot of Galloway right
round to Berwick although Ayrshire is a worry its being a very boring
coastline. But boredom is out of the question. Ayrshire will not be de-
nied. So each return trip might involve say a four month slog if keeping
rigidly to the coast on all minor roads particularly when you consider
Kintyre—or Morven by fuck and even I suppose Galloway itself to some
extent. But that kind of thing is easily resolved. I dont have to restrict
myself to mapped-out routes from which the slightest deviation is
frowned upon. On the contrary, that last minute decision at the country crossroads can only enhance the affair. And certain items of clothing are already marked out as essential items. The stout boots and
gnarled staff to ward off country animals after dusk. A hat & coat for
wet weather. The Imitation Crombie may suffice. Though an anorak to
cover the knees would probably reap dividends. And after a few return
trips—and being a circular route no such thing as a return would exist
ie. I would be traveling on an arc—the farmfolk and country dwellers
would know me well, the goodwives leaving thick winter woollies by the

side of the road, flasks of oxtail soup under hedges. Shepherds offering shelter in remote bothies by the blazing log fires sipping hot toddies for the wildest nights and plenty of tobacco always the one essential luxury, and the children up and down the land crying, Mummy here comes the Scottish Coastroad Walker, while I would dispense the homespun philosophies of the daisy growing and the planet as it revolves etc. A stray dog joining me having tagged along for a trip at a safe distance behind me I at last turn and at my first grunt of encouragement it comes bounding joyfully forwards to shower me in wet noses and barked assurances to stick by me through thick & thin and to eternally guard my last lowly grave when I have at length fallen in midstride plumb tuckered out after many years viz 12 round trips at two years a trip. Yet it might be shorter than that. While the hot days in central summer are the busloads of tourists arriving to see me, pointed out by their driver, the Legend of the North, the solitary trudging humpbacked figure with dog & gnarled staff just vanishing out of sight into the mist, Dont give him money Your Lordship you'll just hurt his feelings. Just a bit of your cheese piece and a saucer of milk for the whelp. Group photographs with me peering suspiciously at the camera from behind shoulders at the back or in the immediate foreground perhaps, It is rumored the man was a Captain of Industry Your Grace, been right round the Scottish Coastroad 28 times and known from Galloway to Berwick as a friend to Everyone. Yes, just a pinch of your snuff and a packet of cigarette-papers for chewing purposes only. No sextants or compasses or any of that kind of shite but

the paperbag

What was the point anyway, there didn't seem to be any at all. I footered about with the newspaper, no longer even pretending interest. It was useless. I felt totally useless—I was useless, totally. I crumpled the newspaper in both hands, watching it, seeing the shapes it made, the way its pages became.

I would go on a walk; that was what to do. I uncrumpled the newspaper and rolled it into a neat sort of bundle, to carry it in my right hand, and then began walking. O christ but it was good to be alive—really. Really and truly. I felt magnificent. Absolutely wonderful. What was it about this life that made a body feel so good, so absolutely fucking wonderful. Was everybody the same. Now I was chuckling. Not too loudly but, no point worrying folk. A woman approached, her message bags not too full, preoccupied, the slight smile on her face. Where else could it be? Her eyes. Her eyes could be smiling. Is that possible. I was chuckling again. And then the mongrel appeared. I recognized it right away: a stupid kind of beast, even how it trotted was a bit stupid—plus that something about it, that odd look it could give—as though it was a fucking mule! Mule. Why did I think of that, mule. Well it was a beast and it was stupid-looking—or rather, it behaved stupidly, the way it looked at folk and didnt do as they desired, they wanted it off the pavement out their road but it never went off the pavement out their road, it just carried on trotting till sometimes they even had to get out of *its* road. Amazing. Imagine giving it a kick! Just going up and giving it a kick. Or else poisoning it. Taking it away on a long walk and then dumping it— maybe on a bus journey right out the other side of the city, pushing it off and shutting the door, leaving the thing yelping in astonishment. What'll happen to me now! Christ sake the dirty bastard he's pushed me off the bus and shut the door and I dont know where I've landed!

Imagine being a dog but—murder! people taking you wherever they like and you dont have a say in the matter. Here boy, here boy. I would hate to be a dog like that, getting ordered about by cunts without knowing what for, not having a genuine say on the matter. Horrible, really fucking horrible. And then getting put down for christ sake sometimes for nothing, no reason, just for doing what dogs do. Biting people!

Crazy, walking along the road thinking about such stuff. Absolute fucking nonsense. Mongrels by christ! But that's what happens. And thinking of that is better than thinking of nothing. I would say so anyway. Or would I? The trouble with being useless is this thinking; it becomes routine, you cannot stop yourself. I think all the time, even when I'm reading my newspaper. And the things I think about are fucking crazy. Imagine going up to somebody and saying Hey, have you ever felt like screwing the queen? Just to actually say it to somebody. Incredible. This is the kind of thing I can think about. I cannot help it. I didnt always think like it either. I used to think about ordinary things. Or did I? I find it hard to tell.

Then she was coming towards me but I didnt notice properly till there we were having to get out each other's road. Sorry, I said and I smiled in a hopeful manner. I was lost in abstraction. . . .

And then I smiled coyly, this coyliness compensating for the use of the long word, abstraction. But everything was fine, everything was fine, she understood. It's okay, she replied, I was a bit abstracted myself.

And of course she was! Otherwise she'd've fucking bumped into me if she hadnt been careful to get out my road while I was getting out of hers!

Then she had dropped a paperbag and was bending down to retrieve it; and once she had retrieved it she opened it and peered inside.

And so did I!

I just fucking stretched forwards and poked my head next to hers—not in any sort of ambiguous way but just to peer into the bag same as her. She glanced at me, quite surprised. Then we smiled at each other as though in appreciation of the absurdity of my reaction. And yet it had been a true reaction. Normally I'm not a nosy person. But having said all of that I have to confess that it maybe was a bit ambiguous, maybe I was trying to get a bit closer to her because it should be said that she was nice, in fact she was really nice. The way she was standing there and then bending to get her paperbag etc., the smile she had, and above all that understanding, how she had eh o christ o christ, o christ and there wasnt anything I could say, nothing, nothing at all because I was without funds, absolutely fucking without funds. So after a wee moment I smiled, an unhealthy smile—even at the actual instant it was happening I was thinking how it would be to have a blunderbuss whose muzzle I could stick my head into and then pull the trigger.

It was a surprise to see her still standing there. How come she was still standing there the way things were. I didnt even know her. I had never seen her before in all my life. I said: Eh d'you live eh roundabout? But she didnt reply. She was frowning at something. She hadnt paid the slightest attention to what I had said. And no wonder, the things I say, they're always so fucking boring, so fucking boring. Why am I the most fucking boring bastard in the whole fucking world? Her cake was bashed. Inside the paperbag was a cake and it had become bashed because of falling on the pavement. I could have mentioned that to her. That was something to say, instead of this, this fucking standing, just fucking standing there, almost greeting, greeting my eyes out. I was just standing there having to stop myself greeting like a wean, looking at her, trying to make her see and by making her see stopping myself and making everything fine, everything fine, if she would just stay on a minute or two and we could maybe have a chat or something—just a couple of minutes' chat, that would have worked the oracle, maybe, to let her see. Because after all, she hadnt been put off by the way I had peered into her bag; she had recognized it as a plain ordinary reaction, the sort of thing that happens out of curiosity—a bit stupid right enough, the way a kid acts. And yet she hadnt been put off. Not even as a person had I put her off. She smiled at me, a true smile—there again, it had happened at the point of departure

for yes, that moment had indeed arrived and was gone now, gone forever. And so too was she, trotting along the pavement, away to a life that was much better than this one. If I could run after her and clasp her by the hand.

I had unrolled the newspaper and was glancing at the back page, an item of football news. I could just have run after her and said Sorry—for having almost bumped right into her and making her drop the paperbag. But what was the point of it all? it was useless, totally fucking useless. I crumpled the newspaper in my right hand then grabbed it from there with my left, and continued the walk.

In a betting shop to the rear of Shaftesbury Avenue

Heh John! John . . . I grinned: How you doing?

He made to walk past me.

John, I said quickly, how's it going—I thought you were in Manchester?

What . . . He looked at me. My name's no John. He sniffed and glanced sideways, then muttered: McKechnie.

McKechnie! Christ. Aye . . . I thought you were in Manchester? How you doing man?

He looked away from me. I've no been in Manchester for years. And again he made to walk past, but I stepped slightly to the front.

Christ, so you left!

Aye, years ago. He sniffed, gazed round the interior of the betting shop. It was a poky wee dump of a place and with nearly quarter of an hour till the first race only a couple of people were about. McKechnie looked at them. He was holding a rolled newspaper in his left hand.

So how long you been here then? you been here long?

What . . . naw. He glanced up at the board to where a clerk had gone to scribble the names of the day's nonrunners. He glanced across to the counter; the two women were eating sandwiches, sipping at cups of tea. Then he glanced back to me, and he frowned momentarily. He said: Mind that wife of mine? I'm in for a divorce off her. She wants the wean, but I'm getting the wean. Lawyer says I'm a certainty. And these lawyers know the score . . .

Aye.

He nodded.

After a moment I said, Aye—these lawyers!

He nodded again. The door opened and in came a punter, then another. McKechnie had noticed them and he moved slightly. And then the knocking sound from the Extel speaker and through it came the first betting show of the day.

The other people were now standing gazing at the formpages tacked onto the walls; up at the board the clerk was marking in the prices against the listed runners, he held a fresh cigarette cupped in one hand.

McKechnie unrolled his newspaper.

So you left then?

What . . .

Manchester, you left?

He nodded without taking his gaze from the newspaper, not even raising his head. But he muttered, Aye—I went to Sheffield.

Sheffield!

Mmhh.

Christ sake!

At this point a further betting show came through. When it was over I said: Sheffield!

Mmm. He sniffed, still gazing at the racing page.

Did you never think of going back then? to Manchester I mean—did you ever think of going back?

What . . . He shook his head, and he grunted: Hard race this.

I shrugged. Favorite cant get beat, it's a good thing.

Aye . . . He indicated the selection of one of the racing journalists. That's what he says and all. I dont know but, I hate backing these fucking odds-on shots. It's one to beat it I want . . . And he glanced at me, and added: Warrior Chief's supposed to be the only danger . . .

Aye, it's got a wee chance right enough. Heh d'you ever see Tommy on your travels?

Tommy? His forehead wrinkled as he glanced at me again.

Tommy, christ, you must mind him—used to work in the building game. Carried the hod or something.

Aw aye, aye, I mind him. Subbied.

You're right! Hh! I laughed. That's right man—Tommy, christ: lucky bastard eh! must've made a real few quid, no having to pay any tax or fuck all.

McKechnie nodded; then he sniffed and indicated the comments on the race by the journalist. According to this cunt, Warrior Chief's the only danger.

Aye, it's got a chance. Heh, I wouldnt mind a start subbying somewhere myself, eh—that's the right way if . . .

Hard race but, McKechnie muttered, a lottery, fucking lottery.

Another betting show was in progress and I altered my stance a bit, to be able to see the racecard in his newspaper. Then when it was over I said: What about yourself man, you working?

Who me . . . He sniffed, he glanced up at the board, rolling up his newspaper at the same time. Hang on a minute, he said, I need a pish.

And he walked off immediately.

I went to the nearby wall; the front page of the *Chronicle* was tacked here and I read the postmortems on yesterday's results. A couple of minutes before the *off* I looked up. I noticed McKechnie, he was standing right beside two old codgers who didnt look to have the price of a packet of Rizlas between them.

And it dawned on me: there wasnt any toilets in this fucking betting shop.

I crossed the floor. He had taken a brand-new packet of cigarettes from his pocket and was unwrapping the cellophane. He looked at me and extended the packet. Ta, I said. When we were smoking I smiled: To tell you the truth man, I never even knew you were married never mind in for a divorce!

What! christ, where've you been? Married—I've been married for years.

Hh. Who to? that wee thing back in Manchester?

He glanced at me: I was well married before I hit that fucking place. He sniffed. She thinks she'll get the wean but she's got no chance.

Good . . . I nodded. But still and all, sometimes . . .

Hang on a minute, I'm just . . . He turned and squinted at the form-page on the wall. Then he was edging along to where another punter stood and I could hear him mutter, This Warrior Chief's supposed to have a chance of upsetting the favorite . . .

I stepped over and peered at the form. Could do, I said, but the favorite's got a good bit of class about her. Won hell of a comfortably last time out and the way I heard it she won hell of a cleverly, a hands and heels game.

The punter was maneuvering himself to write out his line in such a way that nobody would see what he wrote. Suddenly McKechnie thumped the page on the wall. That's the thing I'm feart of, he said.

Dark Lights?

Dark Lights. He nodded, and he grinned briefly. Dark Lights . . .

Hh.

Aye, he went on, they've just stuck it in here.

What?

Aye, fucking obvious.

I nodded. It's got a chance right enough. But you cant always rely on winning form out of *maiden* races; I mean this is the first time it'll have run in a *handicap*, and you know as well as . . .

Hang on a minute, he said. And he walked to a different wall, to where a youth was standing gazing at another formpage; I could see him begin muttering.

Then the runners were being loaded into the starting stalls and the youth strode to the counter to place his bet; and shortly afterwards McKechnie had scribbled down his own bet and was striding to the counter just as they were set to come *under orders*. And when the woman had returned him his change and receipt he went to the other side of the room.

It was no a bad nightlife in Manchester, I said when I got there.

What . . .

The nightlife—Manchester. Mind you, it's no bad here if you know where to go. Murder when you're skint but.

He nodded.

Aye, I said.

He sniffed: I've no been here that long.

What! christ, ach dont worry, dont worry man I mean you'll soon find your way about—once you get the hang of their fucking tube system. And then, when you've got a few quid you can always . . .

I'm going up the road the morrow.

Eh?

Edinburgh. I'm going to Edinburgh.

Edinburgh! Christ sake. Edinburgh . . . I nodded. Aw aye, I'll tell you . . .

OFF BRIGHTON: THEY'RE OFF BRIGHTON: RUNNING 2.17: AND ON THE OFF THEY BET FOUR TO NINE NUMBER THREE, FIVE TO TWO BAR . . .

The race was over the minimum trip and soon they were entering the final stretch; taking the lead at the distance the favorite won going away—exactly the style in which an odds-on shot should win.

A horse by the name of Lucy's Slipper ran on to snatch second place close home. Neither Warrior Chief nor Dark Lights had received a mention throughout the entire commentary.

But McKechnie was grinning all over his face. Told you, he shouted, I fucking told you—that favorite: couldnt get beat—a fucking certainty! I knew it.

I nodded. Trained at Epsom as well if you noticed. These Epsom runners usually do good here, the track, nice and sharp, fast. And . . .

The forecast! McKechnie was laughing and he elbowed me in the ribs: I've dug out the forecast!

What?

The forecast—I've dug it out, that Lucy's Slipper! a certainty for second place, I knew it, I fucking knew it.

Hh.

He winked. I'll tell you something: the shrewd money, all the shrewd money's down to it. Know what I mean? they've just stuck it in here—for the forecast. Fucking obvious. Think they're going to take odds-on on a single when they can lift five or six to one on a fucking forecast? you kidding!

Aye, eh.

Kept saying it all morning to myself: look for a forecast I says, look for a forecast, this favorite cant get beat, look for a forecast. McKechnie grinned and shook his head. And after a moment he glanced to the pay-out window. The youth stood there, holding a receipt in one hand. McKechnie walked across; he was still grinning; then I could hear him say: So you got it?

The youth nodded, and they began comparing notes on the following race in between congratulating each other on the last, as they waited for the *weigh-in*.

McKechnie copped the next three winners but the youth didnt return to the payout window. It had become difficult to tell where he was getting his selections; various people were going to the payout and McKechnie seemed to be in contact with most of them. He kept edging his way in and out of places, eavesdropping here and there. He had this peculiar kind of shuffle, dragging his heels as if his shoes were hell of a heavy—he probably kept a reserve fund stuffed inside his socks the bastard.

I went out for a breath of fresh air. I walked up and down the street a couple of times. Back inside he continued to dodge me but then I stepped right in front of him and said: A nicker, just a nicker, that's all, I'll give you it back man, honest.

Aw I cant, he said, no the now—I'm going to stick the lot on this next favorite. I'll weigh you in after but, dont worry, you'll be alright then—a nicker? Aye, no bother, you'll be alright for a nicker.

He about turned and walked to study a formpage, close in beside the two old codgers. Then just as the first show of betting came through on the next race I noticed him glance at me. Moments later he did a vanishing trick out the door. He probably thinks I didnt see him but I did.

O jesus, here come the dwarfs

When the dwarfs appear everything is at an end. All you ever fixed. The lot. All gone. On the Thursday night they are there. The process of rapid disintegration then follows. Until that point problems do not exist. Problems? what are they at all! no such things. Afterwards there is nothing else.

Dwarfs never have anything fixed, plans have not been laid down, there are no "eventualities." They have nothing whatsoever. Yet they come and they take over. And they look at each other as though joined at the nose, while the feet are being cawed from the very ground you walk on. Nothing can remain the same. Tents will have started collapsing. Those previously occupied are mysteriously empty. Dustbins have been overspilling their contents into the long grass. Television sets explode without causal explanation. And the swimming pool is become infested by insects and wee dods of animal shite. Moles. Moles are burrowing beneath groundsheets apparently. All the things, they all stop working. Continual reports of blocked toilet bowls and sinks; and a pile of pots has been found behind the kitchen area, these pots used to be fine but are now food-encrusted beyond repair; and the smells, all the smells, now encroaching throughout the walking area. And into this same walking area come farm animals, bleating. And the site shop seems to have ceased trading: the wee woman from the village no longer arrives first thing in the morning—that great wee woman who always gave you the cheery nod and allowed you the couple of grocery items plus tobacco on tick till wagesday no problem if the coast was clear.

All gone. All of it.

Yet though holidaymakers may grumble the dwarfs will remain silent. Dwarfs dont grumble. They just smile, are humble, are thoughtful to others. They go dashing around endeavoring to help, ostensibly existing for your especial convenience whereas the reality: you are being set fair for a corner wherein the possibility of laying down your life is advancing. Do not believe in their smile. It is not happy-go-lucky. They have arrived in the pub on Thursday evening because tomorrow you get your wages. When first you bear witness to the voices your puzzled but immediate response is to fuck off home to the tent. This you will not do, having some vague notion that by remaining aloof you must influence events; thus you stand there, awaiting the barman, gradually becoming aware that a cloud of staggering proportions has settled above your head. It is all over. Chance could have reaped a future as secure as this. Aye, of course your defenses were down. A Thursday evening. You are tired out, just managed to tap Pierre for the price of a couple of pints, enough to see you through the evening in a quiet way.

With determined nonchalance you will carry your pint to the domino table to sit on the fringe of the onlookers. But the nodded greeting to such as Emil or Jaques was perfunctory, you are totally preoccupied by something you arent quite able to grasp. Then you are amazed to realize that some sort of inflection of the voices at the bar was giving you to understand that you were supposed to be charging across the room crying: Welcome dwarfs welcome! It is incredible. You lean forwards, place your pint on the ledge beneath the table, rest your elbows on your knees, attempting to devote your complete attention to the game of dominoes. But this is not the weekend, it is Thursday evening and the bar is not full to bursting with exuberant holidaymakers. Voices echo. The dwarfs know fine well you can hear them. It is what they intend. They intend that you hear them, that their voices can and must be heard. At this stage you are not quite admitting your quandary and are willing to indulge in such internal asides as: Am I hearing things! hoping against hope that the consequent ironic smile about your mouth will be noticed. But so what if it is? And why are you in this position in the first place? Is there anybody there to answer such questions? How come you are having to ask them? What the fuck is it? What is going on? Maybe you are hearing things after all. Thursday night, you've been tired out, too knackered even to cook yourself a proper meal, you just washed and came straight down the pub; maybe you're fucking hallucinating. No matter, for by this time you are unable to contain the pressure—your belly, it has been churning—the beer giving you heartburn, the tobacco maybe, burning your lips and causing that dryness in the mouth and you're having to tighten your lips and close your eyelids, trying to suppress the rage. It is rage; you are raging, you have lifted your pint but your hand is shaking and you slam the pint glass down onto the table and jump to your feet and go marching across to deliver the most bitter diatribe ever heard in the pub. But the dwarfs are just sitting there, occasionally drawing their noses together. Are they naive? Is that all it is? How can you tell? You cannot tell. There is no surefire way of knowing. And you are sitting at their table. Here you are on a chair adjacent to theirs. And the questions are coming at you from all angles and if you dont put a stop immediately you are seconds away from giving a moment by moment account of all, all the things. Those pauses occurring in the conversation. Aye, you were about to speak. You must be alert, you have to sit there saying nothing, turning pauses into longer pauses. Or questions into questions: you can turn questions into questions. Tax them on their existence, on their experience, their expectations—above all else their expectations. What precisely is it they are demanding of you? What is it that you are to be having done? Well for starters: consider the things you never classed as problems because of your studied attention to possible eventualities—the things you classified under the banner "impossible." Not only have the dwarfs encountered such things as problems, they have surmounted them. Apparently without having realized it. They havent even realized those things were problems, they just fucking went ahead and got beyond them. And they are gaping at you, at your irritation. They have no comprehension of its cause, and will look to each other as though joined at the nose. Meanwhile you do not feel a mug. Somehow you are given to understand that you yourself are the one individual present who genuinely is aware of the central ins and outs. Only you know the truth, that you are a fucking mug, that you have never known anything, nothing, nothing whatsoever. It is odd. You will sit for a moment, gazing into space, then jump up and rush to the domino table to collect your pint and your tobacco and matches, and back with the dwarfs you . . . Back with the dwarfs? Aye, exactly, of your own volition. It really is fucking incredible. You will look at them for signs of guilt but why should there be? Do they have cause for guilt? It was you returned to sit beside them. You stare at them, and discover that the pint you are holding contains a fresh quantity of beer; it's not the same pint at all—you swallowed the remains of your first in a gulp and the dwarfs have bought you a new one. There is no deceit. Everything is out in the open and being accomplished fairly. They are actually insisting that they dont want a drink in return. They dont want one. They maybe know you are skint because it's a Thursday evening and are quite rightly opposed to you letting yourself in for taking favors from the barman. He's a taciturn old bastard and you hate having to ask for credit even though it's in his own interest, which is why you prefer tapping Pierre although it means that extra 20 percent on the loan, but there you are, and across at the bar a few folk are waiting to be served—unusual in itself considering the day of the week it is—which makes it difficult to signal the old cunt and when finally you do he comes over and will make it necessary to raise your voice so that almost every customer in the fucking place is now aware you've been asking for tick, and for that reason alone you're somehow obliged to add to your order at the last minute; you call for whiskies as well as the beer. Now obviously the dwarfs didnt want any fucking whisky and neither did you and there is no satisfactory explanation as to why you will have done it, but you will have fucking done it and that's that. Down on the table you thrust the drinks, right under the dwarfs' noses, not able to say a word. If you so much as glance at them you will end up having to punch them, you will kick fuck out them, you will smash a bottle across their bastarn skulls. What you do is settle on your chair and stare at the whisky, eventually shuddering in anticipation of that horrible boke ahead, when the first drop of whisky hits at your tastebuds, all the time knowing how the dwarfs will gulp at theirs and express an honest relish of the flavor. Moments later you have invited them back to the site.

The possibility of spare tents. Who was mentioning that in an absentminded manner? The very question must send you into a reverie on the nature of dualism. Meanwhile, the dwarfs are trying to stop themselves bounding up and down on their chairs. Their studied, unclamorous display of thanks cannot be properly described. Yet you will recognize its truth. The dwarfs mean no harm. Nor is there any side to them. They make their feelings manifest in the only way they know. You attempt to lay the blame on their shoulders but know fine well that it is all down to you. It is a total waste of time. It is a fraud. Everything is a fraud. Every last thing is a fraud. And on you go for the next few minutes inventing different ways of saying the same thing, till finally your head develops its own release and suddenly the noises of the pub bring you back to reality: you leap up off your chair and shout it is time to be going! if you dont leave at once the tents must no longer be available! The dwarfs will look at each other behind your back, indicating the drinks on the table and whether they swallow what remains or not can never be known for you are already outside the door, gasping at the fresh air, clawing for the stillness of the evening, those quiet, distant sounds of the countryside after dusk.

The doors bang open, and click shut; the dwarfs are beside you, waiting in silence, gazing over the fields in the direction of the site, enjoying the scene, its tranquillity. Now you will tell them the tent can be theirs for one night and one night only because as far as authority is concerned yours is less than fuck all if truth be told and you are really only doing this as a favor for some reason or another you're not quite sure except that you cannot take any chances because the camping site proprietor is a funny kind of cunt who takes instant dislikes to people for no apparent reason. And come morning they must bolt the course at all costs—either that or they'll have to seek an interview with the man himself because you'll have nothing more to do with it. Sorry, but that's that. You carry on talking like this, any kind of rubbish will do, just so long as it offers the slim possibility of them deciding against the site. And without warning you march off down the lane, clattering your boots to keep from hearing their footsteps behind you. And what about their fucking goods and chattels you're thinking. Surely they've fucking brought something with them! Are they just going to come straight down the lane after you without even having to stop off and collect a bundle of suitcases from beneath a fucking bush! What is it with these dwarfs you're thinking. What in the name of christ is it all about? The went-befores! This is what you're looking for. But there arent any went-befores. Nor is it a simple matter of faith in you as the kind of total stranger who doesnt mind putting oneself about on behalf of a fellow human being. Not at all. What is it then? Fuck knows, you dont have an earthly. Maybe they are Christians you think, who can tell with dwarfs. And then, as though wafting on the breeze one matter-of-fact voice is remarking to another on some remote question such as the itness of the stars and since you will have come in at the end and not really heard you'll toss out some sort of daft comment such as the funny thing about stars is you never hear anybody remarking on them in a specific sense but only as some kind of vaguely collective unity viz O look at the stars—but never O look at that particular star up there to the right-hand side of the bastarn moon. And then the reply, the reply you receive. Have you never heard of the Pole? Or the Plowe? What about the Plowe? The Plowe by christ! But you have been so tightly, so tightly, so—knotted, so tightly knotted up inside that you havent a fucking clue about the Plowe at all until they spell it out as p-l-o-u-g-h and then you remember all about the fucking thing but in so exasperated a fashion you will demand to know why it is called the Plough and not just plain ordinary plough plural since there is a fucking cluster of the bastards—jesus christ you're shouting why do they not simply say there's Plough instead of fucking the Plough. And before you know where you are you're off and charging home to the tent. Home to the tent. What a fraud. This tent was never home. You only labeled it home for some fanciful notion you had about watering holes and final resting places. In fact, this tent in which you are currently dwelling is situated on a camping site you have yet to admit is falling down about your ears. Aye, precisely, the camping site has been disintegrating: you were ignoring it, probably hoping the problem would go away. But the very presence of the dwarfs is enough to establish the reality. And for some reason you will now go off at a tangent, raving at the dwarfs on the subject of necessities; of the need to keep tents clean, of not smoking under canvas, of rolling up one's walls in the morning to let in the fresh air because everybody knows there's nothing worse than stuffy tents at the height of summer. Not so bad if you are on your tod as the likes of yourself but hopeless when there's more than one sharing. And what about the needs of the third party. On a camping site a great many people live and all it requires is one bad apple and the whole place takes a nosedive. Consider for example tidiness: it isnt a question of being fucking neat, it all has to do with hygiene. If you forget to clean your fucking pots and pans you wind up getting mice and rats and christ knows what else. The same applies to the swimming pool. You go walking about all day in the middle of fields in your bare feet and then jump in for a swim and what happens? fucking obvious. And holidaymaking weans just run about here, there and everywhere, and there's no point telling the parents cause they just fucking look at you, and the same applies to chucking food away into the long grass, as if it's going to disappear. That is the kind of thing that happens. This is why you have to be tidy. The chores must be done. It is necessary. You glance at the dwarfs to see whether they are appreciating the point. They will be walking beside you—not exactly parallel because they dont like being forward, a couple of steps to the rear they will be. And they pause significantly while you unbolt the fence into the walking area. At this point you know you've been talking a load of rubbish. They will enjoy doing the chores. Chores shall be done without a grumble. It isnt that dwarfs enjoy chores. In fact they do not do chores because chores do not exist. Chores? what are they at all! They just see themselves as performing a lot of wee actions. They perform this list of wee actions they see as necessary if ever they are to become fully fledged campers. Jesus christ. And now you glimpse your tent, away to the rear of the field, where you had figured isolation a certainty until the day the first holidaymaking family had arrived and pitched their tent next door, under the misapprehension some sort of prearranged order had been given. Behind you the hinges of the gate creak as the dwarfs footer around, letting you hear that they are well up on country matters and are bolting the lock on the fucking fence. The door of the Ladies Washroom opens and out steps a mum. She will be a young mum and this is the end of her second week, she leaves on Saturday morning. She always wears a thin summer dress and goes about barelegged and has taken on a great tan while her husband has remained a peely wally white no matter how often he lies out in the sun on that inflatable rubber mattress. And even so, the most she has ever given you is a nodded good morning or good evening without once saying hello. And here she is bestowing a beaming smile on the dwarfs and all they do is grin idiotically. There's no fucking point any longer. You pause a minute in case she thinks you're following her and then wave your arm in the direction of the tents, before leaving the dwarfs to take their pick. And you walk by a roundabout path to your own tent, knowing that come a certain stage they should be unable to see you in the dark. And even if you're fucking luminous, so what? The dwarfs have arrived and there are empty tents, the game is up. Your part is at an end. From hereon you have become redundant. You are no longer required. They see that you have no authority. They must do as they please, they can come or go and stay or leave. What they do has become their own affair. Aw jesus you think, they're off my back at last; and inside the tent you bury yourself beneath a pile of blankets and just manage to set the alarm before falling completely asleep. It is Thursday night after all, and you've been tired out, up since half five in the morning and out working a 12-hour shift in the fields. Not even the dwarfs can keep you awake.

The next day is very strange indeed. Unfathomable matters are somehow in motion. Things are taking place slightly beyond arm's reach.

It is funny. Out in the field you are smiling to yourself quite frequently. It is no surprise to discover you have had a bad morning. The frenchmen are frowning; you arent picking your fair share of the crop. But there again, your back and shoulders are more knackered than usual and once you've had your dinner you'll make it all up in the afternoon session. But you will find yourself lagging behind yet again. You were in a reverie. What the hell was it about? You cannot remember; it is all hazy, something to do with green fields and blue skies and walking down to a sandy beach, arm in arm with a young woman dressed in a summer dress, a bikini on underneath. Now that you dwell on it you vaguely recollect having listened in on the conversation you both were having. What was it about? It was probably important. Up ahead the lorry has arrived and the frenchmen are carrying the crop across to it—Emil and Jaques are already there and loading. Normally you would be there also. You like to be first and to be seen doing the heavy work. Fuck it you're thinking, you cannot be bothered today. Yet this is Friday. Glorious Friday. Of all the days this is the day, the one you get weighed in with the wages and see yourself fixed for another week. Even forming the words makes it seem ridiculous. Your trouble is you're a dreamer. You have been carrying on as though things are remaining the same. But even in the act of admitting this to yourself you are aware of the smile lurking about your mouth. The truth is you dont fucking care, you arent really bothering. If you were bothering why are you here when you could be home guarding your interests? The farmer would have given you the day off if you had asked. In fact, you preferred to come in and spend the day picking spuds; you knew it would allow your brain to take off, it would allow you the opportunity of ignoring the dwarfs—an opportunity which you werent slow to accept. Ah well you're thinking, that's it all fucking finished now, and thank christ for that. Aye, precisely, that's what you are thinking at this very point. You will be doing nothing whatsoever. You will be stuck in the middle of a field doing nothing whatsoever. Meanwhile the frenchmen are nudging each other and wondering what is going on. And meanwhile the dwarfs are on the camping site wreaking their own particular form of havoc. A group of holidaymaking dads is discussing the dreadful condition of the place, the dreadful amenities being offered, the dreadful state of the swimming pool into which their weans are plunging, these bastarn television sets always conking out; supposedly sturdy tents that keep collapsing, a plague of moles and field mice and all the litter abounding among the long grass and hedges surrounding the cooking area. On and on it goes, their list, lengthening; the whole fucking site is a shambles. In the background the dwarfs are nodding deferentially because they are somehow linking you with the carry-on and doing their best to stick up for you, they dont fucking realize you arent the fucking proprietor and it doesnt have anything to do with you in the first place except insofar as you were attempting to be a permanent resident, you were referring to the dump as home, charging around with your head stuck in the grass, lapsing into reveries connected with watering holes and final resting places, while all about you things were disintegrating. The dwarfs were only a reply. And yet, you will say, if they hadnt arrived it wouldnt be happening. They are to blame. While you were at work they've been charging around the site sowing seeds of discontent among the holidaymakers. Not by intention—granted, there is no malice, okay, you can accept that but still and all, still and all: they have come and they've taken over. They did not know what they were doing. They probably thought they were just being polite when chatting to the dads about the semi-detached villa on the outskirts of Burnley. They couldnt comprehend that this would result in a dialogue, that the holidaymaking parents would wind up getting together, comparing notes on their so-called camping site and its so-called amenities which are rubbish when you consider what is being offered across on the west coast at little or no difference in cost.

And now you are aware of why you have not been working properly this morning. Even your reveries were fraudulent. It was always there; you were always thinking about it—your thinking was just at so deeply set-back a stage that you werent aware of it. This is why you lagged behind the frenchmen, the gaffer frowning at you, wondering if you really are up to it after all. You haven't enjoyed the morning. Normally a Friday is good but today has been terrible, you are suffering; and meanwhile a deputation is being formed by the holidaymaking mums and dads, to march right in and confront the camping site proprietor first thing tomorrow morning. And this camping site proprietor . . . Camping site proprietor! what a joke. Because he owns a camping site he gets labeled that. He knows next to nothing about camping sites. The whole kit and caboodle would have collapsed weeks ago if you hadnt been dropping hints via the wee woman from the village—between the two of you you kept it going. And now she's fucked off and left you to it. But what more could be done you're saying, what more could be done!

That is for you to say. But you will be aware of a peculiar diffidence on the part of the farmer when collecting your wages later. He seems not to want to look at you. And the frenchmen hang back, waiting for you to leave before going to collect theirs, as though they dont want to be tainted by the bad luck surrounding you. Well, maybe that's a bit strong but such an inference could be drawn. And your face will be red; you'll want to walk off immediately, preferably without comment although you'll attempt a matter-of-fact cheerio, before strolling to the side of the barn for a quick wash at the outside tap. You have decided against returning to the site; you're heading straight for the pub. Fuck it you're thinking, I feel like a drink. And the way you've been suffering you're entitled to one. The fucking dwarfs! You smile to yourself, amazing how they can come and just take over! Funny. Just when you think you've got everything fixed, then bang, finished, all gone, all of it.

You have been walking now. You have been walking for quite a while. You have walked way beyond the pub; a car whizzed by, and as its sound decreased you became aware of it and thus of yourself there, way beyond the pub, you were walking, just walking. Now here you are. What will you do? will you go back to the pub or continue walking; you could be in town in another half hour—even less should a bus appear; on this part of the island buses appear infrequently but more often on Friday nights and the weekend; or you could thumb a lift, or just walk the whole way. It is a nice day, a nice day for walking; also the kind of day you enjoy being on the site, having returned home from work and cooking a few spuds, lazily, not bothering too much; the cries of the weans from the swimming pool and the play area, the holidaymaking parents sitting outside their tents relaxing after the evening meal, music quietly in the background, from the radio or cassette recorder: Friday night. And you will return to the pub; you still have to weigh in Pierre with the couple of quid you borrowed. And anyway, you arent really dressed for town, still being in the working togs—different if you had gone home first and had a decent wash and shave and so on. In fact, this carry-on about going into town, it is familiar. You have been meaning to go into town much more often.

You pause, keeping in to the side of the road as a pair of cyclists pass, then you take out your tobacco and sit on the grass by the side of the ditch. Aye, you were meaning to go into town more often. Just the time it takes, getting back to the site and washing and eating and getting your-self ready and then having to hoof it down the lane to the junction and wait for a bus, usually finding you had just missed one or something, so you nearly always stepped across the road and into the pub. It was handy—too handy! You smile wryly; you stop it at once, rising immedi-ately and striding back to the pub. But it is annoying you're thinking, this not making it into town more often. You'll need to make more of an effort in future. The local's all very well but a change is as good as a rest and so on. Seeing the same old faces all the time—especially that cunt of a barman who seems in the wrong job altogether. What is it with him at all the way he serves people? If he doesnt like serving people how come he works in a fucking pub! that superior smile on his face all the time. No wonder you . . . Jesus christ, that couple of quid you borrowed off him. But it wasnt off him you borrowed it, it was the brewery; he just makes you feel that way, that's why you hate getting tick in the place. Fucking dwarfs. Fucking bastarn dwarfs, those fucking bastarn dwarfs coming here by christ you're fucking sick of them. Wee bastards. What is it with them? the way they look at each other all the time, christ—in-credible, it really is incredible, the way they come and just take over. And they're probably out looking for you right now you're thinking. Of course they are. It's because they are loyal and thoughtful to others. They want to advise you of the goings-on up by at the site. It isnt a question of them not wanting you to think they're working behind your back be-cause that never occurs to them because they arent, they are entirely above-board and out in the open. They want to fill you in on what has been happening. Amazing they'll say, these poor holidaymakers, we never knew it was as bad as it is, really dreadful, Tommy Jackson—he's from Burnley you know, a nice fellow, lovely wife he's got and a couple of smashing weans—he was telling us about the amenities, really fuck-ing dreadful so they are, did you know? Did you know! what a joke. What a fucking joke. No you say, I didnt. And they look at each other as though joined at the nose. They are standing by where you are sitting; they have their pints in their hands. One of the holidaymaking dads re-alized they were skint and offered them a couple of quid till they landed their first job. They didnt ask. And one of the holidaymaking mums has been feeding them all day—after the chores they've been getting through she thought they deserved it. They were really going at it ham-mer and tongs, you should've seen them, charging about here, there and everywhere cleaning up the site, mending fuses and getting all sorts of insects out the swimming pool. They even fixed an appointment with the fucking camping site proprietor for tomorrow morning's deputation. Aye, they just marched right up to the door and chapped it, and the cunt answered. According to rumor he's about to offer them the job of running the site shop but they will refuse; they'd prefer the wee woman to return and unless he's any objections they're going to charge down to the village first thing Monday morning and drag her back if need be. And they seem hopeful; they reckon she must listen to reason. And you know fine well she will listen to reason; not only that but she'll invite them in for their fucking breakfast. It really is funny. In some ways you have to admire them. Do they have something special? What is it they've got? because they've definitely got something. There's Pierre telling a couple of the frenchmen to squeeze up so the dwarfs can sit down next to you and be able to watch the dominoes. And they do want to watch the dominoes. They're trying not to seem too keen in case you're offended but back where they come from they used to play the game regularly and aye, when somebody asks if they want to sit in, aye, they will, if nobody's got any objections.

You have to hand it to the wee bastards. You shake your head, smiling. In fact you'd probably quite like them if you werent so fucking . . . so fucking—so fucking what? You are frowning; you glance sideways. There they are there right beside you, taking the spectators' part in the game as energetically as any of the frenchmen, grinning and yapping and gesticulating away, and now smiling at you because you smiled at them but they dont really realize you are smiling at them, they probably think you're just glad to be alive. And two of the holidaymaking dads have entered and are trying to attract the dwarfs' attention—Billy and Dan, they're supposed to be meeting the dwarfs for a pint but now when they spot them here with the locals they feel a bit sheepish and dont want to be pushy although at the same time they're secretly proud to know them. In a couple of minutes one of them'll arrive with the pints he has bought them; he'll walk with determined nonchalance to place them on the shelf beneath the domino table and pause a moment, to study the game. Then, after a decent interval, a dwarf will glance upwards and say: Ta, and return his attention to the next domino being played. Then almost at once he will say: O—how's your wee boy? is his knee any better? This wee boy cut his knee earlier on; he fell in the long grass,

landed on a bit of broken glass or something, a nail maybe. Aw he's fine
now, says the holidaymaker, last I saw he was plunging into the swimming pool. Then he gives them a friendly grin and a brief nod at the
game, and returns to his mate at the bar who is waving and smiling. It
is all a load of shite you're wanting to yell across, dont fall for it. But for
one reason or another you will not do that. You dont have the energy
for a start. But aside from that, aside from that you feel more inclined
to burst out laughing. You clear your throat, move your shoulders, you
sip at your beer, calming yourself down—it would be pointless doing
anything daft. Aye, suddenly you find yourself aware of the possibility.
It's because the place is so crowded you think. There arent even enough
seats to go round. Friday night of course, the start of the weekend, and
it is always busy. A great many holidaymakers are here, from different
parts. Quite a few have stepped off their boats. You spot them immediately by the way they dress but even without that they cant be mistaken, the way they stand there gabbing so loudly just to let everybody
know. They seem to think they own the fucking place. The ordinary holidaymakers are fine; it's these weekend boat sailors you're opposed to—
another reason for making more of an effort to get into town in future.
You have turned to the dwarfs and begun telling them about this. They
nod. They are not a hundred percent interested. In fact, they are genuinely interested in the game. You will pause and they dont realize you
arent speaking. No wonder; what you were saying is boring, even to yourself. You smile ruefully. Emil smiles back at you. He is one of the players and he thinks you're smiling because you've spotted the bad domino
he laid down; his smile is also rueful and he shakes his head and says
something in french, all set to lose the game.

When it ends you go for another pint and ask for a whisky as well,
and as an afterthought you get whiskies for the dwarfs because they already have fresh pints lying. The barman looks at you. There is something about the look, a puzzled quality, and not just to do with the
additional drinks. For a moment you think you've been misjudging the
man; maybe he just has that kind of face and he isnt really a taciturn old
bastard. How would you like to be cooped up here all day you're thinking, and having to serve these fucking boat sailors! It's no joke. When
he returns to give you your change you smile and he ignores you and
wins again. You are definitely going to start going into town, starting from
tomorrow, as soon as you finish your work you're going straight home

for a wash and a shave and a change of clothes. No question. And there can be no excuse either because Saturdays you only work half the day. You glance quickly at him before lifting the tray of drinks: he's staring into space while pouring a pint for somebody. Even if the job's as bad as that you're thinking, it's useless taking it out on the customers, far better just leaving. If you had a job like that you would just leave, you wouldnt start taking it out on people; one of these days somebody's going to stick one on the old cunt's chin and nobody'll jump in to give him a hand, least of all you—in fact, it'll probably be you sticking the one on him! The thought makes you grin, then laugh quietly; you clear your throat, but continue grinning. The dwarfs look at you, smiling politely. Aye you say, and begin telling them about a funny thing that happened while picking spuds recently. A lot of funny things happen in the fields and you mention a few of them. They show interest. All in all you say, there's a lot worse jobs than picking spuds—being out in the fresh air and that, there's a lot to be said for it. Even if jobs were plentiful you reckon you would probably prefer the one you have. Of course there isnt much of a choice nowadays. There used to be but not now. The dwarfs nod. You're glad to see they appreciate the point because quite a few folk land on the island thinking the farmers'll be queuing up to offer them work. The same applies to fixing yourself with a roof. A great many cunts come here thinking it's straightforward, but it isnt, it's nowhere near straightforward; it used to be, but not now. If you dont get things fixed then you're bang in trouble; it's a question of knowing the ins and outs; you have to consider the eventualities, sort out what is possible and what is not possible. Take yourself for instance: when you came here you had your eyes open, none of that romantic shite about tropical paradises, you knew you would have to graft, that it was down to you to make things work because one thing you've learned in life and that is if you want to do something then do it yourself because no cunt's going to do it for you. That's a fucking beauty! That could make you laugh aloud. You dont. What you will do is raise your pint glass and sip slowly, gazing at the dwarfs over the rim. And they are gazing back at you. They are next on at the dominoes and are wanting to return their attention to there but are unsure whether they should continue listening to you. And they make their decision; they continue gazing at you. They are expecting something. You are to speak. What are you to say? They are waiting for you to say something. What is it you . . .

O jesus.

It'll be a beautiful summer's evening outside. One of those where you get that amazing expanse of sky and then when it darkens a shade you see the stars, an infinity of them. It always looks special when you're on an island and standing looking from the middle of a field; the sky, it's like a blanket or something. This is what you say to the dwarfs, about the sky at night, it looks like a blanket or something, with thousands and millions of shining stars and each moment you witness the thing another one explodes into life. It is amazing. Yet so many people dont even bother looking at the stars. They come to a place like this and go walking about with their head stuck in the grass. The dwarfs arent like that. They genuinely appreciate the value of things, same as yourself. If you have any criticism to make of them it has to do with their naivety. It isnt so much that they are naive in the ordinary sense—otherwise they wouldnt be here and making a go of things as well as they are—it is more to do with faith or something. The way they look upon you for instance; you can understand why they regard you as highly as they do but all in all you'd advise against it in future.

Christ, you stop talking; you shake your head, there's a lump in your throat. You stare at your whisky, not wanting to be seen. The dwarfs have coughed and shifted on their chairs so they cannot see you without turning their heads. They are good people. They are thoughtful and they are fucking loyal, you dont care what anybody says. And yet it's funny how it happens you're thinking, and you smile then offer them your job. You're not a hundred percent certain the farmer'll take them on because there was only one of you but you reckon they could do a lot worse than give it a try, and once he sees how well they get on with the frenchmen . . . well, you're sure it'll be okay. There are other problems—well, not really problems, more to do with irksome chores; things like the deputation. The most important thing to remember is the camping site proprietor himself: whatever you do you must not put the jitters into him. He's so fucking incompetent and so fucking aware of being incompetent that at the slightest show of being thought incompetent he'll run for cover, he'll close down the site and head for the mainland. You've seen cunts like him before and so have the dwarfs, there's no real need to tell them, you just thought you'd mention it. O, and the holidaymakers, there's quite a bit to be said about them and you start in on that for a time, until gradually the dwarfs are turning their heads from you; the game of dominoes currently in progress is due to finish any minute. And anyway, what you are saying is fairly boring—not completely boring because it must be of some value; but all in all, all in all . . . And it's hell of a noisy in this place—Friday night, the jukebox going constantly and the boat sailors seem to have bribed the barman into turning up the volume; a couple of the females are now dancing a bit while the males are sipping at their half pint shandies. It wont be long now till you apply the method. This is it: a dwarf will rise to his feet to go to the bar and while maneuvering his way through he will accidentally rub against one of the dancers and one of the males will pass a comment. One thing leads to another. The upshot is that you, being the tallest member of the present company, will challenge the tallest boat sailor to go to the boxing games. At this a great tumult shall occasion. People are on all sides of you, many of whom you recognize, as though trying to paw at you. They are excited by the prospect ahead. You hear them discuss this that and the next thing with some of the female boat sailors trying to play matters down but the males arent letting them; they want to prove themselves—although they act as if they own the fucking place they are in reality very insecure and hate it when they enter an out-of-the-way pub like this only to receive cheek from taciturn barmen and have their females ogled by the regulars. You can hear what sounds like holidaymaking parents attempting to pacify them but to no avail, and then an indistinct voice is calling for a more sporting contest, something less violent, maybe a swim or some fucking thing. Great you shout, and make a lunge at the tallest boat sailor: Me and you outside in the fucking Ocean ya bastard! And this does the trick. The silence lasts for several moments before the tumult continues—it appears to be a kind of vote. It is a vote. A great cheer goes up when a voice calls: Carried! And then by your side you feel hands tapping your shoulder in a furtive way; it's the dwarfs; they are attempting to dissuade you. At first this seems a contradiction, a paradox maybe, you arent sure, there isnt time, you look at them. No they cry, you shouldnt be going out swimming on a night like this with all that beer and whisky in your belly. Out my road you shout, out my road. And a couple of holidaymakers are there also, including a young mum in a summer dress who looks very worried, her hand to the side of her mouth, clutching a hankie. For christ sake! Too late, too fucking late you're shouting, too fucking late. You're just wanting out there, nothing else matters, nothing. Where's that fucking boat sailor who insulted

your wee pal the dwarf? that's what you're wanting to know. He's waiting outside with his cronies. And you might've known, the cunt's got a
pair of swimming trunks. Ah well. And there's the frenchmen laying
bets—Pierre's making a book—and glancing with interest as you go
charging down the beach with the dwarfs scurrying alongside, trying to
keep up. The boat sailor's there already with a couple of his mates; one
of them's testing the temperature for him and he's saying: Not as cold
as when you swam the fucking channel Bertie! Aw good, says the boat
sailor, glad to hear it. But you're straightening your shoulders and marching right past him, way beyond him, and the Ocean's lapping up by your
ankles and you pause a moment to kick off your working boots. You can
hear indistinct voices from the shore. Is it cheers you wonder. Who cares
you say, and when the water comes up beyond your knees you immediately plunge in and begin a hectic breaststroke in a direction sou' sou'-
westerly.

A Nightboilerman's notes

The bunker faces outwards, away to the far corner of the ground surface area. When it requires replenishing (twice nightly) I push the bogey out into the corridor and through the rearmost swing doors, down the steep incline onto the pathway by the canal, along to where the coalmountains pile some thirty yards from the embankment. It is good to walk here, the buckled rattle of the bogey wheels only emphasizing the absence of noise. The Nightoutsideman has charge of this area. I used to envy him. His job has always seemed so straightforward in comparison to this one of mine. He sits on his chair to the side of his hut door, gazing to the sky or to the canal. I walk past him but he doesnt look across, not until he hears that first strike of my shovel into the coal, when he turns and waves.

It takes 4 bogey loads to replenish the bunker. I could manage it with 3 but the incline up into the factory is too steep to push the bogey comfortably if fully laden. And there is no need to rush. This is a part of the shift I like. Once the 4th load is in the bogey I leave it standing and go over to have a smoke with the Nightoutsideman. We exchange nods. I lean my back against the wall on the other side of the hut door from him; sometimes I lower myself down to sit on my heels. Due to the configuration of warehouse and factory buildings there is never any wind here (a very very slight breeze, but only occasionally) and the canal is still, its water black, gray foam spreading out from its banks.

He will have been waiting for me to arrive before making his next cigarette. He used to make one for me but I prefer my own. I strike the match; while I am exhaling on the first draw I flick the match out onto the canal, watching for its smoke but there never is any; if there is I havent been able to see it. He raises his eyebrows, a brief smile. He smiles a lot, speaks very rarely; he just likes to sit there, watching the things that happen. Most of the buildings are unoccupied during the night and their differing shapes and shadows, the shades of black and gray, red-tinged. Now and then he will gesture at the sky, at the bend in the canal, sideways at one of the buildings, to the one where jets of steam suddenly issue from escape pipes, and to high up in the same building, at the large windows where headlike shapes appear frequently. I never quite grasp what he is on about but it probably has to do with plain truths, and I nod, as though acknowledging a contrast. Then when I finish the smoke I flick the dowp out onto the canal, listening for the plop which never comes (which never could come, not in any canal). I wait on a few moments, before going to get the bogey. I like this last push up the incline, that rutted point near the top where the wheels seem to be jamming and the bogey halts and

I cannot hold it any longer! All my strength's gone! The load's going to roll back down and crash into the canal!

and then I grin; I breathe in and shove, continuing on up and through the swing doors into the corridor, still grinning.

I have charge of the boilers. Their bodies are situated in the basement and their mouths range the ground surface area, shut off by solid square hatches with set-in rings. The floor is made of specially treated metal plating so that although it is still very hot it is never too hot such that it is impossible to walk upon when wearing the special boots (metal studded, and perhaps the uppers are of a special substance?). When I arrive with the 4th load of coal I wheel the bogey past the bunker and go straight across to begin stoking. I have a crowbar to insert in the rings to wedge up the hatches which settle at an angle of 100°. With the hatch raised the heat and light from the boiler is tremendous and I have to avert my face while stoking. Asbestos gloves are there to be used but I work without them, simply taking care not to touch the metal parts of the shovel. It is habit now and I cannot remember the last time I burnt my hands. There is an interesting thing that a child would like to see; this is the coaldust dropping from my shovel during the stoking, it ignites simultaneously to touching the floor so that countless tiny fires are always blazing, and it looks startling (diamonds that sparkle). Then I have finished and kick down the hatch, and that thud of impact separating the loud roaring of the open boiler from the dull roaring of the closed boiler that I can never quite anticipate. And I move onto the next. Finally, when I have finished them all, I wheel off the bogey to its position by the bunker then return with the wirebrush to sweep clean the floor of the ground surface. Coalbits will be lying smoldering or burning nearby the hatches; I sweep them straight across and into the water trench next to the basement entrance. Towards the end of the shift I rake out the trench and use what is there on the last stoke. Whenever I forget to do this the trench is full when I come in next evening. The Dayboilerman is responsible. This is his way of reminding me not to do it again.

From a distance the entrance to the basement resembles another boilermouth but it is set away to the side of the ground surface, and its hatch is permanently raised. There is a step ladder going down, the top of which is welded onto the inside panel of the hatch. I enjoy descending. I grip either side with both hands, sometimes scurrying down to break the existing speed record, other times I go stepping very very slowly, very deliberately, as though engaged upon ultra serious business to do with submarines or spaceships. I can be standing watching myself from way over beyond the bunker, seeing my head sink from view, vanishing, wondering if it cracked against the edge of the metal plated floor but no, always I just avoid that by the briefest margin possible, gglullp. gone. Then I poke out my head again. Or maybe remain exactly there, just beneath the surface, counting 25 and only then will I reappear, and back down immediately.

Nowadays I appreciate no tasks more than those that have me down in the basement. It did use to have its frightening aspects but my imagination was to blame. The black holes is the best example. I would step past them and pretend they were not there, or if they were, that I was not particularly bothered by them. This was daft and I knew it was daft but I was just working out a method of conquering myself. At that time I was having to actually force myself to enter the basement. I would say inwardly; these black holes, they are ordinary black holes, ordinary in the sense that they are man-made, they only exist because of the way the walls have been designed. (They also exist as they do because of the effect the lighting system has on the boilerbodies: permanent shadows.)

The basement is a sealed unit, built to accommodate the boilers; the only entrance/exit is by way of the step ladder. Firstly the boilers were sited then they built the basement, and the rest of the building. It took me a while to understand that fully. And when I had I think I was either over my fear or well on the road to it. It was pretty bad at the time. I had to force myself to sit down beside them, the holes, facing away from them, not able to see them without turning my head. I would sit like that for ages, thinking of horrible things, but not being aware of it till later, sometimes much later, when walking home. One morning the Dayboilerman found me. It was a terrible shock for him. The sound of his boots on the steps of the ladder had reached me but could scarcely correspond to anything I knew so that I wasnt really aware of it beyond my thoughts. Then he was there and his eyes staring as though seeing a ghost, seeming about to collapse with a heart attack. Yet he had been looking for me. I hadnt clocked out at the gate and the timekeeper had asked him to check up. So he was looking for me and when he found me reacted as though I was the last thing he expected to see sitting there. He told people I looked like a zombie. A zombie! But eventually it made me realize he had never managed to conquer himself. He must have been really nervous, terrified about what he *might* find.

The switches for the basement lighting are on the wall behind the ladder so they can be turned on before reaching the bottom, but they are supposed to be kept on permanently. I think the reason for this has to do with the idea of one man being down and then another man coming down without realizing the first is there, and returning back up and switching the lighting off, leaving the first man in total blackness. That would be a horrible thing to happen, particularly to someone new in the job. But I have to admit here and now that I do play about with the switches, sometimes leaving the lighting off during the times I'm away from the basement. I think about how it all looks down there, different things. Also, there is that incredible sensation when switching them back on again later. I go stepping off the ladder with my back to the inner wall, facing away from the shaft of light above, right out into the blackness. Occasionally I will walk 3 or 4 (5 at the most) paces until that feeling of narrowness has me stock-still and trying to reflect on a variety of matters, maybe wondering how it would be having to work in such conditions forever (a miner whose lamp keeps going out?). And I continue standing there, thinking of different things, then slowly but surely I notice I am moving back the way, sensing the approach of that strange feeling of being buried in cotton wool and I am turning to reach for the switches calmly, not panicking at all, getting my bearings from the shaft of light high above at the entrance. And the lighting is immediate throughout the basement, and the noise of everything now audible apparently for the first time, that deep deep humming sound.

The boilerbodies dominate the basement. I can stand watching them. They are large, their shadows rigid but falling on each other (it can seem as though your eyes are blurring). There is a complex of narrow passageways between them, just wide enough for a man to walk, carrying a crate of cinders and a rake and shovel perhaps. I used to think a bogey might be adapted to fit the passageways but this is not at all necessary; it is possible the idea only occurred to me because of movable objects—I thought it would be good to have one. There are 4 tools: 2 crates plus a rake and a shovel. There are also 2 pairs of boilersuits, 1 for the Dayboilerman and 1 for me; they have to be kept in the basement, if we want to wear boilersuits on the ground surface we have to order different ones for the purpose. I also keep a towel down here which I find necessary. Although the atmosphere is not stifling it must be akin to tropical. I think of equatorial forests full of those peculiar plants, gigantic ones, with brightly coloured buds the size of oranges hanging down the middle, and that constant dripping. But there isnt any dripping in the basement, nothing like that. There is water in the trenches of course, which surrounds the bottom of the boilerbodies. Cinders fall through to here somehow and I rake them out and carry them in a crate to the foot of the ladder, dumping them into the other crate which I will carry up later on, for eventual use in the last stoke. I enjoy carrying the crate between the boilerbodies. I take different routes and go quickly or slowly, sometimes very very slowly, studying my boots as they land at that point on the passageway nearest to the trench. Even though I work naked I continue to wear the boots. I once tried it barefoot but the edges of the trenches get quite slippery when I'm raking the cinders out; also a daft thing, I was being continually tempted into the water, just to dip my feet (but if I had succumbed to that I would maybe have gone in for a swim!).

The trenches are narrow and they slope in below the bottoms of the boilerbodies so that cinders can become stuck, and stuck fast, there seems to be a great many crannies. I know most of them through having used the rake so often. This part of the job is good, the raking noise and my own silence, that clung of the rakehead below the surface of the water on the sides of the trench, the scraping noise of its teeth in the crannies. I could have expected both that and the sense of touch to grate on me but they dont, perhaps because they come from outside of me altogether. I work silently, and in silence. It is an important point. The idea of the work noise is funny, how it would appear to somebody (not the Dayboilerman) poking his head down the ladder, seeing how all the objects and everything are so stationary, just taking it for granted for a spell while not being conscious of anything else, not until that moment he has become aware of something, of an unexpected noise, rhythmic, and I couldnt be seen from there because of the shapes and shadows, only the clung and scraping sound; after a moment the person would react by snorting, maybe giving himself a telling off for being so daft, and then he would climb back up and out as quickly as he could, trying to kid on he wasnt bothered by it.

But nobody from outside ever comes down into the basement. Firstly the ground surface area needs to be crossed and it cannot be crossed without special footwear. If anybody wishes to attract my attention they either shout or batter the floor with a crowbar. It happens only rarely and I seldom respond since it is always to advise me that the pressure isnt being maintained. This I discover myself sooner or later because of the safety precautions. I might be wrong not to respond. I sometimes wonder whether to ask the Dayboilerman what he does. But his perception of the job will differ radically from my own. It cannot be avoided, he is on constant day and I am on constant night, we each have our own distractions. Yes, I can still be distracted; in some ways it is essential to the work; but I cannot be distracted against my wishes. If I think of things they must be things I wish to think of.

I used to make myself sit by the black hole farthest from the entrance; it lies on the same side but to reach it I have to walk to the wall opposite the ladder then follow the passageway there, right around and into the corner. I would bring the boilersuit to sit on and the towel to lean my back on against the wall; then I lit a cigarette. Smoking is frowned upon down here but I've always done it; I really enjoy it, finishing a particular part of the work and sitting down quietly and lighting one. Sometimes when I sit down I leave the cigarettes and matches beside me for a while before smoking; other times I'm smoking even before sitting down. One thing I used to do in the early days, I used to push the matches and cigarettes inside the hole. I sat there for a long period afterwards, till finally I knelt and withdrew them without looking in, just using my hand to feel around.

There is nothing extraordinary about these black holes, they are cavities and short tunnels. I found them of interest because they had never been seen into since the factory's original construction. I still find the idea quite interesting. When I first found them I thought they were just inshots, little gaps, and I sat by them not bothering. Then one night after sitting a while I suddenly was kneeling down and peering in and I couldnt see anything, nothing at all. I struck a match and the light scarcely penetrated. It was really funny. Then I had to push in my hand; I discovered the wall, and then a tunnel veering off at a tangent. I could have brought in a torch or a candle, and a mirror maybe, but I never did. If I remember correctly I was wanting to check the dimensions of the wall in relation to it, the cavity and tunnel. I knew it had to be some sort of double wall, but probably a triple one, as part of the safety precautions. I went round by the canal pathway to look at the outside of the building but that told me nothing. On this particular side of the factory the pathway only goes along a few yards before narrowing and tapering out altogether, with the wall going straight down into the water.

There were quite a lot of things about it that bothered me at the time but nowadays it all seems hazy. But I think the main factor must connect to the idea of isolation, maybe bringing on a form of deprivation or something. It wasnt good when I had to sit by the black holes at first, some of my imaginings were horrible. I just had to stick it out and conquer myself. I had to succeed and I did succeed. It taught me a lot about myself and has given me confidence. Sometimes I feel a bit smug, as if I've reached a higher level than the others in the factory; but I dont speak to many of them, I just get on and do the job, enjoying its various aspects.

Old Francis

He wiped the bench dry enough to sit down, thrust his hands into his jacket pockets and hunched his shoulders, his chin coming down onto his chest. It was cold now and it hadnt been earlier, unless he just wasnt feeling it earlier. And he started shivering immediately, as if the thought had induced it. This was the worst yet. No question about it. If care wasnt taken things would degenerate even further. If that was possible. But of course it was possible. Anything was possible. Everything was possible. Every last thing in the world. A man in a training suit was approaching at a jog, a fastish sort of jog. The noise of his breathing, audible from a long way off. Frank stared at him, not caring in the slightest when it became obvious the jogger had noticed and was now a wee bit self-conscious in his run, as if his elbows were rotating in an unnatural manner. It was something to smile about. Joggers were always supposed to be so self-absorbed but here it seemed like they were just the same as the rut, the common rut, of whom Francis was definitely one. But then as he passed by the bench the jogger muttered something which ended in an "sk" sound, perhaps "brisk." Could he have said something like "brisk"? Brisk this morning. That was a fair probability, in reference to the weather. Autumn. The path by the side of the burn was deep in slimy leaves, decaying leaves, approaching that physical state where they were set to be reclaimed by the earth, unless perhaps along came the midgie men and they shoveled it all up and dumped it into the midgie motor then on to the rubbish dump where they would sprinkle aboard paraffin and so on and so forth till the day of judgment. And where was the jogger! Vanished. Without breaking stride he must have carried straight on and up the slow winding incline towards the bridge, where to vanish was the only outcome, leaving Francis alone with his thoughts.

These thoughts of Francis's were diabolical.

The sound of laughter. Laughter! Muffled, yes, but still, laughter. Could this be the case!! Truly? Or was it a form of eternal high jinks!!

Hearty stuff as well. Three blokes coming along the path from the same direction the jogger had appeared from. They noticed Francis. O yes, they soon spotted him. They couldnt miss him. It was not possible. If they had wanted to miss him they couldnt have. And they were taking stock of him and how the situation was in toto. They were going to get money off of him, off of. One of them had strolled on a little bit ahead; he was wearing a coat that must have belonged to somebody else altogether, it was really outlandish. Francis shook his head. The bloke halted at the bench and looked at him:

You got twenty pence there jim, for the busfare home?

Francis was frowning at the bloke's outfit. Sorry, he said, but that's some coat you're wearing!

What?

Francis smiled.

Funny man.

Sorry, I'm no being sarcastic.

A funny man! he called to his two companions. He's cracking funnies about my coat!

Surely no! said this one who was holding a bottle by its neck.

Aye.

That's cheeky! He swigged from the bottle and handed it on to the third man. Then he added: Maybe he likes its style!

The first bloke nodded, he smiled briefly.

And he wants to buy it! Heh, maybe he wants to buy it! Eh, d'you want to buy it?

Frank coughed and cleared his throat, and he stared at the grass by his shoes, sparish clumps of it amid the muddiness, many feets have stood and so on. He raised his head and gazed at the second man; he was dangerous as well, every bit as dangerous. He noticed his pulse slowing now. Definitely, slowing. Therefore it must have been galloping. That's what Francis's pulse does, it gallops. Other cunts' pulses they just fucking stroll along at a safe distance from one's death's possibility. What was he on about now! Old Francis here! His death's possibility! Death: and/or its possibility. Was he about to get a stroke? Perhaps. He shook his head and smiled, then glanced at the first bloke who was gazing at him, and said: I didnt mean you to take it badly.

What?

Your coat. Frank shrugged, his hands still in his pockets. My comment . . . he shrugged again.

Your comment?

Aye, I didnt mean you to take it badly.

I never took it badly.

Frank nodded.

The second bloke laughed suddenly. Heh by the way, he said, when
you come to think about it, the guy's right, your fucking coat, eh! Fucking comic cuts! Look at it!

And then he turned and sat down heavily, right next to him on the
bench; and he stared straight into his eyes. Somebody whose body was
saturated with alcohol. He was literally smelling. Literally actually
smelling. Just like Francis right enough, he was smelling as well. Birds
of a feather flock together. And what do they do when they are together? A word for booze ending in "er." Frank smiled, shaking his
head. I'm skint, he said, I'm out the game. No point looking for dough
off of me.

Off of. There it had come out again. It was peculiar the way such
things happened.

The two blokes were watching him. So was the third. This third was
holding the bottle now. And a sorry sight he was too, this third fellow, a
poor-looking cratur. His trousers were somebody else's; and that was for
fucking definite. My my my. Frank shook his head and he called: Eh
look, I'm no being sarcastic but that pair of trousers you're wearing I
mean for God sake surely you could do a wee bit better, eh?

He glanced at the other two: Eh? surely yous could do a wee bit better than that?

What you talking about? asked the first bloke.

Your mate's trousers, they're fucking falling to bits. I mean look at
his arse, his arse is fucking poking out!

And so it was, you could see part of the man's shirttail poking out!
Frank shook his head, but didnt smile. He gestured at the trousers.

He is a funny man right enough! said the second bloke.

Instead of answering him the first bloke just watched Frank, not
showing much emotion at all, just in a very sort of cold manner, pas-
sionless. If he had been unsure of his ground at any time he was definitely not unsure now. It was him that was dangerous. Of the trio, it was

him. Best just to humour him. Frank muttered, I'm skint. He shrugged and gazed over the path towards the burn.

You're skint.

Frank continued gazing over the path.

It's just a couple of bob we're looking for.

Sorry, I really am skint but.

The second bloke leaned closer and said: Snout?

Frank shook his head.

You've got no snout! The bloke didnt believe him. He just didnt believe him. He turned and gave an exaggerated look to his mates. It was as if he was just not able to believe it possible. Frank was taken aback. It was actually irritating. It really was. He was frowning at the fellow, then quickly he checked what the other one was doing. You never know, he might have been sneaking up behind him at the back of the bloody bench! It was downright fucking nonsensical. And yet it was the sort of incident you could credit. You were sitting down in an attempt to recover a certain inner equilibrium when suddenly there appear certain forces, seemingly arbitrary forces, as if they had been called up by a positive evil. Perhaps Augustine was right after all? Before he left the Manicheans.

Twenty pence just, said the first.

Frank shook his head. He glanced at the bloke. Look, I'm telling you the truth, I'm skint.

You've got a watch.

What—you kidding! Frank stared at him for a moment; then he sniffed and cleared his throat, gazed back over the path.

He has got a watch, said the second bloke.

And now the third stepped across to the bench, and he handed the bottle to the first. Frank had his hands out of his pockets and placed them onto his kneecaps, gripping them, his knuckles showing white.

Did you miss your bus? asked the first.

Did you miss your bus! laughed the second.

And the third bloke just stared. Frank stared back at him. Was he the leader after all? Perhaps he was the one he would have to go for first, boot him in the balls and then face the other pair. Fucking bastards. Because if they thought he was going to give them the watch just like that then they had another think coming. Bastards. One thing he was never was a coward. Bastards, he was never fucking a coward. He flexed his fingers then closed them over his kneecaps again, and he sighed, his shoulders drooping a bit. He stared over the path. It was as if they were aspects of the same person. That was what really was the dangerous thing.

The second bloke was speaking; he was saying, I dont think he even goes on public transport, this yin, I think he's a car-owner.

A car-owner! Frank grinned. I'm actually a train-owner! A train-owner! That was really funny. One of his better witticisms. A train-owner. Ha ha. Frank smiled. He would have to watch himself though, such comments, so unfunny as to approach the borderline.

What borderline? One of irrationality perhaps. A nonsensicality. A plain whimsy. Whimsy. There was a bird whistling in a tree nearby. D d d dooie. D d d dooie. Wee fucking bird, its own wee fucking heart and soul. D d d dooie. What was it looking for? It was looking for a mate. A wee female. A wee chookie. Aw the sin. My my my. My my my. And yet it was quite upsetting. It brought tears to the eye. If Frank could just heave a brick at the tree so it would get to fuck away out of this, this vale of misery. God. I need a drink, said Frank to the first bloke. He gestured at the bottle: D'you mind?

The man handed him the bottle.

The second looked at him, biding his time, waiting to see the outcome.

And the third bloke put his hands into his trouser pockets and strolled across the path, down to the small fence at the burn, where he leant his elbows.

The noise of the water, the current not being too strong, a gush more than anything, a continuous gushing sound, and quite reassuring. This freshness as well, it was good. The whole scene in fact, was very peaceful, very very peaceful; a deep tranquillity. Not yet 10 o'clock in the morning but so incredibly calm.

There was no label on the bottle. Francis frowned at this. What happened to the label? he asked.

It fell off.

Is it hair lacquer or something?

Hair lacquer! laughed the second bloke.

It looks like it to me, replied Francis.

You dont have to fucking drink it you know!

Francis nodded; he studied the bottle. The liquid looked fine—as much as it was possible to tell from looking; but what was there could be told about a drink by looking at the outside of its bottle? He couldnt even tell what color it was, although the actual glass was dark brownish. He raised the neck of the bottle, tilted his head and tasted a mouthful: Christ it was fiery stuff! He shook his head at the two blokes, he seemed to be frowning but he wasnt. WWhhh! Fucking hot stuff this! he said.

Aye.

Francis had another go. Really fiery but warming, a good drink. He wiped his mouth and returned the bottle. Ta, he said.

I told you it was the mccoy, said the second bloke.

Did you?

Aye.

Mm. It's fucking hot, I'll say that!

Know what we call it?

Naw.

Sherry vindaloo!

Francis smiled. That was a good yin, sherry vindaloo. He'd remember it.

The first bloke nodded and repeated it: Sherry vindaloo.

The second bloke laughed and swigged some, he walked to hand it to the third who did a slightly peculiar thing, it was a full examination; he studied the bottle all round before taking a sip which must have finished it because the next thing he was leaning over the fence and dropping the bottle into the burn. Francis glanced at the first bloke who didnt say anything. Then he shivered. It was still quite cold. High time that sun put in an appearance, else all would be lost! Francis grinned. The world was really a predictable place to live in. Augustine was right but wasn't right though obviously he wasnt wrong. He was a good strong man. If Francis had been like him he would have been quite happy.

The first bloke was looking at him. You'll do for me, he said.

What was that?

I said you'll do for me.

Francis nodded. Thanks. As long as you didn't take offense about that comment.

Och naw, fuck.

Francis nodded. And thanks for the drink.

Ye kidding? It's just a drink.

Aye well . . .

The bloke shrugged. That's how we were wanting to get a few bob, so's we could get a refill.

Mm, aye.

See your watch, we could get no bad for it.

Frank nodded. There was no chance, no fucking chance. Down by the fence the second bloke was gazing at him and he shifted on his seat immediately so that when he was looking straight ahead he was looking away from the three men. He didnt want to see them at the moment. There was something about them that was frightening. He was recognizing in himself fear. He was scared, he was frightened; it was the three men who were frightening him, something in them together that was making him scared, the sum of the parts, it was an evil force. If he just stared straight ahead. If he stayed calm. He was on a bench in the park and it was 10 a.m. There was a jogger somewhere. All it needed was somebody to touch him perhaps. If that happened he would die. His heart would stop beating. If that happened he would die and revelation. But if he just got up. If he was to just get up off of the bench and start walking slowly and deliberately along in the opposite direction, to from where they had come. That would be fine if he could just do that. But he couldnt, he couldnt do it; his hands gripped his kneecaps, the knuckles pure white. Did he want to die? What had his life been like? Had it been worth living? His boyhood, what like was his boyhood? had that been okay? It hadnt been too bad he hadnt been too bad, he'd just been okay normal, normal, the same as anybody else. He'd just fallen into bad ways. But he wasnt evil. Nobody could call him evil. He was not evil. He was just an ordinary person who was on hard times who was not doing as well as he used to and who would be getting better soon once things picked up, he would be fine again and able to be just the same, he was all right, he was fine, it was just to be staring ahead.

The one with the dog

What I fucking do is wander about the place, just going here and there. I've got my pitches. A few other cunts use them as well. They keep out my road cause I lose my temper. I've got two mates I sometimes meet up with to split for a drink and the rest of it. Their pitches are out the road of mine. One of them's quiet. That suits me. The other yin's a gab. I'm no that bothered. What I do I just nod. If anybody's skint it'll be him. He's fucking hopeless. The quiet yin's no bad. I quite like the way he does it. He goes up and stares into their eyes. That's a bit like me except I'll say something. Give us a couple of bob. The busfare home. That kind of thing. It doesnt fucking matter. All they have to do is look at you and they know the score. What I do I just stand waiting at the space by the shops. Sometimes you get them with change in their hands; they've no had time to stick it back into their purses or pockets. Men's the best. Going up to women's no so hot because they'll look scared. The men are scared as well but it's not sexual and there's no the same risks with the polis if you get clocked doing it. Sometimes I feel like saying to them give us your jacket ya bastard. It makes me laugh. I've never said it yet. I dont like the cunts and I get annoyed. Sometimes I think ya bastard ye I'm fucking skint and you're no. It's a mistake. It shouldnt fucking matter cause you cant stop it. There's this dog started following me. It used to go with that other yin, the quiet cunt. It tagged behind him across in the park one morning and me and the gab told him to fucking dump it cause it must belong to somebody but he didnt fucking bother, just shrugs. One thing I'm finding but it makes it a wee bit easier getting a turn. But I like it following me about. I dont like that kind of company. I used to have a mate like that as well, followed me about and that and I didnt like it. I used to tell him to fuck off. That's what I sometimes do with the dog. Then sometimes they see you doing it and you can see them fucking they dont like it, they dont like it and it makes them scared at the same time. I'd tell them to fuck off as well. That's what I feel like doing but what I do I just ignore them. That's what I do with the dog too, cause it's best. Anything else is daft, it's just getting angry and that's a mistake. I try no to get angry; it's just the trouble is I've got a temper. That's what the gab says as well, your trouble he says you've got a fucking temper, you're better off just taking it easy. But I do take it easy. If they weigh you in then good and if they dont then there's always the next yin along. And even if you dont get a turn the whole fucking day then there's always the other two and usually one of them's managed to get something. That's the good thing about it, having mates. What I dont understand I dont understand how you get a few of the cunts going about in wee teams, maybe four or five to a pitch, one trying for the dough while the rest hang about in the background. That's fucking hopeless cause it just puts them off giving you anything and sometimes you can even see them away crossing the street just to keep out the way, as if they're fucking scared they're going to get set about if they dont cough up. It's stupid as well cause there's always some cunt sees what you're up to and next thing the polis is there and you're in fucking bother. What I think I think these yins that hang about in the background it's cause they're depressed. They've had too many knockbacks and they cant fucking take it so what they do they start hanging about with some cunt that doesnt care and they just take whatever they can get. If it was me I'd just tell them to fuck off; away and fuck I'd tell them, that's what I'd say if it was me.

Forgetting to mention Allende

The milk was bubbling over the sides of the saucepan. He rushed to the oven, grabbed the handle and held the pan in the air. The wean was pulling at his trouser-leg, she gripped the material. For christ sake Audrey, he tugged her hand away while returning the saucepan to the oven. The girl went back to sit on the floor, glancing at him as she turned the pages of her coloring book. He smiled: Dont go telling mummy about the milk now eh!

She looked at him.

Aye, he said, that's all I need, you to get into a huff.

Her eyes were watering.

Aw christ.

She looked at him.

You're a big girl now, you cant just . . . he paused. Back at the oven he prepared her drink, lighting a cigarette in the process, which he placed in an ashtray. Along with the drink he gave her two digestive biscuits.

When he sat down on the armchair he stared at the ceiling, half expecting to see it bouncing up and down. For the past couple of hours somebody had been playing records at full blast. It was nearly time for the wean to have her morning kip as well. The same yesterday. He had tried; he had put her down and sat with her, read part of a story: it was hopeless but, the fucking music, blasting out. And at least seven out of the past ten weekdays the same story. He suspected it came from the flat above. Yet it could be coming from through the wall, or the flat below. It was maybe even coming from the other side of the stair— difficult to tell because of the volume, and the way the walls were, like wafer fucking biscuits. Before flitting to the place he had heard it was a good scheme, the houses designed well, good thick walls and that, they could be having a party next door and you wouldnt know unless they came and invited you in. What a load of rubbish. He stared at the ceiling, wondering whether to go and dig out the culprits, tell them the wean was supposed to be having her midmorning nap. He definitely had the right to complain, but wasnt going to, not yet; it would be daft antagonizing the neighbors at this stage.

Inhaling deeply he got up and wiped the oven clean with a damp cloth. Normally he liked music, any kind. The problem was it was the same songs being played over and over, all the fucking time the same songs—terrible; pointless trying to read or even watch the midday TV programs. Maybe he was going to have to get used to it: the sounds to become part of the general hum of the place, like the cars screeching in and out of the street, that ice-cream van which came shrieking I LOVE TO GO A-WANDERING ten times a night including Sunday.

A digestive biscuit lay crunched on the carpet by her feet.

Thanks, he said, and bent to lift the pieces. The carpet loves broken biscuits. Daddy loves picking them up as well. Come on . . . he smiled as he picked her up. He carried her into the room. She twisted her head from side to side. It was the music.

I know, he said, I know I know I know, you'll just have to forget about it.

I cant.

You can if you try.

She looked at him. He undressed her to her pants and vest and sat her down in the cot, then walked to the window to draw the curtains. The new wallpaper was fine. He came back and sat on the edge of the double bed, resting his hands on the frame of the cot. Just make stories out of the picture, he told her, indicating the wall. Then he got up, leaned in to kiss her forehead. I'll away ben and let you sleep.

She nodded, shifting her gaze to the wall.

You'll have to try Audrey, otherwise you'll be awful tired at that nursery.

Sitting down on the armchair he lifted the cigarette from the ashtray, and frowned at the ceiling. He exhaled smoke while reaching for last night's *Evening Times*. The tin of paint and associated articles were lying at the point where he had left off yesterday. He should have resumed work by now. He opened the newspaper at the sits. vac. col.

The two other children were both boys, in primaries five and six at the local primary school. They stayed in at dinnertime to eat there but normally one would come home after; and if it happened before one o'clock he could send the wee girl back with him to nursery. But neither liked taking her. Neither did daddy for that matter. It meant saying hello to the woman in charge occasionally. And he always came out of the place feeling like an idiot. An old story. It was exactly the same with the headmistress of the primary school, the headmistress of the last primary school, the last nursery—the way they spoke to him even. Fuck it. He got up to make another coffee.

The music had stopped. It was nearly one o'clock. He rushed through to get the wean.

The nursery took up a separate wing within the building of the primary school; only a five-minute walk from where he lived. Weans everywhere but no sign of his pair. He was looking out for them, to see if they were being included in the games yet. He had no worries about the younger one, it was the eldest who presented the problem. Not a problem really, the boy was fine—just inclined to wander about on his tod, not getting involved with the rest, nor making any attempt to. It wasnt really a problem.

The old man with the twins was approaching the gate from the opposite direction; and he paused there, and called: Nice to see a friendly face! Indicating the two weans he continued, The grandkids, what a pair! No twins in the family then all of a sudden bang, two lots of them. My eldest boy gets one pair then the lassie gets another pair. And you know the worrying thing? The old man grinned: Everything comes in threes! Eh? can you imagine it? three lots of twins! That'd put the cat right among the bloody pigeons!

A nursery assistant was standing within the entrance lobby; once she had collected the children the old man said: Murray's the name, John, John Murray.

Tommy McGoldrick.

They shook hands.

I saw you a couple of days ago, the end of last week . . . went on the old man. I was telling my lassie, makes a change to see a friendly face. All these women and that eh! He laughed, and they continued walking towards the gate. You're no long in the scheme then Tommy?

Naw.

Same with myself, a couple of months just, still feeling my way about. I'm staying with the lassie and that, helping her out. Her man's working down in England temporarily. Good job but, big money. Course he's having to put in the hours, but like I was saying to her, you dont mind working so long as the money's there—though between you and me Tommy there's a few staying about here that look as if a hard day's graft would kill them! Know what I mean? naw, I dont know how they do it; on the broo and that and they can still afford to go out and get drunk. Telling you, if you took a walk into that pub down at the shopping center you'd see half of them were drawing social security. Aye, and you couldnt embarrass them!

They were at the gate. When the old man made as though to continue speaking McGoldrick said, I better be going then.

Right you are Tommy, see you the morrow maybe he?

Aye, cheerio Mr Murray.

Heh, John, my name's John—I dont believe in the Mr soinso this and the Mr soinso that carry-on. What I say is if a man's good enough to talk to then he's good enough to call you by your first name.

He kept a watch for the two boys as he walked back down the road; then detoured to purchase a pie from the local shop, and he put it under the grill to heat up. At 1:20 P.M. he was sitting down with the knife and fork, the bread and butter, the cup of tea, and the letter-box flapped. He had yet to fix up the doorbell.

The eldest was there. Hello da, he said, strolling in.

You no late?

He had walked to the table in the kitchen and sat down there, looking at the pie and stuff. Cold meat and totties we got, he said, the totties were like chewing gum.

What d'you mean chewing gum?

That's what they were like.

Aye well I'd swop you dinners any day of the week . . . He forked a piece of pie into his mouth. What did you get for pudding?

Cake and custard I think.

You think? what d'you mean you think?

The boy yawned and got up from the chair. He walked to the oven and looked at it, then walked to the door: I'm away, he said.

Heh you, you were supposed to be here half an hour ago to take that wean to the nursery.

It wasnt my turn.

Turn? what d'you mean turn? it's no a question of turns.

I took her last.

Aw did you.

Aye.

Well where's your bloody brother then?

I dont know.

Christ . . . He got up and followed him to the door, which could only be locked by turning a handle on the inside, unless a key was used on the outside. As the boy stepped downstairs he called: How you doing up there? that teacher, is she any good?

The boy shrugged.

Ach. He shook his head then shut and locked the door. He poured more tea into the cup. The tin of paint and associated articles. The whole house needed to be done up; wallpaper or paint, his wife didnt care which, just so long as it was new, that it was different from what it had been when they arrived.

He collected the dirty dishes, the breakfast bowls and teaplates from last night's supper. He put the plug in the sink and turned on the hot water tap, shoving his hand under the jet of water to feel the temperature change; it was still a novelty. He swallowed the dregs of the tea, lighted a cigarette, and stacked in the dishes.

A vacuum cleaner started somewhere. Then the music drowned out its noise. He became aware of his feet tapping to the music. Normally he would have liked the songs, dancing music. The wife wouldnt be home till near 6 P.M., tired out; she worked as a cashier in a supermarket, nonstop the whole day. She hardly had the energy for anything. He glanced at the fridge, then checked that he had taken out the meat to defrost. A couple of days ago he had forgotten yet again—egg and chips as usual, the weans delighted of course. The wife just laughed.

He made coffee upon finishing the dishes. But rather than sitting down to drink it he walked to the corner of the room and put the cup down on a dining chair which had old newspaper on its top, to keep it clear of paint splashes. He levered the lid off the tin, stroking the brush across the palm of his hand to check the bristles werent too stiff, then dipped it in and rapidly applied paint to the wall. It streaked. He had forgotten to mix the fucking stuff.

Twenty minutes later he was amazed at the area he had covered. That was the thing about painting; you could sit on your arse for most of the day and then scab in for two hours; when the wife came in she'd think you'd been hard at it since breakfast time. He noticed his brushstrokes were shifting periodically to the rhythm of the music. When the letter-box flapped he continued for a moment, then laid the brush carefully on the lid of the tin, on the newspaper covering the chair.

Hi, grinned a well-dressed teenager. Gesturing at his pal he said: We're in your area this morning—this is Ricky, I'm Pete.

Eh, I'm actually doing a bit of painting just now.

We'll only take a moment of your time Mr McGoldrick.

Aye, see I've left the lid off the tin and that.

Yeh, the thing is Mr McGoldrick . . .

His pal was smiling and nodding. They were both holding christian stuff, Mormons probably.

Being honest, said McGoldrick, I dont really . . . I'm an atheist.

O yeh—you mean you dont believe in God?

Naw, no really, I prefer taking a backseat I mean, it's all politics and that, eh, honest, I'll need to get back to the painting.

Yeh, but maybe if you could just spare Ricky and myself one moment of your time Mr McGoldrick, we might have a chat about that. You know it's a big thing to say you dont believe in God I mean how can you know that just to come right out and—hey! it's a big thing—right?

McGoldrick shrugged, he made to close the door.

Yeh, I appreciate you're busy at this time of the day Mr McGoldrick but listen, maybe Ricky and myself can leave some of our literature with you—and you can read through it, go over it I mean, by yourself. We can call back in a day or so, when it's more convenient and we can discuss things with you I mean it seems like a real big thing to me you know the way you can just come right out and say you dont believe in God like that I mean . . . hey! it's a big thing, right?

His pal had sorted out some leaflets and he passed them to McGoldrick.

Thanks, he replied. He shut the door and locked it. He remained there, listening to their footsteps go up the stair. Then he suddenly shook his head. He had forgotten to mention Allende. He always meant to mention Allende to the bastards. Fuck it. He left the leaflets on the small table in the lobby.

The coffee was stone cold as well. He filled the electric kettle. The music blasting; another of these good dancing numbers. Before returning to the paint he lighted a cigarette, stopping off at the bathroom on his way ben.

Cute Chick!

There used to be this talkative old lady with a polite English accent who roamed the betting shops of Glasgow being avoided by everybody. Whenever she appeared the heavily backed favorite was just about to get beat by a big outsider. And she would always cry out in a surprised way about how she'd managed to choose it, before going to collect her dough at the payout window. And when asked for her nom-de-plume she spoke loudly and clearly: Cute Chick!

It made the punters' blood run cold.

The Small Family

J suppose it is best not to say what the name of the station was but if I mention it was the one that got "swallowed" up then the majority of folk familiar with the old subway system will have a fair idea of the one in question. Although lying underground it was one of those which seemed very close to the surface in a strange sense. Actual daylight always appeared to be entering though from where I don't know and people somehow assumed the outer layer of corrugated roofing explained everything. I also remember when I was a boy I was absolutely fascinated by the inordinate amount of dripping. Water seemed to come from anywhere and everywhere. As a result, I was ready and willing to believe anything. Especially was I willing to believe that the tunnel beneath the Clyde was full of rotting timbers and set to collapse at any moment. This was the yarn told me by my older brother. I doubt whether the fact that it actually was a yarn fully dawned on me for a further decade.

Those familiar with the station must readily recall its peculiar hallmark, a weird form of illusion; its main ground resembled a large mound or hill and from the bottom of the long flights of stairs intending travelers would find themselves "walking up" a stiffish gradient along the platform. Such a gradient was a physical absurdity of course but this did not stop visiting travelers from experiencing the sensation. I have to confess that I was as guilty as the next regular in the enjoyment I gained from observing the unwary.

Another hallmark of the station, though the term is somewhat inappropriate, was the Small Family. As far as many people are concerned when we speak of the station we are speaking of them, the Small Family, but I am not alone in the belief that had the peculiar "mound" or "hill" not existed then the Small Family would have associated itself with another station. Individually members of the family were not especially small, rather was the phrase applied as a simplified form of reference by the regulars which in the first instance must have derived from the little mother. There was no father, no male parent, and the female—the little mother—was very small indeed, birdlike almost. Yet be that as it may this tiny woman most certainly was a parent who tended her young come hell or high water.

Of the four children in the family group I chiefly recall the eldest, a large boy or young man. He had the appearance of being big and strong but at the same time with a form of "lightness" of the brain, a slightly brutish quality. I once heard a traveler describe his walk as "thick" and this to my mind was very apt indeed. The other children were aged from infancy to pubescence but at this juncture I am unable to recollect their sexes; they would walk to the front of the mother with the large boy bringing up the rear, often carrying a long stick which he let trail on the ground.

When regulars spoke of the Small Family they did so in a wryly amused fashion. In those days an odd camaraderie existed between us. I am of the opinion that this was the case because of the tacit assumption that in stations like ours the queerest occurrences might take place right beneath one's nose but that in the very act of perception the substance of such an occurrence would have slipped, as it were, "round a corner." I should point out that I am very aware of the pitfalls in nostalgia. But I doubt whether it is necessary to state that the Small Family in itself was never a source of amusement to us. The truth of the matter is that we regulars admired if not marveled at them. Above all did we esteem the little mother. In conversation with an old friend recently we were discussing this; he made the strong point that simply to have been a parent of the large boy would have tested a man's resources. This is not, of course, in any sense, to excuse the absence of a male parent; it was intended as a testimony to the character of the tiny woman. In those days things were more tough than they are now and she could not have had an easy time of it. My friend reminded me that the family seemed to earn its living by gathering and that often they were to be seen carrying large bundles of soft goods. It is possible they may have kept a stall in one of the lesser street markets in the area to the south of the Tron.

I told my friend of a dream I used to have in which the large mound or hill in the station had become hollow and was fashioned out as a makeshift home for the Small Family. Inside it the floors were carpeted and the kitchen contained every domestic and labor-saving convenience.

The rationale of the dream is fairly obvious but my friend also pointed to an element of reality insofar as the back end of the mound would have afforded a degree of shelter. He also reminded me that any form of shelter was always welcome in the old station because of the tremendous rushes of air. This most definitely was the case and of the more amusing side effects of the illusion, as experienced by visiting travelers, perhaps the most striking was the sensation that true equilibrium would be achieved only by crawling on all fours.

I had wanted to speak to my friend of an incident that occurred many many years ago. In matters like this it is far better to move straightaway to the core of the subject otherwise we run the risk of losing our way. My desire was basic, to have the subject aired. It is my opinion that to air a subject, to present the question, is to find oneself on the road to solution. I may well be wrong. In itself the incident is of no major significance, neither then nor now. But it is one that remains to the forefront of my memory and has done for more than thirty years. It concerns my own children.

I have had five children, the eldest of whom is a daughter. At the time I speak she was nine or ten years old but even then had looks of a striking quality. She also regarded herself as quite grown up, as quite the young lady. I must confess that both myself and my wife regarded the girl in a similar light which is not at all uncommon, she being the eldest of the five.

The day of the incident was a Sunday and my wife was not feeling a hundred percent; she decided to remain home with the youngest two while I set off with the other three on a visit to an elderly relation. All children loved the old subway system and mine were no different. Even yet I can recall their excitement as we tramped downwards, down the long flights of stone steps, thoroughly enjoying the onrush of air, the strange smells and echoing sounds. Once onto the platform we "ascended" the large mound or hill to stand hand in hand, peering into the blackness of the tunnel, awaiting the arrival of the next train.

In our group as a whole I should say there had been close on twenty folk, and by "group" I simply refer to those on the platform who were intending passengers, as opposed to the Small Family. They had appeared suddenly, from nowhere it seemed. I myself traveled but rarely on Sundays and I confess to rather a shock on discovering they were here in the station on that day as though it were any other. The other travelers must have been experiencing an unease similar to my own. Not to put too fine a point on it there most certainly was a general strain, and we stood as though rooted to the spot. But gradually I became aware of a pressure on my hand. It was being caused by the child whose hand I held and she in turn was being affected by the child whose hand he was holding who in turn was being affected by my eldest daughter's hand. My eldest daughter was very uncomfortable indeed, but not agitated and by no means in any distress. It was the large boy, he was staring at her. He had halted at the rear of his family and was standing stock-still, staring at her in an entirely unselfconscious manner. It was the most peculiar thing. I see the moment clearly and distinctly and the two figures are in isolation. Beyond that is a blur, until I hear my daughter's voice:

'Dad, I want to put her on the mantelpiece!' and she pointed to someone in their group, either a child or I suppose, perhaps, the tiny woman.

There are many aspects of this incident I regard as worthy of comment, as worthy of discussion. Over the years I have dwelt on the matter periodically but without ever allowing it to become an obsession. I would like, however, to speak of it with my friend. I have wanted to do so for quite some time but the subject I find difficult to approach, that is, the core of the subject, for I find it all too easy to discuss topics peripheral to it.

As the years pass I have become close to overwhelmed by an ever-increasing burden of guilt. There is no one cause. I think that if I could isolate different events, the experiences I derived from them, if I could bring these out into the open then perhaps I would be on the road to assuaging such feelings and ridding myself of the burden. I am also aware that the sensation of guilt—even chronic guilt—is part and parcel of the ageing process and in neither case does a cure exist. Ultimately, however, to have said that is to have said very little.

Half an hour before he died

About half an hour before he died Mr Millar woke up, aware that he might start seeing things from out the different shapes in the bedroom, especially all these clothes hanging on the pegs on the door, their suddenly being transformed into ghastly kinds of bodies, perhaps hovering in mid air. It was not a good feeling; and having reflected on it for quite a few minutes he began dragging himself up onto his elbows to peer about the place. And his wrists felt really strange, as if they were bloodless or something, bereft of blood maybe, no blood at all to course through the veins. For a wee while he became convinced he was losing his sanity altogether, but no, it was not that, not that precisely; what it was, he saw another possibility, and it was to do with crossing the edge into a sort of madness he had to describe as "proper"—a proper madness. And as soon as he recognized the distinction he began to feel better, definitely. Then came the crashing of a big lorry, articulated by the sound of it. Yes, it always had been a liability this, living right on top of such a busy bloody road. He was resting on his elbows still, considering all of it, how it had been so noisy, at all hours of the day and night. Terrible. He felt like shouting on the wife to come ben so's he could tell her about it, about how he felt about it, but he was feeling far too tired and he had to lie back down.

The Red Cockatoos

That moment after sunrise I saw the troop of figures appear, then round the head of the loch, the Red Cockatoos. I was totally enraptured of the scene, unable to even reflect on how my own feelings were. The morning was so mild, so very mild and clear, perhaps the most mild and most clear of the entire summer. There too was the strange purity of air, almost an emanation from the pure loch water. If this scene could have reminded me of anything it could only have been of the Horsemen of Harris as witnessed by Martin Martin more than two hundred years ago. And yet, perhaps I speak only of the day itself, the actual atmosphere, the light and aural texture, for what could ever be likened to the figures I was now seeing? I was an intruder, and beholding a vision so awful that at once I myself had been transformed into victim. I could see them distinctly, the troop of almost thirty, the red circles of their faces, the unquiet, seeming to contain a frenzy. And a figure had moved too quickly and bumped into the figure in front and the laughter of the pair was immediate, and nervous too, scarcely controlled at all, revealing the anticipation of an event so horrible that hackles arose on the back of my neck, the hairs rising, on the back of my neck; and a shiver crossed my shoulders, I was having to fight hard to resist it, this terror. And were they now moving in single file? They were; rounding the head of the loch still, their hats prominent, and their old-fashioned frock coats. I was seeing them from the rear, their voice-sounds muted but already having taken on a new air, a new sense of something, some unknown thing perhaps and yet known too, as though from the depth of a folk memory, the metamorphosis now reaching the later stages. When they vanished I had to jump onto my feet and twist and turn this way and that in my effort to find them; but they were there, they were there, only behind some foliage, not by intention hiding, being unaware of we watchers.

I relaxed and prepared to wait, sitting now with my elbows resting on my knees, gazing lochwards, away from the retreating figures. And gradually my mind had discovered its own concentration. I remembered Miller's tale of the loch wherein lies an island and on that island is a loch wherein lies an island and on that island is a loch wherein lies an island and so on and so forth to that ultimate island. And I envisaged the ancient female seer on that ultimate island's throne squinting at the world with—yes, her irreverent twinkle but also a coldness there too, for the fallibility, the presumption. When I arrived in the glade an elderly woman was there amongst us who did remind me of the ancient seer for she too had a coldness about her that might well have taken my breath away on a different occasion; and lurking there too was an amused expression which I did not like, I could not have liked. This elderly woman was a person set back a pace from the main body, preferring to allow others to take the floor.

But take the floor we did. There was a beautiful girl to the side, modest, her gaze downcast, to the grassy mounds on the edge of the area. She would be mine. Her hair had the sheen and her breasts the concealed manner I knew so well, her body lightly lined beneath the loose cotton dress, and the breeze to her, the lines of her knees and thighs. I could hold her so gently, my hands touching the small of her back, her forehead to my shoulder, dampening my shoulder. There is a life there, a life strong and not to be spent. I put my hands to the small of her back, my palms flatly now to her kidneys, a body of flesh and blood, the warmth of her breasts and the warmth of her breath through my shirt onto my shoulder. And too the others, the others being there too—for now she was thrusting me back from her and laughing quietly; but as excited a laugh as could ever be imagined, as ever could be imagined; and in the laughter a mischievousness there for me, a mischief, I would try to be catching her and always be missing her by a hairsbreadth. And the others dancing now, the figures of humans, men and women, from the young to the old, all dependent on such as myself and the elderly woman whom I could see seated beside an old man with a brosy complexion, his fine head of pure white hair, listening to her animated chatter with great attention, his hand to the crook of her elbow as though to steady her, to pacify her. Was the elderly woman like me?

But the girl wanted me. She urged me on, urged me on. And I was dancing her on a circle, a reel; and our laughter amidst the laughter of the
others, the couples, indistinguishable. It was a rage. It was a fire. We
were on fire. We were clinging together. I was holding her so tightly, to
keep her now, to keep her safe forever. For it was time, it was the time.
And my memory is of a total rapture: the memory of such a moment
but without the moment's memory for I cannot recollect that moment,
only of having had such a moment, of our total rapture, the girl with the
dark hair and myself.

We were apart now, inches, inches and feet and then yards, and her
hands upraised in a question, her frown being followed by a look of an
almost sickening resignation; uncomprehending, she cannot comprehend why this is to be, why they are to be in this way, that she is here
for this one day, this only day, forever, this poor Red Cockatoo. And I
can stare and stare at her, the tears tucked behind my eyes now as they
seem always to have been since first I glimpsed the troop at sunrise, my
chest and throat of an acidulous dryness.

The others were with her. They were standing to the rear of us in their
own grouping, fidgeting, muttering unintelligibly. But soon they were
become silent and those who had been staring at the ground now raised
their heads. We humans were the interlopers, myself and the elderly
woman, the others. And we were having to stand there in our own isolation, watching this heartbreak, these poor Red Cockatoos, their moment having come and now gone, concealing nought from each other,
not now, not any longer. And we must continue our watching as this further stage advanced, their thin arms stretching out to one another; and
they cling hand to hand in a curious, orchestrated fashion, not looking
to one another, as though a certain form of mutual recognition might
destroy some very remote possibility of staying the process. And the
process cannot be stayed. Even then were their hands tearing from
each other as they fought to control their faces, and I searched for my
girl but could not distinguish her, for the faces were now all of the uniform red circles, this bodily transformation seeming to induce a mental calm; but even so, there was an air of bewilderment amongst them,
and a vague self-consciousness, their feet twitching uneasily, twitching

uneasily. I had to turn my face away, glimpsing only the hurried movement of the elderly woman as she did likewise. But for an instant were
we looking into the other's eyes? I do not know, for the screeching had
begun and it was all to be over, within a brief few seconds these poor
Red Cockatoos would cease to exist.

Dum vivimus, vivamus

This whole business is getting on my nerves. I was ploughing my way through these St. Machar legends when right in front of me appeared what can only be a reference to that bastard Brendan O'Diunne. I dont like calling him that. Up until recently I reckoned him the greatest Scotchman to ever live and the greatest Scotchman who ever could live, in a logical sense. If writing this a couple of years back I would probably have been beginning in a manner approaching the following:

Ancient Schottisch Writtaris have chronicklt that which the Illustriss Buchanan has richtly acknowledgt "ane strange gamyn richt eneuch."

A load of shite. Pointless carrying on from an opening like this because it leads to greater expectations of consistency and coherence whereas the entire thing is an utter mishmash, a shambles. This is why I discontinued the project when I did. It also explains why the old George fellow finally, and not too reluctantly, allowed his own welter of research to "slippit intill the muddis of auld annallis." Of course he hesitated for ages but it has to be remembered the sort of person he was. And then as well, any writer as disciplined as that must readily— Ach. Who cares. And Boswell! Not to be spoken of in the same breath I know, but how come he fails to even rate it a mention? Especially when that English sidekick of his allows a reasonable-sized paragraph to "the peculiarly Scotch game"? It could be he just wasnt present while the shepherd was recounting the tale. Perhaps Johnson had refused him attendance, lest he made the shepherd so nervous he might have been unable to communicate. Or maybe it is simply the case he had gone off on his own to ferret a dinner invitation from one of the local highland bigwigs. The point being that had he been there in the bothy we could have found ourselves in the possession of a genuine exposition of the game's mechanics. As matters stand it would appear that either Johnson received a full and proper oral account of the game which for some reason best known to himself he neglected to record, or else he did not receive an account at all, and I am inclined to plump for the latter. The actual odds about the shepherd's having had any detailed knowledge of the game's mechanics are very very long indeed. And even if he did have such knowledge, so what? Does that really suggest he would have felt the need to pass it on to the good Doctor? Apart from anything else, as far as the shepherd was concerned, the whole point of the carry-on lies not so much in the game itself but in its extraordinary and magnificent termination, for without that there is almost nothing at all—and certainly no rational explanation of how come the memory of an ancient game should yet be lingering in the mind of a people. And that to me is the crux of the problem. Other aspects are of interest but to regard any as crucial seems a psychological nonsense. Obviously to gain an understanding of how the game was played would be interesting for its own sake, and I for one would travel a long distance to find such a thing out, but that is as far as it goes. I used to take it for granted that the old commentators were assuming a working knowledge of the game's mechanics, but I now know differently—and that's being kind about it. The simple fact of the matter is that they didnt have a clue. It was always total guesswork—the slippery slopes of inference, some of the more common theories deriving from that astonishingly scientific premise that games in antiquity were much more liable to be of a physical nature. And even supposing that to be true, so what? Success at physical games need not entail having the build of an ox. It is certainly the case that by all accounts Brendan was a "greit baist of a man" but this type of stuff is banal and leads to all sorts of wild conjecture, and I would prefer not to be involved in that. A quick instance of what I'm talking about, a "mathematician" of early last century (whose name it is nicer not to mention though he seems to have accomplished some pioneering work in the science of phrenology) makes a grand case for O'Diunne's having been a weedy individual because of the startling rigidity of the game's rule structure. Fine, is about all you can say to that. But it is a truism that the game's limits were rigidly defined. There again though, insofar as this concerns the nature of Brendan's skull, the guy makes the elementary error of confusing termination with inception, always a risk when somebody in that field strays beyond the somatic hedge. No wonder you start getting involved in discussions on the nature of the cranium! Too much. And yet to some extent he has to be given the benefit of the doubt; he was truly seeking after a disciplined approach and once that is begun every pathway, no matter how shady, seems an obligation. It would have been interesting to see his notes though, I have to confess. Better still but, seeing old George's. What I really would like to know is where his first written reference comes from. I have always thought it would turn out to be via the Achnasheen Monk which if true presents us with quite an irony. There again, I just dont have the patience any longer. I'm also beginning to believe those who handle it in a quasi-humorous way have got the right idea. But Buchanan couldnt manage that and neither can I. And why bother criticizing the likes of Achnasheen? Is it really an accident that he appears not to feel the need of dwelling at length on the famous exhortation? In fact, I'm beginning to think it might be a bit unhealthy to do so. In saying this I've got to remind myself there would be very little without it, at least nowadays. My own interest is well on the wane. Sometimes I just think, leave it to the linguists. But no. Definitely not. So much of it is just— Who cares. There again, I know that when Brendan leaves the field of play Achnasheen has him crying: Dum vivimus. It is all fine and good but the fascinating question here is not so much whether the "vivamus" had already been dropped from the popular saying without affecting its sense but whether Latin was used at all. Did the Monk simply translate O'Diunne's utterance from the Gaelic? Yes, and it would be nice to know what old George's thoughts were on this specific point. Perhaps especially to know if he would have considered such thoughts as valid. Obviously too, it is worth bearing the matter in mind in regard to Boswell's absence during the interview with the shepherd. And here I refer to his sidekick's notorious rejection of the very possibility of Gaelic as a literary form. My own gut reaction is to oppose the good Doctor at all costs but on this particular issue I have to say no. I reckon Achnashseen was recording what he saw as a fairly amusing albeit minorish local legend and that he was recording it as roundly as he could, in other words, no translation. I am well aware that it has become a more controversial aspect than previously but I have to stick with it at this late stage, otherwise—who cares about the otherwise. I'm just sticking with it and that's that. And how in the name of heaven anybody can accept that silly theory now being pushed by those taking a lead from Ghrame and the Latheron X11 I dont know. It just seems to me daft. As far as I can make out it hinges almost completely on the Abbot of Tain and his "dulce est desipire in loco." And I know fine well that the existential mark of the "dum vivimus" has to appeal to one and all. But surely that is the very strength of the argument? When O'Diunne leaves the field of play he does so in such a manner that the game terminates, never to be played again. I say this, that if he really had gone off in the huff then he would have been met by scorn. It is as simple as that and as basic as that. And never, not in ten thousand years, could such a legend have come about. For one thing, the game would have continued—if not on that selfsame day then the next one, or the next one, but certainly at some future date. And to so much as even suggest that the action might have been premeditated is a nonsense. No premeditated act could ever effect such a consequence. Ordinary people just arent so readily impressed. It had to be something else altogether. For what we are here dealing with is very close to a sort of universal appreciation of an absurdity; an immediate and absolute recognition of the validity of one individual's action: a revelation. And revelations are by definition irrational. According to Martin the final day's play occurs somewhere in the Caithness region and although his evidence is based on the same sources nobody raises any serious objections. I think this is the correct approach and I have nothing to criticize in it. Several months ago a Gaelic-speaking pal of mine spent a few days in Barra and got speaking to a very old lady. Out of it came the following, that her people hailed from a small island which has been formally uninhabited since the late seventeenth century, and that to the best of her knowledge the ancient Gaelic saying for "fair play" on this island was always *cothrom na Dhiunne* and not "cothrom na Fiunne" as it is elsewhere. Now at the time I was less interested in this than my pal because of course the great Finn had a cousin whose name was Dhiunn. Then this latest turn-up in these St. Machar things. I'm still not going to get involved either. I feel like wrapping the lot up in a brown paper parcel and dropping it off the Kingston Bridge, except with my fucking luck it would land in a rowing boat. But fair enough I suppose.

Getting Outside

J'll tell you something: when I stepped outside that door I was alone, and I mean alone. And it was exactly what I had wanted, almost as if I'd been demanding it. And that was funny because it's not the kind of thing I would usually demand at all; usually I didnt demand anything remotely resembling being outside that door. But now. Christ. And another thing: I didnt even feel as if I was myself. What a bloody carry-on it was. I stared down at my legs, at my trousers. I was wearing these corduroy things I mostly just wear to go about. These big bloody holes they have on the knee. So that as well. Christ, I began to think my voice would start erupting in one of these bloodcurdling screams of horror. But no. Did it hell, I was in good control of myself. I glanced down at my shoes and lifted my right foot, kidding on I was examining the shoelaces and that, to see if they were tied correctly. One of those stupid kind of things you do. It's as if you've got to show everybody that nothing's taking place out the ordinary. This is the kind of thing you're used to happening. It's a bit stupid. But the point to remember as well; I was being watched. It's the thing you might forget. So I just I think sniffed and whistled a wee bit, to kid on I was assuming I was totally alone. And I could almost hear them drawing the curtains aside to stare out. Okay but I thought: here I am alone and it's exactly what I wanted; it was what I'd been demanding if the truth's to be told. I'll tell you something as well: I'm not usually a brave person but at that very moment I thought Christ here you are now and what's happening but you're keeping on going, you're keeping on going, just as if you couldnt give a damn about who was watching. I'm not kidding you I felt as great as ever I've felt in my whole life, and that's a fact. So much so I was beginning to think is this you that's doing it. But it bloody was me, it was. And then I was walking and I mean walking, just walking, with nobody there to say yay or nay. What a feeling thon was. I stopped a minute to look about. An error. Of course, an error. I bloody knew it as soon as I'd done it. And out they came.

Where you off to?

Eh—nowhere in particular.

Can we come with you?

You?

Well we feel like a breath of fresh air.

I looked straight at them when they said that. It was that kind of daft thing people can say which gives you nearly nothing to reply. So I just, what I did for a minute, I just stared down at my shoes and then I said, I dont know how long I'll be away for.

They nodded. And it was a bit of time before they spoke back. You'd prefer we didnt come with you. You want to go yourself.

Go myself?

Yes, you prefer to go yourself. You dont want us to come with you.

No, it's not that, it's just, it's not that, it's not that at all, it's something else.

They were watching me and not saying anything.

It's just I dont know how long I'll be away. I might be away a couple of hours there again I might be away till well past midnight.

Midnight?

Yes, midnight, it's not that late surely, midnight, it's not that late.

We're not saying it is.

Yes you are.

No we're not.

But you are, that's what you're saying.

We arent. We arent saying that at all. We're not caring at all what you do. Go by yourself if you like. If you had just bloody told us to begin with instead of this big smokescreen you've always got to draw this great big smokescreen.

I have not.

Yes you have. That's what you've done.

That's what I'd done. That's what they were saying: they were saying I'd drawn this great big smokescreen all so's I could get outside the door as if the whole bloody carry-on was just in aid of that. I never said anything back to them. I just thought it was best waiting and I just kind of kidded on I didnt really know what they were meaning.

Greyhound for Breakfast

onnie held the dog on a short lead so it had to walk on the edge of the pavement next to the gutter. At a close near the corner of the street two women he knew were standing chatting. They paused, watching his approach. Hullo, he said. When they peered at the greyhound and back to him he grinned and raised his eyebrows; and he shrugged, continuing along and into the pub.

The barman stared while pouring the pint of heavy but made no comment. He took the money and returned the change, moved to serve somebody else. Ronnie gazed after him for a moment then lifted the pint and led the dog to where four mates of his were sitting playing Shoot Pontoon. He sat on a vacant chair, bending to tuck the leash beneath his right shoe. He swallowed about a quarter of the beer in the first go and then sighed. I needed that, he said, leaning sideways a little, to grasp the dog's ears; he patted its head. He maneuvered his chair so he could watch two hands of cards being played. The game continued in silence. Soon the greyhound yawned and settled onto the floor, its big tongue lolloping out its mouth. Ronnie smiled and shook his head. He swallowed another large draft of the heavy beer.

Then McInnes cleared his throat. You looking after it for somebody? he asked without taking his gaze from the thirteen cards he was holding and sorting through. Ronnie did not reply. The other three were smiling; they were also sorting through their cards. He carried on watching the game until it ended and the cards were being shuffled for the next. And he yawned; but the yawn was a false one and he sniffed and glanced towards the bar. Jimmy Peters had taken a tobacco pouch from his pocket and started rolling a fag. Ronnie gestured at it. Jimmy passed him the pouch and he rolled one for himself. He was beginning to feel a bit annoyed but it was fucking pointless. He stuck the finished roll-up in his mouth and reached for a box of matches lying at the side of the table. Heh Ronnie, said Kelly, did you get it for a present?

What?

I'm saying did you get it for a present, the dog—a lot of owners and that, once their dogs have finished racing, they give them away as presents—supposed to make rare pets.

Aye. Ronnie nodded, inhaled on the cigarette.

I'm serious.

Aye, said Tam McColl, I heard that as well. Easy oasy kind of beasts, they get on good with weans.

Ronnie nodded. This is a good conversation, he said.

Well! Tam McColl grinned: You're no trying to tell us it's a fucking racer are you! McColl chuckled and shook his head: With withers like that!

Withers like that! What you talking about withers like that! Ronnie smiled: What do you know about fucking withers ya cunt!

The others laughed.

My auld man used to keep dogs.

Aye fucking chihuahuas!

Are you telling us you've bought it? asked Kelly.

Ronnie did not reply.

Are you?

Ronnie dragged on the cigarette, having to squeeze the end of it so he could get a proper draw. He exhaled the smoke away from where the greyhound was lying. Jimmy Peters was looking at him. Ronnie looked back. After a moment Jimmy Peters said, I mean are you actually going to race it?

Naw Jimmy I'm just going to take it for walks.

The other three laughed loudly. Ronnie shook his head at Peters. Then he gazed at the dog; he inhaled on the cigarette, but it had stopped burning.

Does Babs know yet? asked McInnes.

What?

Babs, does she know yet?

What about?

God sake Ronnie!

Ronnie reached for the box of matches again and he struck one, got the roll-up burning once more. He blew out the flame and replied, I've just no seen her since breakfast.

Tam McColl grinned. You're mad ya cunt, fucking mad.

How much was it? asked Kelly. Or are we no allowed to ask!

Ronnie lifted his beer and sipped at it.

Did it cost much?

Fuck sake, muttered Ronnie.

You no going to tell us? asked Kelly.

Ronnie shrugged. Eighty notes.

Eighty notes!

Ronnie looked at him.

Jimmy Peters had shifted roundabout on his seat and he leaned down and ruffled behind the dog's ears, making a funny face at it. The dog looked back at him. He said to Ronnie, Aye it's a pally big animal.

Ronnie nodded. Then he noticed Kelly's facial expression and he frowned.

Naw, replied Kelly, grinning. I was just thinking there—somebody asking what its form was: oh it's pally! a pally big dog! Fuck speed but it likes getting petted!

That's a good joke, said Ronnie.

The other four laughed.

Ronnie nodded. On you go, he said, nothing like a good fucking joke. He dragged on the roll-up but it had stopped burning once again. He shoved it into the ticket pocket inside his jacket then lifted his pint and drank down all that was left of the beer. The others were grinning at him. Fuck yous! he said and reached for the leash.

McInnes chuckled: Sit on your arse Ronnie for fuck sake!

Fuck off.

Can you no take a joke? said Jimmy Peters.

A joke! That's fucking beyond a joke.

Kelly laughed.

Aye, said Ronnie, on ye go ya fucking stupid bastard.

Kelly stopped laughing.

Heh you! said McInnes to Ronnie.

Ah well no fucking wonder!

Kelly was still looking at him. Ronnie looked back.

McInnes said, You're fucking out of order Ronnie.

I'm out of order!

Aye.

Me? Ronnie was tapping himself vigorously on the chest.

Aye, replied McInnes.

It was just a joke, said Jimmy Peters.

A joke? That was fucking beyond a joke. Ronnie shook his head at him; he withdrew the dowp from his inside ticket pocket and reached for the box of matches again; but he put it back untouched, returned the dowp to the ticket pocket, lifted the empty beer glass and studied it for a moment. He sniffed and returned it to the table.

The others resumed the game of Shoot Pontoon.

And after two or three minutes Tam McColl said, Heh Ronnie did you see that movie on the telly last night.

Naw.

We were just talking about it before you came in.

Mm. Ronnie made a show of listening to what McColl was saying, it was some sort of shite about cops and robbers that was beyond even talking about. Ronnie shook his head. It was unbelievable. He stared at the cards on the table then he stared in the direction of the bar, a few young guys were over at the jukebox.

Jimmy Peters was saying something to him now. What was it about, it was about fucking the football, going to the football. Ronnie squinted at him: What?

Three each, said Jimmy, what a game! Did you see it?

Ronnie shook his head. He glanced at the shelf in beneath the table, the four pint glasses there, dribbles of beer in each. It was fucking beyond belief.

That last goal! said Jimmy.

Ronnie nodded. He clapped the dog's head, grasped its ears, tugging at them till at last it shook his hand away. He sniffed and muttered, I'll tell yous mob something: see if this fucking dog doesnt get me the holiday money I'll eat it for my fucking breakfast.

The others smiled briefly. And Kelly said, So you are going to race it?

Ronnie shrugged. He didnt feel like talking. It was time to leave. He felt like leaving. It would be good to be able to leave; right now. He reached to clap the dog, smoothed along its muzzle.

Heh Ronnie, said McInnes. Where you going to keep it?

Ronnie wrapped the leash round his hand and he nodded slightly, lifted the box of matches.

No in the house? grinned Tam McColl.

There was a silence.

You're fucking mad!

Whereabouts in the house? asked Jimmy Peters.

Ronnie struck the match and tilted his head while getting the roll-up burning; he exhaled smoke: The boy's room, he said. Just meantime. He's no here the now. He's away with a couple of his mates. Down to London . . . He sniffed and dragged on the dowp again.

The others had been sorting the cards out after a new deal.

We never knew he was going, said Ronnie, no till the last minute. One of his mates got a phone call or something so they had to move fast.

Move fast? said McInnes.

It was a job they were after. They had to move fast. Otherwise they wouldnt fucking get it.

Aw aye.

Ronnie shrugged.

Kelly glanced at the greyhound and said, What you going to call it? You got something fixed?

Eh . . . I dont know. The guy I got it off says it's up to me. The way it works, most of them's got two names, one for the kennel and one for when it races.

Kelly nodded. Has it definitely raced Ronnie I mean I'm no being cheeky?

Aye Christ it's qualified at Ashfield and it's won three out of ten at Carfin.

Honest?

Aye, fuck sake.

What'd they call it?

Ronnie sniffed. *Big Dan.*

Big Dan? Tam McColl was grinning.

What's up with that ya cunt ye they've got to call it something! Ronnie shook his head, and he glanced at Kelly: You heard of it?

Eh naw, no really.

Ronnie nodded.

I've never been to Carfin but; never I mean—have you?

Naw.

You sure it's won there? asked Jimmy Peters.

Aye Christ he showed me, the guy; it's down in black and white.

Whereabouts? asked Kelly.

Whereabouts? Ronnie squinted at him.

Where's it written down?

The fucking *Record*.

Aw.

Kelly said, You talking about the results like? On the page?

Ronnie looked at him without saying anything in reply. He lifted his empty beer glass and swirled the drop at the bottom about, put the glass to his mouth and attempted to drink, but the drop got lost somewhere along the way. He said, Plus I saw its form figures and that on a racecard.

Kelly nodded.

Both McInnes and McColl and now Jimmy Peters were looking at him. Ronnie said, In the name of fuck! What yous looking at!

Aye, well, muttered McInnes, Your boy's fucked off to England and you've went out and bought a dog.

What?

There was no further comment. Ronnie shook his head and added, For fuck sake I've been wanting to buy a dog for years.

Aye, well it's a wee bit funny how it's only the now you've managed it.

What?

Your boy goes off to England and you go out and buy a dog . . . McInnes stared at Ronnie.

Who was it you bought it off? asked Kelly.

What?

Who was it you bought it off?

Away and fuck yourself, muttered Ronnie and he stood to his feet and jerked at the leash, the greyhound getting quickly up off the floor; and he walked it straight out the pub, not looking back.

Once through the park gates he let more slack into the lead before continuing on up the slope, the big dog now trotting quite freely. But the exercise he was giving it just now wasnt necessary. He was only doing it because he needed time to think. Babs would not be pleased. That was an understatement. It was something he had managed to avoid thinking about. And he was right not to have. If he had he would probably never have bought it. It was a case of first things first, buy the dog and then start worrying.

It stopped for a piss. Ronnie could have done with one himself but he would have got arrested. When they resumed he watched it, its shoulders hunched, keeping to the grass verge, sniffing occasionally and looking to be taking an interest in everything that was going on. It was quite a clever beast, the way it paid attention to things. And as well the way it moved, he was appreciating that; definitely an athlete—sleek was the word he was looking for. It described the dog to a tee. Sleek. That way it gave a genuine impression of energy, real energy—power and strength, and speed of course. The thing was every inch a racer.

Leaving the path he crossed the wide expanse of grass, heading down by the bowling greens. It was late spring/early summer, getting on to the middle of May, still a bit cold when the sky clouded; but just now it was fine, the sun shining. More than half of the bowling rinks were occupied. Ronnie paused by the big hedge, peering over, and recognizing a few faces. But he was not going to go in. He wasnt in the mood for more slagging. Sometimes you got sick of it, you werent able to fucking, just to cope with it, it was difficult. You felt as if you'd had enough of it.

Beyond the bowling greens lay the flowerbeds. A lot of prams and pushchairs were in the vicinity, and on the benches women mainly, with the wee toddlers staggering about here and there, looking as if they were going to fall and bang their heads on the paving. But they were always okay; it was fucking amazing. He took the leash in to have more control of the dog but it seemed not to notice anything, not to be in the least nervous, even when one of the toddlers made a lunge at it.

Along by the pond he spotted a bench where a middle-aged guy was seated alone in the center, a folded newspaper and a plastic bag of messages beside him. He had a bunnet on his head, a fawn trenchcoat, a scarf; probably the same clothes he would have been wearing in January.

Ronnie sat down, he sighed. He was aware of a tension easing out of his shoulders and he deliberately made them droop so he could relax even more, feeling a sort of twinge at the top of his spine which made him shiver. He glanced at the middle-aged man and nodded. Nice day, eh?

The man's head twitched in agreement.

Ronnie brought the cigarette dowp out from his inside ticket pocket and he gestured with it. You got a light at all? he asked.

Dont smoke. I chucked it ten year ago.

Aw. Wise man.

The middle-aged guy nodded at the pond: I mind the day it was chokablok with boats—big yins; yachts and all kinds.

Ronnie looked at him.

Beauties. You'd be lucky to get sailing at all unless you were up early! What?

Now it's paddleboats for weans. Pathetic, bloody pathetic.

Aye . . . Ronnie looked away. It was models he was talking about. His attention was attracted to a couple of boys who were fooling about on one, a paddleboat, right away out, rocking the thing from side to side until it looked like the water would go over the top. Their laughter was loud; it was yells more than anything, really noisy. Fucking terrible. Ronnie grunted and shook his head, glanced at the middle-aged man. And then he said, Look at them. Pair of bloody eedjits. They're going to wind up capsizing the thing—look at them! Christ Almighty!

The middle-aged man was staring off in the other direction altogether.

And the dog had started tugging at the leash. It was behind the bench and moving about, and now doing a shite, straining and doing a shite. Ronnie smiled and shook his head. Life just continued, it was fucking crazy how it went. He faced the front again, seeing the two boys, laughing and rocking the boat, one of them trying to paddle at the same time. But there were stacks of broken glass at the bottom of the pond, that was what they failed to realize. It wasnt just him being totally out of order and losing his temper with them. If one of them fell in he could really hurt himself, he could cut himself quite badly, that was what happened, something fucking silly, turning into something serious. Weans! He shook his head and glanced at the middle-aged guy. Weans! he said, Bloody awful!

The man nodded slightly and sniffed.

I've got three of them, said Ronnie, smiling: A boy and two lassies.

Mm.

Ronnie looked at him for a few moments, seeing something in his face that made him think he probably didnt know what he was talking about, that he didnt understand because he didnt have any kids of his own. They're a fucking problem at times, he said, weans. Bloody awful! He grinned and then sighed and after a brief look at the greyhound he got up and tugged on the leash, headed off towards the exit. And the middle-aged man hadnt even acknowledged him. A moaning-faced old bastard he had been anyway. It was funny how some folk ended up like that. All fucking screwed up and tight and not able to open out with people. Chucked smoking ten years ago. No wonder he was so fucking bad-tempered! Ronnie had tried to chuck it twice and each time it was Babs told him he'd be as well starting again because he was making every cunt's life a misery! But if he had succeeded she would have been delighted. She only said it to give him the excuse for starting again, because she thought he was suffering. And she was right! He was fucking suffering! No half! And yet, there again, he could have put up with it; he was putting up with it. Maybe she should just have kept her mouth shut, if she had kept her mouth shut and let him fucking get on with it, if she had just let him get on with it then maybe he would have fucking knocked it off, he might've chucked it. But what was the point of making excuses? He was good at that. That was one thing he was always good at, making fucking excuses, he was smashing at that.

It was half past four. He saw the time through the window of a shop.

He had bypassed his own street and kept on towards the Cross. The traffic was heavy; lines of buses at the terminus. People who still had jobs. He led the greyhound on across the road and down by the newish housing development. The dog was probably getting quite tired now. He had it back on a short lead, it was walking where he wanted it to. It was a nice big thing. He liked it. There was something about it; it made him feel a bit sorry as well, a kind of courage in the way it walked, its head quite high. He was not scared to face Babs. Even though she had this habit of always being right!

It was just that he wanted to have things clear in his head first. So that he would have an answer; that's all. She was too good at arguing, Babs, too good at arguing. She was liable to make him totally speechless. This is because she was always right. She just had the knack of finding that one thing, that one thing he could never get the answer for. That one thing, it always seemed to be there. But the only way he ever found the fucking thing was once it came up, once she brought it up or it came out, sometimes it just came out, while the argument was happening, and that was him, stuck for words.

He had arrived at the pier. It was derelict. He stood by the railing peering through the spikes. The ferryboat went from here to Partick. Old memories right enough! Ronnie smiled. Although they werent all good. Fuck sake. They werent all good at all. And then these other memories. And the smells. And the journey twice a day six days a week. These smells but of the river, and the rubbish lapping at the side of the steps down, and at low tide the steps all greasy and slippery, the moss and the rest of it. Did folk fall in? It always looked like that. It always looked as if folk would fall in. Fucking dangerous—especially for auld people with walking sticks. Even just the rain, that made the steps slippery.

The greyhound was looking at him. It had tugged on the leash to make him notice. A big whitish dog with a lot of black markings. Now standing squarely, like a middleweight boxer; and its long thin tail curling down to between its hind legs. So placid. It was strange. Sometimes when you saw them at the track—especially after the race—they were fierce, really fierce; going for each other, fangs bared inside the wire muzzles. Even just now, seeing its shoulders and that barrel chest, the power there, so palpable, the power, it could have stepped right out the fucking jungle. And its walk, that sort of pad pad pad—athletic wasnt the word.

Ronnie felt in his pockets for a loose match but there was none. He hadnt a light! He smiled. But one of the obvious factors was money. It cost a fortune to keep a dog. And you had to look after it properly otherwise what was the fucking point? you'd be as well keeping a stupid wee pet, a poodle or something. Stew twice a day was what the guy had advised, unless of course it was running that night. If that was the case you gave it nothing, not till after the event, not unless you were wanting it to lose. In which case you fed it five minutes before the fucking *off!*

There were other things he would have to find out about. Although some of it he would really only find out at the actual track, when he was along there giving it a time trial on Sunday afternoons. He was looking forward to that, it would be quite good. And he would be keeping his ears open and his mouth shut. Maybe get to know a couple of folk, and they would keep him straight at the beginning. Which was one of the reasons he had been hoping that bastard Kelly would've got involved. Kelly knew guys who were into different things and as well as that he used to like going over to the track. Between the two of them they could start finding out the right ways of working it. There was a lot more to the game than fucking exercise. Kelly was a bastard.

Ronnie paused. He had been walking a wee while, as far as the town hall. He crossed at the zebra crossing, making for Copland Road. His tea would be ready right at this minute and Babs would be wondering. But it was still too early; he was not prepared enough. And his fucking feet were beginning to feel sore. And if *he* felt like that what about the dog? A sitdown would have been nice. He did have the cash for one more pint; also over and above that he had enough for 10 smokes. Not buying the packet earlier had been intentional, for obvious reasons: he would maybe only have had 2 or 3 left by this time, plus if he had crashed them in the boozer for fuck sake he would've had fuck all, maybe just the same roll-up dowp! Now, if he watched himself, he could buy the 10 and even put one aside to wake up with the morrow morning, when Babs got the Family Allowance money—the giro wasnt due till next Wednesday.

The leash was jerking. The dog knew how to get his attention alright!

It was across the road: a guy walking three greyhounds at once, two from one fist and one from the other—them all looking well-groomed, taken care of. Sleek. Ronnie nodded. He called over: Nice day!

Aye!

As long as the rain keeps off!

Aye! When the man made to continue on Ronnie called:

You getting a turn?

The man shrugged. He indicated the dog walking alone: This yin goes the morrow night!

I'll keep my fingers crossed!

The man nodded.

Whereabouts? Ashfield?

But the other guy made no reply to this; instead he continued on with the three dogs without glancing back over to Ronnie. Ronnie shook his head but he grinned briefly. Typical dog owner! They were notorious for it. And any information they did give out had to be treated with caution; in fact you were probably better just to consider it as useless, as not worth bothering about.

He went into a wee shop and bought the 10 fags and a book of matches and he was puffing when he appeared on the pavement. Farther along there was another guy with a dog, an elderly man—he looked like an old age pensioner. That was another thing about this, how it could keep you active and fit, and still involved.

At one time this district had two greyhound stadia to itself. Ronnie had been well acquainted with the last that closed down. The White City. It had been a licensed track and he used to go quite regularly, even as a boy; him and his pals used to have this way of skipping in down by the dummy railway. It had been great, evenings like this, the sun shining and the rest of it. The other track was the Albion, a flapping gaff. Ronnie had been too young for that one but the old-timers yapped about it still, how it was the best of the lot and all that sort of shite.

He just wasnt ready to go home yet, not yet, not quite; he would be soon. At least it wasnt raining; if it had been raining it would've been terrible, even for the sake of the dog just. Kelly was a disappointment. So was the other three. But it was hopeless dwelling on that; you had to do things for yourself in this life; nobody was going to do it for you. It was him that had bought the dog, and he would have to fucking take care of it, just take care of it, it was down to him. The lassies would give him a hand; they would like being able to take it out for walks and the rest of it. They wouldnt think he was daft, it was Babs just, she would think he was daft. Other people would think he was daft as well. Was he daft? Maybe he was daft; he was always fucking—what was he?

He could just go home for his tea. No, not yet. He couldnt get it right. He still needed to think things out. Where to keep the dog for instance. The boy's room. Could he keep it there? Would Babs accept it? Would she fuck. She would just fucking, she would laugh at him. Quite right as well. What did he actually go and buy it for? Stupid. That would be her first question too and he couldnt fucking answer it, her first fucking question, he wouldnt be able to answer it, he wouldnt be able to give a straight answer to it. Thirty-five years of age, soon to be thirty-six, married for nearly nineteen years, a son of eighteen—a fucking granpa he could be.

He needed time to think. He just needed time to think. And what was the fucking time anyway? it must've been after six. The tea would just go back in the oven; the tea would go back in the oven.

Ronnie jerked at the dog; he had wound the leash round his knuckles and was clenching his fist as he walked, and he transferred it to his left hand.

The same guy served him as at dinnertime but this occasion he did speak; he frowned and he muttered, They'll no like you bringing it in too much.

What?

The barman nodded, looking up from the pint he was pouring: A lot of folk bring in theirs as well Ronnie, know what I mean? Just ordinary pets I'm talking about—in other words, wee yins!

Dont give us that, replied Ronnie. What about these big fucking alsatians! You're feart to walk in here sometimes in case you step on a tail and get fucking swallowed.

The barman nodded, smiled slightly.

Ronnie sniffed; he glanced at the greyhound by his feet: He wouldnt hurt a flea.

The barman shrugged. I'm just telling you Ronnie, they'll complain.

Okay, I hear you . . . Ronnie sipped at the pint, awaiting his 2 pence change; when the barman passed it to him he dropped it through the slot of the huge bottle of charity money, and he went to the toilet. The dog was quite the thing on the floor when he came back.

He should have come to another pub. That would have been the best idea. He glanced about; a couple of curious stares at the dog. Fuck them all. The dog wouldnt harm a flea. It was just a big—Christ! it was just a big pet.

Across at the rearmost table Jimmy Peters and McInnes were sitting on their own. Ronnie arrived and put his pint down, tucked the leash beneath his right shoe heel, and he nodded towards the bar: According to that yin there's going to be all sorts of complaints about the dog.

That right? said Jimmy Peters.

Too wild or somefuckingthing! Ronnie grinned and sipped at the beer. You want to have seen it in the park as well, with all the wee weans! Ronnie grinned: I mean they were fucking poking it and everything and all it did was look at them, it didnt even notice.

The other two nodded.

I mean I've been with it all day and it's fucking . . . Ronnie stopped and shook his head, he grinned. He brought out his fags and gave one to each: It's just won its first race!

Fucking must've! chuckled Jimmy Peters, taking the cigarette and looking at it.

But it didnt stretch to a pint! added McInnes.

Ronnie nodded. It was a wee race!

You've cheered up since this afternoon.

Me?

Me! said McInnes.

Well . . . Ronnie sniffed.

You were like a fucking bear with a sore head, said Jimmy Peters. No wonder, I came in for a pint and I got a fucking row!

Jimmy Peters chuckled.

McInnes said, Naw you didnt.

Aye I did, grinned Ronnie. I mean I fucking expected it right enough, the slagging.

It wasnt a slagging.

Aye it was.

McInnes pursed his lips.

Let's face it, said Ronnie, it was a slagging.

Eh . . . began Jimmy Peters. Ronnie looked at him and he shrugged.

Mind you, said Ronnie, I was expecting a wee bit of interest, just a wee bit.

Och come on, muttered McInnes.

Well, replied Ronnie, just a wee bit would've been fucking something; better than nothing. But naw; fuck all, just the four of yous trying to take the piss out me.

We werent trying to take the fucking piss out you! Jimmy Peters replied.

You were.

We fucking werent!

Aye you fucking were Jimmy—the two of yous were in it just as much as McColl and Kelly.

Jimmy Peters stared at him then looked away. But McInnes sniffed and leaned closer to Ronnie, and he said: I'll tell you something man you better screw the fucking nut cause the way it's going you're going to wind up bad news, bad news. I'm no fucking kidding ye either.

What?

McInnes sat back and grunted, That's all I'm saying.

What're you meaning but?

McInnes shook his head.

Eh?

I'm no saying anything more Ronnie; you fucking know what I'm meaning.

Ronnie continued to gaze at him, then he frowned at Jimmy Peters and reached for the beer, sipped at it and put it down, lifted it again and sipped some more, gulping it down this time. He inhaled on the cigarette and stared towards the clock. And his hand lowered onto the head of the greyhound, and he grasped its ears.

Dont take it personally for God sake, said McInnes.

Naw.

Jimmy Peters said, It's just you're fucking, you're under pressure and that. The young yin, have you heard from him? the boy.

Ronnie shrugged. Then he said, Look, you dont really think I went out and bought the dog because of that, the boy, because he's away; eh?

Naw, Christ.

Cause I've been wanting a dog for ages. Fuck sake.

Jimmy Peters nodded.

And I'm no the only one—Kelly, he's fucking been on about it more than me. Eh?

Aye.

Ronnie shook his head: I mean I've got to laugh at yous cunts. All talk. All fucking talk.

McInnes was looking at him. Ronnie looked back at him. McInnes said, This is you out of order again.

What?

This is you fucking out of order, again.

What d'you mean?

The way you go on . . . McInnes shook his head and stared at the floor.

Ronnie stared at him.

Aye, God sake, the way you go on!

What! Ronnie's face screwed into a glare.

Leave it.

Leave it?

McInnes looked at him then looked away. Jimmy Peters was looking away too. Ronnie sniffed and glanced at the dog, it was asleep, poor big fucking beast, sound asleep. Greyhounds were short-haired. The top of its head was really smooth. He reached to stroke it, it didnt feel like hair at all, more like a kind of material. He took a long draw on the cigarette, ground it out beneath his shoe on the floor.

Jimmy Peters said, I see the Celts're going to sign that Thomson?

Ronnie nodded.

No a bad player.

Aye.

No Celtic class, muttered McInnes.

It needed a feed as well, it was probably starving. That was another thing about greyhound owners, how they were really tight, they treated their dogs like racing machines, no sentiment. The guy he had bought it from probably never fed it because he knew he was selling it, so it was probably fucking starving.

That movie . . .

Ronnie frowned slightly, then nodded. What time does it start? he asked.

Jimmy Peters smiled. Naw, he said, I'm talking about that one that was on last night—fucking brilliant, did you see it?

Nah.

Were you out? asked McInnes.

What?

I was just asking if you were out, last night; you were no in here?

Naw.

McInnes nodded. Oh by the way, he said, that fucking *Hammurabi* won again!

What! You're kidding?

7 to 1.

For Christ sake!

7 to 1 . . . McInnes smiled, shaking his head. They're sending it to Royal Ascot.

Many's that it's won? Jimmy Peters asked.

Four.

Four on the trot, added Ronnie.

Jimmy Peters grinned. Pity you couldnt've bought a horse!

Ronnie looked at him.

Imagine coming in here with it! Peters laughed: Imagine the faces!

For fuck sake! Ronnie began chuckling.

McInnes was smiling.

A pint and a barrel of oats! cried Peters. Heh barman, a pint and a barrel of oats!

The three of them were laughing now. Gradually they stopped. Ronnie began stroking behind the dog's ears and it opened its eyes for a moment, made a movement in its mouth as if it was thirsty. It would be thirsty. When had it last had a drink? Ronnie hadnt given it one. And the guy he'd bought it from, probably he hadnt either. The truth of the matter is Ronnie was feeling bad. He probably shouldnt've bought the dog, if he wasnt going to look after it properly. It just wasnt fair. The lassies would help right enough. They were good, they helped. They would take it for walks. Babs would just—she wouldnt bother, she would be okay. He was just fucking, it was him, he was daft, stupid, coming home with a greyhound, it was out of order. Jimmy was talking. Ronnie nodded, acknowledging something; he didnt know what the fuck it was he was acknowledging but he was fucking acknowledging something! He smiled, he raised the pint to his lips and swallowed beer. Jimmy pushed the tobacco pouch towards him and he rolled himself a smoke. It was time to leave. He struck a match, lighting his own before offering the light to Jimmy; then he finished off the beer and wiped his mouth quickly. Okay, he said, lifting the leash. And he got to his feet.

You off? asked Jimmy Peters.

Aye.

I'll be heading that way myself, said McInnes, glancing towards the clock.

See you the morrow, said Jimmy.

Aye . . . Ronnie gave a slight tug on the leash and the dog rose from the floor. And he left the pub quickly, in case McInnes came along the road with him. They both lived in the same street. He didnt want McInnes to know, that he wasnt going home just now. He wasnt going to go home just now, definitely not. He wasnt feeling right for it. That was it in a nutshell. What was that thing about Hamlet? Like a king. Something. Ronnie just felt fucking, he felt lousy. He hadnt been feeling as lousy as this before. Last night for instance he had been feeling good. He had made the phonecall and he knew he was the only one who had made any inquiries. And eighty quid as well; it was about exactly what he had saved up, almost the total sum. Everything just seemed spot on. And the guy himself seemed okay. If it was possible to trust a doggie-

man! Ronnie grinned. They couldnt all be fucking rogues. Surely to fuck!
Heh Ronnie!

It was McInnes out from the pub and waving to him and coming
along after him. Ronnie waved back and continued, and on round the
next corner and he started walking fast, and then round the next corner, and away.

He liked McInnes, he wasnt fucking, it wasnt as if he was trying to
avoid him, especially; he just didnt want to fucking speak to anybody,
not anybody. Nobody. Fucking nobody. He didnt want to speak to any
cunt at all. And not McInnes, a good pal, he didnt want to speak to the
likes of him at all. And not fucking Babs either. Babs least of all. And
the weans, he didnt want to speak to them, not to even see them, he
couldnt face them; he actually couldnt face them. He couldnt face them,
the wife and weans, that was it, in a fucking nutshell.

It was fucking really terrible. The truth of the matter is he was feeling
really terrible. How the fuck was he feeling as terrible as this? And there
was the big dog! So fucking placid. That was it about these animals, how
placid they were and then when you see them at the track they're so
fucking fierce, so fierce-looking; fangs bared and fucking drooling,
drooling at the mouth and ready to fucking—bite, kill, kill the hare except its a bundle of stupid fucking rags. Imagine being as easy conned
as that! Letting yourself get lulled into it, racing round and round and
fucking round just to catch this stupid fucking bundle of rags. It made
you feel sorry for it. Dogs and all the rest of the animals. And people of
course, they were no different—they seemed different but they werent;
they seemed as if they were different but they werent; they really fucking werent, they just thought they were, it made you smile. Because
there they were, running round and round trying to fucking catch it, a
crock of gold, and did they ever catch it, did they fuck. The boy was like
that, off to London; and what would happen to him, fuck all, nothing.
He would just wind up getting a job somewhere and it would be fucking awful, and maybe he would just stay in London or else he'd come
back. And if he stayed in London that'd be that and he probably'd hardly
ever see them again. It was fucking strange. And Ronnie actually felt
like doing himself in. It was a feeling he'd had, creeping up on him. He
was actually feeling like doing himself in. What a thing. What a fucking

thing. It was because he felt like a, well, because he felt like he'd fucking let them down, he'd let them down, it was because he felt like he'd let them all down, the whole lot, the lassies and Babs and the boy. Jesus, he'd really fucking let them down. What did he do it. What did he do it. What was the thing. There was water at the edges of his mouth, and he wiped it off along his left forefinger and it made him feel better. The dog still walking there, that courageous picture. Because it was going into the fucking unknown! That dog! Getting led by him and not knowing where in the name of fuck it's going. Stupid. And the fucking power, letting itself get led. It was funny how human beings came first, and even one of these wee weans in the park could walk up and take over the lead, and the dog would just let it probably, just let it, itself be led.

Ronnie was walking quickly now, the greyhound trotting to remain abreast of him.

It was maybe good to change speed like this so it kept more alert, especially with it being so tired—and hungry. The thing must have been starving. That was him walking it since fucking what? 10 o'clock in the morning for fuck sake! Poor bastard. Of all the owners to get it gets him. Ach well. The tea in the oven. Babs would have switched it off now and she'd be wondering what the hell, how come he had got money; because she would just assume he was in the pub and in the process of getting totally paralytic. And a drink of water, it hadnt even had a drink of water. For fuck sake. It was actually worrying; it was more than just, it was more than just thinking it was thirsty it was actually thinking it might be getting bad because of it, the dog might actually become ill or something, because of the lack of water; it was possible. What he could do was just throw it in the fucking Clyde! then it'd get bags of water! That old joke about falling into the river, you didnt drown, you died of diphtheria. It was true but you couldnt see into it. Ronnie minded well as a boy when he used to hang over the side and see if he could see any fish, and he couldnt see anything it was so cloudy, so fucking mawkit. Christ! And yet that smell, it was a great smell, and fresh and what else could it be but the sea air, the smell of the sea. Yes. A fucking tang, it was the sea. It was fucking—Jesus, it was fucking great; it was just fucking great. And these other smells working in the leatherworks across in Partick, making football bladders and stuff like that. What a fucking job; that twice-daily journey six days a week and the rain pelting down, and the wind biting your ears going across in the ferry; walking up the steps at the other side and then the cobbles, that terrible monotony, the wooden fence, spar after spar. The good bit about it was the race, every cunt racing each other but kidding on they were just walking fast. Maybe they were walking fast. Maybe he was the only person racing. Not at all. Everybody was at it, seeing who'd be first to reach Dumbarton Road. And anybody who ran was fucking cheating! Comical! Ronnie laughed, shook his head. It was just so fucking comical. Stupid. The greyhound was looking at him and it had tugged the leash. It was going to do another shite. The guy must have fed it after all otherwise there would've been nothing more to come out. Poor bastard. It wasnt much of a shite right enough. *Big Dan;* it was squeezing out this wee skinny shite. Maybe he would give it another name. He could call it whatever he liked. *Shitey!* He could call it *Shitey.* But that wouldnt be allowed, unless he changed its spelling. *Iteysh.* Something like that. Or *Keech!* Outside of Glasgow nobody knew what the fuck it meant. *Big Keechy.* Ronnie shook his head, transferred the leash to his other hand and brought out the cigarette packet and matches. There were only two left. It was unbelievable how they went. Two before going into the pub; three in it; then this was the second since leaving. Which makes seven. He must've smoked another one somewhere else.

The dog was sitting at the gutter, staring down in the direction of the river. It was wondering what was happening. And Babs as well. And the lassies maybe; them thinking he was in the boozer.

The pier was derelict around here, it was a pity. At one time the steamers pulled in on their way down the Firth. And boats went to America, £5 for the one-way trip. When was that? That was fucking years ago. The turn of the century.

Ronnie peered through the fence; he tied the leash round a spike and rubbed his hands together. The wind coming down the Clyde; he moved his shoulders into a hunch. The cigarette packet and matches were back in his pocket again. He was going to save them for later. He didnt need a smoke just now. It was just habit. But he did need another pish. And he would have to wait a minute because there was a couple walking past, man and a woman with the arms linked. And the way they stared at the greyhound it was as if they thought it was there by itself. Ronnie stared after them and there was something in the way they walked that made him think they were wanting to look back but were doing their best not to. It was funny the way people were, how they acted, always so fucking self-conscious and embarrassed about things. All they had to say was, Is this dog yours? And he would've said, Aye. And that would've fucking been it, end of story.

But people didnt do things like that. They didnt do things as simple as that. They had to do it in a devious sort of—they had to be devious, that was it, they just had to be fucking devious. That was it, that was human nature, they just had to be fucking devious. Even the boy—eighteen years of age and just as devious as the rest of them. All he had to do was tell them and that would've been that. But no; what he does is fuck off and then gives a phonecall from a fucking motorway cafe. And Babs is up to fucking high doh worrying about it. Unbelievable. Just like a fucking wee wean. Eighteen years of age! Ronnie had been his father at that age. Eighteen! Fuck sake. It's no that young. It's young, but no that young. Eighteen. Christ Almighty.

It was getting dark. What time was it? When he was in the pub it was 7. It was after that. Nearer 8, when he left. Probably it was 9, it'd be 9 now. And they'd think he would be really paralytic. It could even be after 9.

Heh Ronnie!

Christ! McInnes! McInnes had come after him. McInnes. Where was he? He wasnt here at all. It hadnt been a shout. But it was like a shout. As if somebody had shouted on him. An apparition. A fucking ghost! The docks was a creepy place but, deserted and fucking derelict. And this pier, how you could see the actual particles of coaldust lapping in on the surface of the water, onto the steps for fuck sake, if you wanted to commit suicide you'd choose a better place, you wouldnt want to fucking choke, if you wanted to fucking choke you'd do something else altogether, a bottle of fucking pills maybe.

What did he buy it for? He shouldnt've bought it.

Ach well. It was too late. He had it and that was that. Poor old bastard. Maybe he wouldnt race it at all, maybe he *would* just keep it as a pet, and fuck them. Bastards.

Here was somebody else coming. Another couple.

That was funny how the shout had happened, it sounding like a shout, from inside the head. And it was McInnes; it was his voice. It wasnt Babs for instance, if you'd expected that, because maybe to do with telepathy, her thinking he was about to do himself in or somefuckingthing and so trying to reach out to him, the way twins are supposed to.

She would maybe be worrying about him now. Would she? Aye, she would be, she would be worrying about him because he hadnt phoned. Fuck sake, of course she would; what was the fucking point of fucking, trying to fucking keep it away, of course she'd be fucking worrying about him. On top of the boy; on top of the boy she would now be worrying about him. And the lassies, they'd know something was up because they'd see the way she was looking; if they were watching the telly, they'd see she wasnt really seeing what was on, her attention would be fucking, it would be nowhere near it, wondering if the phone was going to ring; and the boy as well, if he was okay—London for fuck sake, what could happen down there, things were bad down there, weans on the street, having to sell themselves to get by, the things that were happening down there, down in London, to young lassies and boys, it wasnt fucking fair, it was just fucking terrible, it was so fucking terrible, it was just so fucking terrible you couldnt fucking man you fucking Jesus Christ trying to think about that it was Christ it was so fucking terrible, it was so bad. Ronnie had the cigarette packet in his hand and he opened it and took out one; when he was smoking he returned it and the book of matches to his pocket. He inhaled twice without exhaling, let it all out in a gasp. He leaned his shoulder against the fence, inhaled again, exhaling the smoke through his nostrils. He would just tell Babs something or other, what the fuck he didnt know, it didnt fucking matter; what did it matter, it didnt fucking matter.

Pictures

He wasnt really watching the picture he was just sitting there wondering on things; the world seemed so pathetic the way out was a straight destruction of it, but that was fucking daft, thinking like that; a better way out was the destruction of himself, the destruction of himself meant the destruction of the world anyway because with him not there his world wouldnt be either. That was better. He actually smiled at the thought; then glanced sideways to see if it had been noticed. But it didnt seem to have been. There was a female sitting along the row who was greeting. That was funny. He felt like asking her if there was a reason for it. A lot of females gret without reason. The maw was one. So was the sister, she gret all the time. She was the worst. Whenever you caught her unawares that was what would be happening, she would be roaring her eyes out. The idea of somebody roaring their eyes out, their eyes popping out their sockets because of the rush of water. Or maybe the water making them slippery inside the sockets so they slipped out, maybe that was what it was, if it was anything even remotely literal. No doubt it would just prove to be a total figure of speech: eyes did not go popping out of sockets. There was a sex scene playing. The two actors playing a sex scene, the female one raising the blanket to go down as if maybe for oral intercourse, as if maybe she was going to suck him. Maybe this is why the woman was greeting along the row; maybe she once had this bad experience where she was forced into doing that very selfsame thing, years ago, when she was at a tender age, or else just it was totally against her wishes maybe. And she wouldnt want reminding of it. And look what happens, in she comes to see a picture in good faith and innocence, and straight away has to meet up with that terrible ancient horror

or else she enjoyed her feelings of anguish and had come along because of it, a kind of masochism or something, having heard from one of her pals about the sort of explicit—and maybe even exploitative—sex scenes to expect if she did. That was the director to blame anyway.

In the pictures he was involved in something like this usually happened, and there was usually violence as well, like in this one murder. And people would end up in bad emotional states. Was it right that it should be like this? It was okay for somebody like him—the director—but what about other folk, ordinary folk, them without the security, the overall security, the ones that actually went to watch his fucking pictures! The thought was enough to make you angry but it was best to just find it funny if you could, if you could manage it. He nodded and started grinning—it was best to. But it wasnt funny at all in fact it was quite annoying, really fucking annoying, and you could get angry about it, the way these bastards in the film industry got away with it.

And there was that female now, her along the row. He felt like shouting to her: What's up missis? Something wrong?

God Almighty but, the poor woman, maybe there *was* something bad up with her; he felt like finding out, maybe he should ask, maybe it was some bastard in a chair nearby, maybe wanking or something because of the sex scene, and here was the woman within perception distance—listening distance—having to put up with it, and it maybe reminding her of a terrible time when she was younger, just a lassie, and was maybe forced into some sort of situation, some kind of similar kind of thing. So fucking awful the way lassies sometimes get treated.

But it had to come back to the director, he it was to blame, it was this movie making the guy wank in the first place, if he hadnt been showing the provocative sexy scenes it wouldnt be fucking happening. There was a lot to be said for censorship. If a censor had seen this he would have censored it and then the woman maybe wouldnt be greeting. But no, it was more serious than that. Definitely. It was. She was definitely greeting for a reason, a real reason, she had to be—it was obvious; it had just been going on too long. If it had stopped once the scene changed then it would have been different, but it didnt. And the woman actor was back up the bed and her and the guy were kissing in the ordinary mouth-to-mouth clinch so if the oral carry-on had been the problem it was all over now and the woman should have been drying her tears. So it was obviously serious and had nothing to do with sex at all—the kind that was up on the screen at least. Maybe he should ask her, try to help. There were no attendants about. That was typical of course for matinee programs, the management aye worked short-handed, cutting down on overheads and all the rest of it. This meant attendants were a rarity and the audience ran the risk of getting bothered by idiots. Once upon a time a lassie he knew was a cinema attendant. She used to have to walk down the aisle selling ice creams, lollipops and popcorn at the interval; and they tried to get her to wear a short miniskirt and do wee curtsies to the customers. But they obviously didnt know this lassie who was a fucking warrior, a warrior. She quite liked wearing short miniskirts but only to suit herself. If she wanted to wear them she would wear them, but it was only for her own pleasure, she would please herself. She used to get annoyed with the management for other reasons as well; they used to get her to wear this wee badge with her name on it so it meant all the guys looked at it and knew what it was and they shouted it out when they met her on the street. Heh Susan! Susaaaaan! And then they would all laugh and make jokes about her tits. It was really bad. And bad as well if you were out with her if you were a guy because it meant you wound up having to get involved and that could mean a doing if you were just one against a few. She was good too, until she fucked off without telling him. He phoned her up one night at teatime and she wasnt in, it was her flatmate. And her flatmate told him she had went away, she had just went away. She had been talking about it for a while but it was still unexpected when it happened. Probably Manchester it was she went to. He had had his chance. He could have went with her. She hadnt asked him, but he could have if he had wanted. It was his own fault he hadnt, his own fault. She had gave him plenty of opportunities. So it was his own fault. So he never heard of her again. It was funny the way you lost track of folk, folk you thought you would know for life; suddenly they just werent there and you were on your ownsome. This seemed to happen to him a lot. You met folk and got on well with them but then over a period of time yous drifted away from each other—the same as the guys you knew at school, suddenly yous never even spoke to each other. That was just that, finished, fucking zero. It was funny. Sometimes it was enough to make you greet. Maybe this is what was up with the female along the row, she was just lonely, needing somebody to talk to God he knew the feeling, that was him as well—maybe he should just actually lean across and talk to her. Could he do that? So incredible an idea. But it was known as communication, you started talking to somebody, your neighbor. Communication. You took a deep breath and the rest of it, you fucking just leaned across and went "Hullo there!" Except when it's a male saying it to a female it becomes different. She had the hanky up

at the side of her eyes. She looked fucking awful. He leaned over a bit
and spoke to her:

Hullo there missis. Are you okay?

The woman glanced at him.

He smiled. He shrugged and whispered, You were greeting and
eh . . . you alright?

She nodded.

I couldnt get you something maybe, a coffee or a tea or something,
they've got them at the foyer . . .

She stared at him and he got a sudden terrible dread she was going
to start screaming it was fucking excruciating it was excruciating you felt
like stuffing your fingers into your ears, he took a deep breath.

There wasnt anybody roundabout except an old dear at the far end
of the row. That was lucky.

Maybe there *was* something up with her right enough. Or else
maybe she was fucking mental—mentally disturbed—and just didnt
have anywhere to go. Genuine. Poor woman. God. But folk were getting chucked out on the street these days; healthy or unhealthy, it didnt
matter, the powers-that-be just turfed you out and they didnt care where
you landed, the streets were full of cunts needing looked after, folk that
should have been in nursing homes getting cared for. She was maybe
one of them, just in here out the cold for a couple of hours peace and
quiet. And then look at what she has to contend with up on the bloody
screen . . . ! God sake! In for a couple of hours peace and quiet and you
wind up confronting all sorts of terrible stuff in pictures like this one
the now. Maybe censors were the answer. Maybe they would safeguard
folk like this woman. But how? How would they do it, the censors, how
would they manage it? No by sticking the cinemas full of Walt Disney
fucking fairyland. Who would go for a start? No him anyway, he hated
that kind of shite. Imagine paying the entrance fee for that, fucking car-
toons. He leant across:

Ye sure you dont want a coffee?

She shut her eyes, shaking her head for a moment. She wasnt as old
as he had thought either. She laid the hand holding the hanky on her
lap and the other hand she kept at the side of her chin, her head now
tilted at an angle. She kept looking at the screen.

I was going to get one for myself. So I could get one for you while
I was at it . . .

She turned to face him then; and she said, Could you?

Aye, that's what I'm saying.

Thanks, you're a pal.

Milk and sugar?

Just milk.

He hesitated but managed to just get up, giving her a swift smile and not saying anything more, just edging his way along the row. He had to pass by the old dear sitting in the end seat and she gave him a look before holding her shopping bags in to her feet to let him past, and he nodded to her quite briskly. He walked up the aisle and down the steps, pushing his way out into the corridor. Thick carpets and dim lighting. He grinned suddenly, then began chuckling. How come he had nodded at the old dear like that? She was as old as his grannie! God Almighty! But it was to show her he was relaxed. That was how he had done it, that was how he had done it. If he hadnt been relaxed he would never have bloody managed it because it would have been beyond him.

Cinema 2 was showing a comedy. He had seen it a week ago. He wasnt that keen on comedies, they were usually boring. He continued past the corridor entrance. There was an empty ice-cream carton sitting on the floor in such a way you felt somebody had placed it there intentionally. Probably they had. He used to have the selfsame habit when he was a boy—thirteen or something—he used to do things to make them seem like accidental events. If he was smoking and finished with the fag he would stick it upright on the floor to make it look like somebody had just tossed it away and it had landed like that as a fluke.

He used to go about doing all sorts of stupid things. Yet when you looked at them, they werent all that fucking stupid.

What else did he used to do? He used to leave stuff like empty bottles standing on the tops of stones and boulders, but trying to make it look like they had just landed that way accidentally. To make folk imagine alien things were happening here on planet Earth and they were happening for a reason, a purpose.

He was a funny wee cunt when he was a boy. Looking back you had to admit it.

The woman at the kiosk passed him the change from the till; she was in the middle of chatting with the cashier and didnt watch him after she had put the money on the counter so he lifted a bar of chocolate, slid it up his jacket sleeve. One was plenty. He took the two wee containers of milk and the packet of lump sugar for himself.

It was raining outside. He could see folk walking past with the brollies up. And the streetlights were on. It would soon be teatime.

He didnt take the chocolate bar from his sleeve until along the corridor and beyond the Cinemas 1 and 2, which were the most popular and had the biggest auditoriums—but there were usually cunts talking in them, that was the drawback, when you were trying to listen to the movie, they held fucking conversations. He had to lay the cartons of coffee down on the floor, then he stuck his hand in his side jacket pocket, letting the bar slide straight in from the sleeve. He was going to give it to her, the woman. He wasnt that bothered about chocolate himself. And anyway, in his experience females liked chocolate more than males. They had a sweet tooth.

That was one of these totally incredible expressions, a sweet tooth. What did it actually mean? He used to think it meant something like a soft tooth, that you had a tooth that was literally soft, made of something like soft putty. When he was a boy he had a sweet tooth. But probably all boys had sweet tooths. And all lassies as well. All weans the world over in fact, they all liked sweeties and chocolate, ice cream and lollipops, popcorn.

She was sitting in a semi-motionless way when he got back to the seat and it was like she was asleep, her eyelids not flickering at all. Here's your coffee, he said, milk with no sugar, is that right?

Ta.

He sat down in his old seat after an eternity of decision-making to do with whether or not he could just sit down next to her, on the seat next to hers; but he couldnt, it would have been a bit out of order, as if just because he had bought her a fucking coffee it gave him the right of fucking trying to sit next to her and chat her up, as if he was trying to get off with her—which is what women were aye having to put up with. The best people to be women were men because of the way they were, the differences between them, their sexuality, because they could get sex anytime they like just about whereas men were usually wanting it all the time but couldnt fucking get it—it was a joke, the way it worked like that, a joke of nature, them that wanted it no getting it and them that didnt want it having to get it all the time. The bar of chocolate. He took it out his pocket and glanced at it; an Aero peppermint; he passed it across, having to tap her elbow because she was staring up at the screen.

Here. It's a spare one. He shrugged, I'm no needing it. I'm no really a chocolate-lover anyway, to be honest, I've no got a sweet tooth, the proverbial sweet tooth. He shrugged again as he held it to her.

Oh I dont want that, she said out loud, her nose wrinkling as she frowned, holding her hand up to stop him. And he glanced sideways to see if folk had heard her and were maybe watching. He whispered:

How no? It's alright.

Oh naw pal I just dont eat them—Aero peppermints—any kind of bar of chocolate in fact, being honest, I dont eat them.

Is it a diet like?

Aye. Thanks for the coffee but.

That's alright.

You're no offended?

Naw. I'll eat it myself. On second thoughts I'll no, I'll keep it for later. He stuck it back into his pocket and studied the screen while sipping the coffee which was far too milky it was like water. Funny, how they said something was coffee and then sold you a cup of fucking water with just a splash—a toty wee splash—of brown stuff, to kid you on. Total con. They did the selfsame thing with tea, they charged you for tea but served you with milk and water and another wee splash of brown, a different-tasting one. You couldnt trust them. But it was hard to trust people anyway, even at the best of times. You were actually daft if you trusted them at all. At any time. How could you? You couldnt. Cause they aye turned round and fucked you in some way or another. That was his experience.

The film would soon be done, thank God. It was a murder picture, it was about a guy that was a mass murderer, he kills all sorts of folk. A good-looking fellow too, handsome, then he goes bad and starts all the killing, women mainly, except for a couple of guys that get in his way, security men in the hostel, it was a nurses' hostel, full of women, and a lot of them fancy him, the guy, the murderer, he gets off with them first, screws them, then after he's screwed them he kills them—terrible. And no pity at all.

But sometimes you could feel like murdering somebody yourself in a way, because people were so fucking awful at times, you helped them out and nothing happened, they just turned round and didnt thank you, just took it like it was their due. His landlord was like that, the guy that owned the house he stayed in, he was a foreigner, sometimes you helped him out and he didnt even thank you, just looked at you like you were a piece of shite, like you were supposed to do it because you stayed in one of his fucking bedsits, as if it was part of your fucking rent or something.

He was sick of the coffee, he leaned to place the carton on the floor beneath the seat. He grimaced at the woman. She didnt notice, being engrossed in the picture. To look at her now you would hardly credit she had been greeting her eyes out quarter-of-an-hour ago. Incredible, the way some females greet, they turn it off and turn it on. He was going straight home, straight fucking home, to make the tea, that was what he was going to fucking do, right fucking now. Hamburger and potatoes and beans or something, chips. He was starving. He had been sitting here for two hours and it was fucking hopeless, you werent able to concentrate. You came to the pictures nowadays and you couldnt even get concentrating on the thing on the screen because

because it wasnt worth watching, that was the basic fact, because something in it usually went wrong, it turned out wrong, and so you wound up you just sat thinking about your life for fuck sake and then you started feeling like pressing the destruct button everything was so bad. No wonder she had been fucking greeting. It was probably just cause she was feeling so fucking awful depressed. About nothing in particular. You didnt have to feel depressed about something, no in particular, because there was so much of it.

The bar of chocolate in his pocket. Maybe he should just eat it himself for God's sake! He shook his head, grinning; sometimes he was a fucking numbskull. Imagine but, when he was a boy, leaving all these dowps lying vertical like that, just so somebody passing by would think they had landed that way! It was funny being a wean, you did these stupid things. And you never for one minute thought life would turn out the way it did. You never for example thought you would be sitting in the pictures waiting for the afternoon matinee to finish so you could go fucking home to make your tea, to a bedsitter as well. You would've thought for one thing that you'd have had a lassie to do it for you, a wife maybe, cause that's the way things are supposed to be. That was the way life was supposed to behave. When you were a boy anyway. You knew better once you got older. But what about lassies? Lassies were just so totally different. You just never fucking knew with them. You never knew what they thought, what they ever expected. They always expected things to happen and you never knew what it was, these things they expected, you were supposed to do.

What age was she? Older than him anyway, maybe thirty, thirty-five. Maybe even younger but it was hard to tell. She would've had a hard life. Definitely. Okay but everybody has a hard life. And she was on a diet. Most females are on a diet. She wasnt wearing a hat. Most females were these days, they were wearing hats, they seemed to be, even young lassies, they seemed to be as well; it was the fashion.

The more he thought about it the more he started thinking she might be on the game, a prostitute. He glanced at her out the side of his eye. It was definitely possible. She was good-looking and she was a bit hard, a bit tough, she was probably wearing a lot of makeup. Mostly all females wore makeup so you couldnt really count that. What else? Did she have on a ring? Aye, and quite a few, different ones, on her different fingers. She shall have music wherever she goes. Rings on her fingers and rings on her toes. Bells on her toes. She had black hair, or maybe it was just dark, it was hard to see properly because of the light; and her eyebrows went in a high curve. Maybe she *was* on the game and she had got a hard time from a punter, or else somebody was pimping for her and had gave her a doing, or else telt her he was going to give her one later, if she didnt do the business, if she didnt go out and make a few quid. Maybe her face was bruised. Maybe she had got a right kicking. And she wouldnt have been able to fight back, because she was a woman and wasnt strong enough, she wasnt powerful enough, she would just have to take it, to do it, what she was telt, to just do it. God Almighty. It was like a form of living hell. Men should go on the game to find out what like it was, a form of living hell—that's what it was like. He should know, when he was a boy he had once went with a man for money and it was a horror, a horror story. Except it was real. He had just needed the dough and he knew about how to do it down the amusements, and he had went and fucking done it and that was that. But it was bad, a horror, a living hell. Getting gripped by the wrist so hard you couldnt have got away, but making it look like it was natural, like he was your da maybe, marching you into the toilet, the public toilet. Getting marched into the public toilet. People seeing you as well, other guys,

them seeing you and you feeling like they knew, it was obvious, him
marching you like that, the way he was marching you. Then the cubicle
door shut and he was trapped, you were trapped, that was that, you were
trapped, and it was so bad it was like a horror story except it was real, a
living hell, because he could have done anything and you couldnt have
stopped him because he was a man and he was strong and you were just
a boy, nothing, to him you were just nothing. And you couldnt shout or
fucking do anything about it really either because

because you were no just fucking feart you were in it along with him,
you were, you were in cahoots, you were in cahoots with the guy, that
was what it was, the bad fucking bit, you were in cahoots with him, it
was like you had made a bargain, so that was that. But him gripping you
the way he was! What a grip! So you had to just submit, what else could
you do. You had to just submit, you couldnt scream nor fuck all. Nothing like that. Men coming into the urinals for a pish, no knowing what
was going on behind the door and him breathing on you and feeling you
up, and grabbing you hard, no even soft, no even caring if he had tore
your clothes. What the wonder was that nobody could hear either because of the rustling noises the way he had you pressed against the wall
and then you having to do it to him, to wank him, him forcing your hand
and it was like suffocating him forcing his chest against your face and
then coming over you, no even telling you or moving so you could avoid
it it was just no fair at all, all over your shirt and trousers, it was terrible, a horror story, because after he went away you had to clean it all up
and it wouldnt wipe off properly, all the stains, the way it had sunk in
and it was like glue all glistening, having to go home on the subway with
it: broad daylight.

For a pile of loose change as well. How much was it again? No even
a pound, fifty stupid pence or something, ten bob. Probably no even that,
probably it was something like forty pee, he just stuck it into his hand,
some loose change. What did prostitutes get? what did they get? women,
back then, nine year ago. It was probably about five quid if it was a short
time; a tenner maybe if it was all night. That was enough to make anybody greet. But you could spend your life greeting, like his fucking sister. Because that was the thing about it, about life, it was pathetic, you
felt like pressing the destruct button all the time, you kept seeing all
these people, ones like the woman, the old dear at the end of the row,
plus even himself as a boy, you had to even feel sorry for him, for him-

self, when he was a boy, you had to even feel sorry for yourself, yourfuckingself. What a fucking joke. A comedy. Life was a comedy for nearly everybody in the world. You could actually sympathize with that guy up on the screen. You could, you could sympathize with him. And he was a mass murderer.

He glanced at the woman along the row and smiled at her, but then he frowned, he glared. You shouldnt be sympathizing with a mass murderer. You shouldnt. That was that fucking director's fault. That happened in his pictures, you started feeling sympathy for fucking murderers. How come it wasnt for the victims. They were the ones that needed it. No the actual perpetrators. That was probably how she had been greeting, the woman, because of the fucking victims, she was a victim, and that's who it was happening to, the fucking victims. He wanted to go home, right now, he wanted out of it, right fucking out of it right fucking now it was a free country and he wanted to get away home for his fucking tea. He glanced along at her, to see what she was doing. She was still holding the carton of coffee, engrossed in the picture. The old dear as well. It was just him. He was the only one that couldnt concentrate. That was that nowadays, how he never seemed able to concentrate, it never fucking seemed to work anymore, you couldnt blank it out. He kicked his coffee over. It was a mistake. But he was glad he had done it. He wished they had all fucking seen; it would sort them out, wondering how come he had done it, if it was meant; he got up off the chair and edged his way along to the end of the row, watching he didnt bump into her as he went; she never so much as glanced at him, then the old dear moving her bags in to let him pass, giving him a look as he went, fuck her, even if he stood on one of them with eggs in it, bastard, he just felt so fucking bad, so fucking bad.

A walk in the park

She was coming towards him and he hesitated, she had yet to see him. But then he stepped out the close and he smiled the welcome while taking her by the arm. Beyond the park gate they continued round the corner and along in the direction of the main road. He said nothing to her. He noticed when she became aware of the fact. He glanced at her, seeing a certain look on her face; she was trying to hold it to herself, but she didnt succeed and she frowned at him and stopped walking: Is there something up? she asked, but she smiled to make it sound less dramatic.

Naw, no that I know of.

She studied him.

I'm just no feeling very talkative.

Mmm. She smiled, I dont really believe you.

Is that right? Well it's quite straightforward. He laid both his hands on her shoulders. He was about nine inches taller than her. He stared at her without smiling, then he relaxed and grinned. But she didnt. And she wasnt going to again, not until she knew there was something to warrant it.

Ach, he said, christ, I dont have any cash.

Oh.

Aye oh.

So what are we going to do?

I dont know.

I've hardly got anything either. Did something happen?

Happen? What d'you mean?

She looked at him.

Sorry. Naw, nothing happened. I'm just skint. People are skint these days you know.

Why are you being sarcastic?

Oh fuck sorry, sorry.

And now you're swearing. Are you worried about your son?

Naw.

Did the doctor come?

He stuck his hands into his trouser pockets, sauntered a few steps forward then turned to her: Doctors dont come these days, that's how they sell invalid chairs with fucking caster wheels on them! Sorry . . . Christ! He turned away from her again, stared into the shop that sold antiques. It was a shop she liked to look into. He saw her reflection in the window. For some reason he felt very angry. He still had his hands in his trouser pockets; now he brought out his left one and rubbed his brow and left eye. When she reappeared beside him he put his arm round her. Ach, I'm just no in a cheery mood. I'm sorry, too much on my plate . . .

It's okay.

He nodded then sighed. Where can we go?

I dont know.

They stood staring at each other for several moments. Then she said: The library?

Nah.

A walk in the park?

Uch naw.

We could go into town.

Into town?

See the shops . . . Dont look so excited.

He glanced at the antiques in the window: What about this shop here, can we no just look in it?

. . .

Ach, sorry. But I mean it'd just be a case of walking about.

Well that's better than nothing.

He sighed again.

What is it?

Ach nothing. Nothing.

Is something wrong?

No.

She studied him.

He shrugged and stepped away from her. I mean if you really want to go into town . . . I mean, if you do it's fine, just say.

It was only a suggestion.

Aye, fair enough, I know. He sniffed, gazing along the road, and wondered if she did have any cash. And if she did and it was enough to take them both for a coffee then how come she was not offering. Economics entered everything. It had caused the collapse of his marriage. At least it had as far as he was concerned. Who knew about the wife, she went her own way, had her own thoughts, you never knew what she was thinking. You never knew what anybody was thinking, that was the problem, the same applied everywhere. She was looking at him. He said, Do you want to go up the town?

She didnt answer.

Eh?

No.

He grinned suddenly and touched her arm. Give us a smile!

She didnt smile.

I'm sorry, I'm just . . . Ahh! He shook his head. He rubbed his hands together and blew out sharply. Bloody cold! Time we were going somewhere.

Did he let you down, the guy that owes you the money?

Yeh.

I might've known.

He was supposed to meet me but he never turned up.

Mmhh.

I thought he would.

Did you?

Now it's you that's being sarcastic.

Oh I'm sorry . . . She smiled, reached up and kissed him on the mouth, thrust her tongue inside.

They looked at each other as they parted.

Well? she said.

What about your sister?

I cant ask her.

Definitely?

No.

He nodded.

I cant.

Ah well. He turned abruptly: Christ . . . ! I'm gasping for a fag! He grinned: I says I'm gasping for one no I'm going to smoke one. There's a big difference you know!

I dare say it'd improve your temper.

He smiled at her. He liked her, he really did, he really did bloody like her. He wanted to put his arms round her and hold her, he wanted to give her a cuddle, a real cuddle, he wanted to hold her and give her a really big cuddle.

When she raised her right hand and touched his chin with her fingertips his eyes closed. She cupped both hands round his face. He opened his eyes and said, Let's walk.

Yeh.

They walked hand in hand, firmly. It was a thing he liked about her, how she held his hand, it was always so tight and he felt like it meant she was wanting to make sure of him, that he was there and that they were together. It was some time before either spoke. She said, I know you've got a lot on your plate.

It's okay.

You have though.

Ah well so have you, so have you.

Not so much as you.

He shook his head. I disagree. And he felt her grip on his hand tighten, and it sparked the muscle in his cock. He only had to look at her, that was the problem. I'll end up getting an erection, he said.

She smiled.

I cant help it.

She withdrew her hand and dug him in the ribs.

It's no my fault! He grinned.

Ssh. And come on! She took his hand.

Right, right! Will we go through the park?

If you want, it's up to you, I'm no the boss.

Ah well neither am I.

No but just decide.

Can you no.

Tch!

I want a rest. I spend my life making decisions. That's how I like being with you!

You trying to say I'm bossy! She grinned.

They crossed the road into the park, past the line of red sandstone villas—Victorian, four bedrooms maybe plus lounge, dining room, kitchen and bathroom; with probably an extension built out the back garden—maybe even with the attic kitted out into a wee annex bedroom and play area for the kids. And kids liked that kind of space, the adventure of it, even going to bed in itself, that became exciting. One of his wife's aunties lived in a big house. Not a great big house but big enough, big enough to get a bit of privacy. Wee rooms to go and sit in, empty rooms, ones that had fireplaces and standard lamps, you could sit there and read a book, on your own, really good; the sort of place you dreamed about owning, plenty room, not tripping over one another; you could keep cats if you wanted, cats and dogs, all the pets you felt like—plus the privacy, that much space you could go away and be by yourself, you could be alone, you could just sit and think, work things out.

She broke the silence. She spoke without turning her head to him: Was your wife down at the weekend?

She was, aye.

Did you see her?

Well I had to to give over the wee yins.

Yeh . . .

Christ! It really is freezing! His shoulders moved as though in a shiver. He saw her watching him now. What about your boyfriend? he said.

What about him?

That's what I want to know, what about him?

Nothing.

Nothing?

Nothing.

Great. Life is so wonderful.

Dont complain.

I'm no.

It could be worse.

Could it?

It could be worse, of course it could.

Aye, I suppose so . . . He shivered again. You no cold?

No, because I'm wearing a coat. Which is what you should be doing, but you arent.

Glasgow macho . . . aye. He put his arm round her then his teeth started chattering; and he laughed, exaggerating the noise of it till eventually she also laughed. He pointed out the red sandstone villas. I'll get one of them and fill it with servants. To hell with the social conscience, I'm sick of it.

So am I!

I'm going to become a smug capitalist.

She laughed. She linked arms with him as they continued on over the brow of the hill.

I was reading John MacLean this morning, he said.

I havent read him.

What a life he had! How they treated him as well! Bloody disgraceful. Sick. The authorities, sick.

Mm.

A woman was walking along towards them, leading two small terrier dogs on leashes, they both had tartan jackets tucked round their bodies. Caricatures, he said, *Sunday Post* specials.

Yeh. Who's pulling who eh?

He smiled in answer.

The path stretched beyond a clump of trees for about quarter of a mile. There was nobody about. Two other directions were possible. The woman with the dogs had taken one of them.

Will we go the long way round, he asked.

What?

Will we go the long way round?

I dont care.

D'you just want to go the short way?

I'm no bothering. Then she added: I thought I smelt smoke on your breath?

Ha, I wish to God you had! That'd mean I was a cheery smoker, a cheery dier of cancer!

Have you no been smoking then?

Naw.

Honestly?

Well I've had a couple.

Ah.

A couple.

D'you mean two?

Aye.

Honestly?

You and your bloody honestly!

D'you mean two?

I said yes didnt I!

That's all?

That's all.

Good . . .

It's bloody hard but know what I mean? He shook his head. When he saw she was still looking at him he asked her the time. She unlinked her arm to pull back her coat sleeve. Quarter to three.

Christ!

Time passes.

No half!

When you're enjoying yourself.

He put his arm round her again and he kissed her on the side of the mouth. She turned into him. But quarter to three, he said, moving from her slightly, that's hellish I mean you'll have to go back soon.

No for a bit yet.

Naw but soon.

She shrugged. Not for a bit.

He nodded. She smiled suddenly. I once smoked you know and it was in a park.

What! You! My God! Smoking? I cant bloody believe it!

It was no laughing matter either, believe me!

Whereabouts? No in here?

Whiteinch.

Whiteinch! What age were you?

I was thirteen; we were over watching the boys play football.

My God!

D'you know where the pitches are there?

Naw, no really.

Behind the pond. You walk towards your left, if you're coming from the dressing rooms it's your right.

From the dressing rooms?

Where the boys played football, where they got changed. They had to change in there before going to the football pitches to play.

Aw aye, now we're hearing the awful truth I mean did you watch to see if you could see anything when they were changing! Is that what yous were up to!

Tch.

He laughed.

We werent that bad!

A likely story! So tell us about the smoking then, did it make you sick?
Yeh, it did, it did!

Ha ha!

She punched him in the ribs and he let her go, stepping away from her, still laughing: I might've known. Females, you cant handle it!

That's right, we're no macho enough . . . It was bloody awful but, I thought I was going to pass out. We had two cigarettes and we smoked them one after the other, sharing them between us, taking draws each.

You and the boys?

Me and my two pals. Lassies . . .

I see, mmhh, on you go, but I warn you, I'm taking all this down to use in evidence at a later date.

And I mind as well how they were all soggy. Bits of the tobacco was in your mouth. Uch! It was awful. Disgusting.

Bits of tobacco? That means it was plain fags.

What?

Fags without tips?

I cant remember.

Must've been, if they were all soggy like the way you're saying. Hell, you must be older than you look.

Shut up.

Naw but honest, no kidding.

I think somebody had stole them off their dad.

God, thieving as well! What next! Dont tell me—with all these boys about!

You've got a dirty mind.

He smiled, but only for a moment. He looked at the grass.

A joke, she said, want to hear it?

Aye.

She let go his hand and walked on a pace, stopped and turned, trying to keep her face straight. You're laughing already! he said.

Because it's funny.

He chuckled.

If it wasnt I wouldnt tell you it.

Ah but it puts me under pressure.

Charlie's daughter told me it.

Charlie's daughter?

I knew it already. You probably know it yourself.

Naw I dont.

You will when you hear it.

Tell me then.

After a moment she said: What's yellow and very dangerous?

I dont know.

Shark-infested custard!

Christ!

She smiled.

Where do they get them!

Och it's an old one, I think I heard it at school myself.

Aye. He turned from her and stared along the path. There was a group of people in the distance—teenagers; they had a ball. He sighed.

What's up? She had touched him on the elbow.

Och . . . He smiled for a moment, then gazed into her face; she was just so bloody beautiful. She was. And he was just fucking . . . hopeless, he was just fucking hopeless. He couldnt bloody cope, that was the problem, he couldnt bloody cope, with life. The expression on her face had been serious; she relaxed now and smiled for a moment, she gripped his hand tightly, put her other arm round his waist and spoke his name, but he shook his head in answer.

Dont worry. She whispered, Things arent as bad as that.

Och I know I know.

Well then.

Yeh. Yeh.

She was staring right into his eyes.

A situation

Different incisions seemed to have been cut into the wall and from inside one of them an insect was peering at him. The insect reminded him of a flea, the curved part of its body, even down to its blood tan color. The middle finger of his right hand began to drum on the edge of the table, he was frowning. What if for every incision one such insect was lodged? Mind you, they were so minute, these insects, that he was not afraid. He could ignore them easily. Or else he could get a spray gun and blast them all to smithereens. But what was the use of fantasizing. He was not going to do anything. He couldnt do anything. He was stuck fast on this wooden chair, surrounded by everything hostile you could possibly conceive of in the universe. And as well as that it was like he could hear a scraping noise coming from somewhere too so no wonder he couldnt concentrate. Or was it just his ears? The finger drumming stopped but he continued frowning at the insect. Its toty brain would be working overtime. Who is this giant staring at me? Is he going to kill me? Somebody as big as him could squash me in a tick! Will he leave me alone? Forget all about me? Because if he does then I can continue crawling up the wall. Or down the wall; maybe it was going down the wall. Or else burrowing deeper into the hole, the incision. Maybe it and its relations, its ancestors—bearing in mind that each day is probably a lifetime and thus you have a state of affairs where four weeks ago is prehistoricity:

the world of the insect is of an eternity undreamt by man.

He shook his head to clear the brains into some sort of order, some sort of cohesion, so that he could think properly, he had to think properly. Life wasnt as good as all that just now. Not at present. But he couldnt afford to get more panic-stricken than he currently was. On top of all the studying he had to meet the girlfriend in next to no time and he had had sex with her sister less than four hours ago. It was the sort of factual statement you had to present so coldly to yourself, so coldly. What was that bloody insect doing? Maybe burrowing deeper, trying to find a way of escaping out through the damn wall. That reminded him of himself. He spoke aloud: Make it big enough for the both of us, me as well as you. He could imagine hearing the insect's voice in answer. It would of course be squeaky, in keeping with its size. Unless it was an ironic bass baritone. Why ironic? Because of its size obviously. And what was that scraping noise, was it the actual burrowing sound? Surely no. But where was it coming from? He stared hard at the wall. It was just a wall. As walls go it was simply one of them. It was neither up nor down. Walls are walls, the prison bars make them. That was a line from somewhere, a poem or a song. Prison bars make them. Prisons do not a prison make, walls and bars, cells. He had never been in a cell, a jail; it was an experience he hadnt had. And didnt want. Not at all, why should he? Why should he want to end up in a cell? He had never done anything remotely worthy of such a crime, charge, jail, that sort of castigation.

Nor do insects have heads wherein brains are tick-tocking thus they do not worry about minor tragedies, only the major ones such as food and sex, the impetus for survival.

He sighed so loudly he glanced immediately over his shoulder to see if he had been heard, sitting there alone, in his poky wee room, feeling oh so tired, drained and exhausted. It wasnt his fault he had slept with Jeanette. He was up in her flat to give her some advice on something and she just more or less offered herself. She did. She offered herself to him. Probably the pair of them had had a big fight or argument or something, her and Deborah. Mind you, as far as he had been given to understand they were always the best of pals. They seemed to get on fine the gether. He gazed at the wall. It was actually covered in these incisions. Tiny toty wee holes. Oh Lord. Lordie Lordie. Lordie Lordie Lordie.

The A4 folders. Ah dear. All the A4 folders, and the trade brochures.

A4 folders and trade brochures. Life was a series of A4 folders and trade brochures. Cardboard and glossy paper. Pens and pencils. Stamped addressed envelopes and gummed labels, invoices.

His eyes had just about closed there. God. But he was knackered. He was. He was drained and exhausted, feeling like a quick forty winks. He needed it. Plus it was a good way out of a problem, to sleep on it.

But this was a genuine tired feeling with a genuine real cause. There had been no time for rest and recuperation after the Jeanette performance because her own boyfriend was coming home and he had had to get out fast, fast. Which was not as bad and decadent as it sounds. She was wanting to dump the bloke, she really was—she just didnt fancy him anymore, but found it difficult saying the magic words of release. He was hell of a clingy Benny—Benny being her boyfriend's name. Poor old Benny. The two males had met on a couple of occasions, plus they had gone out on a foursome once with the sisters, to a pub up the town. It hadnt been a great success because the two females had had an awful lot to speak about—family stuff and that kind of thing—whereas the two men had had nothing at all, they had just sat there, not even any music to listen to, having to discuss football and general things about society. Except later on when the women went off to the *Ladies*, Benny had confided. Insecurity and an inferiority complex with women. These were the guy's problems. Imagine confiding in somebody who was a stranger to you! My God. Even the insect was laughing at that one. He could see it poking its napper out the incision on the wall again. He put his thumb up and squashed it. It made him wince. It was awful. His stomach felt queasy. It was just an insect and he had squashed it with his thumb. Why worry? But why do it why did he do it, why did he do it? Why did he do it, in the first place, take away its life? The stain of it on his thumb, a brown brackeny-colored substance. Here he was having just had illicit sex with his girlfriend's sister

fiancée's sister. She was his fiancée's sister. Deborah was his fiancée: and now into the bargain he had squashed a living creature. And God would rightly be angry. Nobody likes their creations getting killed.

And what was that when you come to think about it but blasphemy, talking about God like that, in that tone of voice.

So here was now the third mark against him this day.

But he was a male and the sexual needs of the male are so horrendously hard to contain. Everybody knows that. And he had let himself fall into her web. Jeanette was a spider. She drew him in in that willowy winsome way and then let him have it, her bending down like that in front of him etcetera etcetera, an old trick which he was delighted to have played on him let us be honest, let us be good and damn honest about it he thought she was an extremely sexy lady and always had done since first they had been introduced. So what now what now. Killing a creature for no reason, just a silly absentmindedness. But wanton all the same. He had killed one of God's creatures through an act of wanton absentmindedness. Yes He would be angry with him and would make him fail tomorrow's test and he would then be forced into a life of continuous penury. He would have to go out working the road for a living instead of just training other folk to do it. That is what happened when you crossed the Lord.

That was him blaspheming again. Upon this day he had committed what amounts to adultery, and murder, and blasphemy. There was no fun in the thought. In fact it demanded an honest appraisal of himself, his entire life. If he couldnt manage an honest appraisal then the future was definitely bleak. He was doomed, he was doomed to become an ordinary salesman, a cynical salesman, somebody who held no truck for half measures and had absolutely no compunction whatsoever in destroying people who were customers, they would destroy all the resources of the world if they could get away with it, all on behalf of the selling racket. It was so bad. And yet it was the corollary of the downward spiral. It began with minor atrocities like the destruction of insects and the destruction of love, both earthly love and spiritual love. And the mark of the beast was on his thumb. And he needed rid of it. He got up and went to the toilet and washed his hands thoroughly. If he had had a bath he would have bathed. If he had had a shower he would have showered. He had neither of these facilities. Jeanette had both in her flat. It belonged to the two of them, her and her boyfriend, and they were able to bathe together and play sexy games. He would have wanted the same sort of fun and nonsense. But he and Deborah didnt do it, they didnt play sexy games. There was something that wasnt just right for it, something between them. Something that seemed to stop such an enjoyable interlude from happening. Plus his room was only big enough for what his grandpa used to call a jawbox, a sink in the wall, and this was where the diverse functional uses for water were put to the test, from shaving the chin to washing the socks through the doing of the dishes, given that the owners of the property were so totally greedy and so directly opposed to the whole concept of cooked food where tenants were concerned, so he didnt have that much crockery, and there was nary a pot and nary a pan, and normally a rinse of cold water was ample for everything. There was a bathroom. But it was outside on the next landing, shared by folk upstairs and down, including wheezing old McAllister who spat into the washhand basin there and never sluiced it out properly and you could always see the telltale signs. Plus there was always sticky things on the linoleum floor and even if you were having a bath you felt like wearing shoes. The idea of Deborah and him getting up to anything in there was beyond imagination. Deborah!

Lord, oh Lord, Lord please help me, have mercy, I am a soul in need of succor.

Two other women shared Deborah's flat with her and it was really short on privacy. Nice women, but they were never out the place if you were sitting watching television. So there was never any

But most of all it was his fault! The pair of them should have been married by now and then they would have had privacy and everything would be fine, fine: and none of this would have happened. It wouldnt have. It wouldnt have happened if they had been married. But they werent married because she had said no to his first proposal and he hadnt made a second. That was six months ago. She had said no the first time so that was that, he hadnt asked her again. And maybe he never would, they would just have to wait and see. Everybody. That included his parents and her parents and all their acquaintances and everybody else they knew throughout the world, them all, they would all just have to wait. You cannot just go about refusing things and expect life to remain the same. If and when he and Deborah were ever to share a flat together they would no doubt install a proper bathing service. Of course they would. Once he got round to asking the question again and if things worked out then that sort of pleasurable life facility could be taken for granted. But he was not going to ask the question just now, he was just not going to. And anyway, things were too upside-down at the moment, he just didnt know where his head was with all this product study and memorizing he was having to do. The job was driving him nuts.

And what would happen now with her sister oh Lord Lord what was now going to happen, now, after that please God please God oh please God.

It was all so amazing. Life. Life was so amazing, it was just so incredibly amazing.

But for heaven's sake he was so sick of this poky wee room where insects crawled out of the wall and stared at you as if you were an object of derision; or an object of contempt, of horror even. As the killer of one's fellows

bearing in mind that the insect he had murdered was probably about to copulate and be responsible for the birth of a million eggs, a hundred thousand of which would survive to become fully fledged members of the beetle race. It was like committing genocide. He needed coffee. Coffee coffee coffee. The caffeine was good for him. His adrenaline. It would assist him in thought and he did require assistance in just that direction, because he needed to think, to think to think to think, he needed to bloody think, he needed to think. These bloody test questions required consideration. If he did not consider these bloody test questions with the utmost bloody care he would wind up failing tomorrow and therein lay his doom, to exist for all eternity as an ordinary guy on the road, and he would grow into a tired and clapped-out old chap with ulcers and heart attacks. And God would be angry because he hadnt put his talents to good use.

The idea of sitting snugly in a toty wee cavity though, secure on three out of four sides, and then coming towards you is something in appearance similar to a meteorite, it getting huger and huger as it rushes towards you. And you are mesmerized by it. All you can do is stay stuck fast in your cavity; and then glulp, you're squashed. It doesnt bear thinking about. He didnt want to think about it. He had no time to. He had to do his studying. All the A4 folders,

And in less than half an hour for heaven's sake in would come Deborah.

And what would happen if she expected to stay the night he would not be able to have sex with her because of his condition, the way he was now, at this moment, at this moment in time. Because Deborah would know! She would know! She would guess. She was too percipient! Percipient? That isnt even a word. Dictionaries dictionaries dictionaries. Plus the fact he wouldnt be clean, he would have to go and have a wash. That is what he would do, he would go and have a wash.

He went to the sink and put on the kettle for a cup of coffee then cleared the dishes and made space for himself, taking the trousers down to his ankles and setting the towel over them between his feet. Nor did he wish to think about Jeanette who was a very sexy lady and her thighs.

The water was freezing! My God!

In fact he *was* slightly tender around the genital region. He hadnt been aware of it till now. To tell the truth he was a wee bit sore; a wee bit sore.

The cold water now quite soothing.

Yes and it *was* adultery. A fiancée was as good as a wife any day of the week so who was he kidding there was just no way out of it in that direction as far as the morals went.

Plus vanity. That is what it was, vanity. Otherwise they would now be married, a married couple.

But she had refused the first proposal and he was not giving her a second chance, arrogant vain bastard that he was. So conceited. So damn conceited. But it was her own fault. If she hadnt fancied the idea then it was nothing to do with him. He had tried to persuade her but she was resolute. So how could it be him to blame? It couldnt. It wasnt his fault at all, if he had proposed and she had deposed, deponed, said no,

Yes it was. It was. Of course it was. You have to be honest in this life and not fool yourself and here was one occasion he was not about to: it was him; he was to blame, for the transgression in question. Pride. Plus now another three of them, transgressions, another three transgressions oh Lord three more of them, transgressions. Sex and murder

and what was the third?

blasphemy for heaven's sake imagine forgetting that which some would say was the worst most grievous charge of all. Certainly ministers of the church would say so. Mind you, they were biased; making out blasphemy was the worst was just an unsubtle way of asserting how important they were themselves. It put them a cut above lawyers for instance because look at the judge they had to intercede with: the good God Himself! Then they would shove adultery next in line because of the taboos and how it affected so many more people than murder. Quantity is what counts. No matter the business you're in. The more souls you save the better. And far fewer people get affected by murder in comparison to the vast multitudes who get directly affected by sex, including most especially themselves, the clergy.

But there's no time to think of that though even worse if it had been priests and the involvement was with the Roman Catholics, and he had been one of them, a Roman Catholic. But no time to think of that either. And look at that the purplish red patch on the right testicle there a purplish red patch; that was odd. What was that about the purple red patch on the right testicle? Unless he had been scratching, but he hadnt been scratching, not that he could remember, not like this, to have had this effect. My God. It wasnt so good. Probably it had just kept rubbing against Jeanette's thigh. Was that it? Jeanette's thigh. Rubbing against

Jeanette's thigh, soft upper. If that was it. It was so

But she had fancied him, it wasnt the other way about; so dont go blaming him, it wasnt his fault; if you're going to blame somebody blame her. Okay he had looked, but who wouldnt? It was her made the actual move, the first actual move. He shouldnt have allowed it though, his fiancée's sister. How come she had done it; there must have been a feud, they must have had a fight. Oh God he didnt feel good he just didnt feel good he needed to sit down quickly, quickly. He was just a bit dizzy. Just feeling a bit dizzy. Black dots in front of the eyes, plus whitish, a whitish

If he hadnt reached the chair he would have fainted, he would have fallen down. Probably it was a castigation, a punishment, a retribution, a righteous chastisethment. He had been bad and now he was getting made to suffer. Murder, adultery and blasphemy. Plus of course the pride of vanity. The vanity had been first and then

what was the time what was the time! Deborah had left her house she had left her house. She had been away seeing her parents today. She was now getting the train. She was at the station and getting the train. Her parents lived nearby a railway station, so it was good and convenient. The train let her off in the city center and then she got a bus from behind St Enoch's subway station straight to his place. Who in heaven's name was St Enoch? Where had he come from? Was he even a man! She would be here in half an hour. Unless she was late oh please God make her late if she was just late for a little bit, to let him think straight and get his mind on things and how he was to handle what he would say to her because he had never been what you would call a good teller of tales, teller of lies, of fibs, i.e. never any good at it, at telling them, so he needed out of selling, out of the selling racket all together, he was no good at it, he wasnt, it wasnt his forte; he would be much better at training others, if he could just get onto that training course. He would be good at it. He would be good. He would try so bloody hard. Plus his memory was fine and it was a memory you needed.

The A4 folders spread out on the table. All the mumbo jumbo. Because frankly this is what it was, a load of mumbo jumbo, and high time somebody informed Head Office of the fact. He should actually just burn it all and run away. He had no chance of passing tomorrow with flying colors. He didnt, he just didnt have any chance. He was doomed to lead a life of terrible distaste, a guy for whom life will never ever be a time for fun, trying to survive on the road and failing failing failing thus back on the broo and having to face up to the people down at the DSS office, how they would just ignore him and humiliate him all day long because here he was seeking handouts from a decent Government agency like them. Why had he thought so badly of them! They were just doing a bloody job same as him if he was doing it, he would just be doing a job, it wasnt his bloody fault

Oh God, he just wasnt any good at it it was all his own fault, how in the name of heaven had he left college why had he been so bloody damn daft and absolutely stupid and damn stupid naive that's what he was oh God, he just wasnt any good at it, he wasnt—

I'm not. I am not any bloody good at it. Please help me. I am having to face up to those who hate me. They dont mean to but they do. I do not blame them because they sin, because they sin against me. Please to help me overcome, amen.

He wasnt any good at it. He would be better if he was doing something different. Or else out of it altogether. It was best he resigned in advance. If only he could have made better use of his education and stuck it all out instead of leaving when he had, if he had stuck it through to the bitter end. But even if he had gone into the Post Office bank like his dad had advised him to do: and so strongly. That was his experience talking. If he had just listened to him, but he hadnt, he just hadnt bloody listened because he had wanted bloody out, because he had hated the place and he just couldnt get his heart in it he just couldnt like it at all, what he was doing there, what they were asking him to do and all that stupid damn studying for no reason, it was all just bloody nonsense and difficult and even if it had been difficult and had a purpose but it didnt, it was just for nothing, graphs and statistical analysis, and nobody ever talking to you, it was like they all knew each other from years ago, except him, he was a sore thumb, he was a sore thumb, or else he would have done it properly, he would have stuck in and just managed it, he would have concentrated hard, hard.

How come he had not bloody done it when he had the chance! He was just a damn fool. He had always been a damn fool. His dad knew it, he knew it; you could tell by the way he looked. And probably mum secretly agreed although she made excuses for him. And Deborah knew it as well, she did, it was bloody obvious, he was just a damn bloody fool. She would maybe forgive him his trespass if he told her truthfully, if he explained it, all he had to do was explain it and then she would see because it was her sister, her own sister: it was her led him into the spider's web and trapped him and it was just male sexuality and her breasts and stockings and her thighs.

And there was just no possibility of her staying the night for heaven's sake that just wasnt on. How could it be it couldnt be it just was beyond anything, even having washed.

The thing about Deborah of course her character trait it wasnt so much her temper but her stubbornness, how stubborn she was. It was just so bad; she had to learn to control it, she really did—otherwise it would definitely cause her problems in life. Maybe that had something to do with Jeanette, the way Jeanette had acted with him, if she had maybe been upset by Deborah if they had had a fall-out, and this was her taking revenge, seducing him, her sister's fiancée, the future brother-in-law. But had it been on the cards you could say it had been on the cards. Things had been

Well it was that selfsame very sister's own fault. It was, it was her own damn fault, damn and bloody blast. Her own mother had even referred to that awful bloody stubbornness which was surely something because normally they stick together mothers and daughters

At that moment a loud chap-chap at the door just about gave him a heart attack, he nearly toppled over, having returned to the sink, the trousers still at the ankles but he very quickly got himself ready and glanced into the mirror to see he was okay, steadying himself, he closed his eyes for some moments because life, because

he wasnt good he just wasnt good, he wasnt, he felt so bloody, so damn

the chap-chap at the door again. He walked forwards and turned the handle. It was a small elderly old woman. It wasnt Deborah. His head craned over her. He felt like the Blackpool Tower and she was a wee midget. She spoke to him; what she said was something like, I'm your neighbor up the stairs if you mind son myself and my husband moved in last week.

Pardon?

You gave us a wee hand up with our suitcases and our bags.

Yeh, yeh.

If you mind the housing put us in after we got decanted out our own place.

Aye, aye, that's right that's right, yeh . . . He stared at her then stepped out and peered sideways. He said, Go on, the coast being clear. Go on, he said, yes, what is it?

The woman studied him, evidently thinking he was being uncalled-for abrupt and hostile to her.

Sorry. Sorry sorry sorry. He didnt mean it at all. He really didnt. I've got a sore head just now, he told her, I'm studying for a test tomorrow for my work. It's an in-house thing and it's really

He frowned at the woman: what the hell was he telling her for! He said: What is it you want, is it something you want?

My husband would like you to come up the stair a minute, he would like a word with you.

Pardon?

If you wouldnt mind. He's just awful worried the now about something and he'll no tell me . . . And onto her face appeared a kind of—what look? a something look, it would have flummoxed you. He stared at her and then glanced away in case something bad happened. And she said, You know how he's an invalid.

Aw aye, yeh, that's right, an invalid—he's got a walking stick or whatever it is one of these three-angled triangular frame things whatever you call them, sorry, I mean . . . Is he wanting me to do something?

He'll tell you himself.

Yeh but missis it's just I'm so busy the now, I'm just so busy, I've got all this, God, stuff I'm studying and having to learn, to memorize, for the morrow morning, first thing . . . And he was about to fling back the door and show her but no, no, she was the last person he wanted to see inside his room, the last person, somebody like her, unspotted, untainted, such a fresh old lady with her invalid husband who never had had a bad thought in her entire life, who had never ever periodically once upon a time ever felt or saw, thought or spoke an evil word, deed or action please the Lord.

The woman nodded but she took him by the elbow and he was powerless to refuse because how do you know it might well have been a chastisethment, something like that he was suffering and had to endure as a penance: but then he frowned at her a moment later and tried to pull himself clear because she could be a malevolent demon or something it seems stupid but who knows who knows the way things were and how life was turning against him, old-age pensioners plus her being a woman and maybe the wrath of a female because of what had just so lately taken place—he glanced down the stairs. I'm waiting for my fiancée, he said. He shrugged and smiled for a moment; We're getting married, I'm just having to pass this wee test first, for my promotion, and then after that we'll be putting the mortgage down for a house, a flat, a wee room and kitchen or something, a place of our own . . . He grinned at her.

You'll just be a minute, she said. Honestly. It's because you see my husband gets agitated sometimes, he gets things on his mind and they'll no let him go. She then made a brandishing motion with her right hand as if an indication of it, of how the things went inside her husband's mind: He's a worrier. He never used to be. Telling you son he was aye about the most relaxed man you could meet, but no now. Us being stuck in this lodging house just makes it worse.

Yeh . . . He stared at his arm as she held it, leading him across the landing and up the stairs to the room directly above his own and therefore likely to have very similar walls and incisions; she held the door open for him to enter. The odor of something like ancient bodies filled the doorway. It wasnt a vile stench although he breathed in and out through his mouth to avoid it. The invalid husband was waiting. He had his three-angled contraption there which he was leaning on from the inside; he wore a dark-brown serge suit with outsize lapels and quite smartish-looking although it was creased as if he had been sitting in a certain way for too long, maybe like he had fallen asleep, dozed off, his bad leg resting maybe up on a stool, and further when you looked at the suit you could see it was greasy, shiny.

Here he is, said the woman.

What's your name young fellow? asked the invalid.

My name's eh . . . He paused. He was wondering why he should be giving his name to a complete stranger. He couldnt remember helping him up the blasted stair last week with no blasted suitcases either—neither him nor his damn wife, this old woman and her quasi-humble politeness. Edward Pritchard, he said, emphasising the two ards as he used to do many years ago when he was in primary school, about eight years of age or something and thought such a remarkable poetic feature just had to be a personal and secret message from Jesus setting him apart from his fellows, it was pathetic, pathetic—as if he had any reason to be famous, because all he was cut out for was what he was about to receive for his sins, sent out on the road as a working sales for the rest of his days, whenever he could bloody get a damn job and lump it, just bloody lump it, he was never going to be anything special, nothing, he wasnt going to amount to anything really at all, these silly stupid dreams, none of it was worth a damn, because he had ruined it all, his entire life, and that was that, he was finished, it was over, he was never going to make it at all, you would be as well laughing at the very idea, because he was a malcontent who committed transgressions in the name of the Lord and was therefore doomed.

You go away Catherine, the invalid commanded.

His wife looked at him as if she was trying to figure out what he was thinking.

Go a message, he said. I want to have a word with the young fellow. The invalid had taken one of his hands off from the contraption now and was waving at her to leave and you felt you hoped he wouldnt fall down and hurt himself his hands were so shaky. What could he want maybe it was a male problem or something to discuss or else to give him a hand in some way, shave him or something the old guy because he needed a shave he looked like he hadnt shaved for a couple of days, and if his hands were suffering from too many twitches

The old woman was now pulling on her overcoat, a quite smart one for rainy weather, pink and gray, and her legs were short. Some people had funny short legs thank the Lord it wasnt him he couldnt imagine it, walking down the road having to step over puddles, big puddles with your wee toty stride, how could you manage it it would be so bloody difficult you had to admire her, she was so strong in the face of the world, that was a trait though in old women he found, they were so brave, his grannie was like that; plus his other one who was now dead; they had come through the mill—this old woman especially with her invalid husband, having to take care of him what the hell did he bloody want! My God he didnt even look worried, no really. And when the door closed behind his wife he started gesticulating. Sit down! he commanded, imperious old bugger, glancing roundabout and then maneuvering his way to a chair nearby the window. He got himself seated and sighed deeply. And he looked at Edward.

Edward wanted to have something to say but there was nothing, there was nothing at all and his brow became furrowed.

See young fellow what it is, I've got a confession to make and I dont want Catherine to know.

Edward felt his head go funny at this but he kept his eyes open and concentrated hard.

Poor old sowel she's got enough on her plate, she works hard and she looks after me you see, she looks after me. The invalid breathed in sharply, then sighed. Edward had been watching him very attentively and he too breathed in sharply but via his nostrils and it was terrible. The smell was a fuisty one of dirt, and it was definitely coming from the old bloke. A fuisty smell of dirt—or excrement! Shit, old shit. God! Maybe he needed his bum cleaned and was too proud to tell his wife. Oh dear. Oh dear. Edward just couldnt cope with that, he couldnt, he just couldnt cope with it if he was maybe not able to attend to himself for heaven's sake did they not have home-helps, had the government stopped home-helps now and strangers were getting called in to wipe folk's bums, old invalid people who couldnt manage it theirselves and were wanting to hide it from their nearest and dearest so the neighbors, now having to get called in. He ran his hand across his forehead, opened his eyes widely.

You see young fellow I've got this confession to make. What's your name? No, dont tell me, it's best I dont know. Now pay attention: before they invalided me out my job of work I used to be involved in what some people would call malpractice; some other people would call it sabotage and other people again, well, they would call it something else all the gether. What I used to do you see was the spanner-in-the-works carry-on; I used to stop the line. Understand me? That was what I did, wherever it was I was working, I used to bring things to a halt—I tried to anyway. That's the shape my politics took and that's the shape they were; and I cant help it and nor did I ever want to help it, and I've never wanted to change things neither. But as a way of living my life so to speak what it means is I've aye had to do what my conscience tells me. There's no an in-between. Now . . .

The invalid stopped there and he studied Edward as if wanting to make sure who it was he was telling all this.

But Edward's face was expressionless.

Now the last place I worked in was a firm by the name of eh Gross National Products which, as you probably guess, is a made-up name. I dont want to tell you the real one because you never know you might be a police informer.

Edward smiled after a moment, shaking his head.

The invalid's hands started waving about furiously: But never mind that never mind that—and never mind me neither because I get nervous and I get agitated.

And the way he pronounced "agitated" sounded funny although Edward didnt acknowledge this. And the old invalid was looking at him with maybe a bit of impatience or something maybe just wanting to know who it was he was confiding in, because how do you know who you're talking to in this world you dont, you just dont know, it could be anybody; it was the very same when you were out on the road trying to talk your way into some office or garage or factory. Even when you were down at Head Office with the other sales teams you werent free, you had to watch it; you had to say nothing and keep your distance while at the same time try not to appear too stand-offish because that was bad points and you knew they were always watching and taking notes—especially if your figures werent that good, if they had been on the decrease, during the last four-week period even although the area he had to work was nothing like the density of other areas, and you would expect such things to be taken into consideration, but no, they were treated like they just didnt matter, which was a strange way to run a business. But the selling game was a funny business. That's exactly what it was, a funny business; the way it operated.

which happened to me, said the invalid.

What

something that I ended up doing as well and it's caused me a lot of pain and suffering, a hell of a lot . . . The invalid smiled, he waved at his contraption: I wasnt always pushing one of them about you know.

Edward nodded. What is it you call it?

But the invalid just gave an impatient shake of the head and continued talking: Now what happened you see, I've got to fill you in, I was keeping a low profile because they were after me, I'm talking about the bigwigs, they were out to get me. And they were using a fellow who was a mucker, a pal. Mind you he was a waster the same man, if I'm to be honest about it, and you dont like saying that about anybody never mind when he's your mate. But this yin was the sort that winds up changing colors, he joined the enemy, he was a turncoat. That happens a lot in this life: traitors.

Edward stared hard at the old invalid, concentrating on each word he spoke, noting the way his head twitched this way and that, he looked like he was wanting a place to spit into:

Bad bastard that he was. And to think you took him into your home and gave him your hospitality. And his wife and mine became friends too and my Catherine, poor old sowel, she used to look after their weans like they were her own. But that was who it was, the very one they sent to get me. They had chose him because they knew we were close. Ahh! It's a world of conspiracies out there.

Pardon?

But I soon knew the situation anyway. Too many ears to the ground young fellow . . . You probably dont know that yet but you will soon enough. Wait till you get to my age, then you'll find out. The invalid winked and tapped the side of his nose. Then he smiled, waved his hands in a dismissive gesture. But there's much more you've got to understand and I'm no wanting to get us bogged down in the petty stuff. Come and sit next to me so I dont have to bellow.

I'm fine here though.

No but I want to tell you a secret young fellow, and walls have ears.

What?

The invalid squinted at him: I thought you'd have kenned that by now, you being a student and aw that.

But I'm no a student, replied Edward, frowning, I'm in the selling game. I'm just studying for a work test, it's a kind of I dont know what you would call it, mainly it's product memorizing I've to do. I think it's what's known as a Retraining Schedule. In reality it's to do with re-grading, if you dont pass it you stay where you are. And that's like a de-motion. In fact it is a demotion. In fact, this test isnt really to pass onto greater things at all, it's just to avoid the pit.

The pit?

Yeh.

The old woman says you were a student.

Did she? I wonder how she thought that.

She'll have keeked in the door and seen you at your lessons.

Pardon?

Cause that's how she does it. She's good so she is. You just wouldnt have heard her at all but what she'll have done she'll have lifted the flap of your letter box and just looked through to see what you were doing. The invalid chuckled. I aye wished I'd had her for a partner at the "spanners"! She would've been rare at it—better than me. And I would say I was one of the best though as a masculine model my limitations were there, they had to be. Masculine models and limitations mascu-line models and limitations. These facets we are born with—faculties I mean—man. Man is born with definite limitations. We attempt to set out and change the world but then we get bogged down in the microcosmic ephemera of getting to B from A. You have your goal. You go to college and you take a wee look about. You think the road ahead is signposted—not so much signposted as like the conditions are set for you. You find a lass and the two of you set out as partners in the face of a hostile and aggressive world; and that includes your parents. Because the harsh truth is that most parents hate their children, just like Romeo and Juliet, wherefore art thou, they hate them actively and discourage them from doing the things they want, if you want to change the world you're no allowed to, they dump you down so you have to take what you're given, and then you end up with things you dont really want but are just settling for and it isnt your fault at all because you are doing your best, trying your damnedest to please and to settle down properly with your loved one in your nest, when you are married, when you are given the proper chance, the nettle, grasping that opportunity

Edward had a look on his face, it was a smile, his eyelids were closed and he shook his head. An overwhelming sensation of relief. Utter and total relief. Oh Lord, Lordie Lordie, it was so good sitting there, just sitting there, so good just sitting there—here, I find it so relaxing, he said, opening his eyes and grinning at the invalid: I just wish I had a cigar! But no, honest, being serious about it, it's just so soothing, for my head— and for my brains, giving them a rest like this, not having to worry about things, you see my fiancée eh was coming, she's about due to come.

Ah . . . ! So you've a fiancée, that's even better. That shows you're responsible. I like to see responsibility in a young fellow. What's your name?

. . .

You're no going to tell me eh?

I told you before.

Did you?

Yeh, it's Edward Pritchard, I dont mind you knowing at all.

The invalid nodded, and he said slowly, Edward Pritchard. He pursed his lips. My name's Robert Parker, Bobbie—like the boy who used to play for Falkirk or was it the Hearts?—big right back if you remember, I think he got a cap for the Scottish League team, maybe even the full national one.

Edward shook his head.

Before your time I dare say. The invalid continued speaking: There's a confession I need to make you see. I need to make it because I've got a feeling something impending is going to happen . . . I dont know like it's as if maybe you think you're about to get knocked down by a lorry or a bus or a taxi—

Pardon?

Well you see sometimes they go careering down the road and they dont see you if you're an invalid, you're walking that slow they fail to take you in on their line of vision. And you cant but take a stride without doing so with that very reckoning and you're darting a look this way and that or else trying no to, you just keep your face fixed to the front and try no even to listen for the roar of the engine—the thing that's coming to mow you down.

My God!

Yeh.

That sounds like an awful nightmare. Edward's left hand went to his face and he covered then rubbed at his left eye.

It's like they think you're a pillar or a post.

Surely no!

Aye! The invalid waved his hand, then signaled the need for silence and he whispered, Come here till I tell you. You're no a religious young chap, are you?

I believe in God if that's what you mean.

Do you? The invalid sat back on his chair and he studied Edward.

Well I hope I do I mean I hope I do . . . And I'm no ashamed of it. I used to be an agnostic. But no now, I'm back to believing. Edward gazed at the invalid and suddenly felt very sad. His parents were getting old and no doubt they would be dead eventually, just like everybody else, his good old grandpa as well. And it wasnt long since Deborah's grannie had died, he remembered the funeral quite vividly, the two sisters taking charge of doing the food, and they did it really terrific, rolls and different scones and things, bowls of nuts and crisps— better than if they had gone for a meal in a hotel.

My parents are churchgoers, he told the invalid. But I'm no. When I was a boy I was, but I've no been for years apart from when my fiancée's grannie died last March. I felt a hypocrite . . . Edward stopped and frowned: Did I though? Maybe I didnt. Maybe I just thought I should have felt a hypocrite, because that's . . . He glanced at the invalid: I've been involved in some things recently that I think really are sins, to be honest, I dont mind telling you Mister Parker and I can only hope I'll be forgiven, I hope nothing's going to get held against me although if it does I'll no complain, if I've to suffer a chastisement. If I can only make up for it, maybe by doing my test properly tomorrow, if I can only manage that.

He punched his right fist into his left palm and cried: That's all, that's all I want!

You will pass it, the invalid said.

What!

You will. You'll pass your test and you'll get your promotion.

Edward stared at him and was immediately suspicious. Somewhere there was a line between making a slight fool of somebody and genuine fellowship and good company like the way at the fortnightly sales-team talks when the guys made jokes about one another and you didnt quite were sure, you never quite

You just couldnt laugh. But the jokes always seemed to be so damn unfunny. How was it possible to laugh? Edward could hardly even smile let alone throw the head back. It was terrible. He hated it.

The invalid was speaking:

Somebody that's as diligent a studier as you, he's the kind that deserves to succeed. And you will succeed. I'm convinced of that.

Edward coughed to clear his throat. Ah but I'm no that diligent, he said, my concentration's nil . . . He wet his lips and swallowed, his mouth seemed to have gone dry; then he glanced sideways for some reason but everything was fine, fine.

The invalid was frowning at him: Although with me mind you there's aye the wish that a young fellow like yourself could one day take up the cudgels where me and the muckers left off. But these battles have finished, just like the days they happened in are finished, and the kind of future that sorts itself out on the past isnt the kind of future we fought for—and I'm no a supporter of such things—none of us were, no in the slightest. You understand me?

Edward hesitated.

Ah you will young fellow you will. And now if you'll no come to me then I'll come to you.

And so saying the old invalid got himself up onto his feet with the aid of the contraption and he made his way over to sit down on the chair next to Edward and Edward hoped so strongly that he wouldnt put his hand on his knee because he hated that being done he just couldnt stand it, couldnt cope with it and knew his face would just get so crimson, so awful crimson

And the invalid whispered: Now young fellow, my confession, afore Catherine comes back; when I worked in whatever you call it, Gross National—which is twelve years ago now—the country was in a state of economic decline, everything was to pot. You're a bit young to remember that eh?

Edward felt nauseous, he felt sick sick sick, he needed to vomit, he needed to spew, to spew. He clamped shut his nose by squeezing it with his right thumb and forefinger. He breathed out loudly, clearly, to prepare for the refreshment of his lungs, breathed deeply in; he opened his eyes and stared at the frayed carpet on the floor. His room was better than this, it was bad, but not this bad. But maybe the old couple had something special that made it better and evened things out, although the light was terrible, and the walls and ceiling were just as crappy-looking and it was so heavy an atmosphere—that dull yellow everywhere and it all so damn unhealthy and just damn bloody ungood.

But Lord Lord Lord was it a smell of shite right enough? Ohhh. But it might just have been sweat, the old invalid male having been using such tremendous exertions in merely getting to B from A about the room, even toing and froing re the cludgie. So he was bound to get sweaty.

Always he had to think the worst about folk, that was his problem; even with Deborah for heaven's sake how come he was always blaming her for everything? And he was. No matter what it was he blamed her. It was just so uncharitable and wrong. Pride. That's all it was. Conceited buggar. Pride.

but the pong from this old bloke sitting next to him he felt like he was going to keel over off the chair, he would topple over onto his doom and he would just die here in this room with an ancient stranger as a companion, somebody who could have devised an unheard-of method for removing fresh limbs from a young person's body in order to weld them onto an elderly sick person, an invalid—spare-part surgery, and here he was about to become a human trunk with no limbs like that horrible story he had once read about a man getting mutilated by evil slavers for some purpose he couldnt remember, set in the Sahara region, and these armless and legless beggars in third-world countries who have to get wheeled about in bogies in an effort to pay off loans to the IMF and the World Bank. God he was so cold now, cold, he was so cold. No bloody fire, why was there no bloody fire, rabbiting on like this about all these factory incidents from a forgotten past and all his gesticulations it was so difficult to even listen because of it.

You did your best.

. . .

. . .

Still silence. Had he finished? What did he mean "you did your best"? Edward was almost scared to look up from the carpet. But he managed it, and found the invalid staring straight at him. It was such a strong stare. You would like to have looked at this stare but it would have been a stare-out contest if you had and he would have lost. He was no good at that kind of thing. It reminded him of these facetious mockups they had to play out at the monthly interdistrict meetings. Awful, so awful. You felt so self-conscious and not just for yourself but for them as well, all the other salespersons. He was the only one seemed to have that kind of response. Then there was that funny sadistic aspect about it. He just wasnt into it, and not the humiliation side either. It wasnt something he enjoyed at all. These games were just a kind of psychology. That's all they were. And he didnt have the mentality needed if you were ever to excel at them. It was a certain kind you required. And he didnt have it. The other blokes did have, they had the right sort of makeup, they were the right mettle, it was him that wasnt, that was how he had to get out from it.

Plus he couldnt reach a closure anymore. That was the real truth, he couldnt close a sale, he just couldnt close a sale. And that meant he was a goner because if there was one thing you needed in the selling game it was the closure knack, how to close a sale, how to stop talking and point the customer's pen at the dotted line. He had been great for the first few weeks. He seemed able to sell anything to anybody. No now. He was rubbish now. A dumpling. That's the truth, he was a dumpling.

But he could train others. He could definitely train others. He knew what the correct procedure was; and his product knowledge was good— all of that side of things.

But talking to potential customers, he couldnt bloody manage that either, the theory yeh, but not in actuality, when face to face with them, as individual human beings. What was that poem by William Wordsworth?

Jeanette had just happened to flash her breasts at him and he was a goner—then also her stockings, he knew she wore stockings and not tights when she was bending.

The invalid was looking at him.

What is it?

I was just saying to you when the old woman comes back we've got to speak about other things, maybe the facilities in this place.

Pardon?

I'm meaning when Catherine comes back, she's a habit of sneaking up on you. If she does then just you should start talking about the facilities here—I mean what you're supposed to do for grub and so forth because you're no allowed to cook in your room as far as I hear. That right?

Edward nodded.

Start talking about that then. Because it's a hell of an irritation, especially to her. No me so much cause I'm no what you'd call an eater, but she gets all het up about it and you cant blame her, poor auld sowel, she's used to an oven and a cooker and what-have-you. So if you start talking about the facilities you see I dont want her knowing what I'm going to tell you. I want that to be a secret between me and you. The invalid gazed at Edward then sighed. And he sighed again.

But it was like there was something underhand going on and Edward couldnt put his finger on it. Was it like a form of sarcasm against him? It was. It was actually like a form of sarcasm. Just the way all this was happening, like it was all falling into place. And he was a culprit.

A lot of different things, nothing you could just put your finger on.

Such an incredible cheek really. You had to just sit there with your mouth hanging agape. Then you felt like getting up and letting him see you knew what was going on. Edward smiled to himself, shaking his head. But imagine his dad hearing about it! What would he do! It was like a slur being cast on him, not just him, his entire family.

He glanced sideways at the invalid who was now gazing round the four walls in a very intentional and deliberate way. He gazed at the window in particular—as if expecting a snooper to be hanging outside on a painter's platform. And then he started talking but it was so difficult to hear him properly with all his wavering and his gesticulating plus as well the terrible terrible fuisty pong that came from him. He seemed to be speaking about a horrendous and wicked horrible incident in a factory, something bad and evil he had been involved in that drove somebody off their mind and destroyed them, and killed somebody else, an accident or something, and related groups and even families as well as different industrial stresses were involved, and it was turning to center on one of these wee boyish kind of apprentice lads that everybody's supposed to like—naughty and full of devilment etc. etc. It was just so awful and impossible to hear. In fact Edward was going to leave right now. His head was spinning. It was too much. How was he supposed to cope with it, it just wasnt bloody feasible when he was supposed to be studying because either one thing or the other but not both; that was too much, too bloody much, just too damn bloody much. Damn and bloody blast. Edward stared at the invalid.

What happened you see I was working in this place where a spanner had just been tossed.

A spanner had just been tossed. He stared at the wide lapels on the invalid's jacket; there was a stain down one of them.

a very big spanner, one of the biggest seen in this country for quite a number of years—me and a couple of blokes working the gether for it, a team effort—and I reckon it must have cost maybe one point seven five million for final rectification see young fellow because we had it worked so the bigwigs never found out it was deliberate—no even that it was an accident.

If it was an accident . . . ?

No, said the invalid, that's what I'm saying. I'll tell you something you'll maybe no quite understand except maybe you might: you see they never found out that it happened at all. You get it? They just thought there was something wrong with the entire works, and I'm no talking about safety measures because safety measures dont make that much difference as well you'll know, but just that a general improvement would need doing, right the way through all their factories—and I'm here meaning across the whole of what you call the "free world";

It's a hoax!

That's how it cost so much to put right you see because you're talking Thailand, Indonesia, India, Zambia, Kenya, Korea, Vietnam, Scotland.

It's a hoax!

Denmark, the Irish Free State, Wales, Pakistan, Australia, Iceland, Sweden—wherever GNP Plc used to exist it no existing now of course because it was taken over by a big conglomerate back in the time of the conspiracy trials. Then it went itself in the Throgmorton Crash if you mind, and you had the Makgas Consortium stepping in, government funding and CNI money, headed by a noted patriot—though you understand young fellow that the patriot's real name is something different to anything I might tell you so what's the point of me telling you anything at all. Unless you rather you heard everything, but that sort of information isnt classified I mean it's freely available elsewhere and if you would rather hear than no hear then you should go and check it out, you'll find most of it down the Advocate's Library.

Edward looked up from the floor. He looked the invalid in the eye. As much as you could tell he was the real mccoy. You would never know for sure of course. But how could you know anything for sure in this world since it was full of illusion. His dad used to tell him as a wee boy that if ever he found himself in dark trouble it would pay to tell the truth and if God really was there—and we knew that He was—then everything would turn out fine. Because He would look after you.

That was the route Edward would have taken away before he left off being a believer. And now he was back to it again he knew the course of action was right. It was right and it was good. But it was difficult. Telling the truth as an adult male was different from telling the truth as a boy.

After a moment he said, It's a world I dont know Mister Parker. I wish I did but I dont. I've never really been able to get the hang of it—it's like the international news in the quality Sunday papers, all these places and names you can never remember, they go hazy as soon as you look at them. I'm sorry. Honest. My mind's good at some things but no at others. I wish it was different: I wish I could just bloody I mean it's concentration, it's just concentration, I dont seem able to concentrate beyond about five minutes at any given point—even when I was at college it was the same, I think there's something up with me.

The invalid was watching him and he had a frown on his face.

Edward cleared his throat before continuing: I just do my best at my job of work without hurting too many people, although you've got to appreciate about it that being on the road, what I do, as a sales rep what you've got to do, anybody, you've got to gyp folk because that's the nature of the game, salesmanship, you have to gyp people into buying stuff they dont like. Silly buggers. How come they buy all that junk! I've never been able to work it out. Even my own mother, with all her experience through having a salesman for a son, this guy comes to the door a week ago and he sells her some insurance that's more or less useless, in fact it's absolutely useless, it's no good at all, if I'd had been there I'd have bashed him one on the jaw. Bloody stuff! I went through it to check. Rubbish! Absolute rubbish! And I mean

The invalid stopped him from talking by waving his hand. Young fellow, were you the lad that helped me up the stair the other day?

Edward couldnt answer because this was part of the hoax and it was a trap question.

Were you?

Your wife says so but you'll have to work it out for yourself, it's no good asking me because how do you know about me you dont know nothing quite honestly, quite frankly, when you come to think about it. She says it was me, she says it was but I wouldnt actually believe her, how do you know, she might be lying, just because she's elderly and small and acts like she's the epitome of truth and wisdom therefore she has to be a paragon, but how do you know the devil hasnt entered her soul and she's only there to draw us all into evil ways?

He stopped speaking. Then he said, I obviously only mean that as a for instance; I dont really think it—I mean how could I! Obviously I couldnt.

The way the invalid was staring at him, his eyes set, set fixed and firm.

Look, said Edward, I'm just trying to be honest. I dont know anything about industrial sabotage or industrial injuries, I dont know anything at all, if somebody has to suffer a terrible horrendous agony just in order that others might go free, that's just the same as happens to other people—it happened to Jesus Christ, He had to be crucified, so maybe it was like what you're saying, for the sake of the good of mankind as a whole, if that's what you're talking about, about somebody having to get killed instead of something else. Well there's other sins people have to atone for, it's no always just your own. I think that's a mistake a lot of folk make, especially males like us, men, I think we're very often mistaken at the very root of our own existence as human beings.

The invalid was squinting at him. He shook his head: I'm no following your drift.

Well look I mean you asked if I believed in God. I do, I really do. I stopped it for a while but now I'm back to having the faith. I feel on my best behavior because of it and having everything to overcome. The world's just such a big place I find with people suffering the wide world over. I find it hard. You help the one person are you supposed to help them all? And then how are you supposed to keep on living your own life into the bargain? Cause nobody helps you. Know what I mean? That's all I'm saying, it's no because you're selfish, you just dont have the power or the control except maybe a wee minuscule slice, and then you wind up getting squashed, just like a wee beetle—that's what happened to a friend of mine . . . when we were at college, he started to get involved in charity work for foreign countries and then he ended up in trouble.

You're misjudging yourself young fellow.

Pardon?

I was beginning to guess that just after you came in. But there again it's my own fault; I tend no to get things right either.

Edward scratched the side of his head.

And then you see I've got to trust whoever she trusts; my missis, I have to rely on her for my character judgments. Of course it's this bloody thing here . . . ! He shook his head, staring at the contraption. If it wasnt for it I'd be able to give more time to things, I'd be able to do my own thinking when it comes to getting things done, and that's what's important. Ach . . . The invalid's head drooped and he sighed.

Edward nodded, he studied the frayed bit of the carpet, how its wee threads were spread so very haphazardly and you could just reach down and straighten them out, get them into a neat wee row. This was a memorable meeting but it wasnt nice at the time. He would always take pains to remember that. It was a promise. He had promised, and he would do it. Even when he would tell a friend about how all this had happened he would make sure he added on about it not being nice when it happened, actually was happening at the time; it was very uncomfortable—not even the chair was good to sit on and plus as well you had the very proximity of the old man, how him being an invalid meant you got this old smell which was really quite fuisty and you hate to say it but almost nearly what you would call a stench, when you came to think about it, like as if he hadnt washed or perish the thought cleansed himself the last time he visited the toilet etcetera etcetera though you dont like saying that because he was a genuine and good old guy that you had to respect for his integrity down through the years, him being involved in politics in an active way on the factory floor, you had to really respect him. There was the door! Deborah! Deborah . . .

Oh Lord Lord Lord.

Edward had started up from the chair, he glanced this way and that; but whosoever was outside on the stair landing must have continued on to some other destination. He relaxed, settled himself back on the chair again.

Where was she though? She was late. Usually she was on time, she was quite a precise person. In fact that was quite a good thing about her and fitted in with him; they were quite alike in that sense, him also being a person who was quite precise or tried to be. That side of things was fine but not an especial plus, not in the selling line, it was definitely not an especial plus in the selling line: you could be as late as you wanted as long as you knew how to close a sale.

Deborah:

He really thought she was a great lassie, really great. It was just she didn't have the best of manners. This bad habit she had of—it was like not having a sense of humor maybe, to do with that—quite a nasty tongue even, in some ways, you had to admit it. Even her own mother said it about her, and that was something surely. And maybe as well, and it was terrible to say, and it wasnt a criticism at all but just if she maybe just learned to wear better clothes, a wee bit more stylish, if the truth be told, maybe like Jeanette who was called Jinty by people. You couldnt call Deborah anything like that. She didnt like him calling her Debbie for instance and Debs just sounded stupid

Edward got to his feet.

Because it was time to go. It really was time to go. He had all these bloody things to learn before morning came, never mind prepare his head for her, get his head right, get things sorted, get the things worked out because of

God, he just didnt know what to do, he didnt, he didnt know what to do. He had no idea. He just had no idea. He was in a terrible state, situation, it wasnt something he didnt know how to get out, what he could do, and she would be here she would be here, she would be here, she would be here

Just sit down a minute, the invalid commanded.

Edward shook his head.

Just for a minute.

I cant, I just cant.

You can.

I've got to go.

I've a need to tell you something. It's a kind of confession.

Edward gazed at him.

I've got to talk things out with you.

But you've done that already, have you no?

No.

I thought you had.

Look young fellow talking it out in that certain way I'm meaning *is* a confession; that's what a confession *is*. And I'll know when I've done it, because you always do, once you've made it you know you've made it. Your mind feels easy.

Edward paused. He was looking to say something. There was something he was to say and he was looking to say it, it was maybe to do with guilt, because he knew about that, a wee bit at least. Although he was so much younger that didnt mean he didnt, because it was a thing you could feel even as a boy.

The invalid was waiting to speak.

Sorry, said Edward.

The invalid frowned and made a gesture with his hand: You see I'm no able to speak unless you're willing to listen, you've got to be able to hear what I'm saying but you're no always willing to do that.

Yeh but Mister Parker I'm sorry eh it's just that my fiancée's due at any minute.

The invalid glanced at the door, then said, She'll know where you are, Catherine'll tell her.

Will she?

Aye, she'll be back soon herself . . . And again the old invalid glanced at the door.

Edward nodded; he sniffed, breathed in deeply and raised his head, at the same time making a gulping noise like as if his Adam's apple was stuck, then the tears started in his eyes and he was blinking to keep from crying.

What's wrong?

Jees I'm just in awful trouble Mister Parker, awful trouble.

Sit down a minute.

Yeh but I'm just in so much trouble.

Sit down a minute then. Sit down. Maybe we can share it. Sometimes you share a problem you swop it, and in the swopping it gets lost.

Edward had his face in his hands.

Dont get yourself into a state . . . He leaned forwards, grasping Edward's right shoulder: Edward's a king's name by the way, did you know that?

Edward shook his head.

Come on, at your age it cant be that bad, it'll be a personal thing, personal things are easy. Just sit down a minute and tell me what it is. I was going to tell you mine so you can just tell me yours—see! if you tell me I'll tell you, that's what I mean by a swop.

Edward dragged the cuff of his sleeve across his face, wiping his eyes as he sat down.

I'll take on your problem if you'll take on mine. You hear me out and then I'll hear you out.

Yeh but . . . Edward now rubbed quickly at his eyes with the palms of both his hands.

In that way you see we'll both have things into the open, we'll have shared what's troubling us . . . If I start worrying about your problems you start worrying about mine. You get it?

Edward shifted on his chair enough to see the door. She was coming along the street, he knew it. There was no time at all now. He was sunk. What was he going to say to her because he couldnt think of anything, and he wasnt clean. What could he do? He hadnt given it any thought, none, none, he was just relying on something, chance maybe oh more than that more than that he had been praying, he had prayed for assistance, because he needed help, help, he needed help, help help help help please the Lord, oh God but he needed help from Our Father who art in heaven, hallowed be thy name, thy kingdom come, thy will be done

Edward closed his eyes and he put his hands next to each other, not clasping them.

I slept with my fiancée's sister, he said. He raised his head, opening his eyes, but not looking at the invalid. I slept with her. I didnt mean to. I dont know what to do about it. I just dont know.

Mm.

I've never done it before, never, it just bloody happened it was just bloody out the blue, I think maybe it was me with my head full, all the worries I've had cause of this damn test, my job, the whole lot.

Mm.

Edward gazed at him. I just didnt mean it, it just happened.

Aye it's a difficult one that.

Is it?

Questions of loyalty young fellow, they're aye difficult.

Yeh, Edward sighed.

And she doesnt know?

What?

You're wife's no found out?

It's no my wife it's my fiancée; I'm no married.

Aw.

Edward paused. I suppose they're the same really anyway, if you're married or engaged. I am wanting to get married to her. In fact I actually asked her and she said no.

She said no?

Yeh. I asked her. Hh, she didnt want to.

Aw.

I dont know how. I thought it was good you know I mean I thought it was fine, but it wasnt, she just said no. It was a shock.

Oh well, aye. Had you been planning it for a while?

No, no really, I just actually popped it out one night. I hadnt thought of it happening, her saying no. I suppose it's ego, you just dont think of it, you always think it's you, you always think you've got to make the decision. And that's that. Then you find out it isnt, the other people have got their own minds, and what they say for themselves you dont find out till you've asked . . . Eh . . . I know this is a personal question Mister Parker but I was wondering . . . I'm only meaning how it's as though here we are meeting up with each other at a time when we need a way out of a problem.

Edward paused. The old invalid had his hand raised and was waving:

Mine isnt really a problem, he said.

Oh.

It's different to that.

I see.

But on you go anyhow and say what you were saying.

Edward wasnt going to but then he resumed talking. I dont mean like fate, he said, us meeting, because I know God doesnt arrange things just for our benefit in that way I mean that's even a bit like blasphemy to think that, I'm thinking more in the way you get led along a road, it's like how you see a road in the country going over a hill in the distance where the fields look rectangular with their hedgerows and you're going to a village to do a bit of business and there's no avoiding it even although you hate the very idea because the road leads you there and you know you're to have to grit your teeth but you're used to that because that's what you do all the time when you meet these clients even if they're old and valued ones I mean you're always gritting your teeth anyway and then having to go and do it because that's the way things are, you've always got to go straight in and start off the chat as if it was the first time in your life. But maybe things are going to happen to you along the way. Maybe you start to get a blind panic settling in cause that can happen too, that can happen too—it happens to me, sometimes. There's all kinds of trials and tribulations. You see in some ways today has been awful bad for me. I'll no bore you with all the sorry details, it's just personal stuff mainly, and maybe that kind of thing's best not to get aired. You have to remember I'm younger than you I mean you know what like it is nowadays anyway, folk just dont talk about serious things, they dont want to, they only talk about things like television and videos and football, rock bands, that side of things, media personalities and high financiers, big businessmen, big fat cats who work down the Stock Exchange in London, all these big high financiers who get the great big sums of money.

facilities young fellow

What you were saying there a wee minute ago . . . The invalid was staring at Edward. About the facilities, mind? Just tell us about them.

There was something in the invalid's gaze and he turned swiftly to see Deborah. Deborah and the old woman. Both standing there just in from the doorway.

Deborah smiled briefly.

Hiya . . . Edward continued to sit, then he coughed and made to rise from the chair but didnt. For one split second he felt so comfortable and nervous at the self same moment he wanted to rush straight across and take her by the hand and drop to his knees and ask her to marry

him right there and then but something was stopping him and he felt
like bursting out crying again because he seemed to have failed he
seemed to have failed and it was in so dramatically and so suddenly and
in so unforeseen and unexpected a way it was just so amazing and so ultimately stupid, it was just stupid, there was just something so up with
him, something so just

He was telling me about the facilities Catherine. Some funny rules
they've got in this place! Eh young fellow?

Oh yeh, yeh . . . He raised his head and looked directly at the old
woman, and he tried to swallow saliva but his throat was as dry as a bone.

Tell us again, asked the invalid.

Yeh, said Edward.

They're strict eh?

Yeh.

Tell her about what people do.

Edward nodded. You mean the other tenants or just me myself?

Just how you all get by for your meals and the rest of it.

Edward addressed the old woman: Some people I think just eat cold
stuff; cheese and slices of cold meat, tins of beans unheated, that kind
of thing. Bread and butter. Or chips or maybe kebabs or pakora from
the carry-out shop.

She nodded.

Other people have got an electric kettle and what they do is boil eggs
and cook things preserved in salted water, like these wee hot-dog
sausages you can buy out Presto's and sometimes I think some of them
heat up these wee fish done in tomato sauce—pilchards.

He's talking about himself, said Deborah, giving Edward a look, and
then he makes a cup of tea without rinsing out the kettle so it's all
tomato sauce left inside—even vinegar sometimes.

Edward avoided looking back at her she sounded so honest and
good, he felt so badly sick, so badly sick. And he had to say something
they were waiting. She's just saying that, he said, and smiled, she's just
saying that.

And he twisted a little bit on his seat as if he was trying to glance at
her somehow like he was not able to the way he was at present and he
saw her frowning and puzzled. And he cleared his throat at the invalid
and he carried on speaking about maybe even soup could be done in
your kettle, he said, especially if it was really clear and no full of veg-

etables. As long as the owners dont find out, what they dont know wont hurt them.

Mm . . . The elderly woman grimaced from him to her husband: If he was fit and healthy we wouldnt be in this state. We would have a proper cooker with an oven and I could make proper meals. She was looking at Deborah now: You see he was on the injured pensioners' income supplement but they took him off it because it'd become a condition, so that's us now until he gets better, if he ever will. And he's the only one that says he will, cause the doctor says he'll no.

That's bloody appalling, said Deborah. She glanced at Edward, shaking her head.

Edward stared at the carpet.

It's bloody appalling.

He raised his head and peered at Deborah, his eyebrows sticking out in front of his eyes, the hairs, as if he was getting old before his time, bushy eyebrows. He said to the old woman: I'm sorry missis I'll have to go back down the stair now because I've got my studies to attend to.

He's got his test tomorrow morning, said the invalid.

Did you tell him about your cousin Jim?

No.

You should have.

Och he's no wanting to hear about him.

It's only because things are so rushed, said Edward, plus as well I was thinking of setting my alarm early, so's I could get up and do an extra bit of studying the morrow morning.

You'll pass young fellow so dont worry.

I hope so, Edward said, smiling but feeling hopeless. And he knew his forehead was falling, falling flat—how it would be flat and he would droop there to everybody, them knowing his state, and he stood up and stepped to the side of Deborah, speaking while he passed: Will we go then?

Alright.

I thought you would feel like something to eat . . . Do you? he said to her.

Do *you?*

Well if you do.

Deborah sighed.

I'll maybe pop down later then like we agreed, called the invalid.

Pardon?

Maybe the back of nine, when you're knocking off for a coffee. Or else will you just come up here?

Eh

Well I'll just pop down then?

Eh, what about I mean . . . ?

It'll be alright. I just have to rest now and again. Have you got a chair?

Yeh

He's a stubborn old besom, said his wife. You know you're no supposed to be walking too much!

I'm only going up and down the one flight of stairs Catherine.

Aye well you're no supposed to.

Edward grasped Deborah's arm but released it at once.

That was a bit rough, she said.

Sorry.

The elderly woman had opened the door for them. He ushered Deborah out then followed. 'Bye, he said.

The door closed.

It was a hard grip, said Deborah.

I didnt mean it, sorry.

She nodded.

So where did you meet Missis Parker?

On the pavement. Outside the front close.

Mm . . .

Why?

Oh nothing I mean it was just, a bit strange.

What were you talking about when we came in? it seemed interesting. You just switched subjects; one minute you were talking about fate and big business and then you went to making tins of soup in your electric kettle.

We were having a conversation. Edward shrugged. That's all—it wasnt really strange. Just me. It was just me.

How d'you mean?

He looked at her. Och, nothing. She was somebody he didnt know but knew as well as anybody in the whole world. There she was in front of him. How she had been a minute ago with the elderly couple. Then there she was with her family. He didnt know her at all. She was just the way she was, whatever that might be. Then her and her sister, how they would also be together, that kind of faith maybe or loyalty. Something. They would have it between them. And it was now broken. He had broken it, he had come between them. Before him it was fine. Now it wasnt. He wanted to lift her up and protect her from all the dangers and pitfalls. If ever she was to get a happy outcome to her life she needed some advice, guidance, she needed to have her faith restored as well, once the truth came out. He felt abased in front of her. Plus she had a certain look in her eye. He could easily push her in the back when she was going down the stairs.

Did you get a sleep? she said when they reached his landing.

No. Did you?

I did, yes, eventually. Did you see my sister?

Yeh.

Was it alright?

Yeh.

Can you help her?

I think so.

Edward that's good.

Yeh.

It is, she'll be so relieved.

Aye . . . He grinned at her. If they went out for a meal it would be fine they would just be fine and the things to talk about, different things to do with different things. He gulped for air. He needed to open the door to the room because now she was waiting for it and he hadnt done it yet. I'm just worried about the test, he said.

Well you shouldnt be.

But it's important.

I know it's important but it's not that important.

It is for me.

Yes I know it is.

I've got to treat it seriously, he muttered, getting the key into the lock, it's important, important for me . . . Oh God! He sighed. Life eh? Life. He smiled. An old couple like that too, imagine getting put out their house because of arrears, would it no sicken you? It's appalling, you're right what you said up the stair. Edward turned and frowned at Deborah: Or else do you fancy going out for a meal?

Out for a meal?

We could go for something to eat, I'm starving, quite hungry. He pushed the door ajar and entered, waited for her then shut it afterwards. He sighed again. All the stuff on the table. He walked to it and shook his head and he smiled. Ach I dont know Deborah, sometimes I feel as if I'm just making no headway at all. He breathed to get air he was going to faint, and he had got to get a chair onto the seat to sit down oh God, the Lord my God.

Edward!

Oh m'God.

What's wrong?

So bloody bad.

Edward.

His face down on the table the smell of the paper. I'm so God awful Are you alright?

No, no, I'm no, I'm no feeling good I'm no feeling good I'm no feeling good

What's wrong?

Aw Jesus

She put her arms round his neck and shoulders. You're shivering . . .

He peered upwards from the table. There was a smudge on the wall where he had killed the insect. It was funny how your life went. He was in the tennis league as a boy. He had quite enjoyed it. Him and the others used to have masturbation contests some nights. But if it was possible to give all his woes to this old invalid then that would be that and he would have given them to him and that would be him okay again, like a new start was being made and he would never ever ever again in his whole life ever think of straying again because it was just sex, it was sex, male sexuality and he was sick to death of such things trying to take over your life, trying to dictate the terms of life to you, as if you had no say in the matter and were there just at the beck and call of your erections, any woman who wanted to flash herself at you, and you were finished.

Oh God God God. And it was like it was going to be as if the old guy with the bad legs had been sent down here to help him in his hour of need. That was what it had been like. Edward raised his head and glanced at Deborah's wrists. Because there was something in how that old guy had looked, a sort of honesty, as if there were no clouds surrounding him at all. What like was it it was something

He didnt want to think, he didnt want to

The kind of thing that was difficult.

She wasnt the usual kind of woman how could you say she was, she wasnt. What like was she with her sister? Her smell. Deborah had a smell. It was a smell of skin, how her skin gave a smell that was different. His shoulders were now weak. How they were weak. He also felt cold. One time with the tennis league from school camp they were on this what they called "maneuver," pretending to be commando troops and Bob Finlay had cheroots from Holland he had stolen off a prefect and they had all smoked them. My God was that bad! So terrible and bad and maybe the worst queasiness he had ever experienced. You had to grow up and get involved as an adult, a man, you had to get to be a man, like that old invalid and the troubles all over the world what a span of mind he had, somebody that kept going in spite of his handicap and did all the things he did. Edward just to be honest felt he would never have coped with being shut in, stuck in offices with crowds of folk in shirts and ties and smart outfits and all the pecking orders.

Your memories just come. We dont have any control. The good Lord made us with memory boxes. Inside each one of them as well is the Voice of Conscience. And the Voice isnt your own. As well as that it's in touch with everybody else's. It was part of how the Voice could say what was right and wrong. It had the insight because it had some sort of ghostly communication with everything.

The door opened and Deborah came in. She hadnt been holding him. She must have gone away when he wasnt looking. Now she was back again and holding a cup. Drink this, she said, it's just water. He took the cup and she held it to his mouth as he turned his head to sip it, her face staring at him. You look bad. He closed his eyes.

I feel like a bad sinner he rushed on and gazing straight at her, It's a feeling all day maybe I'm working too hard, no sleeping enough. He stared at her. I dont get on with Jeanette you know I was meaning to tell you that. She's your sister but I dont. I just dont. And I cant help it.

What? What d'you mean?

I dont get on with her and dont want to see her again, that's all. It's like there's something wrong, wrong. He sipped the water then lifted the nearest folder and flicked at a page. He said, D'you want to get something to eat?

But what are you saying about Jeanette?

Nothing.

Yes you are.

I'm not, honest.
You dont get on with her? You're saying you dont get on with her.
It doesnt matter.
It does.
It doesnt.
But it does Edward, it matters, if you dont like my sister.
I dont, it's just—I dont not like her at all, it's just
Just what?
It's just . . . He sighed. I thought we were going for a curry.
Well I didn't know what we were doing.
D'you not want to
Edward, for God sake!

She had taken her coat off. And the kettle was going. He stared into the cup of water. There *was* something wrong with him. He *wasnt* a good man. It was as plain as the nose on your face. He just hadnt *seen* it before. He hadnt *seen*. It had *always* been there but he just hadnt looked. Other people had seen but he hadnt. They all knew it. Except him.

Oh Christ

She had pushed him on the shoulder. What's up with you! she cried.

I'm sorry. I'm sorry. I'm just no well, leave me alone.

What's wrong?

There's nothing wrong, I'm just

She was staring at him.

My head

She was so staring at him.

My head

Her mouth going *what's wrong, what's wrong.* It's my head I've just got a sore head it's so bloody sore and my insides, wracking and dry I'm just all dry inside and I need water. He gulped a mouthful from the cup and it shook in his hand and he put his other round it steadying it, getting it firm but his hands were shaking it maybe he needed food, maybe that's what it was.

But was it him?

Fine

What?

Deborah smiling

What is it? he said, he smiled. It wasnt me, he said, it was her, it was her. If she claims about me, it was her—because

because it was her seduced him, it wasnt him, he didnt seduce her, that was the so bloody unlucky thing about it, the whole business, because he was the man, that's how it went, that was the trials and tribulations of it, just being a man, the maleness; it was so unlucky it

he gestured at the A4 folders. I just dont know what to do with my life.

That's fine but tell me?

I killed an insect earlier on

I dont want to hear about a bloody insect Edward I want to hear about what you're saying about Jeanette!

But Deborah I just squashed the thing, the wee soul, I just actually killed it, in cold blood, just like you would I dont know I was going to say kill a beetle, that's how bad it is for the poor wee creatures. It's become a byword for it all, death and destruction and just wanton brutality, even the way you sell your equipment to people, how the guys just gyp people into buying rubbish they dont want. The whole thing, it's just so awful, it's terrible and wanton and just goes against everything God stands for. People dont want that sort of life. They dont. They dont want it. It shouldnt be forced on us.

You're no listening!

I am

You're not.

I am! It's just the way things are. You take the way I live my life just as an ordinary man; this is an average day and I've committed awful sins. Just like wanton brutality. And I feel so awful . . . just so bad just so awful bad.

God Edward what's wrong with you?

Nothing. He stared at her. She had leaned to gaze into his face and she had placed each hand on his shoulders.

You've not been eating and now your stomach's in knots because of the work you've been doing for tomorrow morning's test.

Yeh, he smiled and laid his right hand on top of her left hand while it still lay on his shoulder. Aw Deborah, he said, aw Deborah.

A woman and two men

Some folk would think it was her keeps them the gether, without her who knows what they would do, making sure they get their grub, whatever it is, the bowl of soup, the sausage and egg, whenever she gets round to making it. But it's all an illusion, it just isnt true. It's sentimentality. It isnt a true picture at all. People just like to think that because they dont want to think something else. You see her, she hardly talks at all. And she never walks in the middle. There is something but right enough, you dont quite know what it is about her. Plus the fact she never seems to hear what the other two are talking about. She has a set look on her face all the time. Probably she knows everything they have to say anyway, their conversation's probably the same all the time. The older guy is about fifty years of age, the younger one about thirty-five, maybe even a nephew, because their relationship appears to be to do with family rather than friendship, but this is guesswork. It looks like the older one has been the longest with the woman, that the younger one just came along and decided he wanted in on the act. Unless it was a case of being invited in by the other two, or just the man, because his nephew, you dont feel he's really up to doing things for himself and neither do you get the feeling about her, about the woman, that she ever gets a say in the matter either, unless maybe she doesnt want one; she has such an inferior way of going about you can hardly imagine her ever saying much at all. But this might no be true, maybe she does, maybe she just gives the impression she doesnt. Whenever they walk down the road people stare at them, and they're open about it, because of the way they look, as if they're full of their own lives, as if what they do concerns them to the exclusion of everything else. Not only does that make them interesting it means folk feel able to stare at them without them noticing which is just as well maybe because the older guy is quite aggressive; you get the feeling about that, there's a nastiness about his face, he's always got a grin. He's definitely the chief. But then one time right enough she was on her own and she walked normal, she was swigging from a can of stout, so she might not be as docile as people think. Somebody looked at her and she looked back. The person had just came out the baker shop near the Botanic Gardens and maybe was having to step out her road—whatever, but the woman just gave her a "look". Somebody told me, apropos of what I dont know, that she "liked the men", meaning she liked to go with men. But that makes it seem she's got choices. It makes it seem like she's been able to make up her mind about things some of the time but maybe she doesnt, folk just like to think about other folk, especially women, they like to think they make up their minds about everything. But they dont, it's a fallacy.

Except I suppose there's the swing of her skirt. That lurching movement makes you think of a piece of material just thick with dirt and that is what you think of that skirt it's like you can imagine the sperm of quite a lot of men. Having said that it's important to say about her how you always think she is the one who is reflective, that it is her who reflects on what is happening roundabout; she's the one that notices what people are signifying when they look at the three of them. Plus if ever you're confronted by them, it's her eyes that stay with you; it's her you see eventually, the one who makes it hard for you. It can start you thinking about things, probably about men and women I suppose, the different types of relationships they have, how you think the women it is who carry the burden yet in such a veiled aggressive way you never feel sorry for them. They know the score. It's as if it's always them that work out the percentages. Even her, this one, the weight of her skirt, you dont for a minute think she is a hopeless victim and you dont think she is as passive as she makes out. Right enough she is a victim in the way she is just one woman having to face up to two men and you dont know quite what goes on in that situation, even if she sometimes has to find a punter if they're in trouble. That time she was overheard when they were seated on the bench down by the River Kelvin, just over by the kids' swing park, and she says something that showed how she felt on her own in the company, what she said wasnt heard by the two guys—or else they didnt pay it any attention, they never "heard" her. They were on the paving stones at the edge of the flower beds, the two of them involved about something or other, or maybe nearer the point, the guy with the permanent girn on his face was talking and the nephew was listening, and then the woman says, It's no like that. Her hair straggling down her shoulders and her mouth gumsy. I think the nephew heard her and the other guy didnt because he just never expected her to speak unless spoken to, something like that. But again you know there's that way you can tell when somebody isnt very bright, maybe just how he sometimes smiles for no reason anybody can see and that nephew was a bit like that, I dont think he was the full shilling. So girny, the older guy, he turns to her: Did you speak there?

Naw.

Aye you did.

I didni.

Aye ye did.

I didni.

Ye fucking did.

Then she just shut up. Girny stared at her and you would have expected him to hit her one. I think he would've if she had said anything more. He was daring her, that's what he was doing. But she never says fuck all. She just stared at the other women, the ones with their kids playing on the swings, and you wondered about that, if she was away thinking about them and relating it to herself, the way she was. It was sad. You felt as if there was this terrible awful gap between them but there wasnt really. It was all a bit weird. I just wish she could have washed her hair. I felt that for her. I felt if she had done that then the gap wouldnt have been so bad and so big, all them with their weans playing in the wee swing park, all standing there having their wee chinwag the way women do, enjoying the sun and all that, while there was this other one, their comrade I suppose in solidarity, there she was, but they werent bothering about her, trying no to see her, then there was girny himself getting up off the bench and giving her the wire, Come on you, he said, not in actual words but just the way he jerked his thumb; the nephew as well, giving her a look, and then they went away down towards the old dummy railway.

Lassies are trained that way

The lassie came in on her own; she glanced roundabout then continued on past the ladies' toilet, heading into the lounge. Minutes later she was back again, squinting this way and that, as if letting it be known she was only here because she was meeting somebody. When she arrived beside him at the bar there was a frown on her face. She asked the woman serving for a gin and orangeade, stressing the orangeade, how she didnt want natural fruit juice or the diluting stuff. She was good-looking. She had on a pair of trousers and a wideish style of jersey. Eventually he spoke to her. He gave her a smile at the same time:

Has he gave you a dizzy?

The lassie ignored him.

Has he stood you up? he said, smiling. Then he drank a mouthful of lager. In some ways he hadnt been expecting any response, even though he was just being friendly, taking her at face value and trying to ease her feelings; get her to relax a bit. This wasnt the best of pubs for single women, being frank about it—not the worst, but definitely not the best.

Her eyes were smallish, brown, nice. He liked her looks. Okay. What is there to that? There can be strong feelings between the sexes. He was attracted to her. Fine. But even more than that: probably if something bad was happening he would have been first there, right at her elbow. It was a big brotherish feeling. He used to have a couple of wee sisters. Still has! Just that they are no longer wee. They are married women, with families of their own. He used to be a married man with a family of his own! Which simply means, to cut the crap, that him and his wife dont see eye-to-eye anymore. If they ever did. She doesnt live with him. And he doesnt live with her. They separated a year and a half ago. He spent too much time boozing down the pub. Too much time out the house. That was the problem, he spent too much time out the house. The work did it. The kind of job he had is the kind that puts pressure on you. And what happens but you wind up in the pub drowning your sorrows.

The lassie with the brown eyes, she was standing beside him. He didnt know what she was maybe she was a student. Although she was older than the usual. But some of the older students came round here. Even during the day, when you might have expected them to be at their class getting their lessons, here they were, having a wee drink. He thought it livened things up. Other folk didnt. Other folk didnt think that at all. They thought it was better to have things the opposite of livened up—deadened down—that's what they thought it was better to have, that was their preference. When they went into a pub they wanted no people, no noise and no laughter, no music, no life, no bloody fuck all, nothing, that's what they liked, nothing, to walk into a pub and get faced by nothing. How come they ever left their place of abode? That was the real question. How come they didnt just stay put, in their bloody house. Then they would give other folk a break. If they were actually interested in other folk then that's what they would do, they would stay fucking indoors and give them a bloody break. But they didnt do that. Out they came. He couldnt be bothered with it, that kind of mentality, he just couldnt be bothered with it. They were misanthropes. The very last thing he ever wanted to be. No matter how bad it got he would never resort to that way of behaving. He genuinely thought people should help one another. He did. He genuinely did. Something that was anathema nowadays right enough, the way things were. But so what? There's aye room for variety. Who wants everything to be the same? Imagine it: a whole regiment of folk all looking the same and then thinking the same thoughts. That would be terrible, absolutely bloody horrendous. You see some blokes going about, their faces tripping them. You wonder how come they ever set foot out the door, as if they just left the house to upset folk. A pain in the neck so they are. The kind that never does somebody a turn unless it's a bad yin. His wife's people were like that. They used to talk about him behind his back. They spoke about him to her, they carried tales. She believed them as well. Plus they did their chattering in front of the wee yins. Bad. If you've got to talk about somebody, okay, but no in front of the wee yins. Bringing somebody down like that. It's no right. There again but his wife didnt have to listen; nobody was forcing her, she could have ignored them, she could have told them to shut their bloody mouth.

The lassie was staring across the bar to beneath the gantry, to where all the bottles of beer were stacked, as if she was comparing all the different labels or something. Because she was feeling self-conscious. You could tell. And there was a mirror up above. She was maybe wanting to look into it to see if she could see somebody but she wasnt able to bring it off in case she wound up catching somebody else's eye. That was probably it. He gave her a smile but she ignored it. He didnt want to feel hurt because it would have been stupid. Not only stupid but ridiculous. She hadnt ignored him at all. She had just no seen him. But she was no seeing anybody. Which is what lassies have to do in pubs. It's part of how they've got to act. He had a daughter himself and that's exactly what he would be telling her next time he saw her. You just cannot afford to take chances, no nowadays—different to when he was young. Aye, he said, young yins nowadays, they have it that wee bit harder.

And he glanced at her but she kept her stare fixed on the bottles beneath the gantry. Which was okay really because he had said it in such a way she would be able to do exactly that, ignore him, without feeling like she was giving him an insult at the same time. That kind of point was important between the sexes, between men and women, if ever they were to manage things together. He gave her another smile and she responded. She did. Her head looked up and she nodded. That was the irony. If you're looking for irony that's it. Plus as well the way things operate in conversation it was really up to her to make the next move, whatever it was, it was up to her.

The woman serving behind the bar was watching him. She was rinsing the glasses out at the sink. Her head was bent over as if she was attending totally to the job in hand but she wasnt, it was obvious. Probably because she knew he was married, thinking to herself: So he's like that is he; chatting up the young lassies, I might've bloody guessed, they're all the bloody same!

And that would make you laugh because he wasnt like that at all. No even just now when he was separated, when he was away living on his own. It was a total guess on her part and she was wrong. But women like to guess about men. They get their theories. And then they get surprised when the theories dont work out. She had seen him talk to the lassie and she just assumed he was trying to chat her up. It can be bad the way folk jump in and make their assumptions about you. And apart from his age what made her so sure he was married anyway? He had gave up wearing the band of gold a while ago and she was new in the

job, still feeling her way; she was still finding out about folk and as far
as he was concerned what could she know? Almost nothing, it was just
guesswork.

The woman was wearing a ring herself but that didnt even mean *she*
was married. As far as a lot of females are concerned a band of gold's a
handy thing to have pure and simple for the way it can ward off unwelcome attention. There again but let's be honest, most men dont even
see a ring, and even if they do, so what? they just bloody ignore it.

The woman stopped rinsing glasses now to serve an auld bloke at
the far end of the bar. He said something to her and she said something
back and the two of them smiled. She had a quiet style with the customers, but she could crack funny wee jokes as well, the kind you never
seem to hear at first—no till after the person that's told you has went
away and you're left standing there and suddenly you think: Aye, right
enough . . . This is the way it was with her. And then when you looked
for her once it had dawned on you she was off and pouring the next guy's
pint, she had forgot all about it. It was actually quite annoying. Although
at the same time you've got to appreciate about women working in a pub,
how they've got to develop an exterior else they'll no be able to cope.
This one for example had a distracted appearance like she was always
away thinking about bloody gas bills or something. Mind you that's
probably what she was thinking about. Everything's so damn dear nowadays. He said it to the lassie. He frowned at her and added: Still and all,
it wasnt that much better afore they got in, the tories.

She looked at him quite surprised. It was maybe the first time she
had genuinely acknowledged he was a person. And it made him think
it confirmed she was a student, but at the same time about her politics,
that she was good and left-wing. He jerked his head in the direction of
the woman serving behind the bar. Her there, he said, I think she's a
single parent; she looks like she goes about worried out of her skull because of the bills coming in—she'll have a tough time of it.

The lassie raised her eyebrows just; and that was that, she dropped
her gaze. In fact she looked like she was tired, she did look like she was
tired. But it was a certain kind of tiredness. The kind you dont like to
see in young people—lassies maybe in particular, though maybe no.

I'm forty going on fifty, he said and he smiled, forty going on fifty.
Naw but what I mean is I feel like I'm fifty instead of forty. No kidding.
In fact I felt like I was fifty when I was thirty! It was one of the major

bones of contention between me and the wife. She used to accuse me about it, being middle-aged. She used to say I was an auld man afore my time. No very nice eh? Accusing your husband of that.

He smiled as he shook his head, swigged a mouthful of beer. Mate of mine, he said, when I turned forty, at my birthday, I was asking him what like it was, turning it I mean, forty, and what he told me was it took him till he was past fifty to bloody get over it!

He smiled again, took his fags out for another smoke although he was trying to cut down. The lassie already was smoking. He lit one for himself. I noticed you come in, he said, the way you walked ben the lounge and then came back here, like you were looking for somebody. I'm no being nosy, it's just an observation, I thought you were looking for somebody.

She had two brown moles on her cheek, just down from her right eye. They were funny, pretty and beautiful. It made him smile.

That was how I spoke to you, he went on, because I thought you were in looking for somebody and they hadnt showed up. I'm no meaning to be nosy, it was just I thought the way you looked, when you came in . . . He finished by giving a nod then inhaled deeply on his cigarette. He was beginning to blab and it was making her uncomfortable. He wasnt saying it right, what he was meaning to say, he was coming out with it wrong, as if it was a line he was giving her, a bit of patter.

She was just no wanting to talk. That was it. You could tell it a mile away. Then at the same time she wasnt wanting to be bloody rude. It was like she maybe didnt quite know how to handle the situation, as if she was under pressure. Maybe she would have handled things better if it had been a normal day, but for some reason the day wasnt normal. Maybe something bad had happened earlier on, at one of her classes, and she was still feeling the effects, the emotional upset. He wanted to tell her no to worry. She wasnt at her classes now.

Unless she thought he was acting too forward or something because he was talking to her—though as far as pubs go surely no, it was just what comes under the heading of being sociable. And we have to live with one another. Come on, if we arent even allowed to talk! Nowadays right enough you cant even take that for granted; it's as if you're supposed to go about kicking everybody in the teeth; you're no supposed to be friendly, if you're friendly they go and tell the polis and you wind up getting huckled for indecent assault. There again but folk have *had* to get that wee bit tougher nowadays, just to survive. He said to the lassie: Do you know what the trouble is? I'm talking about how things have got harder and tougher these past couple of years.

She kept her head lowered. It made him smile. He glanced over the counter but the woman was off serving other folk. He smiled again: You obviously dont want to know what the trouble is! And that's your privilege, that's your right. But I'm going to tell you anyhow!

Naw but seriously, he said, the way things are—society I'm meaning—it's just like auld Joxer says in that play by Sean O'Casey, the world's in a state of chassis. I'm talking about how capitalism and the right-wing has got it all cornered, so selfishness is running amok, everywhere you look, it's rampant—no just here in Scotland but right across the whole of the western world. It's bloody disgusting. Everybody clawing at one another. Nobody gives a shit. We just dont care anymore about what the neighbor next door might be suffering. It's true. They can be suffering. That auld woman up the stair for example, take her, you've no seen her for how long? a week? a fortnight? a bloody month? So what do you do do you go up and keek through the letter box? naw, do you hell; nothing as simple that, what you do is go and phone the bloody polis and get them to come and do it for you. That's the way it is. So you come to rely on people like the polis as if they were angels of mercy—instead of what they are, the forces of law and order for the rich and the wealthy, the upper class.

The lassie frowned.

Sorry, he said, am I talking too loud? I know you're no supposed to nowadays. When you talk about something you're really interested in you're supposed to bloody keep it down, the noise level I mean. So so much for your interest, if it happens to be bloody genuine . . . He shook his head, sighing; he drank from his pint of lager, glancing at her over the rim of the glass, but she was managing not to look at him. Funny how that happened. He could never have managed it himself, to not speak to somebody who was speaking to you. He would have found it extremely difficult, to achieve, he would have found it really difficult. Maybe some folk were mentally equipped to carry that kind of thing off but he wasnt, he just didnt happen to be one of them—not that he would have wanted to be anyhow. Mind you, if he had been a lassie . . . But lassies are trained for it, in a manner of speaking; it's part of the growing-up process for them, young females. It doesnt happen with boys, just if you're a lassie, you've got to learn how not to talk; plus how not to look, you get trained how not to look. How not to look and how not to talk. You get trained how not to do things.

My mother was a talker, he said, God rest her she was a good auld stick. I liked my father but I have to admit it I loved my mother. She used to sing too. She's been dead for fifteen years. Fifteen years. A long time without your maw eh? I was just turned twenty-five when it happened. A long time ago.

The lassie smiled.

You're smiling, he said, but it's true. He tapped ash onto the floor and scraped the heel of his shoe over it, then inhaled deeply. He had loved his mother. It was funny to think that, but he had. And he missed her. Here he was a grown man, forty years of age, and he still missed his mammy. So what but? People do die. It's the way things are. Nobody can change it. The march of progress.

I dont believe in after-lives, he said, and I dont bloody believe in before-lives. Being honest about it I dont believe in any of your bloody through-the-looking-glass-lives at all. And that includes whatever you call it, Buddhism or Mohammedism or whatever the hell. There's the here and there's the now. Mind you, I'm no saying there's no a God, I'm just no saying there is one. What I will bloody say is I'm no very interested, one way or the other. What about yourself?

O . . . She smiled for a moment then she frowned almost immediately; she dragged on her cigarette and let the smoke out in a cloud. Then she dragged on it again but this time inhaled.

He shrugged. It's alright if you're no wanting to speak, I know how things are. Dont worry about it. Anyway, I'm doing enough chattering for the two of us! One thing but I will say—correct me if I'm wrong—your politics, they're like my own, we're both to the left. Eh?

She nodded very slightly, giving a very quick smile. Probably she was a wee bit suspicious. And if she wasnt she should've been; especially nowadays. Because you just never know who you're talking to. He gazed at her. There was something the . . .

And then he felt like giving her a kiss. It was so sudden and what an urge he had to turn away.

And he felt so sorry for her. He really did. He felt so sorry for her. How come he felt so sorry for her? It was almost like he was going to burst out greeting! How come? How come it was happening? He gulped a couple of times and took a puff on the fag, then another one. God. He bit on his lower lip; he stared across the bar to where a conversation was on the go between some guys he knew—just from drinking in here but, he didnt know them from outside—and didnt really want to either. Nothing amazing, he just found it difficult being in their company, it was a bit boring, if he had to be honest, nothing against them, the guys themselves. What was up? What was wrong? He blinked, he kept his eyelids shut for several moments.

A tiny wee amount of gin and orangeade was left in her glass. She was obviously trying to make it last for as long as possible. And she wouldnt allow him to buy her another. That was for definite. It was a thing about females. She was looking at the clock. That was another thing about them! Women! God! Strange people! He grinned at the lassie: Yous women! Yous're so different from us! Yous really are! Yous're so different!

She gazed at him.

Yous are but honest.

In what way?

O Christ in every way.

She nodded.

I mind when my daughter started her period if you dont mind me saying—I felt dead sorry for her. No kidding. Know how? Because she wasnt going to be a boy! He shook his head, smiling.

That's awful.

Naw, he said, what I mean . . .

But she had looked away from him in such a style that he stopped what it was he was going to say. Along the counter the woman serving was setting pints up for a group of young blokes who had just come in. He said, I dont mean it the way it sounds. The exact same thing happens with a pet, a wee kitten or a wee puppy, when it's newborn and it's just like any baby . . .

I dont want to hear this.

Naw but . . .

She shook her head. I dont want to hear it.

Aye but you dont know what I'm going to say.

I dont want to hear it. She smiled, then set her face straight, stubbed her fag out in the ashtray.

He had just been wanting to tell her how the things he liked as a boy he had wanted his wee lassie to get involved in, because he knew she would enjoy them, that's all; nothing else, things like football and climbing trees, jumping the burn; nothing special, the usual, the usual crap, just the things boys did. Of course she would go on and do the things lassies did and she would enjoy them. He knew that. That was what happened. And it was fine. But it wasnt the point. It was something else, to do with a feeling, an emotional thing. Surely you had to be allowed that?

He indicated her near-empty glass. D'you want a drink?

No thanks.

He smiled.

I'm going in a minute.

He smiled again. There's barriers between us, the sexes. But what you cannot deny is that we're drawn to one another. We are: we're drawn to one another. There's bonds of affection. And solidarity as well, you get solidarity between us—definitely . . . That's what I think anyhow—course I'm aulder than you . . . When you get to my age you seem to see things that wee bit clearer.

She looked at him. That's just nonsense.

I'm no saying you see everything clearer, just some things.

She sighed.

I was reading in a book there about it—it was a woman writer—she was saying how there's a type of solace you can only receive from the opposite sex, a man from a woman a woman from a man.

It's nonsense.

It's no nonsense at all.

She paused for a moment, then replied, Yes it is. She looked away from him, off in the direction of the group of young blokes, one of whom stared at her. So blatant too, the way he did it. He just turned and stared at her, then he turned back to his pals. And the lassie shifted the way she was standing. She looked up at the clock and checked the time against her wristwatch.

They keep it quarter of an hour fast, he said. Common practice. A few of the customers complain right enough. But it's so they can get the doors shut on the button else the polis'll come in and do them for being late and they might lose their license. So they say anyway. Mind you it's bloody annoying if you've come in looking to enjoy a last pint and then they start shouting at you and start grabbing the glass out your bloody hand. My auld da used to say it was the only business he knew where they threw out their best customers!

She didnt respond.

He grinned. I mean it's no as if they open quarter of an hour early in the morning! Look eh . . . are you sure I cant buy you one afore you go?

No, thanks.

He nodded.

I'm just leaving.

He never turned up then eh!

No.

Was it your boyfriend?

She shook her head.

D'you mind me asking you something. Are you a student?

Why d'you want to know?

I was just wondering.

Why?

Aw nothing.

She continued looking at him. He felt like he had been given a telling off. For about the third bloody time since she had come in. He swallowed the last of his lager and glanced sideways to see where the bar staff had got to. And then he said, Do you think it's possible for men and women to talk in a pub without it being misconstrued?

She paused. I think people should be able to stand at a bar without being pestered.

O you think you're being pestered? Sorry, I actually thought I was making conversation. That's how come I was talking to you, it's what's commonly known as being sociable. I didnt know I was pestering you.

She nodded.

Sorry.

It's just that I think people should be able to stand at the bar if that's what they want to do.

So do I, he said, so do I. That's what I think. I mean that's what I think. My own daughter's coming up for seventeen you know so I'm no exactly ignorant of the situation.

The woman behind the counter had reappeared and was looking along in his direction, like she had heard the word "pester" and was just watching to see. He shook his head. It was like things were getting out of hand; you wanted to shout: Wait a minute! He frowned, then smiled. When he was a wee boy him and his brother and sisters would be right in the middle of a spot of mischief when suddenly the door would burst open and mammy would be standing there gripping the handle and glowering at them. And they would all be on the confessional stool immediately! She didnt have to fucking do anything! They'd all just start greeting and then cliping on one another! What a technique she had! It was superb! All she had to do was stand there! Everybody crumbled.

He grinned, shaking his head, and he called for a pint of lager. For a split second the woman didnt seem to hear him. Then she walked to the tap, started pouring the pint, staring at the lever very deliberately, as if she was making some sort of point. It was funny. Maybe she was a bit put out about something. Well that was her problem. If you've got to start safeguarding the feelings of everybody you meet on the planet then you'll have a hard time staying sane.

The lassie wasnt there.

Aye she was but she was across at the group of young guys. They looked like students as well. He didnt have anything against students. Although the danger was aye the same for kids from a working-class background, that it turned you against your own people. How many of them were forever going away to uni and then turning round and selling themselves to the highest bidder as soon as they'd got their certificates. Then usually they wound up abroad, if no England then the States or Canada or Australia, or Africa or New Zealand, it was all the same. Then they spent the rest of their lives keeping other folk down.

One of the young blokes laughed. It would have been easy to take it personally but that would have been stupid. Getting paranoiac is the simplest thing in the world. A gin and orangeade was on the counter in front of the lassie but she was paying for it out of her own purse. A young guy glanced across. Another one said something. But there was no point seeing it directed at yourself. The woman behind the bar was away serving another customer. The change back from the money for the pint of lager was lying on the counter. He put his hand out to get it.

Street-sweeper

The sky was at the blueyblack pre-heavygray stage of the morning and the gaffer was somewhere around. This is one bastard that was always around; he was always hiding. But he was somewhere close right now and Peter could sense his presence and he paused. It wasnt a footstep but he turned to see over his shoulder anyway, walked a few more paces then quickly sidled into a shop doorway, holding the brush vertical, making sure the top of his book wasnt showing out his pocket. This was no longer fun. At one time in his life it might've been but no now, fuck, it was just bloody silly. And it wisni funny. It just wisni fucking funny at all. These things were beginning to happen to him more and more and he was still having to cope. What else was there. In this life you get presented with your choices and that's that, if you canni choose the right ones you choose the wrong ones and you get fucked some of the time; most of the time some people would say. He closed his eyes, rubbed at his brow, smoothing the hair of his eyebrows. What was he to do now, he couldni make it back to the place he was supposed to be at, no without being spotted. Aw god. But it gave him a nice sense of liberty as well, it was an elation, quite fucking heady. Although he would have to move, he would—how long can you stay in a doorway! Hey, there was a big cat watching him, it was crouched in beside a motor-car wheel. Ha, christ. Peter chuckled. He was seen by a cat your honor. There he was in a doorway, having skived off because he had heard about a forced entry to a newsagent shop and thought there might've been some goods lying available to pilfer.

Objection!

Overruled.

Ah but he was sick of getting watched. He was. He was fucking sick of it. The council have a store of detectives. They get sent out spying on the employees, the workers lad the workers, they get sent out spying on them. Surely not. The witness has already shown this clearly to be the case your Honor. Has he indeed. Aye, fuck, he has, on fucking numer-

ous occasions, that's how come he got the boys out on strike last March.
Ah.

Naw but he's fucking sick of it, he really is. High time he was an adult.
Here he is forty-seven years of age and he's a boy, a wee lad—in fact,
he is all set to start wearing short trousers and ankle socks and a pair of
fast-running sandshoes (plimsolls for the non-Scottish reader). What was
he to do but that is the problem, that is the thing you get faced with all
the bloody time, wasnt it just bloody enervating. But you've got your
brush you've got your brush and he stepped out and was moving, dragging his feet on fast, dragging because his left leg was a nuisance, due
to a fucking disability that made him limp—well it didni *make* him limp,
he decided to limp, it was his decision, he could have found some new
manner of leg-motoring which would have allowed him not to limp, by
some sort of circumlocutory means he could have performed a three-
way shuffle to offset or otherwise bypass the limp and thus be of normal perambulatory gait. This was these fucking books he read. Peter was
a fucking avid reader and he had got stuck in the early Victorian era,
even earlier, bastards like Goldsmith for some reason, that's what he
read. Charles fucking Lamb, that's who he read; all these tory essayists
of the pre-chartist days, that other bastard that didni like Keats. Why
did he read such shite. Who knows, they fucking wreaked havoc with
the syntax, never mind the fucking so-called sinecure of a job, the street
cleaning. Order Order. Sorry Mister Speaker. But for christ sake, for
christ sake.

Yet you had to laugh at his spirit I mean god almighty he was a spir-
ited chappie, he was, he really and truly was. But he had to go fast. There
was danger ahead. No time for quiet grins. Alright he was good, he was
still doing the business at forty-seven, but no self-congratulatory pos-
turing if you please, even though he might still be doing it, even though
he was still going strong at the extraordinarily advanced age of thrice
fifteen-and-two-thirds your Honor, in the face of extraordinarily calami-
tous potentialities to wit said so-called sinecure. Mister Speaker Mister
Speaker, this side of the House would request that you advise us as to
the appertaining set of circumstances of the aforementioned place and
primary purpose of said chappie's sinecure so-called. Uproar. A Spring-
burn street. Put on the Member for Glasgow North. The Member for
Glasgow North has fuckt off for a glass of claret. Well return him
posthaste.

But the goodwife. Has the goodwife a word to say. Yes, indeed. The goodwife would bat him one on the gub. She thought all this was dead and buried. She thought the sinecure was not deserving of the "so-called" prefixed reference one iota, i.e. sinecure *qua* sinecure in the good lady's opinion.

She wouldni think it was possible but, it's true, she thought it was all over as far as the problematics were concerned. Pussycats pussycats, I tought I saw. But there you are, getting to the doddering stage, being spotted by a crouching cat, so much for his ability to cope, to withstand the helter skelter, the pell mell, the guys in the darkblue and the bulky shoulders. Bejasus he was getting fucking drunk on the possibility of freedom, a genuine liberty, one that would be his prior to deceasement. What he fancied was a wee periscope from the coffin, so he could just lie there watching the occasional passersby, the occasional birdie or fieldmouse:

he was into another doorway and standing with his back pressed into the wall, eyes shut tight, but lips parted, getting breath, listening with the utmost concentration. Nothing. Nothing o christ why was he an atheist this of all times he felt like screaming a howsyrfather yr paternoster a quick hail mary yr king billy for christ sake what was it was it a fucking footfall he felt like bellowing, bellowing the fucking place down, it would show them it would show them it would display it, it would display how he was and how he could bellow his laughter in the face of the fucking hidebound universe of them, fucking moribund bastirts—was it the gaffer? He pulled the brush in, held it like an upright musket of the old imperialist guard, India or Africa yr Lordship.

Carol thought it was all dead and buried. She did, she truly truly did. His eyes were shut and his lips now closed, the nostrils serving the air channels or pipes, listening with the utmost concatenation of the earular orifices. Not to scream. Not to make a sound. Another minute and he would go, he would move, move off, into the graying dawn.

He was safe now for another few minutes. It was over, a respite o lord how brief is this tiny candle flicker. Peasie Peasie Peasie. For this was his nickname, the handle awarded him by the mates, the compañeros, the compatriots, the comrades: Peasie.

It didni even matter the profit but this was the fucking thing! Maybe he got there and the newsagent turned out to be a grocer for god sake how many cartons of biscuits can you plank out in some backcourt!

Fucking radio rental yr Lordship. Mind you the profit was of nay account, nane at all. Neither the benefits thereon. If there were benefits he didni ken what they were. He shook his head. Aright, aright me boy, me lad. There was a poor fucker lying on the grun ahead. There was. Peter approached cautiously. It was a bad sign. It was. If the security forces martialled, and they would, then they would be onto him in a matter of hours, a couple of hours, maybe even one; he would need a tale to tell. Diarrhea. Diarrhea, that savior of the working classes. He had to go to the loo and spend some several minutes, maybe thirty, unable to leave in case the belly ructured yet again. But the body was a bad sign. Poor bastard.

Peter knelt by the guy. He was still alive, his forehead warm and the tick at the temple, a faint pulsing. But should he drag him into a closemouth? No, of course not, plus best to leave him or else

but the guy was on his back and that was not good. Peter laid down his brush and did the life-saving twist, he placed the man's right arm over his left side, then raised and placed his right leg also over his left side, then gently pulled the left leg out a little, again gently, shifting the guy's head, onto the side: and now the guy would breathe properly without the risk of choking on his tongyou. And he would have to leave it at that. It wisni cold so he wouldni die of frostbite. Leave it. You'll be aright son, he whispered and for some reason felt like kissing him on the forehead, a gesture of universal love for the suffering. We can endure, we can endure. Maybe it was a returning prophet to earth, and this was the way he had landed, on the crown of his skull and done a flaky. He laid his hand on the guy's shoulder. Ah you'll be right as rain, he said, and he got up to go. He would be though, he would be fine, you could tell, you could tell just by looking; and Peter was well versed in that. Yet fuck sake if he hadni of known how to properly move the guy's body then he might have died, he could've choked to death. My god but life is so fragile; truly, it is.

And he was seen. The pair of eyes watching. The gaffer was across the street. The game's a bogie. He looked to be smiling. He hated Peter so that would be the case quite clearly.

Come ower here!

Peter had walked a couple paces by then and he stopped, he looked across the road. Giuseppe Robertson was the gaffer's name. Part of his

hatred for Peter was straightforward, contained in the relative weak notion of "age"; the pair of them were of similar years and months down
even to weeks perforce days and hours—all of that sort of shite before
you get to the politics. Fucking bastirt. Peter stared back at him. Yeh
man hey, Robertson was grinning, he was fucking grinning. Ace in the
hole and three of them showing. Well well well.

Come ower here! he shouted again.

He wasnt kidding. Yeh. Peter licked his lips. He glanced sideways,
the body there and still prone; Robertson seemed not to have noticed
it yet. He glanced back at him and discovered his feet moving, dragging
him across the road. Who was moving his fucking feet. He wasnt, it had
to be someone in the prime position.

The gaffer was staring at him.

I'm sorry, said Peter.

It doesni matter about fucking sorry man you shouldni have left the
job.

I had to go a place.

You had to go a place . . . mmhh; is that what you want on record?

Aye.

The gaffer grinned: You've been fun out and that's that.

As long as you put it on record.

Ah Peter Peter, so that's you at last, fucking out the door. It's taken
a while, but we knew we'd get ye.

You did.

We did, aye, true, true true true, aye, we knew you'd err. So, you
better collect the tab frae the office this afternoon.

Peter gazed at him, he smiled. Collect my tab?

Yes, you're finished, all fucking washed up, a jellyfish on the beach,
you're done, you're in the process of evaporating. The gaffer chuckled.
Your services, for what they're worth, are no longer in demand by the
fathers of the city.

That's excellent news. I can retire and grow exotic plants out my window boxes.

You can do whatever the fuck you like son.

Ah, the son, I see. But Giuseppe you're forgetting, as a free man, an
ordinary civilian, I can kick fuck out you and it'll no be a dismissable offense against company property.

Jovial, very jovial. And obviously if that's your wish then I'm the man, I'm game, know what I mean, game, anywhere you like Peter it's nomination time.

The two of them stared at each other. Here we have a straightforward hierarchy. Joe Robertson the gaffer and Peter the sweeper.

Fuck you and your services, muttered Peter and thereby lost the war. This was the job gone. Or was it, maybe it was just a battle: Look, said Peter, I've no even been the place yet I was just bloody going, I've no even got there.

You were just bloody going!

Aye.

You've been off the job an hour.

An hour? Who fucking telt ye that?

Never you mind.

There's a guy lying ower there man he's out the game.

So what?

I just bloody saved his life!

Robertson grinned and shook his head: Is that a fact!

That means I've just to leave him there?

Your job's taking care of the streets, he's on the fucking pavement.

Mmhh, I see.

It was on the streets, past tense.

Aw for fuck sake man look I'm sorry! And that was as far as he was going with this charade, no more, no more.

It doesni fucking matter about sorry, it's too late.

It'll no happen again yr honor . . . Peter attempted a smile, a moment later he watched the gaffer leave, his bowly swagger, taking a smoke from his pocket and lighting it as he went. Death. The latest legislation. Death. Death death death. Death. Capital d e a

He continued to watch the gaffer until he turned the corner of Moir Street.

Well there were other kinds of work. They were needing sellers of a variety of stuff at primary-school gates. That was a wheeze. Why didnt he get in on that. My god, it was the coming thing. Then with a bit of luck he could branch out on his own and from there who knows, the whole of the world was available. Peter cracked himself on the back of the skull with such venomous force Aouch that he nearly knocked it off Aouch he staggered a pace, dropped his brush and clutched his head.

O for fuck sake christ almighty but it was sore. He recovered, stopped to retrieve the brush.

It was bloody sore but christ that was stupid, bloody stupid thing to do, fucking eedjit—next thing he would be cutting bits out his body with a sharp pointed knife, self-mutilation, that other savior of the working classes. O christ but the head was still nipping! My god, different if it knocked some sense into the brains but did it did it fuck.

Who had shopped him? Somebody must have. Giuseppe wouldni have been so cocky otherwise. One of the team had sold him out for a pocket of shekels; that's the fucking system boy no more street-sweeping for you. Yes boy hey, he could do anything he liked. Peter smiled and shook his head. He glanced upwards at the heavy gray clouds. He felt like putting on a shirt and tie and the good suit, and get Carol, and off they would go to a nightclub, out wining and dining the morning away. He liked nightshift. Nightshift! It was a beautiful experience. My god Robertson I'd love to fucking do you in boy that's what I would fucking like. But he had no money and he was eighteen years short of the pension. And he was not to lose control. That was all he needed. The whole of life was out to get you. There's a sentence. But it's true, true, the whole of life. Who had shopped him but for fuck sake what dirty bastirt had done the dirty, stuck the evil eye on him, told fucking Robertson the likely route. Och, dear. I had a dream, I had a dream, and in this dream a man was free and could walk tall, he could walk tall, discard the brush and hold up the head, straightened shoulders and self-respect:

the guy was still lying there.

Ohhh. A whisky would be nice, a wee dram. Peter carried a hipflask on occasion but not tonight, he didnt have it tonight. Ohhh. He paused, he stared over the road, seeing the guy in that selfsame position. Perhaps he was dead, perhaps he had died during the tiff with the gaffer. Poor bastard, what was his story, we've all got them, we've all got them.

Morning has bro-ken.

♫ ♩ ♫

That thread

After the pause came the other pause and it was the way they have of following each other the next one already in its place as if the sequence was arranged according to some design or other, and set not just by the first but them all, a networked silence. It was that way when she entered the room. The noise having ceased right enough but even allowing for that if it hadnt it would have—which is usually always the case. She had the looks to attract, a figure exactly so, her sensuousness in all the moves so that her being there in this objectified way, the sense of a thousand eyes. Enter softly enter softly: it was like a song he was singing. and her smile brief, yet bravado as well, that style some women have especially, the face, the self-consciousness; and all of them being there and confronting her while her just there taking it, standing there, one arm down, her fingers bent, brushing the hem of her skirt. She was not worried by virtue of him, the darkness of the room, any of it. Like a sure knowledge of her own disinterest, his nonexistence as a sexual being, in relation to her, and he grinned, reaching for the whisky and pouring himself one, adding a half again of water, the whisky not being a good one. She was still standing there, as if dubiously. She was seeking out faces she recognized and his was one that she did recognize, lo, but would barely acknowledge, she would never acknowledge. Had he been the only face to recognize; the only one. Even that. He smiled then the sudden shift out from his side jacket pocket with the lighter and snap, the flare in the gloom, the thin exhalation of blue smoke; he sipped at the whisky and water, for his face would definitely have had to be recognized now, from the activity, no matter how softly, softly and quietly, no matter how he had contrived it. Now his elation was so fucking strong, so fucking vivid man, and striking, and so entirely fucking wonderful he wanted to scream he had to scream he really did have to he had to scream he would have to he wouldnt be able to fucking stop himself he was shaking he was shaking the cuff of his sleeve, the cuff of his sleeve, trailing on the surface of the table, his hand shaking, shaking, now twitching and his breath coming deep, and she would have sensed it, sensed it all, and she would be smiling so slightly around the corners of her mouth, the down there, her thick lower lip how round it was, how round it was and mystifying, to describe it as provocative was an actual error, an error, a mistake. But the hesitancy in her movement. That thread having been long flung out now, though still exploratory, but ensnaring, it was ensnaring, causing her to hold there, so unmistakably hesitant now rubbing her shoulder just so self-aware yet in that kind of fashion a woman has of rubbing her shoulder at the slightest sensory indication of the thread, feeling it cling, that quiver and he shivered, raising the whisky to his mouth and sipping it, keeping his elbow hard in to the side of his body, keeping it firmly there because that sickness in the pit of his belly and the blood coursing through his cheeks, and burning, burning, everyone seeing and knowing, he was so transparent, so transparent, she just shook her head. What was she going to do? She just had shaken her head that most brief way, and she turned on her heel and she left, left him there. He couldnt move. He would cry out. But his face was controlled, so controlled, although the color now drained from his cheeks, or else the opposite, was it the opposite? and his hand now shaking, the cigarette lighter on the coffee table.

by the burn

Fucking bogging mud man a swamp, an actual swamp, it was fucking a joke. He pulled his foot clear but the boot was still lodged there like it was quicksand and it was going to get sucked off and vanish down into it forever. He felt the suction hard on his foot but when he pulled, curling his toes as firm as possible, out it came with a loud squelching sound. Thank Christ for that. He shook his head, studying the immediate area, these marshy stalks of grass were everywhere; fucking hopeless. He glanced back across the wide expanse of waste ground and up to where the blocks of flats were. But he had to go this way and go this way right now, he was late enough as it was, he just couldnt afford to waste any time. He continued on, steering clear of the clumps of long weeds, the kind that told you where the worst of it was, but it was bad and each step now his boot sunk in an inch or so, but still not as bad as before. Imagine if he had lost the fucking boot but Christ almighty, hirpling down the road for the train then into the interview office, trying to explain to the folk there how you had just lost your shoe in a fucking swamp. My God, a fucking joke right enough. He stopped to look ahead. Then the rain started again and this time it wasnt a passing shower, the sky was full of dark gray clouds, he turned up the collar of his suit jacket, it was going to get worse, nothing surer. And he would get bloody soaked. What the hell time was it? Aw for fuck sake who cares, he plunged on, veering off towards the banks of the burn. You could actually hear the roar of the water; so it was probably running awful high. So there was no chance of him crossing at the usual stepping-stones, maybe have to skirt right the way round through the wood to get to the bloody bridge. Aw dear. He hated having to go that way. By this time he had reached the last of the marsh and there was the ordinary grass and the short clumps of bushes. He passed the wee tree, most of its branches half snapped and trailing onto the ground. A kid's sock dangled off one of them. Then the slope up to the bank of the burn. It was all slimy mud here and he had to steady himself by using his hand as a prop, stepping up in a kind of semicircle. His hands were all muddy now and he had to pull off a couple of big docken leaves to wipe them clean. The roaring from the burn was really loud, deafening. He waited a moment up on the bank, staring down at the swollen water, it came rushing, spray flying out, so high it looked set to overflow the banks. You couldnt even see the stepping-stones where he would have crossed, probably about two feet of water were covering them. So that was it now there was no chance, the path across the bridge or nothing, that was for fucking definite, he just had no choice in the matter. He sighed, blowing out through his mouth. He felt a wee twinge across his shoulders and that was followed by a shiver. He actually did feel tired although it was only about half eleven in the morning, he felt a bit weak in fact. Then the rain on his head. He felt like going away home again, back to the fire, cup of tea and put the feet up. It was just a joke, the whole fucking thing. Away in the distance he saw a shape looming into view through the trees, then another one. Two blokes. They cut off but, taking a different route to get to the flats, up through the field. The rain now definitely getting heavier. He walked as fast as he could along the peak of the bank without slipping on the fucking mud, arse over elbow into the burn—probably he wouldnt have been able to save himself from drowning for Christ sake. Once upon a time aye, but no now. He glanced down as he went. The water was flowing that fucking fast. It was years since he had had a swim too, years. High time they extended the path along this way for the poor cunts living up the flats, the fucking council, it was out of order the way they didnt bother. They had been fucking talking about it for donkeys. He left the bank at the first opportunity, following a narrow trail into the wood and he took shelter beneath the first big tree. He started shivering again. Just the dampness maybe because it wasnt really cold. And he needed a coat. He really did need a coat man this was just stupid. He had one right enough he just didnt wear the fucking thing, he didnt like it. It was too big for him for a start, it was his brother-in-law's. You could have wrapped it round him twice. But still and all he should have wore it, he could have carried it over his arm and just stuck it on and off, depending on what it was doing, if it was raining or not, he didnt have to wear it all the time. His suit shoulder nudged against the tree trunk now and he moved from it, it was slimy, it was really fucking slimy. He gave the material a good rub but the stain still showed, the mud or whatever it was. He caught sight of his boots, all soaking wet and bits of grass and leaves sticking to them, nettles, the lot. Some picture. The wife would be pleased. Once they dried but they would be alright, brand new—except because of the damp they would turn white probably. They werent that old either, bastard. Just like it when you needed everything to be right, when you needed to be at your best, the way you looked. Fucking Jesus. My God. Never mind. Never mind. They would do for the time being, as long as they stayed damp they would pass inspection. If he ever got out of here! Because the fucking rain was pelting down and thick heavy blotches were dropping through the branches of the tree and landing on his nut. Still another half mile through the wood and he would have to start moving soon, he couldnt afford to wait any longer oh but Christ he didnt want to go he would just have to make a run for it, he would just have to make a run for it, just forget about the rain because it wasnt going to go off now, it was on for the bloody duration. The smell of the tree was in his nostrils, it was like decay or something like it was rotten. A lot of the bark had been cut from the trunk here, peeled off. Somebody with a knife. Wee boys probably. Maybe big ones. He studied the bark that was left, the thick dark green stuff, all crisscross lines and it was like cobwebs inside it, a gauzy sort of stuff; it would be full of beetles, beetles and termites, maggots, all living off it, the bark was there to be eaten, they would eat it. He jumped suddenly out from the tree and started running, keeping his head down. At places the trail got really narrow and it took sharp angles and he had to slow down to avoid the traps, the bent branches and the roots and stumps of trees. It was a joke, it was just a joke. Then he was having to walk, he couldnt go any faster, it was just too thick, it was too thick. He had his hands in his trouser pockets. By the time he arrived in the office he wouldnt be in a fit state for the interview. They probably wouldnt even let him in the fucking door man they would send for the fucking polis, the way he was looking, the suit all fucking mud and the boots turned white because of the fucking dampness man it was just bloody out of order, you just had no fucking chance. He needed a car. Every cunt needed a car. That was what happened when you stayed out in the schemes, it was fine till you wanted to go someplace, once you did you were in fucking trouble. Stupid, it was just stupid. But it was a bastard, it really was a bastard, these bloody fucking bushes and swamps man what could you do, going for a fucking job, just when you needed to look right, it aye happened, that was the way it went, you just couldnt win, you just couldnt fucking win man never, you could never win. He glanced about him. Then he looked back over his shoulder. A funny feeling there. He walked on a few paces then slowed again, he stopped. He stopped and listened, he was feeling a bit funny, like somebody was watching him. It was like there was somebody watching him. He felt the twinge in his shoulders. There *was*. There was somebody watching him. What was it he felt so Christ almighty another shiver, somebody definitely watching him. It was gloomy and dark now with the trees high and affecting what light there was; shadows, all the bushes, all thick. He stood where he was, he just stood there. Then he felt it again, right across his shoulders. It was a chill. He had caught a chill. Definitely. He was damp, he was bloody cold. He was oh Christ almighty and he felt it another time now right across his chest as well a sort of tremor and down his thighs to his knees it was, it was like a tremor, a spasm. But it was his daughter, it was his daughter. Like her ghost was somewhere. He knew it. He knew what it was exactly. Because it was the sand pit. It was right across the burn from where he was standing and if it was winter and the leaves had fell you would see right across and the sandpit was there, it was right there, just on the other side. Aw dear, the wee fucking lassie. Aw dear man aw dear it was so fucking hard so fucking awful hard, awful hard so fucking awful hard. Oh where was the wife. He needed his fucking wife. He needed her. He needed her close. He needed her so fucking close he felt so fucking Christ man the sandpit, where the wee lassie and her two wee pals had got killed. Hiding out playing chases. Aye being warned to steer clear but in they went and then it collapsed on them, and it trapped them, all these tons of earth and they had all got suffocated. Aw dear. Aw dear. He stepped in near a big tree and leaned his arms against it, his forearms, crossed, them shielding his eyes, he was greeting without any sound, he just couldnt handle it. He couldnt. He had never been able to. It used to keep him awake at nights. For ages, fucking ages. He could never get it out his mind. For Christ sake bloody years ago it was, bloody years ago. Oh Christ. She was stronger than him. The wife. She was. She really was. She could handle it. He couldnt. But she could. She could handle it fine. She got by on it. But he didnt. He couldnt; he just couldnt handle it. He never could. He had never been able to, he had just never been able to. He opened his mouth to breathe fresh air. The insides of his mouth ached. Throat dry. A wetness at the corners of his lips: he wiped them with the cuff of his suit sleeve. He had just never been able to handle it; he couldnt come to terms with it at all. These years. All these fucking years. And that wee fucking lassie oh God man he just could never fucking handle it. Plus as well he would have wanted to be one of them that carried her out. No just her but the other ones, her two wee pals. But he wasnt there. He didnt know. He just heard about it later. Him and the wife man they never fucking knew it had happened, no till too late, it was too late when they knew. It had been firemen done it and some other folk who went down. But him and the wife never knew about it till too late, there was nobody telt them. But it was nobody's fault, they didnt know who it was that was buried, no till they got them out. The firemen came and cleared out the rubble, then they found them, the wee souls, they lifted them and carried them. He would like even to have seen it. He telt the wife that at the time as well, just from a distance, it would have been fine as long as he could just have seen them, the wee legs all spindly and them broken like that, their wee bodies. Ah dear, ah dear. He swallowed. The tears were running down his face again. He shut his eyes tight to stop it. He could feel rain down the back of his neck; his throat was so dry. He flexed his shoulders. Just seeing her would have been good, smoothing her head and hair, just smoothing her head and hair, that was all. God. Ah God he was feeling better, it was passed. Poor old wife but it was a shame for her, the missis. She had to carry on. She had to cope. Different for him. Different. He wasnt stuck in the house, he had a job at the time, but she was, she was stuck in the house. Plus she had to look after the other one. That was what kept her going. Christ almighty he could do with a drink. All this rain and he was dying of fucking thirst. It was past now, finished. He felt better. Aye he could do with a drink, of water just. The feeling was away, it had gone. There was another twinge now at his knees but it went as well. He shivered again. He was alone. He had to carry on now. He started walking, following the trail. One thing he did know but, see when he died, he was going to die of a heart attack, he was going to die of a heart attack and he was going to be alone, there wasnt going to be no cunt, no cunt, he was going to be fucking alone, that was the way he was going to die, he fucking knew it, it was a fucking racing certainty.

Acknowledgments

I have included some of my earliest work, published in my mid twenties. In bookform the selected stories first appeared as follows:

"He knew him well"; "An old pub near the Angel"; "Nice to be nice":
An old pub near the Angel: (1973, Puckerbrush Press, Orono, Maine, USA)

"Remember Young Cecil"; "No longer the Warehouseman":
Three Glasgow Writers: (1976, Molendinar Press, Glasgow, Scotland)

"Busted Scotch"; "Acid"; "learning the Story":
Short Tales from the Nightshift (1978, Glasgow Print Studio Press, writers' collective)

"Away in Airdrie"; "The hitchhiker"; "Wee horrors"; "Roofsliding"; "Not not while the giro":
Not not while the giro (1983; Polygon Press, Edinburgh, Scotland)

"the paperbag"; "In a betting shop to the rear of Shaftesbury Avenue"; "O jesus, here come the dwarfs"; "A Nightboilerman's notes":
Lean Tales (1985; Jonathan Cape, London, England)

"Old Francis"; "The one with the dog"; "Forgetting to mention Allende"; "Cute Chick!"; "The Small Family"; "Half an hour before he died"; "The Red Cockatoos"; "Dum vivimus, vivamus"; "Getting Outside"; "Greyhound for Breakfast":
Greyhound for Breakfast (1987; Secker & Warburg, London, England)

"Pictures"; "A walk in the park"; "A situation"; "A woman and two men"; "Lassies are trained that way"; "Street-sweeper"; "That thread"; "by the burn":
The Burn (1991) Secker & Warburg, London, England)